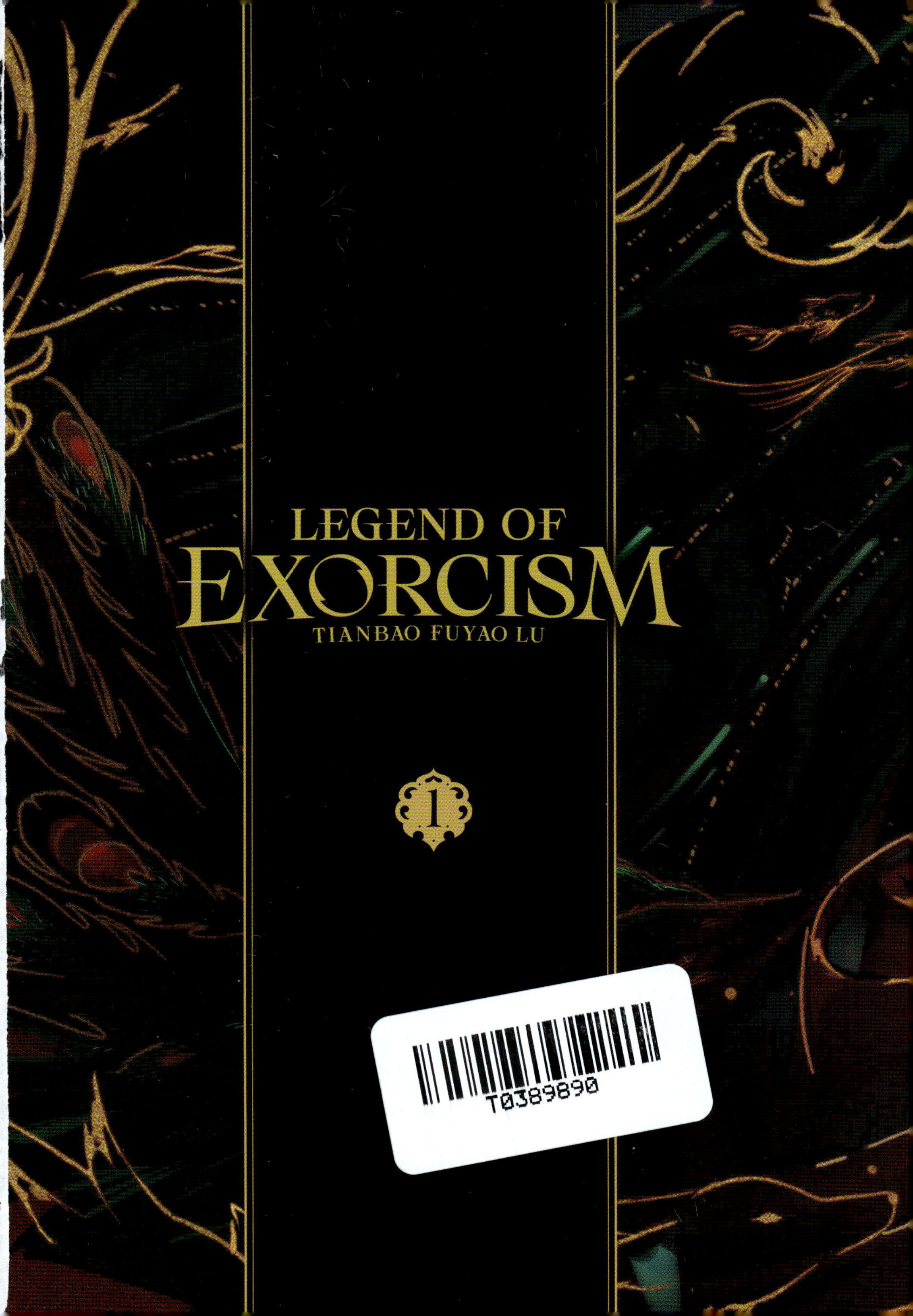
LEGEND OF
EXORCISM
TIANBAO FUYAO LU
1

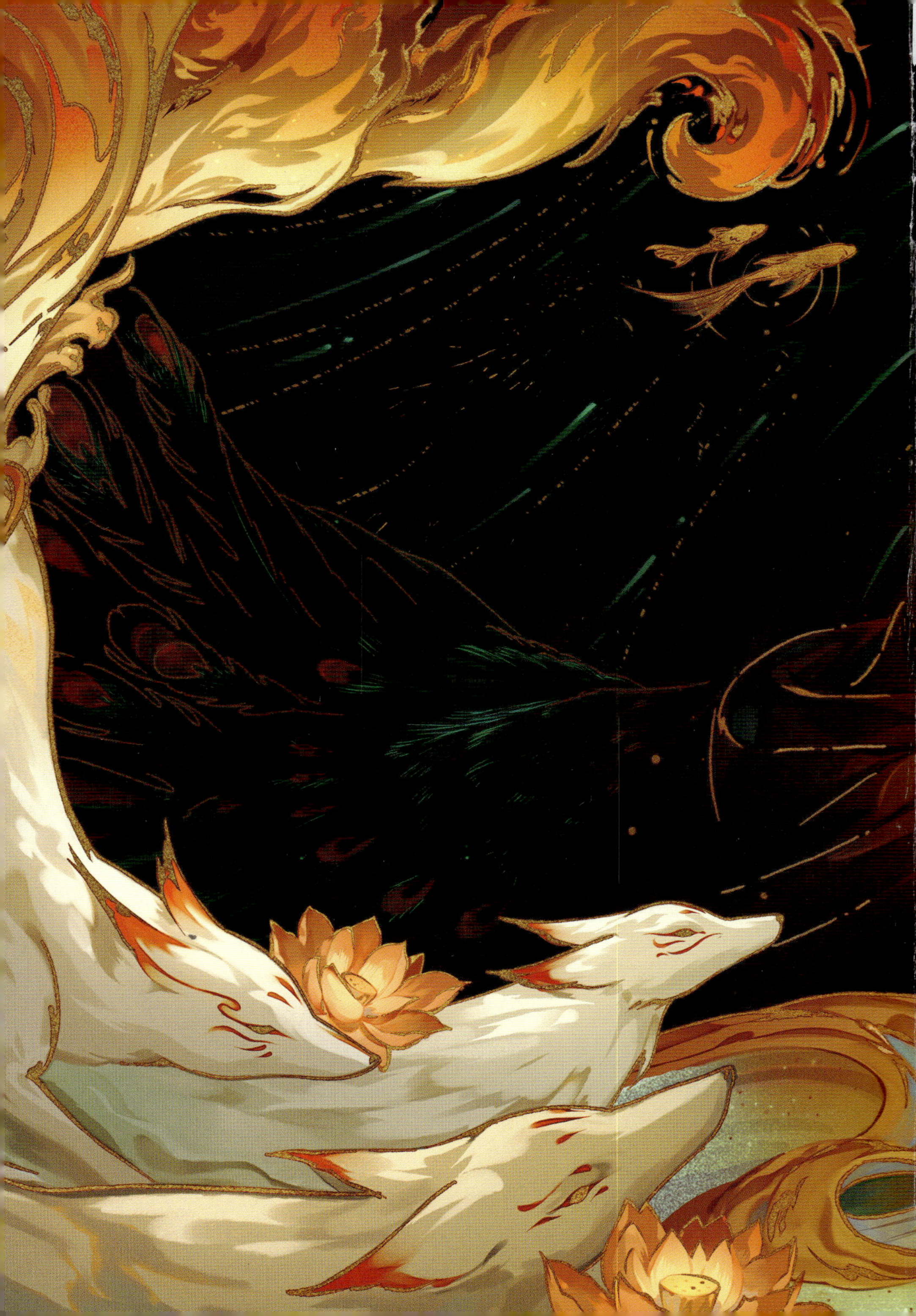

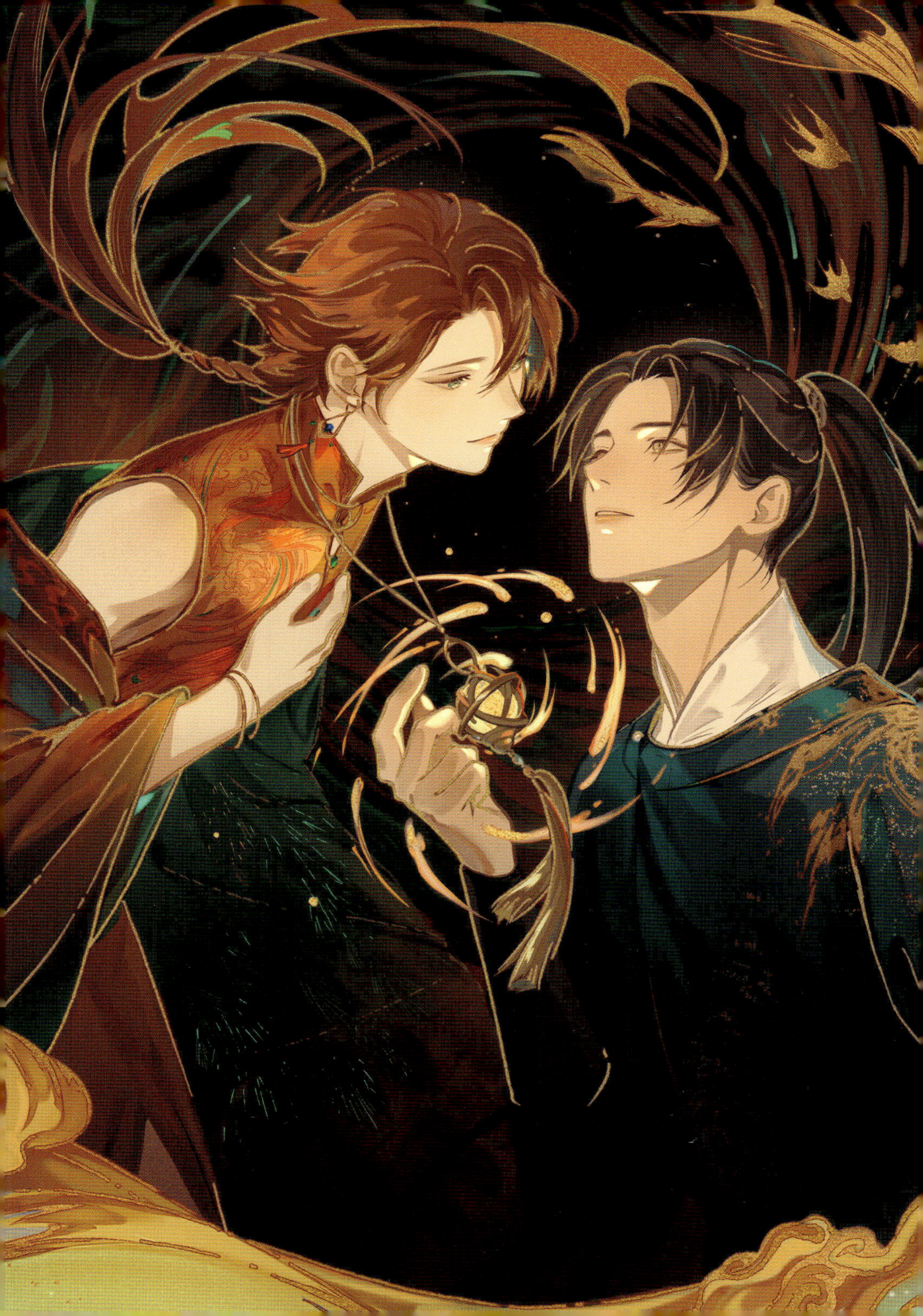

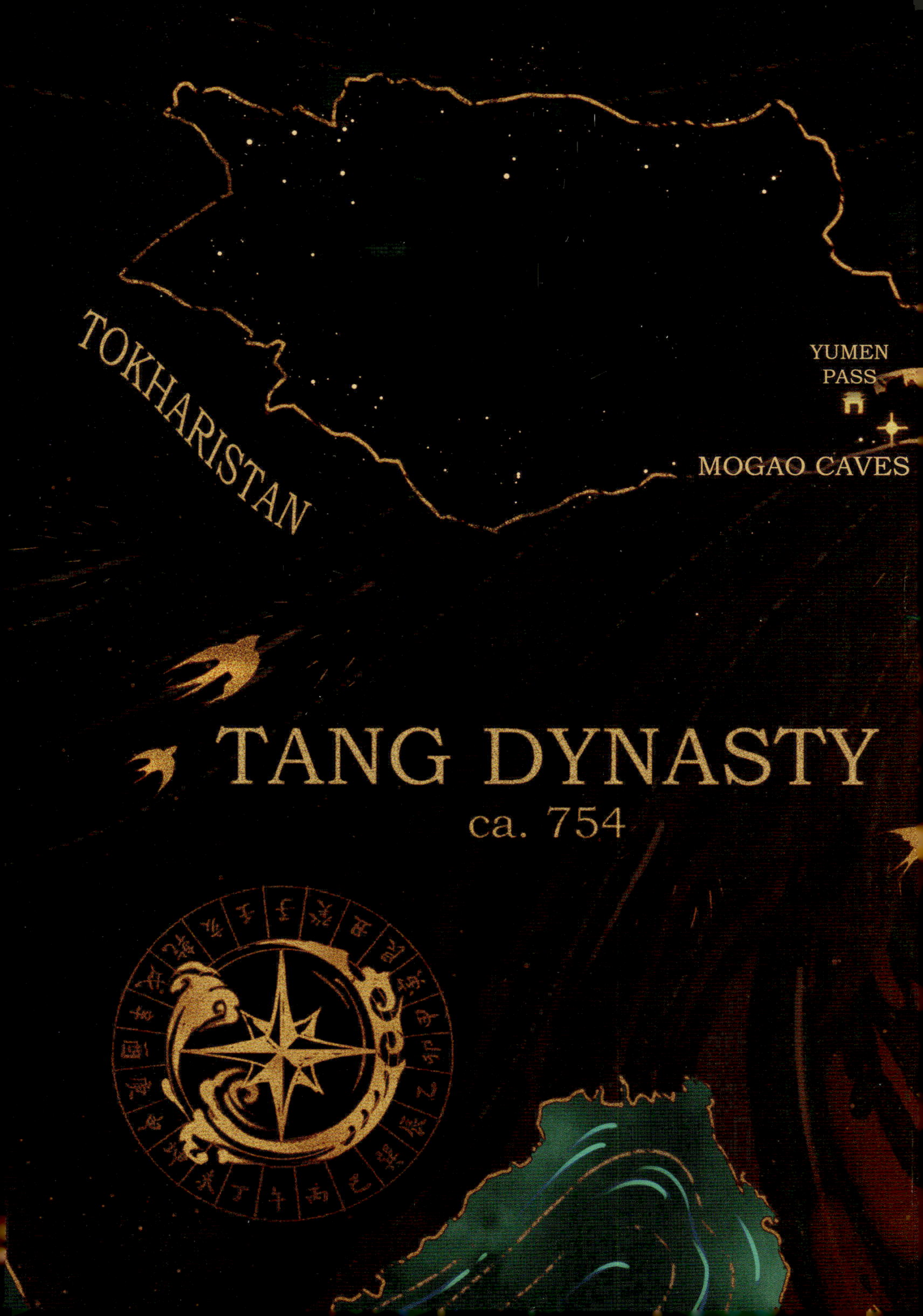
TOKHARISTAN
YUMEN PASS
MOGAO CAVES
TANG DYNASTY
ca. 754

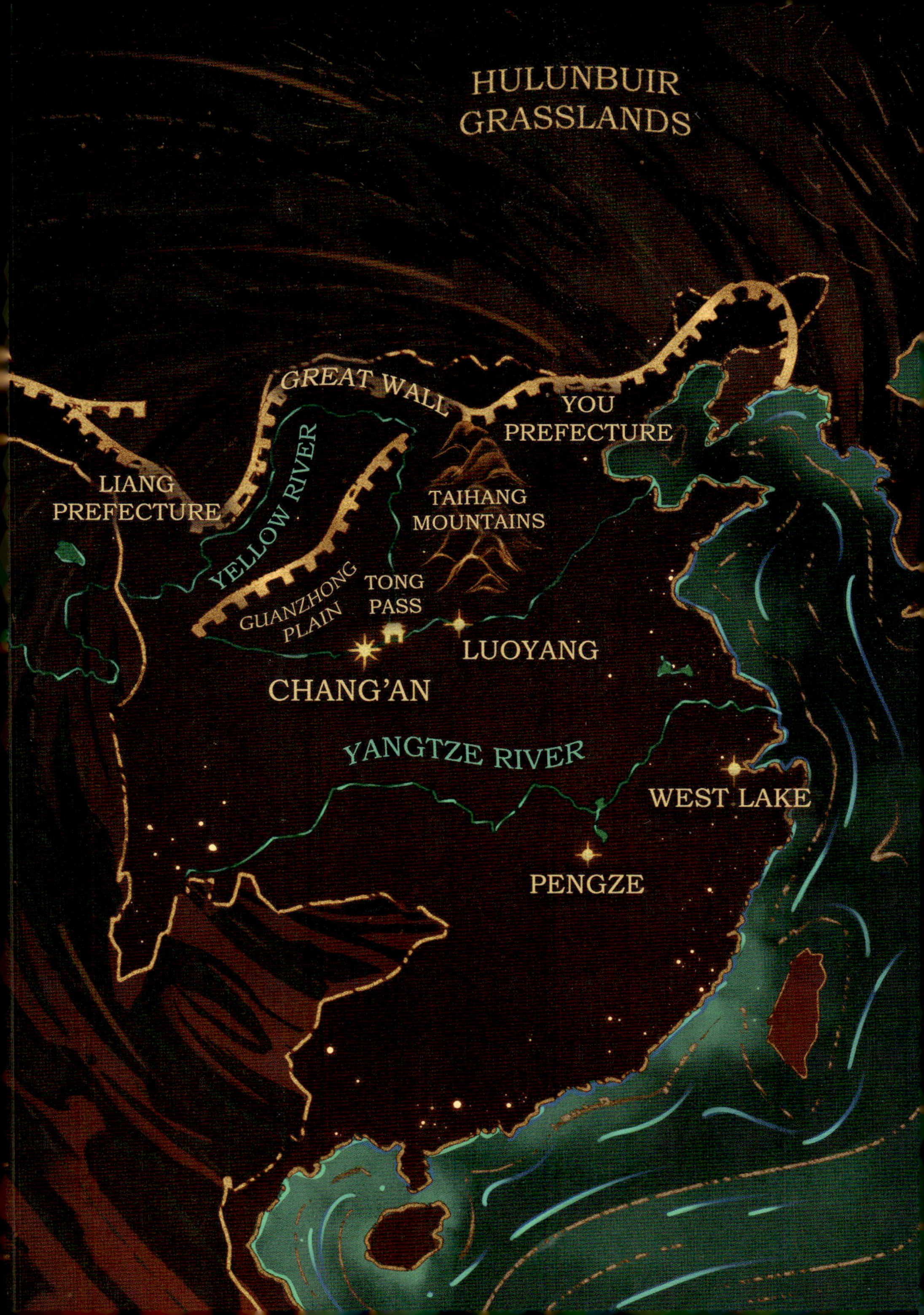
HULUNBUIR GRASSLANDS
GREAT WALL
YOU PREFECTURE
YELLOW RIVER
LIANG PREFECTURE
TAIHANG MOUNTAINS
GUANZHONG PLAIN
TONG PASS
LUOYANG
CHANG'AN
YANGTZE RIVER
WEST LAKE
PENGZE

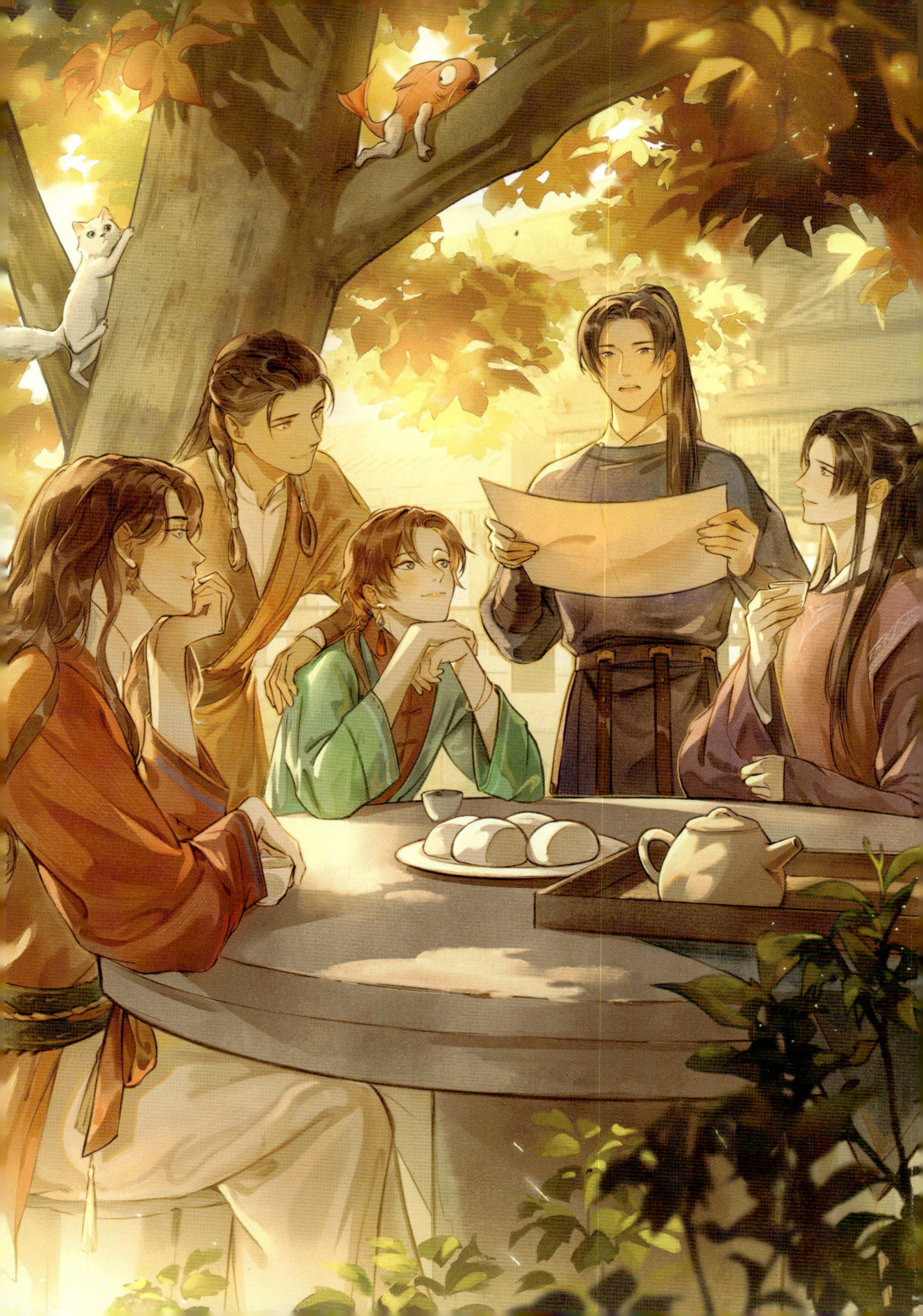

LEGEND OF EXORCISM

TIANBAO FUYAO LU
天宝伏妖录

WRITTEN BY

非天夜翔
FEI TIAN YE XIANG
(ARISE ZHANG)

ILLUSTRATED BY

RUTHIE
(KKCOOCOOL)

TRANSLATED BY

LILY & LOUISE

Seven Seas Entertainment

Legend of Exorcism: Tianbao Fuyao Lu (Novel) Vol. 1
Published originally under the title of 《天寶伏妖錄》 (Legend of Exorcism)
by 非天夜翔 Fei Tian Ye Xiang
Author© 2017 非天夜翔 (Fei Tian Ye Xiang)
Published by arrangement with JS Agency
English Translation copyright ©2025 by Seven Seas Entertainment, Inc.
All rights reserved.

Cover and Interior Illustrations by Ruthie (kkcoocool)

No portion of this book may be reproduced or transmitted in any form without written permission from the copyright holders. This is a work of fiction. Names, characters, places, and incidents are the products of the author's imagination or are used fictitiously. Any resemblance to actual events, locales, or persons, living or dead, is entirely coincidental. Any information or opinions expressed by the creators of this book belong to those individual creators and do not necessarily reflect the views of Seven Seas Entertainment or its employees.

Seven Seas press and purchase enquiries can be sent
to Marketing Manager Lauren Hill at press@gomanga.com.
Information regarding the distribution and purchase of digital editions is available from Digital Manager Kristine Johnson at digital@gomanga.com.

Seven Seas and the Seven Seas logo are trademarks of
Seven Seas Entertainment. All rights reserved.

Follow Seven Seas Entertainment online at
sevenseasentertainment.com.

TRANSLATION: Lily, Louise
ADAPTATION: Samantha C. Allen
COVER DESIGN: M. A. Lewife
INTERIOR DESIGN & LAYOUT: Clay Gardner
COPY EDITOR: Jehanne Bell
PROOFREADER: Ami Leh, Hnä
EDITOR: Kelly Quinn Chiu
PREPRESS TECHNICIAN: Salvador Chan Jr., April Malig, Jules Valera
MANAGING EDITOR: Alyssa Scavetta
EDITOR-IN-CHIEF: Julie Davis
PUBLISHER: Lianne Sentar
VICE PRESIDENT: Adam Arnold
PRESIDENT: Jason DeAngelis

Standard Edition ISBN: 979-8-89160-609-8
Special Edition ISBN: 979-8-89373-557-4
Printed in Canada
First Printing: March 2025
10 9 8 7 6 5 4 3 2 1

TABLE OF CONTENTS

	Preface	11
1	The Three Sage-Kings of Yaojin Palace	15
2	Shadows of the Past	27
3	The Vast World	35
4	The Sacred Light Reemerges	43
5	Commandant Li of the Longwu Guard	53
6	Living Under Someone Else's Roof	63
7	Hai Mie Hou Bi	73
8	Chief Exorcist	85
9	Newcomer	97
10	A Fresh Start	107
11	Divide and Conquer	119
12	Assuming Office	129
13	Return to Pingkang Ward	141
14	The Body under the Bed	157
15	The Hazy Past	171
16	Late-Night Fox Hunt	189
17	Leaving the Bait	205
18	The Palace in the Northern Outskirts	225
19	Fei'ao Slain	241
20	Persian Prince	257
21	The Name of an Ancient Sword	273
22	Yao in the Academy	287

23	Grass Rope and Jade Hoop	301
24	Imperial Audience on Mount Li	317
25	Roundup on the Examination Grounds	333
26	Compassion	347
◆	Character Guide & Glossary	367

PREFACE

I AM THRILLED THAT, seven years after its publication, *Legend of Exorcism* has arrived in North America with an English translation.

In chronological order of publication, this book is the first entry in the Exorcist series. Its story takes place in Tang dynasty China. The deities and demons of ancient eastern legends take the stage in this historical setting, situated around the time of the An Lushan rebellion. Nearly thirteen hundred years ago, the Tang dynasty began its turn from a flourishing empire into abject decline. The nation was set alight by the flames of war, until its remnants fell under the disjointed authority of regional warlords. Thereafter, such prosperity was rarely seen again.

Like a great tower on the verge of collapse, there is an unspeakable beauty in the tragedy of this moment in history. The poet Bai Juyi used it as inspiration to compose the epic poem, *Song of Everlasting Regret*. The line "he searched the dirt beneath Mawei Slope in vain, finding only a desolate grave and not her face of jade" tells the story of how the nation's internal strife prompted the emperor's flight with his noble consort and ultimately resulted in the death of his beloved Yang Yuhuan at Mawei Slope.

The exorcists' maxim in *Legend of Exorcism* comes from a poem written by the Tang dynasty literary giant Li Bai. It represents one of my favorite viewpoints on life and death during the time that I was writing the Exorcist series: Nothing lasts forever; the myriad things and all living beings are only guests on the shore of the winding river of time.

Every feast will come to an end, and flourishing scenes of abundance will one day be things of the past, never to return—but they will leave many beautiful memories we can revisit time and again. Welcome to Great Tang's Department of Demonic Exorcism. Backed by Li Guinian's song, let us do as a certain giant bird said, all together now: Go—go to that vast land of mortals. You won't regret it.

FEI TIAN YE XIANG (ARISE ZHANG)

BOOK 1
VULPINE BEAUTY

THE THREE SAGE-KINGS OF YAOJIN PALACE

*I long to cross the Yellow River, yet my way is choked with ice;
I wish to scale the Taihang Mountains, yet the snow prevents
my rise.*[1]

THE SKY STRETCHED as far as the eye could see, the perpetually snowcapped peaks of the Taihang Mountains merging with the clouds at the horizon. This was a place beyond the reach of ordinary birds; only a few white gyrfalcons braved the bitter winds to wheel high above, a handful of black specks scattered across the deep blue canopy of heaven.

A great bird clutched a cloth-wrapped bundle in its talons as it swept through cloud banks, drawing closer with each beat of its outstretched wings. Bathed in the last glow of twilight, the creature's feathers gleamed liquid gold as it swooped toward a mountain encircled by peaks and enshrouded in mist. The clouds parted to reveal a resplendent palace complex sitting atop its summit. The outer walls glowed red beneath the rays of the setting sun, as if they had been dyed by vermilion flames.

Snow did not gather within the palace complex as it did atop the peaks; instead it was filled with verdant parasol trees. Beneath the dazzling sun, it felt like midsummer. Now, as an evening breeze

---

1 Lines from the poem "The Hard Road" by the Tang dynasty poet Li Bai.

drifted past, the leaves of the trees rustled, shadows dancing in the lingering twilight, as if drawing open the curtains on a majestic dreamscape within this mountaintop residence.

The great bird landed on a platform outside the palace's main hall. With a cry that made the mountains shudder, the creature shook out its shimmering plumage in a dramatic flourish before gathering its feathers into itself. As the plumes dispersed, the figure of a man appeared.

He had a towering stature, deep-set features, and pitch-black eyes that glinted dark gold in the dim light. He wore no clothes on his upper body, showing off a well-defined torso and wheat-colored skin; on his lower half, he wore a regal black qun[2] with gold embroidery that danced in the wind. With his cloth bundle in hand, he slowly made his way toward the main hall.

The palace was a flurry of activity, young men and women coming and going in all directions. Upon seeing the newcomer, they hastily fell to their knees.

"Your Highness, King Qing Xiong."

The man called Qing Xiong strode through the tree-lined courtyard to the main hall, his long, black qun fluttering behind him. Night had quietly fallen, yet the lamps within the main hall remained unlit. Beneath the scattered light of the moon and stars stood three thrones upon a dais, two of which were empty.

The center seat was occupied by a man whose hair and clothes were both a dazzling shade of red. Even in the room's crepuscular light, his hair blazed like a flame, and his royal regalia gleamed a coppery gold, like rosy clouds drifting across the sky at dawn. Fiery tail feathers trailed from his belt to the ground, and his robes were draped loosely over his shoulders, revealing the fair skin and powerful muscles of his bare torso.

---

2   *Indigenous clothing of the Central Plains similar to a wrap-around skirt.*

At the sound of footsteps, the man lifted his head and met Qing Xiong's eyes.

He was the king of this palace, the ruler of this snowy domain and its vast sky. Few in the world knew that this stately man's name was Chong Ming. Nearly two centuries had flown by; dynasties had risen and fallen in the Divine Land in that time, and his fearsome reputation had long since been lost to history.

Chong Ming had a handsome face, with brows sharp as blades and a countenance that inspired both fear and awe in all who looked upon him. A burn scar reached up the side of his neck, ending just below his ear.

After a lengthy silence, Qing Xiong finally spoke. "Kong Xuan is dead. He left behind an orphan son; I'm leaving him with you to raise."

"How did he die?" Chong Ming asked coldly.

Qing Xiong slowly shook his head, and a dark silence settled over the hall.

"His offspring with a human? I'll do no such thing," Chong Ming said, voice flat. "Sheshen Cliff is out back, in the rear mountains—go find somewhere to toss it."

Qing Xiong dropped to one knee and laid down the bundle in his arms. The moment the cloth touched the ground, it began to expand and unfurl, the lotus patterns embroidered on its four corners glowing faintly until the bundle opened to reveal a child lying curled up on his side.

The boy was dressed in a tattered linen robe, his thin chest rising and falling with each of his shallow breaths. His features were delicate, and his little hand clutched something—an object of utmost importance, if the way he curled his body around it was any indication.

"By human reckoning, he should be about four years old," Qing Xiong said.

Chong Ming gazed down at the child in silence.

The boy twitched slightly in discomfort as Qing Xiong picked him up. "He looks just like his dad did as a child," he added.

He walked up the steps of the dais, coming to stand before Chong Ming with the boy in his arms. "Look at his eyes," he said quietly. "His brows."

"I told you to kill it," Chong Ming repeated.

Qing Xiong tried to hand the child to Chong Ming, but Chong Ming refused to take him. Qing Xiong set the boy in Chong Ming's lap instead. The child shifted restlessly, as if about to wake from his deep sleep. Feeling the warmth of Chong Ming's firm chest, he unconsciously pressed closer and fisted a tiny hand in the man's robe. The object in his hand slid from his grip—it was a deep green peacock feather, fashioned out of jade.

"Give him a name," Qing Xiong said, stepping away from the throne. "I'm leaving."

"Where are you going?" Chong Ming asked, his voice frigid. "If you leave him here with me, I'll kill him the next time I remember that woman."

"Do as you like." Qing Xiong turned to Chong Ming and took several steps backward. "Di Renjie is on his last breath. Yao have slowly overtaken the human realm, and Mara's resurrection is fast approaching. I must learn the truth about Kong Xuan's death. I'll be going now."

Qing Xiong took a flying leap, shook out his feathers, and transformed once again into that great black bird. With a thunderous beat of his wings and a resonant cry, he soared into the night sky.

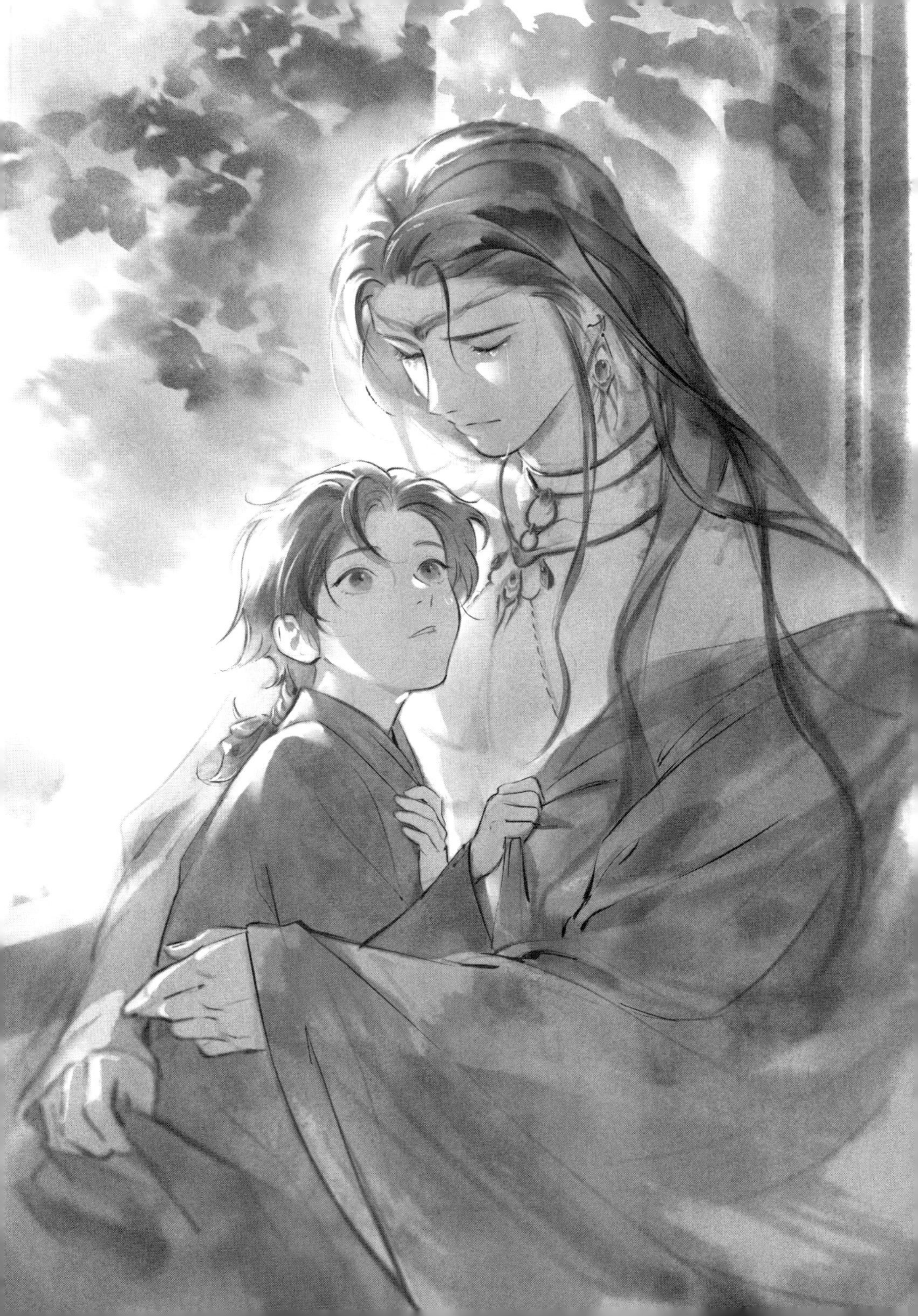

The child startled awake at Qing Xiong's shriek, and the jade feather slid from Chong Ming's lap and fell to the ground with a bright tinkling sound before tumbling down the steps of the dais. Glancing down, the child found that he was clutching at Chong Ming's robes. He looked up once more, meeting the man's eyes.

A hot teardrop fell onto the child's face. He reached out, puzzled, and touched Chong Ming's cheek, wiping away the man's tears. Timidly, the child asked, "Who are you?"

In Hebei, near You Prefecture Terrace, bloodred maple blossoms danced on the breeze as far as the eye could see. A scholarly man and a beautiful woman stood before the grand building atop the terrace and leaned over the balustrade to gaze at the magnificent landscape laid out below.

"Struck by the vastness of heaven and earth, I shed bitter tears as I stand alone,"[3] the man recited offhandedly. "Boyu truly was a genius of unbelievable proportions."

"Waxing poetic all of a sudden?" the woman behind him asked, her voice measured. "Now that Di Renjie is dead, there is no one to stop the yao from overrunning the human realm."

"There's no need to rush," the man muttered. "Who knows what cards that old fart still has up his sleeve? How go the preparations with Mara's vessel?"

"The vessel is willing this time. The integration process has gone exceptionally well. Still, we can't be certain until after the observation period. But aren't you worried about the problems that might arise from killing Kong Xuan? If the master of the Taihang Mountains rallies his strength and enters the fray…"

---

3 Lines from the poem "Ascending You Prefecture Terrace" by the Tang dynasty poet Chen Zi'ang, courtesy name Boyu.

"He would have come ages ago if he had the power to do so," the man said with a laugh. "Fortunes rise and fall with the inevitability of the tides, and Yaojin Palace has long been on the decline. Chong Ming is afflicted with fire venom—he wouldn't have retreated into solitude two hundred years ago otherwise. No—as things stand, Chang'an is ours to rule."

They could hear the sounds of music in the distance. The man stepped closer and ran his fingers through the hair at the woman's temples, studying her beautiful face. "Let's go," he murmured. "His Majesty awaits."

Twelve years later, in Yaojin Palace atop the Taihang Mountains, brilliant midsummer sunlight spilled through the leaves of the parasol trees, casting dappled shadows that swept across the ground like passing meteors.

A youth as beautiful as a jade sculpture perched on the branch of a parasol tree, mixing a bowl of white pollen. He wore a short, sleeveless crimson tunic adorned with embroidery beneath a green robe with a patterned border, tied off at his waist. His clever eyes darted periodically toward the main hall's open window as he worked.

Within the palace, Chong Ming reclined on a couch amid the fluttering gauze curtains, his face turned toward the chain of sunlit mountains in the distance.

"Hongjun!"

"Shh..." The youth named Hongjun glanced down at the base of the tree and lifted a finger to his lips.

The speaker was a yaoguai—a being that had absorbed and refined the energy of the natural world through the practice of spiritual cultivation until it gained a higher level of consciousness—more specifically, a carp yao. He had the torso of a large fish, nearly two feet in length, and the hairy legs of a man, which allowed him to walk on land. His arms, which emerged from behind his pectoral fins, were presently wrapped around the trunk of the parasol tree. The creature looked exceptionally bizarre as he shouted up at the boy.

"Get down from there!" A stream of bubbles poured from his mouth as he spoke. The fish yao swished his tail from side to side. "You don't know how to fly—if you fall and hurt yourself, I'll be in for a beating from His Majesty!"

Hongjun finished mixing his pollen and said quietly, "Dad's been sitting there all day. He refuses to see anyone, and loses his temper whenever anyone goes in."

"He's waiting for someone," the carp yao responded. "His Majesty's in a foul mood today."

"Who's he waiting for?" Hongjun asked.

As the carp yao hemmed and hawed, Hongjun hopped down from the tree and darted around the side of the main hall. One after another, the servants bowed as he passed, calling "Your Highness" in greeting, to which Hongjun replied with a nod. When he reached the back of the hall, he tossed out a grappling hook and swung himself up onto the palace roof.

Kneeling down, he shuffled along the roof in silence until he was right above the spot where Chong Ming was resting. Quietly, he lifted a glazed roof tile, picked up his bowl of medicine, and blew gently at the contents within. The medicinal powder seemed to take on a life of its own, shimmering with white light as it floated down into the main hall. Outside, among the parasol trees, the carp turned aside to watch through the entryway.

Chong Ming was asleep, his face still turned toward the gleaming peaks of the Taihang Mountains, the burn on his neck flashing with red light. The pollen drifted into the room, where it sparkled around Chong Ming like a river of stars before slowly settling against the scarlet burn mark, forming a white layer of frost.

The carp's open mouth gaped wider.

Chong Ming inhaled the pollen as he steadily breathed in and out, still asleep. Then his eyes flew open—an odd expression came over his face.

Success! Hongjun cheered to himself. Jumping down from the roof, he ran around the hall to watch alongside the carp as Chong Ming scrambled to his feet, his eyes darting frantically around the room. His face twitched as he glanced toward the entrance of the palace.

Overjoyed, Hongjun was about to call out to his father when Chong Ming abruptly turned his head away.

"A...*choo*!" Chong Ming gave an earth-shattering sneeze—a fireball the size of a horse cart hurtled from the main hall toward the unbroken chain of peaks beyond, exploding against the mountainside with a thunderous *boom*.

The servants of Yaojin Palace shouted in alarm as the ground bucked violently beneath their feet.

"An earthquake!"

"A...choo!" Another fireball smashed into the white jade pillars of the main hall. Hongjun squawked and grabbed the carp yao, making a break for the courtyard, where he dove headfirst into the pond.

"Achoo—achoo! Achoo!"

Chong Ming sneezed thrice in rapid succession. Fireballs erupted all around him, igniting the parasol trees in the courtyard and engulfing Yaojin Palace in a sea of flames.

"Help! Fire!"

A fireball landed in the courtyard's pond. "Ouch—hot! Hot!" the carp yao yelped. Hongjun sprang back out of the pond with the carp in his arms, scurrying around beneath the flaming parasol trees like a rat. After tossing the carp over the palace wall, he turned and raced back to Chong Ming.

"Dad!" Hongjun burst into the main hall, which was already ablaze. Chong Ming shot Hongjun a glance, his hand cupped over his nose and mouth. "Dad!" he began, "I just wanted to help—"

Chong Ming turned away, sucking in a sharp breath. Unable to hold back any longer, he sneezed explosively. Flames licked at the sky, enveloping the main hall in a sea of fire and surrounding Hongjun in the conflagration. Chong Ming darted forward and dragged Hongjun into his chest, protecting the youth in the circle of his arms.

A strident phoenix cry pierced the heavens as a pair of shimmering, multicolored wings burst from Chong Ming's back, glowing with orange light as they closed over Chong Ming and Hongjun to shield them from the flames. Their clothes burned away, leaving them naked, but Chong Ming was unscathed; as a phoenix, his divine powers of self-protection allowed him to emerge from the blazing inferno without harm.

Hongjun poked his head out and looked around. Lit by the true fire of Samadhi, the main hall of Yaojin Palace burned with unquenchable brightness.

Birds filled the sky, arriving from all directions. Like a waterfall flowing in reverse, they rushed up from the slopes below to douse Yaojin Palace in snow from the Taihang Mountains. The blizzard hissed as it melted, smothering the flames in an instant.

Two hours later, Hongjun stood outside the study, his face still streaked with soot.

"Aiya!" Hongjun yelped as the ruler smacked his palm.

"How many times is this now?!" Chong Ming had changed into casual clothes and was holding the ruler in his hand. "Explain yourself!" he said coldly.

Hongjun faltered; Chong Ming brought the ruler down once more, and the youth cried out again in pain.

"Are you so desperate to burn to death?" Chong Ming demanded furiously. "Stand outside in the front courtyard till nightfall, or there'll be no dinner for you!"

The third time Chong Ming swung the ruler, he used such force that tears sprang to Hongjun's eyes. "Go face the wall!" Chong Ming snapped.

Hongjun could only hang his head, trudge over to the courtyard, and stand facing the wall. The carp scratched his scales and scurried after him. He squatted down beside Hongjun and collected some melted snow to drink.

Chong Ming was fit to be tied. To think that such a disaster should befall him while he was simply lying around at home! Stalking out of the palace, he raised two fingers to his lips and whistled. Birds rose up from all directions to carry away the burnt branches and broken bricks that had been crushed under the weight of the snow.

"I warned you not to be so reckless," the carp yao said beside Hongjun. "How many times has it been? Your dad was already in a bad mood today, too."

"How could I know he would sneeze?" Hongjun protested. "I spent three years scouring the mountain for that snow lotus pollen!"

"The physicians have said it a hundred times," the carp yao responded. "There's no antidote for fire venom, so stop meddling."

Hongjun went silent. After only a few minutes of standing, he began shifting from foot to foot in boredom. He examined the scorch marks on the courtyard wall, where the streaks of ash resembled a landscape painting. Hongjun reached out and rubbed his fingers over the surface, smoothing the silhouette of the mountain until he was satisfied. The result looked rather like a painting rendered in splashed-ink style.

"Your dad's going to scold you again for getting your hands dirty!" the carp yao warned.

"I'll wash them before I eat," Hongjun hastily responded.

Black smoke was still rising over the main hall late in the afternoon. The lingering warmth of the embers had melted the snow, leaving puddles everywhere among the wreckage. Taking in the scene, Chong Ming felt like weeping but couldn't quite muster the tears.

An avian screech split the air as a great black bird draped in golden light winged its way through the Taihang Mountains. Upon landing, Qing Xiong transformed and walked through the courtyard, gaping in shock.

"What happened?" Qing Xiong asked a young attendant, dismayed. "Was there an attack?"

The attendant dared not answer, saying only that His Majesty, Chong Ming, awaited him in the side hall. Qing Xiong turned and strode over.

"Qing Xiong!" Hongjun rushed toward him with a joyous cry. With a flying leap, he hugged Qing Xiong around the neck and clambered onto the man's back.

2
SHADOWS OF THE PAST

Qing Xiong snatched at Hongjun and dragged him off his back. He tickled the youth, eliciting peals of laughter, before forcing him to stand before him properly. "Have you been making trouble again?"

Hongjun's hands were still covered in ash, which he'd wiped all over Qing Xiong's face. He pointed at the dark streaks and broke into another fit of giggles. As Qing Xiong stood bewildered, Hongjun recounted the day's events in vivid detail. Qing Xiong couldn't suppress a chuckle as Hongjun described the way Chong Ming had lost his composure.

They laughed together for a while before Hongjun looked at him seriously again. "What did you bring back for me this time?" he asked. "Hand it over!"

"I brought nothing," Qing Xiong responded.

Skeptical, Hongjun stepped forward to pat Qing Xiong down himself. Qing Xiong always went around bare-chested; the only place gifts might be hiding were his pants pockets. Hongjun was about to start digging when Qing Xiong said solemnly, "I really didn't bring anything this time."

"No books, no food…" Hongjun's face fell.

Qing Xiong laughed. "You've already finished the books I gave you last time?"

"I've read them so many times they're falling apart."

Seeing Hongjun's disappointment, Qing Xiong couldn't resist teasing him. "Where's your Zhao Zilong?"

"He's here." Hongjun called out and the carp yao bounded over. The creature's half-carp-half-man appearance was the result of a failed attempt to cultivate into human form. Hongjun had stumbled across him in the Taihang Mountains five years ago and taken him in. The carp yao's appearance had happened to come just before one of Qing Xiong's visits, during which Qing Xiong had gifted Hongjun a collection of short stories about the heroes of the human realm's Three Kingdoms. In his excitement, Hongjun had promptly named the carp Zhao Zilong after the legendary general of Shu Han, and declared that he would surely leap over the Dragon Gate to become a powerful dragon one day.

With a magician's flourish, Qing Xiong finally produced something from his pockets—a treasure hanging from a gold chain, which he dangled before Hongjun. The moment Qing Xiong took it out, the entire courtyard lit up with a brilliance that matched the blazing sun in the sky.

"What is it?" Hongjun asked in astonishment.

From the chain hung a delicately wrought pendant of metal and stone, ringed with mechanical components that enclosed a tiny crystal orb, which glowed with a soft white light like a lamp.

"I'm leaving this in your care for now." Qing Xiong smiled as he untangled the chain and placed the necklace in Hongjun's hands. "It's a spiritual device. I don't have the nerve to teach you how it works, though... Your dad would rake me over the coals. The crystal is fragile—be careful you don't break it. I'll show you what to do with it later."

Itching to examine his exquisite gift immediately, Hongjun

hastily bobbed his head in agreement before scurrying off with the pendant cupped in both hands.

"He's already sixteen."

Chong Ming had been drinking tea when Qing Xiong entered the ancillary hall. Qing Xiong knelt before the table and shot Chong Ming a glance.

"He decided to wreak havoc again today, so he's being punished," Chong Ming explained dispassionately.

"A youngster like him is bound to cause a little trouble," Qing Xiong said. "The two of us and Kong Xuan were the source of no shortage of chaos back in our day."

Chong Ming arched a brow. "He's not ready yet."

"I received a letter last night from the Department of Demonic Exorcism in the human realm," Qing Xiong responded. "We have less than four years until the heavenly demon Mara returns to this world. The letter is a summons calling young exorcists of talent to gather in Chang'an—presumably in preparation for Mara's resurrection."

Qing Xiong tried to hand Chong Ming the letter, but Chong Ming wouldn't look at it. With a flick of his fingers, a blazing ball of fire shot from his hand. Qing Xiong snatched the letter back to save it from being burned.

"Chong Ming, the yao have run rampant over the Divine Land while those in the Tang dynasty capable of stopping them have grown fewer in number each year. We're out of time."

Chong Ming at last turned to look directly into Qing Xiong's eyes. "Do not forget that we, too, are yao."

"Oh, so you *do* remember," Qing Xiong said. "And here I thought my liege, the yao king, had forgotten."

Chong Ming's aura surged as if flames raged within his body. His brow creased in anger as he glared at Qing Xiong.

In the study, Hongjun was trying to pry the pendant open with two of his throwing knives. When that didn't work, he attempted to cut through the mechanical rings with a pair of sharp shears. Finally, he resorted to smashing the pendant with a hammer, but even after whacking it until sweat dripped down his forehead, he still couldn't extract the tiny crystal in its center.

"Ahhhh—" Hongjun picked up a bronze vase, sorely tempted to smash the little thing with it next.

"Why are you so determined to take it apart?" the carp yao piped up from beside him. "His Highness Qing Xiong told you to be careful with it."

"I just want to take out the crystal," Hongjun replied. "I want to set it in the hilt of my sword."

"That's no ordinary light it's giving off." The carp yao clambered onto the table, hopped atop a book, and flopped down. The radiance of the pendant reflected in his fishy eyes.

Hongjun examined the necklace. "The rings on the outside are charmed, but to do what? Are they a seal? This light is so pleasant."

"Just looking at it makes me feel warm and cozy," the carp yao said. "I can feel my mood improving already."

Hongjun picked up the pendant. "Let's go ask Qing Xiong about it."

"You're not done with your punishment yet!" the carp yao reminded him, but Hongjun had already flitted away with the necklace in hand.

The setting sun bled across the sky and into the mountains as birdsong rose and fell among the peaks. As Hongjun approached the ancillary hall, he heard a fierce argument coming from inside. Startled, he ducked behind a pillar.

"That black jiao is nothing but a usurper, a false dragon—he'll never be a yao king! As if some reptile that crawled out of a cesspool could ever be worthy of that title!"

"But he defeated us in battle—this is an irrefutable fact," Qing Xiong said grimly. "Unless we return and destroy him completely, the entire human realm will turn to ash the day Mara returns to lead the yao!"

"What does that have to do with me?!" Chong Ming shouted. "The humans abandon principles for the sake of profit! They took Lao-san[4] and left his halfling son in my care for twelve years! Why should I have been forced to raise an orphan with human blood running through his veins?!"

"He is still Kong Xuan's child!" Qing Xiong said, his voice low and filled with reproach. "Didn't you have any regrets after Kong Xuan left?!"

"What is it that you think I should regret?!" Chong Ming practically roared his response. "Hongjun wouldn't even *be* an orphan if that human hadn't led Kong Xuan to his death!"

"There are indeed ingrates among the human race who abandon principles for the sake of profit, but there are also friends like Di Renjie!"

"Friends? What friends?!" Chong Ming sneered. "Even if there are, I won't see Hongjun do anything for those humans' sake! My answer is no!"

Qing Xiong's voice trembled. "Kong Xuan possessed the power of both the demonic and the divine. As his child, Hongjun has inherited his pentacolor sacred light. He has the power to help the yao eradicate the black jiao, avenge his father, and destroy Mara's

---

4   *The third eldest among siblings or third-ranked member of a group in terms of seniority.*

reincarnation. Even if you try to keep him here for the rest of his life, it's only a matter of time until he learns the truth!"

"The day we left the Central Plains," Chong Ming began, voice low, "I told you I would no longer concern myself with the survival of the yao. And Mara? I only hope Mara returns and exterminates those damned humans once and for all!"

"Can you not be honest with yourself for once?! Chong Ming!" Qing Xiong stepped forward, his aura billowing outward. The atmosphere within the hall took on a dangerous quality. The teacups on the table clattered softly against each other and the latticed windows rattled in their frames as the two kings stared each other down.

They were interrupted by the soft press of footsteps outside.

Qing Xiong and Chong Ming retracted their auras and turned as one. Qing Xiong hurried to the door just in time to see Hongjun's figure receding into the distance.

He sighed. "The last words you spoke to Kong Xuan all those years ago were 'get out,' and the next thing you knew, you were parted forever. If only you could have said something—anything—to convince him to stay, we wouldn't be in this mess today."

With that, Qing Xiong strode from the hall, leaving Chong Ming to stare out at the twilight beyond the door in a quiet daze.

Night descended, and the sky filled with stars, their silver light cascading like a waterfall over the Taihang Mountains.

The sound of footsteps rose behind him, but Hongjun remained motionless where he lay on a flat slab of rock near Sheshen Cliff. The surface of the rock sloped down toward the cliff's edge; the slightest lapse in focus would send him tumbling into a bottomless chasm.

Qing Xiong climbed up and lay down beside him, and the two stared up at the glittering night sky in introspective silence.

"Is it true?" Hongjun suddenly asked.

"In your heart, you already know the answer."

Hongjun's breathing hitched, and Qing Xiong lifted a hand to cover the youth's eyes. Clutching at Qing Xiong's hand, Hongjun wiped his tears against the man's palm.

"Does my dad hate me?" Hongjun's voice was choked with sobs.

"What he says rarely reflects what he feels," Qing Xiong said pensively. "You mustn't hold his words against him. If he truly doesn't wish to do something, there is no one in the world who can force him. The thing that I gave you earlier—do you have it with you?"

Hongjun shakily held out the pendant.

"You've always wanted to visit the human realm, have you not?" Qing Xiong said, taking the pendant from him. Its soft glow lit up half the mountain, a brilliant match for the star-spangled sky. Bathed in its brightness, Hongjun slowly regained his composure.

"Every time I come to visit, you throw a great tantrum, begging me to take you to the human realm with me," Qing Xiong continued. "Now that you've grown up, I say, very well, go ahead—what have you to fear?"

Hongjun's first reaction was joy, but at the thought of Chong Ming, his expression dimmed. He stared blankly at Qing Xiong, who had turned away to gaze into the pendant's glimmering light.

"There is plenty of good food and fun to be had in the human realm—beautiful women, friends to drink with, music that rings for dozens of miles, lights that burn brightly through the night... So, go—go to that vast land of mortals. You won't regret it."

By the next day, the ancillary hall had been tidied up and the three thrones moved in temporarily. Chong Ming occupied the center seat, with Qing Xiong sitting to his left. Chong Ming's expression was as chilly as ever as Hongjun approached.

Hongjun greeted him before respectfully moving to stand in a corner. "Dad."

"I am not your father," Chong Ming said, his voice devoid of emotion.

"You are," Hongjun said, feeling uneasy as he looked up at Chong Ming. "You're my dad."

But Chong Ming looked away, his eyes falling on the third, empty throne. "You once asked me to whom this final seat belonged," Chong Ming said solemnly. "Now I will give you your answer. Your birth father once sat in this chair. His name was Kong Xuan. Like Qing Xiong and me, he was one of the masters of Yaojin Palace. After he died, Qing Xiong brought you here. Now that you have grown up, it's time you went back."

"Went back where?" Hongjun asked.

"To wherever you came from." Chong Ming's voice was toneless.

"I belong here," Hongjun said. "I'm not going anywhere."

THE VAST WORLD

THE HALL WAS SO QUIET one might have heard a pin drop. At last, Qing Xiong broke the silence. "I hereby order you to travel to the human realm, where you will complete three tasks. Hongjun, your father has raised you for twelve years. Will you help him fulfill his three wishes?"

Hongjun glanced first at Chong Ming, then at Qing Xiong, before turning back to Chong Ming once more. Finally, he nodded. "If you put it that way, then yes, I'll go."

Qing Xiong handed him a letter. "Before passing from this world, Di Renjie established a government office known as the Great Tang Department of Demonic Exorcism. Take this letter and report for duty at the department's headquarters. You must find the culprit responsible for the death of your father, Kong Xuan—this is your first task."

"Did he have any enemies?" Hongjun asked after some thought.

"I don't know." Qing Xiong rose to his feet. A jade peacock feather appeared between his fingertips, which he placed in Hongjun's hands. "The kind of person your father was—the life he led in Chang'an; the people he hated and the people he loved; those who owed him debts of gratitude and those who bore him feelings of enmity—all of it is a mystery to us, so there's nothing we can tell you. You are the only one who can supply the answers to these questions."

Hongjun hesitated briefly before taking the feather.

"Yao are running rampant in Chang'an." Chong Ming tossed him a book, then continued, "You were given a set of immortal-slaying knives as a child. You may kill any of the yao listed in this bestiary."

Hongjun nodded his assent as he accepted the book and cracked it open. He didn't understand a word of what was written about the monstrous yaoguai described within its pages.

"Understood?" Chong Ming prompted.

Hongjun flipped through the bestiary, making a show of carefully examining its contents. He stole glance after glance at Chong Ming atop his lofty perch, but Chong Ming never looked back.

"Who is Di Renjie?" he asked when he saw that Chong Ming's stern expression had eased ever so slightly.

"A human," Chong Ming responded. "An old friend of your father, who also died long ago."

"The Department of Demonic Exorcism is responsible for hunting yao and exorcising demons," Qing Xiong explained. "Once you join, just listen to your superior's orders. The yao occupying Chang'an are the mortal enemies of Yaojin Palace. If you can successfully expel the false yao king of Chang'an, then perhaps one day, your father and I will return to the human realm with you."

Hongjun lifted his head. "Really?"

"When did I ever say that?" Chong Ming's voice was frigid as he glowered at Qing Xiong.

"Two hundred years ago," Qing Xiong continued calmly as he paced around the hall, "a war broke out between Yaojin Palace and the Sacred Kingdom of Mara. After a protracted struggle—"

"There's no need to tell him all this," Chong Ming interrupted. "He will not succeed."

"He is your son," Qing Xiong retorted, "as well as a prince of Yaojin Palace!"

Chong Ming's anger flared. "Enough!"

"I will defeat the yao king," Hongjun said, a smile flickering to life upon his face. "That's the second task, right? It's a promise!"

"I will never return to the human realm, not even if you hack that black jiao into a thousand pieces." Chong Ming gnashed his teeth. "There's no point risking your life for such a useless endeavor!"

Hongjun went quiet.

"There's also this." Qing Xiong placed the pendant in Hongjun's hand. "When you arrive in Chang'an, look for a man named Chen Zi'ang and tell him the Light-Bearer Dipamkara... Never mind, there's no need for you to tell him anything. Just take the pendant and open it like this..."

As Qing Xiong held the necklace between slender fingers, the gold band at the base of the pendant began to glow with magical script before separating from the mechanical rings protecting the luminous gem within. With the charms broken, the bright crystal slowly floated free.

"...then crush this in front of him."

Hongjun's face colored with surprise. "Why?"

"This heart lamp was entrusted to me by the kun[5] king of the Dark Capital," Qing Xiong explained. "It should have been inherited by a member of the Chen family in the human realm. However, due to a small accident two hundred years ago, the power of the heart lamp failed to pass into anyone in the Chen family line... It's time the heart lamp was returned to its rightful owner. When the crystal shatters, the lamp and its power will enter the rightful bearer's body on its own."

---

5   *A legendary giant fish, measuring up to thousands of miles in length, that transforms into an equally large bird known as a peng.*

"Who knows whether that useless mortal is still among the living." Chong Ming sneered.

"There's no need to worry; any descendant of the Chen family will do," Qing Xiong said. "In any case, Hongjun, you must find the rightful inheritor of the heart lamp, befriend them, and give them the light contained within this crystal. That is your third task. Once you have completed all three, you may return to Yaojin Palace. Naturally, if you succeed, your father will never drive you from these mountains again."

"All right." Hongjun tucked the pendant away with care. "Then I'll complete these three tasks and return home within a year."

Chong Ming scoffed, but he couldn't help adding some words of his own. "You have Kong Xuan's pentacolor sacred light within your body; it will protect you. You also have your immortal-slaying knives, which are more than sufficient to defeat any human or yao you might encounter. I have raised you for twelve years. Given the time we've shared, Qing Xiong will surely berate me if I say nothing, so…if you've thought things through and truly wish to go…"

Hongjun stared open-mouthed as Chong Ming finally turned to look at him and said deliberately, "You may choose one thing among the treasures of Yaojin Palace to take with you. Anything that you want; say the word, and it's yours."

Sunlight spilled into the palace hall, bathing the floor that stretched between them in gold. The firmament beyond the skylight was a deep, flawless blue dotted with a handful of snowy white clouds.

After an expansive silence, Hongjun finally said, "I want my dad… I want you to come with me down the mountain—is that okay?"

Chong Ming was still for a very long time. At last he rose to his feet and walked toward the side of the room, turning away.

"No." He didn't look back at Hongjun.

"You said you would give me anything I want," Hongjun said with a smile. "Well, I choose you."

"That's enough," Qing Xiong cut in. "Hongjun, this is for you."

Qing Xiong handed Hongjun a full travel pack. Hongjun slung the bag over his shoulder before slowly approaching Chong Ming, but Chong Ming refused to look at him; he walked instead out onto the hall's outdoor terrace. Hongjun's feet slowed.

"If you don't have anything to ask of me, you may as well leave now," Chong Ming said.

There was a long silence. Then: "There's nothing else."

Hongjun turned and left the ancillary hall, crestfallen.

"He's just like Kong Xuan was back then," Qing Xiong sighed when he had gone.

Chong Ming's shoulders were trembling. When he spoke, his voice was slightly hoarse. "Hongjun is Hongjun; Kong Xuan is Kong Xuan. After all these years, I've managed to move on from the past, yet you're still holding on."

Qing Xiong looked at him in surprise.

Shouldering his little travel pack, Hongjun slowly made his way down the winding footpaths of the Taihang Mountains. The carp yao bounded after him.

"Your Highness! Your Highness—!" The carp gasped for breath. "How could you leave without me?"

Only when Hongjun heard him calling did he realize he had completely forgotten about the creature. "What are you doing here?"

Hongjun asked. "Hurry and go back! Dad said the human realm is full of danger..."

"Master Qing Xiong asked me to come with you." The carp plopped down on a rock and flapped his tail. "Do you know how to get to Chang'an?"

Hongjun scratched his head.

"Do you know how many copper coins make up one tael of silver? Do you know where to buy a horse? Do you know how to order a meal or book a night at an inn? What about how to greet a human? Did you know the best-looking men are the biggest liars? Also—"

"All right, all right, stop!" Hongjun dropped his bag and sat down as well.

But the carp yao was just warming up. "Remember to wash your hands before you eat. Also, make sure you put on an extra layer when the weather cools. The human realm has four seasons: spring, summer, autumn, and winter. Unlike Yaojin Palace..."

In the distance, the rise and fall of birdsong echoed between the misty peaks of the Taihang Mountains, the sea of clouds churning beneath the golden glare of the sun.

The carp yao's lecture seemed to fade as Hongjun thought back on his twelve years in Yaojin Palace. He had never before left his father's side. Yes, he'd always yearned to explore the world of mortals below the mountains, but now that he'd actually left, he found himself unspeakably terrified at the thought of Chong Ming bidding him what might very well be a final farewell. A wave of grief overwhelmed him.

"You can go home after you've finished your three tasks," the carp yao said. "Don't cry."

"I'm not crying!" Hongjun said angrily.

"Then let's go. These mountain roads hurt my feet."

Hongjun picked up the carp yao and stuffed the creature—who had very helpfully tucked his arms and legs against his body—into his travel pack. But he couldn't resist taking a final look at the mountains behind him, his heart filled with an indescribable tangle of feelings.

"Let's get going," the carp yao said. "It'll be hard to travel once night falls."

Hongjun could not reply. He turned his back to those familiar peaks and took the first steps on his journey down the mountain path.

"It's been three days—how are they still wandering the Taihang Mountains?"

Chong Ming stood before a pond in the courtyard of Yaojin Palace, his face written with impatience. Within the pond was an image of Hongjun squatting by a small stream and scooping up a handful of water to drink, his hair and clothes dirty and unkempt.

"I told him not to drink unboiled water, that it would make him sick! He's only just left the mountain—how has he already become so uncouth?!" Chong Ming was beside himself with exasperation.

"He's probably lost," Qing Xiong commented.

"I told you that carp isn't to be relied on!" Chong Ming's cheek twitched in irritation. "Forget it, you go escort him out of the mountains."

"No," Qing Xiong said. "Escort him yourself."

As Chong Ming turned to glare at him, Qing Xiong pointed to the pool. "Look, they're almost back on track. If they follow that path on the right, it'll take them down the mountain."

Chong Ming and Qing Xiong watched as Hongjun stood before a fork in the road and glanced first left and then right.

"Right! Take the right!" Chong Ming and Qing Xiong urged him in anxious unison.

Hongjun did not disappoint; watching him stride down the path to the right, the brothers breathed a sigh of relief.

"There they go," Qing Xiong said. "If they continue along the humans' official roads, they'll reach Chang'an in a month's time."

Hongjun strayed out of the water mirror's range at last, his figure disappearing beyond the final ravine of the Taihang Mountain range. Chong Ming could watch no longer. He turned to leave, alone.

4
THE SACRED LIGHT REEMERGES

ON A PITCH-BLACK NIGHT one month later, rain sluiced over a flat plain, accompanied by deafening crashes of thunder. Lightning streaked across the sky, illuminating the dark earth below.

"Where did it go?" Hongjun swiped rainwater from his face as he scanned his surroundings. There seemed to be countless dangers lurking in the darkness; he could sense yao energy spreading in all directions.

"Stop chasing it!" The carp yao shouted as he scurried after him. "We're almost to Chang'an!"

"A monster is a monster!" Hongjun hollered back. "Every yaoguai we slay counts for something!"

Hongjun stood in the middle of the road, drenched in rain and hair sticking to his forehead, and tried to catch his breath. His clothing had grown tattered during his monthlong trek from the Taihang Mountains to the Guan-Long region, and he was presently covered in blood. The downpour diluted the splotches of red, which ran down his body to soak into the muddy ground.

In his mind's eye, he saw the devastating scenes of huts burning in the Guanzhong Plain and children with their heads bitten off.

He surveyed the area around him. The spatter of relentless rain drowned out the yaoguai's rustling as it wove through the open fields. Each flash of lightning left nothing but darkness in its wake, save for the soft glow that clung to the pendant around his neck.

There was a deep rumble as a giant creature, over twenty feet in length, leapt from the wheat fields at his side. The slick black yaoguai had five bloodshot eyes set in its massive head, its bloody maw filled with viciously sharp teeth. It looked like a catfish the size of a small house—if catfish had four clawed, mucilaginous limbs sprouting from their bodies. The creature lunged at Hongjun, its teeth bared.

"It's an ao fish!"

Hongjun threw up his hands, and a hazy barrier of light unfolded at his fingertips. The ao fish crashed straight into it and went careening backward, howling in pain.

In a flash, Hongjun spun a throwing knife between his fingers and hurled it at the primary eye at the apex of the ao fish's head.

The immortal-slaying knives were a treasure left behind by the cultivator Lu Ya: four deadly throwing knives each imbued with an elemental affinity for wind, water, fire, or lightning. As Hongjun's first blade shot out, a bolt of lightning crashed down from the sky, surging like a waterfall over the horizon.

The ao fish jerked away to avoid the strike, only to be blinded by the knife as it plunged directly into one of its lateral eyes. Howling in pain, it crashed to the ground before burrowing into the mud and out of sight, taking the sparking knife with it.

Dirty water splattered the official road as the ground split open like a breaking wave before the monster. The monster shot into the distance; Hongjun grabbed the carp yao and shoved him into his bag before leaping onto his horse and giving chase.

The storm shrouded Chang'an in a veil of darkness. High on the city wall, sentries in conical bamboo hats were dozing in the shelter of a gate tower's eaves.

THE SACRED LIGHT REEMERGES

A monstrous roar echoed from somewhere outside the city.

"What's going on out there?!"

Startled awake, the sentries gathered on the walls. Lightning forked across the horizon, revealing a spine-chilling scene at the far end of the official road, beyond the city's outskirts. Sludge flew into the air as the earth split open, light flashing from beneath the muddy ground as if an invisible war chariot was barreling toward Chang'an's outer gates.

Chasing after this invisible chariot, another figure in the distance was shouting, "Get back here!"

"Archers, fire! Fire!"

"Chang'an is under curfew—entrance is forbidden—"

But the warnings came too late—or rather, everything happened too quickly. The garrison commander had scarcely finished speaking before the behemoth, invisible except for the crackling of lightning, splashed into the city moat.

With a wild roar, a huge black creature sprang from the water in a flying leap. The sentries on the city wall stood agog as the giant, four-legged ao fish sailed hundreds of feet through the air over their heads with a flip of its tail, its head flashing with electricity. Slicked in mud and algae from the moat, the creature crashed its way into the city, leaving a trail of crushed roof tiles in its wake.

The garrison commander stared in stunned silence.

The stone brick pavement shattered as the giant ao fish reached the inner roads, where it instantly sank back into the earth again, accompanied by sparks of electricity as it dashed down one of Chang'an's main streets. Only when it had disappeared did the several dozen sentries atop the city wall come to their senses, shouting in alarm.

A voice rang out in the darkness beyond the wall. "Stop chasing it!"

"My throwing knife is still stuck in its eye!" another voice shouted back.

"Then recall it! Are you stupid?!"

"I can't! The knife is the only thing keeping it near the surface. The moment I recall it, it'll burrow into the ground and disappear!"

A grappling hook shot out with a hiss and caught on the eaves of the gate tower. Seconds later, an agile figure swung up toward the guards like a celestial deity, lit by the white beams of their searchlights. Chang'an's sentries once again looked on helplessly as Hongjun landed on an overhanging eave and launched himself back into the air, soaring into the city with his arms outstretched like wings.

"N-n-n-notify the Yulin Guard! Hurry!" the garrison commander atop the tower shouted in a panic.

Inside Chang'an, Hongjun once again flung out his grappling hook, snagging it on the roof of a roadside dwelling to slow himself down before softening his landing with a roll.

"Where did it go?" he wondered aloud.

"I told you not to chase it..." The carp yao poked his fishy head out from where he was stowed in Hongjun's travel pack, opening and closing his mouth as he drank the rainwater.

"Well, what's done is done!" Hongjun said. "Can you be any more of a nag?"

"It's behind you! Behind you!" the carp yao cried as he spotted a bolt of lightning swerving into an alley.

"Who dares commit crimes under cover of darkness?!"

"That glowing man over there! Grab him!"

Hoofbeats rang out as the city guard rushed toward them, followed by a rain of arrows.

Yelping in alarm, the carp yao screamed at Hongjun to retreat, only for the youth to sidestep the arrows as he chased the yaoguai into a narrow alleyway. The ground was littered with broken brick and shattered stone, but the ao fish was nowhere to be found, its roar replaced by the screams of the common folk who had been startled awake by the commotion.

Gathering his wits, Hongjun looked up, searching for a place to cast his grappling hook so he could propel himself over the wall in front of him. The alleyway he'd run into was bare on all sides, with no useful eaves or overhangs for him to exploit. "Where are we?"

"Someone's coming," the carp yao said behind him.

Hongjun turned just in time to see the city guard had caught up with him. "We've found him!" their leader shouted. "He's over here!"

Hongjun backed away helplessly. He couldn't kill ordinary humans the way he did yaoguai—but the guards showed no mercy, loosing a hail of arrows with a chorus of twanging bowstrings. Hongjun called on his sacred light, which hummed into place as it formed a protective shield, blocking the projectiles. The deflected arrows flew in all directions, eliciting bloodcurdling screams as they knocked the archers from their horses.

"Is everyone all right?!" Hongjun called out, afraid he'd killed someone by accident.

"Yaoguai!" a clear and resonant voice rang out. "Surrender yourself at once!" The lead guard splashed through the rain and charged directly at Hongjun.

"Stop fighting already and run!" the carp yao cried.

"Run where?!" Hongjun turned aside to avoid the man's strike; he didn't dare use his throwing knives for fear of injuring his opponent. "I'm not a yaoguai!" he shouted.

"You are though," the carp yao corrected from behind him. "Your dad is a great yaoguai, with powerful yao blood running through his veins! How are you *not* a yaoguai?"

Hongjun was speechless.

The guard had no spiritual power, but his martial prowess was undeniable. Hongjun tried time and again to escape the narrow alleyway, only for his path to be blocked by the man's sword. He had no choice but to deploy his sacred light once again to protect himself.

The storm swallowed the earth and sky as thunder rolled overhead.

"I don't want to fight you!" Hongjun shouted as he ran up one of the narrow alley's walls. Kicking off the surface, he leapt over the head of the guard, attempting to flee.

To his surprise, the guard turned and rushed forward with a shout. He hurled himself bodily at Hongjun, his blade ringing as it collided with the sacred light and broke through Hongjun's barrier.

Hongjun had never imagined there was a weapon in the world with the power to pierce his shield of sacred light. He twisted in midair, folding his left arm behind him as he bent backward and raised his right hand to fend off the blade.

The falling rain seemed to freeze in place, each droplet a reflection of the fantastic scene unfolding in the narrow alley. In a thousand drops of liquid radiance, Hongjun met the guard's fierce eyes as the man thrust his sword toward his throat. Hongjun flinched back to evade the strike, and the pendant around his neck swung up on its chain to meet the blade. The thought struck Hongjun like a bolt of lightning—*That's no ordinary weapon!* But it was too late. The sword cleaved through the chain; with a *crack*, the crystal pendant shattered to pieces.

A blinding flash erupted in the alley. Beneath the roiling tempest up above, Chang'an was engulfed in a cyclone of light that rendered the magnificent capital of Great Tang bright as day—

As quickly as it'd come, the intense light vanished with a powerful blast of air that forced Hongjun and the guard apart. The shockwave threw Hongjun backward, slamming him into the ground.

The only sound was the heavy patter of the rain as a hush descended over the city once more.

Hongjun groaned and climbed to his feet with difficulty, swiping rainwater from his eyes. His hand went instinctively to his neck as the realization struck like a thousand bolts of lightning.

The pendant—it's not here. It...broke?

It broke?! It broke!

Crap!

Hongjun's face crumpled. He looked back at the groaning soldiers strewn over the ground before turning to the guard lying motionless before him, seemingly unconscious.

"Are you all right?!" Hongjun cried anxiously as he patted the man's cheek under his black helmet. "Wake up, wake up! Where did my heart lamp go?!"

When the pendant had shattered, the explosion had flung the man into the deepest reaches of the alley. As the sky began to lighten with the promise of dawn, he could hear angry shouts and shrill screams outside the alleyway...

Oh no. The pendant was gone—what was he going to do? No, he had to stay calm. A thousand thoughts and ideas raced through his mind, all converging on the man before him.

Hongjun put all his strength into dragging the guard upright. But it was no use—combined with his iron armor, the man weighed over two hundred pounds, much too heavy for Hongjun to lift. He hurried to strip off the armor, tossing it onto the ground with a series of clangs before mustering all his strength to pull the man onto his own back.

Hongjun peered deeper into the alleyway. At the end of the passage stood a wall nearly ten feet high. He could only guess at what lay beyond it, but he was truly out of options. Hongjun lugged the unconscious guard—so tall his feet dragged on the ground—to the base of the wall, where he fastened his grappling hook around the fellow's waist and slowly hoisted him up into the air.

Over the wall was a garden crowded with overturned flowerpots. Hongjun could hear more pursuers drawing near; he grabbed the guard by the arms and hauled him out of the courtyard, panting from exertion as he went.

As the first glimmers of dawn spread out from the horizon, the storm subsided into a fine drizzle. Most of Chang'an's citizens had yet to wake. Exiting the courtyard residence, Hongjun found himself in a maze of streets and alleyways, each road leading to yet more roads. He was utterly lost.

Great Tang's capital had been personally designed by the master architect Yuwen Kai himself and featured a hundred ten wards enclosed within a thick outer city wall with twelve gates. Hongjun had passed through several rural villages on his way here, but never had he seen such a grand metropolis. He had no idea where he ought to go.

"Hey, Zhao Zilong! Zhao Zilong!" Hongjun glanced back at the three-pound carp tucked into his travel pack. The carp yao lay motionless, eyes bulging and mouth agape—knocked unconscious when Hongjun had crashed to the ground.

"Wake up!" Hongjun was at a complete loss for what to do. He couldn't leave the guard and escape on his own, but he had no idea where to go next.

Another group of soldiers marched by in the distance. Hongjun didn't dare make any more trouble. He had to find a hiding spot, and fast. Casting about, his eye snagged on an open door in the alleyway up ahead. A woman giggled as she walked a portly man out into the street. After a few teasing words, she led out a horse and stood by as the man mounted his steed and rode away.

Dragging the guard along with him, Hongjun hid in the darkness and observed the exchange. The sound of hoofbeats rang louder and louder behind him—the soldiers were closing in. Steeling himself, Hongjun grabbed hold of the guard once more and made a break for the open door.

5
COMMANDANT LI OF THE LONGWU GUARD

Beyond the open door lay the rear courtyard of what appeared to be a family residence. A lotus pond edged with fragrant osmanthus blossoms occupied its center, and despite the light patter of rain, the place exuded the elegant aura of a scholarly home. Hongjun glanced this way and that as he dragged the man through a winding open-air corridor, marveling at the sights. *Wow, this place is gorgeous.*

The main house consisted of two stories. Musical female voices floated down from the upper floor. Hongjun was exhausted; after chasing the ao fish all night and encountering every sort of misfortune, what he most wanted was a place to rest. Finding himself alone for the moment, he plopped down on the ground and leaned back against the railing, gasping for breath.

It was then that a young woman dressed in a pale yellow ruqun, holding a spray of osmanthus blossoms in her hands, entered the corridor and stumbled across Hongjun.

The young woman stared in stunned silence at the tableau before her: the bedraggled youth, the unconscious man crumpled beside him, and the carp head sticking out over his shoulder, its mouth opening and closing.

Hongjun turned. His eyes met hers, his expression lost. Before she could cry out, he made a quick shushing gesture, then leapt to his feet and bowed repeatedly.

After a night of heavy rain, the filth on Hongjun's face from his days of travel had been washed clean. With his fair skin and fine features, he was breathtakingly handsome, and the young woman found herself momentarily dazed.

"Please, could you…let me stay here for a little while?" Hongjun tried.

Hongjun's father, Kong Xuan—known to many as the Peacock Wisdom King Mahamayuri—had once been so famed for his good looks that no one else in the three realms would have dared claim the title of Most Beautiful Man Alive, even if he had relinquished the crown. He was so handsome, celestial maidens scattered flower petals in his honor. Once, five hundred years ago, he had caused a fatal stampede among a great crowd of yao jostling to catch a glimpse of his exquisite face.

Unfortunately, Hongjun had lost his father at a young age and never had the chance to grow up under Kong Xuan's care. Instead, Chong Ming had raised him for twelve years like livestock put out to pasture. Left to his own devices, he'd spent his days running wild through the mountainside, exposed to the sun in the daytime, drenched by rain at night, and sometimes even wreathed in smoke from Chong Ming's ill-tempered fireballs. Nevertheless, he possessed the soft lips, white teeth, and fair skin he had inherited from his handsome father; although the elements had laid waste to much of his beauty, his lovely features and pure, bright aura—a distinctive feature among young men—captivated all who saw him.

"You… What's wrong with him?" The young woman looked from Hongjun down to the unconscious guard. "Isn't that Commandant Jinglong?!" she cried in alarm.

"What's a commandant?" Hongjun was bewildered.

"What's going on?!" A disgruntled female voice floated down from the veranda of the western wing. "Is that Sang-er down there? Did you bring someone home again?"

The young woman, Sang-er, beckoned Hongjun. "Everyone's getting ready to go to bed. Keep quiet and follow me."

Hongjun staggered upright with the man who was apparently Commandant Jinglong in his arms and stumbled up the stairs after the young woman. The man's feet clunked loudly against the wooden steps. Hongjun realized he'd forgotten to take off the man's heavy iron boots. Hurriedly removing them, he carried him more quietly into the room the woman had entered, where he laid him down on a bed before setting his travel pack on a table.

"What should I do?" Hongjun mumbled to himself.

"Is this fish yours?" Sang-er studied the carp spilling out of the pack on the table. Zhao Zilong's gills were still fluttering.

Hongjun nodded. The guard was now wearing nothing but a set of white undergarments. When Hongjun reached out to pat him down, he found an iron token inscribed with the words *Great Tang Longwu Guard Li Jinglong* hanging at his waist. The words meant nothing to him, so he tossed it onto the table before examining the sword that had cut through his pentacolor sacred light and shattered his pendant. It was a simple—but heavy—blade, pitch-black in color and densely etched with small seal script.

Unable to make heads or tails of it, he turned back to Li Jinglong and loosened the man's inner robes, revealing the bare skin of his muscular chest. Li Jinglong had a tall and slender figure, with a well-defined chest and abdomen. His features were deep-set, with a high-bridged nose, a mouth that curved gently upward at the corners, and ink-dark brows as sharp and straight as two swords.

The heart lamp passed down by Dipamkara...

Hongjun replayed the moment the pendant shattered, recalling Qing Xiong's instructions—*When you crush the crystal within the pendant, the heart lamp will enter the body on its own.* The two of them had been the only people present; if the heart lamp hadn't entered Li Jinglong's body, then it should have entered his own.

Hongjun didn't feel any different. But it seemed odd for Li Jinglong to remain unconscious for so long. Even if he had been knocked out by his fall, he should have woken by now... Perhaps it was the heart lamp's doing?

Hongjun didn't know what that bright light was supposed to do when it entered someone. He bent down and pressed his ear to Li Jinglong's chest, listening to his heart. As he turned his head, he caught sight of Sang-er's wide eyes.

"Can you leave us alone for a while?" Hongjun asked.

Sang-er nodded; her expression was strange. "Is Commandant Jinglong injured? Should I fetch the doctor?"

"What's a doctor?" Hongjun blurted without thinking. "No, no, there's no need."

"I'll go get him some water then," Sang-er said before stepping out of the room.

Bursting with anxiety, Hongjun grabbed the carp yao. "Zhao Zilong! Wake up!"

"A doctor is someone who treats sick people." The carp yao had woken up ages ago. "Where are we? What's happened?"

Hongjun had just as many questions as the carp, but he explained what he could to Zhao Zilong. The youth and the fish stared at each other for a fraught moment before the carp yao suddenly started wailing.

"Wahhhhh—you've really done it this time! It's over! What are we going to do?!"

"I don't know either!" Hongjun was beside himself.

"Is he surnamed Chen?" the carp yao asked.

"No!" Hongjun wanted to die. "He's surnamed Li... But wait, what if we made him change his surname to Chen?" Hongjun was struck by a bolt of inspiration.

"Are you an idiot?!" the carp yao demanded. "He's not a descendant of Chen Zi'ang!"

"I'm so dead! What am I going to do?!"

"Kill him," the carp yao advised. "Who knows, maybe the glowy thing will come back out."

"How can I kill him?!" Hongjun protested. "I'm the one who got him into this mess!"

"Life is full of suffering," the carp yao intoned. "He's a fine-looking man, and he seems to possess great talent, but his furrowed brows and the darkness of his Yintang point between them suggest he is destined for failure and misfortune. For someone like him, to live is a torment; you may as well put him out of his misery now."

Hongjun had no idea how to respond.

The carp yao continued, "You gave the heart lamp to the wrong person. This is a huge problem!"

Hongjun picked up Li Jinglong's sword. The carp yao urged him on. "It's not like you're human. Why are you so afraid of killing one?"

"My mom was a human!" Hongjun retorted.

"Well, you've killed yao before," the carp yao pointed out. "Now hurry up! Otherwise, what are we going to do about the Chen family? The heart lamp must be returned to the Chen family line. Only then will Mara..."

Realizing he had let something slip, the carp yao promptly shut his wide mouth.

"Mara?" Hongjun asked in surprise, recalling the conversation he'd overheard between Chong Ming and Qing Xiong. They, too, had mentioned Mara.

The carp yao pressed ahead. "In any case, you must recover the heart lamp! Otherwise, we're all dead! I'm not trying to scare you... Where's your throwing knife? Did you get it back?"

"No... I'm still missing one."

"Ahhhh!" The carp yao lost it. "I told you to stop chasing that thing, but heaven forbid you listen! Now look what you've done! You've lost your throwing knife—and the heart lamp's..."

Hongjun grabbed a pillow cover, rolled it into a slim bundle, and stuffed it with pinpoint accuracy into the carp's mouth, cutting off the endless prattle of this naysayer. It was easy to be right after the fact!

There was a knock on the door, and Sang-er entered carrying a kettle.

"Who are you talking to?" Sang-er asked in confusion when she saw Li Jinglong still unconscious on the bed.

"Just talking to myself," Hongjun said hastily. "Can you give us a little more time?"

Sang-er handed Hongjun a towel, then studied him with a smile. "Oh, all right."

When Sang-er had left the room again, Hongjun wiped Li Jinglong's face with the towel before jumping onto the bed and straddling his torso. Taking a deep breath, he turned slightly and gathered his spiritual power. A wave of his hand called up the pentacolor sacred light, which he pressed to Li Jinglong's chest.

Scrabbling with both hands, the carp yao yanked the pillow cover out of his mouth and shouted, "Hongjun, do not falter!"

Hongjun poured the sacred light into Li Jinglong, feeding his spiritual power into Li Jinglong's meridians. If the power of the heart lamp flowed through this man's body, it should automatically resist the incursion. Yet Hongjun had barely begun when Li Jinglong woke with a shudder.

At the same time, Hongjun heard a disturbance outside.

"The Shenwu Guard is conducting a search of the premises! All civilians, stand back and maintain a safe distance!"

Li Jinglong looked absently down at Hongjun's hand pressed to his chest. Following his arm upward, he met Hongjun's eyes.

The two stared at each other in silence.

Suddenly realizing he was naked save for a pair of pants, Li Jinglong snapped back to his senses. "What are you doing?!" he demanded, furious.

Hongjun hastened to explain. "My heart lamp—you..."

With a great shout, Li Jinglong grabbed Hongjun's hand and wrenched it back, tumbling them both off the bed.

"Wait!" Hongjun cried.

The situation immediately devolved into chaos. Li Jinglong had knocked over the kettle, and the carp yao hastily hopped down from the table. The guards conducting the search outside heard the commotion and shouted, "The room at the end of the hall! Hurry!"

"Hongjun! We need to go! Someone's coming again!" the carp yao cried.

Li Jinglong turned and saw the carp yao. Aghast, he shouted, "Monster!"

Afraid of causing even more trouble, Hongjun grabbed his pack, scooped up the carp yao, and smashed through the window. Hooking a hand on the overhanging eaves, he hoisted himself up and fled across the rooftops, sliding down the glazed tiles to make his escape.

Li Jinglong was left wide-eyed and panting, his sword still in his hand as he gasped for breath. His armor had long since disappeared; he was completely flummoxed by what had just transpired.

An angry shout came from outside. "Who's in there?! The Shenwu Guard is conducting a search! Open the door now or—"

Sang-er's voice joined them. "Wait! Two of our guests are enjoying each other's company in that room! Please don't disturb them…"

The moment Li Jinglong heard the words *Shenwu Guard*, he realized there was no cleaning up today's mess. If he wanted to save any part of his dignity, he had to get out of there. He followed Hongjun out the window—but while Hongjun had sprung up to the rooftops to make his escape, Li Jinglong dropped downward. His bare feet slipped on the glazed roof tiles the moment he stepped out.

Li Jinglong crashed down the side of the roof, clutching his sword with one hand as his other tried and failed to find something to grab hold of. As his legs kicked wildly, he caught sight of the busy street below. By then, it was too late.

While Li Jinglong was unconscious, Hongjun had dragged him into Chang'an's Pingkang Administrative District, also known as Pingkang Ward, famous for its brothels. This particular establishment—known as the Spring Oriole—was one of the city's finest houses of ill repute and just so happened to be located right next to Chang'an's East Market.

The rain had given way to clear morning skies, and a cacophony of voices filled the East Market as it opened for business. Hearing the racket, the pedestrians and street vendors looked up to see Commandant Li Jinglong of the Longwu Guard, in all his bare-chested glory, scramble out the window of the Spring Oriole with his sword in hand. In broad daylight, he slipped violently on the eaves and plummeted into the East Market with a thunderous crash.

Horses and mules screamed in alarm as baskets full of wares went flying across the ground.

"Hey, isn't that Commandant Jinglong?"

"Commandant Li? Ha ha ha ha—"

Disoriented from his fall, Li Jinglong had barely taken a breath before he was swarmed by a sizable crowd. As the Shenwu guards inside the Spring Oriole stuck their heads out the windows, Li Jinglong ducked out of sight, dragging his sword behind him, and disappeared into the throng red-faced with humiliation. The remaining Shenwu guards searched everywhere as the marketgoers burst into raucous laughter.

A group of pedantic scholars discussed the incident with relish.

"I've written a poem, for which I seek critique."

"Go on, then, speak!"

"I've titled it, 'Li Jinglong of the Longwu Guard Departs the Spring Oriole'—

Commandant Jinglong is a man of great virtue;

As dawn breaks over Pingkang, our hero comes to;

Amid broken roof tiles, our strapping young fellow

Sheds bitter tears as he departs the bordello!"

"Genius! Please allow this foolish one to add a worthless addendum to your masterful composition..."

"Please do!"

"The Flying General lives yet again;

He's a man both handsome and tough;

He fears no god yet his armor forgets,

And frolics about in the buff!"

Hidden within a water tank behind the East Market, Li Jinglong endured the mockery in silence. Lifting the lid a crack, he watched the Shenwu Guard march past and finally sighed in utter exhaustion.

6
LIVING UNDER SOMEONE ELSE'S ROOF

The rain had passed, and a clear, blue autumn sky stretched over Chang'an. The fragrance of osmanthus blossoms drifted through the city. Hongjun kicked hard at the trunk of a parasol tree, sending rainwater that had gathered in the leaves overnight splashing down. He washed his face and took a drink before picking a few leaves to press against his lips as a whistle.

Stuffed inside his pack, the carp yao was the picture of misery. "What are we going to do?"

"This city is so big." Hongjun patted his belly. "Let's get something to eat."

"I refuse to eat worms again," the carp yao declared.

"I'll get you some meat," Hongjun promised. "We'll figure things out one step at a time. Ay, why have we had such rotten luck on our way here… Oh? What's that?"

Hongjun set aside his troubles when he saw the dazzling world of the city with all its wonders; he was, after all, a young lad who had just come down from the mountains. He fished out a handful of copper coins and dove into the crowds of the market to buy some breakfast.

"Ever since you left the mountains, you've been eating everything in sight! Careful you don't upset your stomach," the carp yao admonished.

At a restaurant in the market, Hongjun sat with one leg kicked up on the seat next to him and a giant bowl of noodles in his hands, slurping noisily until he'd polished off the whole thing. Food in the human realm was far more delicious than in Yaojin Palace. Deep fried, roasted, pan-seared—the variety was endless. Stewed mutton, Double Ninth cake, sticky rice pastries... The chefs of Yaojin Palace had never made these dishes. Not to mention that he'd been traveling at speed since he left the mountains, surviving only on rations.

Thankfully, Qing Xiong knew him all too well and had provided plenty of valuable pearls for his monthlong journey to Chang'an. Following the carp yao's instructions, Hongjun had traded the pearls with the merchant caravans he'd met along the way for silver, which he'd then exchanged for copper coins to buy his meals. He was ignorant of the ways of human society, but with the carp yao's help, he generally managed to avoid making a fool of himself.

Hongjun was quick and clever; as he stopped here and there on his journey, he had swiftly learned the rules of human interaction. He spoke little but observed what others did and picked things up by example. Seeing a queue of people lined up to purchase steamed buns, Hongjun watched for several minutes before imitating them, lining up and handing over copper coins to buy two buns.

Spotting a street performer breathing fire, Hongjun stopped in curiosity. "What's so special about that? A single sneeze from Dad gets you a way bigger fireball."

The carp yao thought it best not to comment.

Other acts included performers smashing boulders on their chests, bending iron rods with their necks, scaling mountains of knives, and walking through boiling oil. Hongjun couldn't suppress a shudder as he watched. "What's the point of torturing themselves like this?"

"To make money," the carp yao responded. "You wouldn't understand. Life is hard for humans."

As the show came to an end, the performers asked the audience for coin, and the crowd of onlookers began to throw coppers into a bowl. Out of pity, Hongjun tossed in one of his pearls. The carp yao was slung across Hongjun's back and couldn't see a thing. He had no idea what had happened until someone shouted, "A night pearl?!"

The pea-sized night pearl caused an instant commotion. All thoughts of virtue or morality flew out the window as several onlookers rushed forward and groped into the bowl in hopes of snatching away the precious treasure. Others boldly followed suit, and a brawl soon broke out.

"Stop fighting, stop fighting, I have more!" Hongjun cried.

"Do you want to die?!" the carp yao asked. "Run!"

The city guard hurried over as chaos descended on the market. After last night's incident, the very sight of soldiers spooked Hongjun. He took to his heels and fled as quickly as his feet could carry him.

The carp yao hadn't left off carping at him to report for duty at the Department of Exorcism since the rain had stopped. As the day wore on, Hongjun assured him he would go very soon—only to be distracted once again by a busker with a monkey on the edges of the market.

"Don't you think chaining it like that is too cruel?" Hongjun asked the monkey tamer.

The man responded with a glare and a string of curses. The carp yao was about to cry. "Young Master, can we please get out of here already!"

Back in the Taihang Mountains, the monkeys all lived freely. But the skinny little monkey before him was chained up. Not only was it obviously underfed, the poor creature had to run around kowtowing to people for their entertainment.

Hongjun walked a dozen steps past the busker before turning back. After glancing around to ensure no one was watching, he flicked one of his throwing knives out, and the chain in the monkey tamer's hand snapped with a sharp *clang*.

The monkey looked around, momentarily dazed.

"Run!" Hongjun urged quietly.

Seizing its chance, the monkey fled. The monkey tamer cursed and gave chase, causing yet another commotion in the city.

"Hongjun," the carp yao piped up, "put me in front. What's going on over there?"

Hongjun smiled in secret pleasure as he watched the monkey scamper away. He wound his way through the market, slowing to a stop once again before a shopfront with a large horizontal sign that read *A Wealth of Knowledge*. Scholars wandered in and out of the store.

"Is this a bookshop?" Hongjun asked in some amazement.

"It's going to be dark soon…" the carp yao sighed woefully. "Must you wander around at a time like this?"

Hongjun strolled in, unconcerned. A pungent fishy smell immediately permeated the bookshop, and everyone turned to look at Hongjun.

"No fish allowed!" the shopkeeper said. "What are you doing, carrying a fish around?"

"See? Everyone's shunning you," the carp yao said.

"I'm making braised fish for dinner," Hongjun explained. "You know the saying, ruling a large nation is like cooking a small fish…" The carp yao fell silent at once. Hongjun continued, "I'm just taking a quick look around. I'll leave in a minute."

The most popular books in the shop were poetry anthologies. Hongjun flipped through a collection of selected works by Li Bai and promptly forgot his promise to leave as he began to read.

The autumn sun turned blisteringly hot as it began its descent after noon. In the Feng Estate within Chang'an city, the cicadas' droning calls rose and fell as Li Jinglong knelt in the middle of a courtyard, still barefoot and naked to the waist, his black sword pinned beneath his knees.

"You! You're a complete disgrace to your father and ancestors!"

Feng Changqing limped forward. His left hand clutched the token bearing Li Jinglong's name, left behind in the brothel, as he raised a long, flat ceremonial rod in his right. The rod whipped through the air, and Li Jinglong let out a muffled grunt of pain as another searing red stripe marred his shoulder.

Huffing with rage, Feng Changqing tapped the disciplinary rod against the side of Li Jinglong's handsome face. "The streets of Chang'an are buzzing with rumors that you abandoned your wounded subordinates to go whoring in Pingkang Ward in the middle of the night... You...!"

Li Jinglong bowed his head.

"Do you have any idea how much effort it took to land you a position in the Longwu Guard?!" Feng Changqing roared. "Don't you want to better yourself?! Speak!"

Met with Li Jinglong's silence, Feng Changqing went on. "Running around with that rusted sword of yours—don't tell me you fancy yourself some great general of the Yulin Guard? When will you grow up? When?! And get rid of that thing!"

Feng Changqing kicked at the sword beneath Li Jinglong's knees, but Li Jinglong refused to budge.

"The summons for your court-martial will arrive tonight at the latest." Feng Changqing was shaking with fury. "You're sure to be the talk of tomorrow's morning court session as well. What do you expect me to say when you've humiliated me like this?!"

The servants stood beneath the eaves of the corridor and watched with malicious glee. In Chang'an, it was often said that Li Jinglong was an embroidered pillow stuffed with straw: beautiful on the outside, with nothing of substance within. Feng Changqing was his cousin—his paternal aunt was Li Jinglong's mother, who had died when Li Jinglong was young. Four years ago, when Li Jinglong was sixteen, his father, Li Mou, had served under Cen Shen in General Gao Xianzhi's army. Li Mou had followed him into battle beyond the Great Wall, where he was struck by a Xiongnu arrow and died from his injuries. With no close relatives to guide him, Li Jinglong squandered his family's wealth little by little—first by consulting a Daoist priest on matters of divinity and immortality, then by spending a small fortune on a sword that had once belonged to Di Renjie, said to be capable of slaying demons.

There were quite a few young ladies in Chang'an who'd fallen in love with the spendthrift Li Jinglong in those years. But as with his career, he made no progress when it came to settling down and starting a family. He always seemed haughty and standoffish, and he didn't so much as nod when he met with matchmakers. Now twenty years old, he had as yet accomplished nothing of consequence, and thus talks of marriage gradually dried up as well.

Li Jinglong was no longer a child, yet he refused to settle down or build a career. He spent his time loafing around—until last year, when his elder cousin Feng Changqing returned in triumph after defeating the kingdom of Greater Patola in the Western Regions. It was Feng Changqing who, during an audience with Emperor

Xuanzong to reward his great military accomplishments, had arranged a position for Li Jinglong in the Longwu Guard, one of the three divisions of the imperial guard.

For years, Feng Changqing had worried himself sick over his failure of a younger cousin. Now his cousin had become the laughingstock of Chang'an just as the imperial court was preparing to appoint Feng Changqing to a new official position. It wasn't enough for Li Jinglong to bring shame upon the entire family—he had to drag Feng Changqing's career down too! The more he spoke, the angrier he became, the flat rod whipping through the air like the gales of a violent storm.

His wife ran into the courtyard, crying, "Husband, stop! Stop hitting him!"

Feng Changqing's final blow struck with such force it broke the rod in two. Blood oozed from Li Jinglong's forehead and down his face, dripping onto the ground.

"Husband, please calm down!" Madam Feng patted Feng Changqing soothingly on the back.

Feng Changqing turned without another word and limped into the house. When he had gone, Madam Feng instructed the maidservants to bring a cloth to wipe Li Jinglong's face.

"Why are you so stubborn?" she asked. "Your ge[6] wouldn't get so angry if you'd just admit your mistakes."

Li Jinglong said nothing. He knelt until he was cast in the ruddy shades of dusk. The dying light of the setting sun stretched across the ground, blending with the blood stains on the blue-gray brick.

Painted in twilight, Hongjun returned to the East Market with a stack of books in his arms. The vendors had long collected their

---

6 A word meaning "elder brother." It can also be used to address an unrelated male peer, and optionally used as a suffix.

wares, and the crowds had dispersed. Crimson clouds smeared the horizon as the steady beats of the evening drum sounded from a distant tower.

A counterpart to the morning bells, the evening drums of Chang'an signaled that night had fallen. Hongjun yawned expansively. After forgoing sleep the night before, then running around all day, he was weary beyond description. The sunset only heightened his feelings of homesickness as he recalled that he had recovered neither the heart lamp nor his precious throwing knife.

"Hey, Zhao Zilong?" Hongjun patted the pack slung over his shoulder. The carp yao had been motionless, sleeping with his eyes open and jaws agape, but at Hongjun's prodding, his mouth began to open and close again.

"Where's the Department of Demonic Exorcism?" Hongjun asked.

"I don't know," the carp yao answered. "It's been eighty years since I last came to Chang'an."

"Well how did you get here back then? Didn't you take a look around?"

"Last time I was here, I was put on sale in the East Market. I was bleeding with a hook in my mouth. You tell me, how was I supposed to look around?"

Hongjun had no response.

"Does the letter Master Qing Xiong gave you contain an address?"

"Let me see... Where's Jincheng Ward?"

"North of the West Market. Hurry up, let's go. Curfew sets in once the drums stop. We'll be arrested if we keep wandering around after that."

Hongjun quickened his pace. The distance from the East Market to the West was more than half the breadth of the city. The roads of

Chang'an were arranged in a grid pattern, with the different wards separated by busy thoroughfares. Each individual ward was filled with a twisting network of interlinking lanes and side roads. He asked for directions as he went, walking so fast he was soon panting for breath.

By the time Hongjun finally found his way to Jincheng Ward, the night had turned dark, yet he still couldn't find the Department of Exorcism. There was nothing left to do but to head for the closest lit building.

HAI MIE HOU BI

THE WARD WAS surprisingly quiet at night. A handful of dogs barked from time to time, but few houses had lamps lit at this hour. From behind him, the carp yao's lecture continued without cease. "I told you to come earlier, but did you listen? Everyone's gone home, and the streets are so dark you can't even read the signs on the buildings. How do you expect to find this place?"

Hongjun stood still, hesitating. After three hundred beats, the evening drums fell silent, and night closed over the city. At last Hongjun had no choice but to brace himself and start knocking on doors to ask for directions. After several fruitless attempts, his knock was finally answered by a mute old man, who merely waved a lamp in Hongjun's face. Hongjun apologized for the disturbance and left.

He turned down a narrow lane and entered the courtyard of what seemed to be an abandoned residence. The place was overgrown with weeds, and he could only guess how long the building had gone without repairs. Lacking the energy to worry over a little dirt, Hongjun settled onto the floor, so exhausted he fell asleep the instant he laid his head down.

That night, dark clouds swallowed the moon. Deep within Xingqing Palace, a chilly draft set the gauzy curtains to fluttering, and the candles flickered and swayed.

A noblewoman dressed in black robes embroidered with the curling motif of a man-eating beast sat poised at the head of the palace hall. A trio of men stood before her, their features obscured by hooded cloaks. One stepped forward to present a tray, upon which lay a bloodstained throwing knife.

"What is this?" the noblewoman asked.

"This knife struck Fei'ao while he was hunting in the outskirts of the city," the man responded, his voice low. "He's hiding in Daming Palace now while he recovers from his injuries."

The noblewoman lifted the knife with slender fingers and examined it with a deep frown. The sharp blade reflected her devastatingly beautiful face.

"I don't know this weapon." She tossed the knife back onto the tray with a *clang*.

"Someone has come for us," another of the men said.

"To think they would do so after so many years," the noblewoman said coldly. "Present this to His Majesty tomorrow and see what he says. Where is the knife's wielder?"

"Li Jinglong chased him down, and the two of them fought," the third man reported. "We lost them during the chase, I'm afraid..."

The noblewoman laughed contemptuously, her graceful shoulders quivering with mirth. "Fascinating. Does that lunatic Li Jinglong still dream of vanquishing evil?"

"Fei'ao accidentally revealed himself at the city walls last night. Rumors have begun to spread that there are yao in Chang'an," the man said.

"Oh?" the noblewoman's lips curved in a shallow smile. "Yao in Chang'an? That's the first I've heard of this. A virtuous emperor occupies the throne, the world is at peace, and all under heaven willingly bend their knee to Great Tang—how could there possibly be yao here? I'll have a good chat with His Majesty tomorrow. All of you, withdraw for now. Tell Fei'ao to stay out of sight, and in the meantime, look for the owner of the knife. Once you find them, feed them to Fei'ao."

The next morning dawned sticky and hot. A few stray chirps sounded high in the parasol tree outside the dilapidated house, followed by a great flapping of wings as the birds all took to the sky.

A loud noise in the outer courtyard roused Hongjun from his sleep.

The carp yao startled awake as well. Frightened out of his wits, he tumbled out of Hongjun's bag and flopped around with a wet slapping sound. "What's happening?! What's happening?!"

Rolling back onto his hands, he sprang from the ground with a kip-up and landed nimbly on his feet. "Where are we?" he asked, looking around.

"Is anyone here?" A man's voice called out as he pushed open the door to the entrance hall.

Hongjun lifted a hand to shade his eyes. In the hazy sunlight, he saw a tall and slender young man dressed in strange clothes, looking back at him with an expression of surprise.

The two stared at each other in confusion. As Hongjun's eyes adjusted to the light, he saw that the man had deep-set features with high cheekbones, well-defined lips, and brows thick and dark as a hawk's feathers. His skin was the healthy bronze of a man who was exposed to the sun year-round, and his thick black hair was plaited with several thin braids. He wore black hunting boots and a travel pack strapped to his waist over a long, lambskin ao jacket with one sleeve off, revealing his toned right shoulder. The man had an impressive bearing despite his humble attire, with broad shoulders and a narrow waist. A bow and a quiver of arrows were slung across his back; he seemed to be a hunter.

"Good heavens, you nearly scared me to death," the carp yao huffed.

The young hunter started upon seeing the carp. In a flash, he grabbed an arrow from his quiver and drew back his bowstring.

Hongjun dove in front of his companion. "Stop! He's never hurt a human—and I'm an exorcist!" Then, as if afraid the carp might contradict him, he hissed, "Zhao Zilong, stop talking!"

The hunter lowered his bow and eyed Hongjun, still distrustful. "You're an exorcist? Why are you accompanied by a yao? Also... where are we supposed to report for duty?"

"Report for duty?" Hongjun asked blankly.

The young man lifted a hand to point at something over Hongjun's head, motioning for him to look. Hanging high above them in the entrance hall was a horizontal plaque inscribed with the large words *Great Tang Department of Demonic Exorcism*.

Beyond the walls of Xingqing Palace, dark clouds blanketed the sky as the air turned intolerably muggy. In the gardens, Emperor Xuanzong of Tang, Li Longji, found it too hot to hold his beloved consort Yang Yuhuan in his arms. He released her, but soon missed her presence and pressed himself close once again. Although the lovers had been entwining this way for only a short time, they were already covered in sweat. Sipping on glasses of an iced drink made from sour plums, they settled for linking their pinkies together.

Beside them was Yang Yuhuan's elder sister, the Duchess of Guo, busy peeling lychees. She placed the peeled fruit into a colorful glass bowl filled with ice as her cousin Chancellor Yang Guozhong stood by, eating the pale pink fruit by the handful.

"It's nothing but a silly story spun up by that Commandant Li Jinglong of the Longwu Guard," Yang Guozhong said with a laugh. "His subordinates got drunk and started a brawl while he snuck off to go whoring on duty. He knew there'd be no way to clean up his mess the next morning, so he came up with this absurd story."

"This man must be punished," the Duchess of Guo said. "He fails to discipline his subordinates, neglects his duties, deceives the Son of Heaven, and spreads dangerous rumors. It's completely unacceptable!"

"This Li Jinglong…" Yang Yuhuan finally placed the name. "Isn't he General Feng's younger cousin?"

"That's him all right," Yang Guozhong said. "When Changqing returned to court the other day, he submitted a memorial recommending this young man for promotion. He wanted to take him along on a campaign so the lad could be recognized for outstanding military service. The way I see it, the boy's too idle. Consign him to some far-flung military post for a few years and he'll settle down."

Li Longji hummed thoughtfully. Anticipating his response, Yang Yuhuan quickly turned the conversation—she didn't have the heart to let it end this way. "General Feng has just won a great victory for our nation," she said. "To banish his cousin just like that… After all, it's no great crime for a young man to be a bit spirited."

"Duke Di also harped on about yao back in the day, when he'd grown muddled with age," Li Longji mused. "He created a division called the Department of Demonic Exorcism, which was supervised by the Grand Chancellor. When Chang'an became the capital, the department was moved here."

"You know, when I was little—" Yang Yuhuan began.

"How did I know you'd bring up that white fox again?" the Duchess of Guo said with a small smile.

"Speaking of which…" Li Longji interjected. "Once, as a child, when we went to offer sacrifices to heaven and earth with…them, we saw a black dragon's back as it swam through the waters of the Luo River."

"An auspicious omen!" Yang Yuhuan exclaimed with a smile. "The people call these creatures 'yao' because they do not understand their miraculous ways. Isn't such an omen proof that Your Majesty possesses the Mandate of Heaven?"

"Indeed," said Li Longji. "In fact—we've suddenly had a thought. Seeing as Li Jinglong possesses such *remarkable* talents, why not appoint him to lead this Department of Demonic Exorcism?"

All three of his listeners started in surprise. Yang Yuhuan burst into laughter, and the corner of the duchess's mouth twitched as she found herself briefly speechless.

"We've decided," Li Longji said with utmost seriousness. "Who knows where the Department of Demonic Exorcism is currently headquartered, but surely it still exists. It seems that Li Jinglong isn't meant to remain within the Longwu Guard; we shall send him to watch over this Department of Exorcism. We'll have him announce his findings on such auspicious omens to the citizens of Chang'an from time to time and grant Feng Changqing's wish to promote him as well. In that case, his supervision will fall to you, Guozhong."

Yang Guozhong could not think of a reply.

Within the deserted residence, Hongjun and the handsome young hunter stared at each other in bewilderment. *This* was the Department of Exorcism? Given the cobweb-covered entrance hall, it was clear the place had been abandoned for years. The residence, a typical courtyard house with buildings arranged around a square central yard, was surprisingly spacious on the inside; beyond the entrance hall was a large courtyard open to the sky, presently filled with empty, rotting storage trunks.

It turned out that the young hunter was named Mergen, a Shiwei tribesman who had also come to the Department of Exorcism to report for duty. He asked for Hongjun's letter and checked it carefully against his own in the morning sunlight. The two letters were nearly identical: Chang'an, they said, had been taken over by yao and demons, and descendants of the most powerful exorcist bloodlines throughout the nation were called to the Great Tang Department of Demonic Exorcism in Chang'an to report for duty.

While Mergen pored over their letters, Hongjun wandered through the abandoned Department of Exorcism. A parasol tree in the main courtyard stretched high over the eaves, with a large scattering of seed pods surrounding it on the ground below. A wave of familiarity came over Hongjun at the sight of the parasol tree. A pair of winding, open-air corridors with rusty wind chimes hanging from their eaves and an ornate spirit screen standing on either end connected the central courtyard to the eastern and western wings. The windows and doors of the residence's twelve rooms had all rotted, and mice scurried back and forth, squeaking loudly as they went.

Near the back of the complex stood a spacious room that served as the main hall, which contained a large couch fashioned from bamboo with a tea table set before it. They had clearly been abandoned for years; the furniture had long fallen to pieces, and several broken porcelain cups lay in shards beneath the wooden table. A stable occupied the narrow rear courtyard behind the main hall, where Hongjun found a sealed-off back door to the complex.

"Kong Hongjun!" Done examining their letters, Mergen strode swiftly into the entrance hall, the top of his head narrowly missing the lintel. "Our letters are the same."

"Well, that's odd…"

Hongjun had imagined that the Great Tang Department of Demonic Exorcism would be bustling with people. Even if it wasn't like the great government offices he had heard about, he'd expected it to be at least as busy as the relay stations he'd passed on his journey. There didn't seem to be a soul anywhere in these deserted premises— but in that case, where had the letters come from?

Qing Xiong hadn't mentioned the letter's sender before Hongjun left the mountains, nor had he ever said to which powerful exorcist family Hongjun supposedly belonged. But now it seemed someone had personally written and sealed these letters before sending them off one by one—and strangest of all, whoever it was had signed off with the name *Di*.

"Could the sender of these letters be Di Renjie?" Mergen wondered aloud. "But he died years ago, didn't he?"

"Hey, you two, come take a look at this wall," the carp yao called from inside the main hall.

Hongjun hummed curiously and stepped forward to wipe away the dust coating the wall, revealing a faded mural of a seated official attired in stately purple robes. A copper incense burner, now green with verdigris, had been placed on the floor below the man's feet.

"This must be him," Mergen said.

"Could the Department of Exorcism have been moved elsewhere?" Hongjun asked.

"This is the address mentioned in our letters," Mergen responded. "Look at the state of this place. It doesn't look like anyone's been here recently, much less moved out."

The two of them stood before the mural in silence. Hongjun had traveled for weeks and overcome so many obstacles, only to find that his destination was nothing like he'd imagined. He suddenly felt an unspeakable disappointment, as if he had spent hours climbing a mountain only to find that there was nothing at the top.

"Oh my, the door's fallen in. Is there anyone here?"

The voice came from the outer courtyard.

Mergen and Hongjun emerged from the entrance hall to find a young foreign man dressed in sumptuous crimson combat robes in the middle of the yard. He had a lute strapped to his back and was in the middle of paying a pair of porters who had just finished hauling a great number of packages of various sizes through the gates. The young man had a sharp, straight nose, milky-pale skin, and a head of exuberant curls above a pair of deep-set eyes. He wore four rings, one on each finger of a hand that held a sapphire-blue fan, which he shook open to shield his face from the sun as he glanced around in confusion.

"Oh hey!" he cried out, catching sight of Mergen and Hongjun. The pair jumped in surprise.

"Hai mie hou bi!" the young man called enthusiastically, his arms outstretched. "My dear friends of the Great Tang Empire! Hello!" He strode forward and hugged first Mergen, then Hongjun. "My name is Tyropotamia Homihok Hammurabi. But you may call me A-Tai."

A-Tai pressed his hands to his chest before slowly releasing them and performing a graceful bow. "May I please ask whether this is the Great Tang Department of Demonic Exorcism? Here, my referral letter. Which of you is the official responsible for this department?"

Mergen and Hongjun were both flabbergasted. Before either of them could respond, yet another newcomer arrived.

"Is there anyone here?"

Three heads turned as one to see a tall scholar peering in from beyond the doorway.

"My name is Qiu Yongsi, from Jiangnan." The scholar cupped his hands and smiled. "I've come here on my grandfather's recommendation... Um, why are you all staring at me with such strange expressions? Eh?! Why is there a monster inside the department?!"

Fifteen minutes later, everyone had taken out their letters and stood staring at each other in befuddlement.

"But that doesn't make any sense," said Mergen, the Shiwei tribesman. "You're all here to report for duty? Is the Court of Judicial Review in charge of this department?"

"I visited the Court of Judicial Review before coming here," the scholar, Qiu Yongsi, responded. "This department falls outside their purview."

"I asked around the Court of State Ceremonial," A-Tai, the foreigner, added. "They don't oversee this department either."

The four sat down in a circle and settled into silence. Each had received a letter to report for duty, only to be greeted by a deserted and overgrown Department of Exorcism. What on earth was going on?

"There's something I find suspicious..." A-Tai snapped his fingers and got to his feet, pacing the room. Glancing at Mergen, he said, "I was in Tokharistan, our friend Mergen was in the Hulunbuir grasslands, our beautiful young friend here..."

"Hongjun—Kong Hongjun," Hongjun said.

"Where are you from?" A-Tai asked with a brilliant smile.

"The Taihang Mountains."

"And you?" A-Tai turned toward Qiu Yongsi.

"West Lake," Qiu Yongsi responded.

"So then, we must have all received our letters at different times," A-Tai went on, "and traveled here from locations near and far. How can it be that we have all arrived in Chang'an at precisely the same time?"

"You're right!" Hongjun exclaimed.

"Oh?" Qiu Yongsi blinked in surprise. "All three of you arrived just now too?"

"Mm." Mergen nodded slowly. "If we find the person who sent the letters, we'll learn the truth."

If this person could deliver a letter to Qing Xiong, Hongjun wondered, did that mean they knew Hongjun lived in Yaojin Palace? Could they have known Di Renjie and his father, Kong Xuan, and if so, did they know what had happened to them?

He was suddenly struck by another thought: "Maybe more people will come later?"

A-Tai nodded, the corners of his lips curving into a cunning smile. "Indeed. Perhaps all we need to do is wait."

CHIEF EXORCIST

THAT AFTERNOON, four confused young men sat beneath the eaves and watched the rain fall in a continuous patter, bringing with it an unexpected chill.

"My grandfather told me to come to Chang'an to stop the yao," Qiu Yongsi said. He was a baby-faced young man who seemed totally harmless. "He said I would learn to be braver this way. My skills are lacking, so when we go hunting for yao, I ask that you all please look out for me."

"I'm not all that impressive either," Hongjun said. "These two, though…"

"Is this fan your weapon?" Mergen asked A-Tai. "You seem quite skilled with it."

"You haven't yet seen my greatest magical weapon." A-Tai chuckled. "But there's no harm in telling my dear friends about it. It's this barbat."

A-Tai unslung the lute he had been carrying on his back. Hongjun had loved all kinds of magical devices since childhood, but as he had only just met A-Tai, he hadn't wanted to pry. Now that they'd grown somewhat more familiar, he ran his fingers over the instrument appreciatively. "It's a magical weapon?"

"That's right." A-Tai nodded, grinning. "My father gave this barbat to me before he passed. When a monster appears, all I need to do is point this end toward my enemy…"

"And play a song?" Hongjun asked.

"Nope." A-Tai shook his head. "I swing it up and smash my enemy right on the head."

Hongjun was speechless.

"This barbat is as light as a goose feather in my hands," A-Tai said seriously. "But when I smash it down, it's as heavy as Mount Tai. I can kill even dragons with a single blow."

"Please stop talking…" Hongjun pressed a hand to his brow, pushing A-Tai's face away when the man drew too close.

But A-Tai was undeterred, leaning over to stare into Hongjun's eyes. The young man had indigo eyes the deep blue of the sea. Paired with his brilliant smile, they made him practically impossible to resist. "Beautiful didi,[7] is there something that weighs upon your mind?" A-Tai asked tenderly. "Why is your brow always furrowed? Life is so beautiful; why don't I play you a song?"

Mergen couldn't bear to listen any longer. Wrapping one hand around Hongjun's shoulders and holding up the other to block A-Tai, he said, "Stop teasing him. He doesn't understand."

In truth, Hongjun really was feeling rather upset. Glad as he was to have made new friends, all this talk of magical devices had reminded him that the heart lamp was gone, and that he had lost one of his throwing knives. He had no way to fix the mess he had made and had been hoping that once he arrived at the Department of Exorcism and started hunting yao, he'd slowly sort things out. He'd never imagined that instead of answers, he'd find only another mystery.

"It's true that I've…encountered some difficulty," Hongjun admitted.

---

[7] A word meaning "younger brother." It can also be used to address an unrelated, usually younger male peer, and optionally used as a suffix.

"What kind of difficulty?" Mergen asked. "Tell us, and maybe we can help? Is it some sort of monster?"

"A monster?!" Qiu Yongsi straightened up in alarm. "So it's true? There are monsters in Chang'an?"

"It would be my greatest honor to help you," said A-Tai.

Qiu Yongsi shrank into himself. "As long as I don't have to get too close to any monsters, I can help with other things. And, well, I have to learn how to be brave anyway, so…go ahead and tell us, what kind of monster is it?"

"Let me see if I can figure it out first," Hongjun said, deeply touched. "If I'm really stuck, I'll ask you guys for help then."

"That's fair," Mergen said with a smile. "It's better to rely on yourself than to sit around and pray for help. I'm sure you'll come up with something." He patted Hongjun on the shoulder.

The rain gradually tapered off. "Good times mustn't be wasted," A-Tai piped up again. "Why not lift our voices in a song?"

"Let's clean this place up and clear out some of the rooms first." Mergen slapped his hands against his knees and stood up. "After all, we'll probably have to sleep here tonight."

"We'll sleep at an inn," A-Tai countered. "Come on, it'll be my treat."

"I think I should sleep here," Hongjun said. "Zhao Zilong will stink up the place if he sleeps at an inn. I wouldn't want to scare anyone either."

For some reason, he'd already grown rather fond of this broken-down residence. After drifting through so many strange places on his journey here, the sight of the giant parasol tree in the courtyard seemed to ground him. Mergen wasn't picky about lodgings, so he agreed to stay with Hongjun; after thinking it over,

Qiu Yongsi decided to stay as well. A-Tai had no choice but to concede and remain in the ramshackle Department of Exorcism.

As evening fell, rosy clouds veiled the sky over Chang'an. After three days of rain, autumn had officially come to the Guanzhong region.

Feng Changqing limped out of the Longwu Guard Garrison, leaning heavily upon the cane in his left hand as he held Li Longji's imperial decree in his right. Li Jinglong followed, a towering figure with a bedroll tucked under his arm.

Li Jinglong thought his cousin would bring a servant to transport the bedroll home. But Feng Changqing insisted Li Jinglong carry it himself so that he might better receive the gift of the common folks' mocking eyes upon him. It was the ultimate humiliation—catching sight of the wastrel who'd been chased out of the Longwu Guard, the commoners of Chang'an couldn't keep from bursting out in laughter.

"You've been transferred to the Great Tang Department of Demonic Exorcism." Feng Changqing snorted as he hobbled ahead with the imperial edict in hand, though it was difficult to say whether he was ridiculing Li Jinglong or himself. "Truly an outstanding appointment, under the Right Chancellor himself—why, you've risen two ranks overnight!"

"I'm not walking anymore," Li Jinglong said in a low voice.

He could feel the commoners' pointing fingers like sharp blades pricking his back. Feng Changqing turned and struck him with the cane. "Where was your shame when you fled from the brothel in Pingkang Ward?" he demanded furiously.

Li Jinglong was sorely tempted to hurl his bedroll to the ground and storm off, but filial piety was the foundation of good character.

Li Jinglong's parents had died young, and although Feng Changqing was his cousin, it was he who had supported Li Jinglong through the years. If Li Jinglong were to openly defy his elder cousin in the middle of the street, he would never be able to hold his head up again. He could only grit his teeth and endure it.

"Who loses face when you parade yourself through the streets the way you did?" Feng Changqing sighed woefully. "Me! I am the one who loses face!"

Li Jinglong trailed behind Feng Changqing. "Even the virtuous Duke of Zhou feared the power of rumor. Meanwhile, the tyrant Wang Mang maintained a righteous image up to the moment he usurped the throne," he said, stony-faced. "Had either of them died early, no one would have known which parts of their lives were true and which false. Sooner or later, the truth will reveal itself. If you don't believe me, why did you summon so many people to the garrison today to question me? You know perfectly well that I've never told a lie!"

"Then why not show His Majesty the yao of which you speak?" Feng Changqing retorted. "Why not find the mysterious adversary you encountered and go defend yourself before the imperial court? Why don't you go find them and show them to me?!"

Li Jinglong was so angry he was shaking. Standing in the entrance of an alley, he said with all the solemnity he could muster, "One day, you will see."

Feng Changqing said no more. The two of them walked almost halfway across Chang'an, Feng Changqing making a point of leading Li Jinglong through the West Market.

As they came to an intersection, Li Jinglong turned into an alleyway with his bedroll in his arms. Feng Changqing drew himself up. "Where are you going?"

Li Jinglong ignored him. He had no desire to return to Feng Changqing's home where they'd only end up fighting again; he'd rather go straight to his new assignment. Feng Changqing leaned on his cane and staggered after Li Jinglong, who continued to stride forward without a word.

A bright melody floated out from the alleyway; someone nearby was singing at the top of his lungs. The setting sun dyed the brick road red and dragged Li Jinglong's shadow across the ground. An autumn breeze swept past, clutching at their clothes with its dismal chill.

"Where are you going?!" Feng Changqing repeated as he chased after him.

Ashen-faced, Li Jinglong forged ahead until he reached a doorway at the end of the alley. He pushed on the dilapidated double door, and the left leaf immediately toppled inward.

The door fell with a resounding *boom*, revealing the scene within.

At the center of the courtyard of the Department of Exorcism, A-Tai was playing his barbat, Hongjun was drumming on the bottom of a chipped bowl with a pair of chopsticks, Qiu Yongsi was striking at a large rock with a pair of bamboo pipes to emit hollow thunking noises, and Mergen was twanging rhythmically at the string of his great bow. The four of them sat in a circle around a wooden basin half filled with water, at the center of which stood a carp with human arms and legs. With one foot propped up on the lip of the basin, the creature swung its arms back and forth, evidently in the middle of a rousing dance.

The four exorcists and one fish froze as the door fell in, turning to stare at Li Jinglong and Feng Changqing behind him with befuddled expressions.

Li Jinglong stared back.

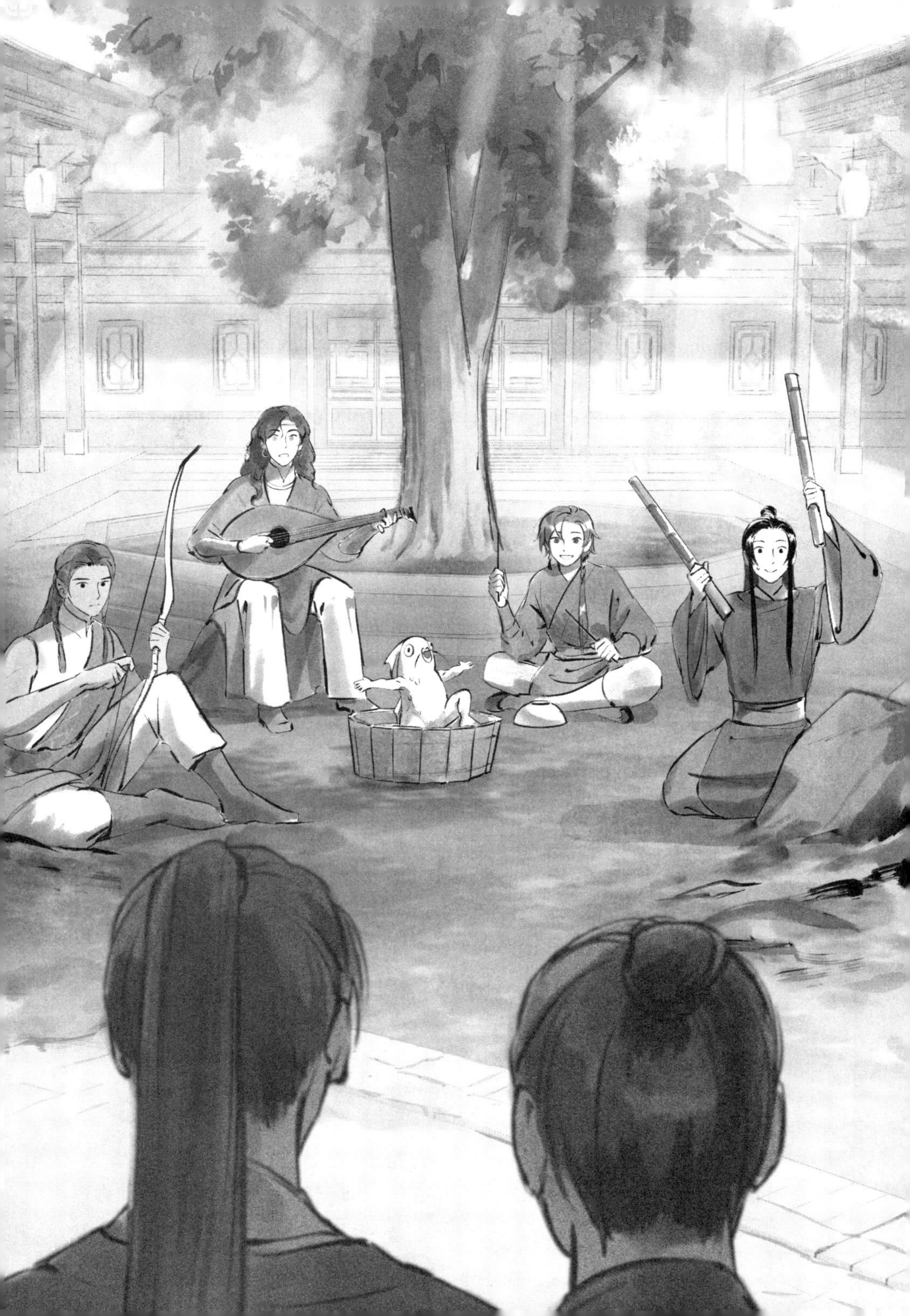

That which arises from fate cannot be decided by the will of man. Li Jinglong was still ignorant of the many fantastical forces that had mysteriously and inexorably steered his life to this point. It was as if everything he had experienced in his twenty years on this mortal plane had been for the sake of today—a string of curious coincidences that led him to push open the door in the alley.

A fleeting glimpse of fate, of a bond formed and then broken—until he looked into the eyes of that beautiful young man. The world seemed to fade, leaving only a single, unforgettable face.

If only all of life could be like a first meeting: What seems to be an ordinary encounter at the time turns out, years later, to be something else entirely. Emotions beyond counting swirled in Li Jinglong's heart, becoming a violent storm with strength to cleave the heavens. It crashed through the embankment of his reason and good sense, until everything he wanted to say was distilled into a handful of furious words:

"Give me back my virtue—!"

With an enraged roar, Li Jinglong drew his sword and lunged toward the group before him. Before the rest could react, Hongjun was on his feet, jumping backward to dodge.

"Wait! Don't hurt the yao!" Mergen shouted.

"My friend! There's no need to panic!" A-Tai cried.

"Don't be scared!" Qiu Yongsi added.

But instead of striking out at the carp yao, Li Jinglong swung directly for Hongjun, aiming to kill. The other three cursed; A-Tai whipped open his fan, Mergen stepped forward to shield Hongjun behind him, and Qiu Yongsi drew his own sword, all three moving as one to stop Li Jinglong.

Even this was too slow. Li Jinglong had already crossed the outer courtyard and arrived before Hongjun.

"He's an ordinary human!" Hongjun shouted to his friends. "Don't hurt him!"

Hongjun was deeply wary of Li Jinglong's sword, for it had been this very weapon that had shattered his pentacolor sacred light. He had replayed the scene countless times in his mind over the last two days. Naturally, he did not make the same mistake twice; he blocked the long, black blade with two crossed throwing knives as he sailed through the air.

The knives chimed against the sword as the divine weapons resonated with each other. Li Jinglong's pupils contracted. Before he could change tactics, Hongjun locked Li Jinglong's sword between his throwing knives with a twist of his wrists and swung his arms in a wide arc. The web between Li Jinglong's thumb and forefinger burned as his sword flew from his hand.

Mergen, A-Tai, and Qiu Yongsi cheered. Hongjun slammed into the ground, landing hard, and before he could make sense of what had just happened, his friends had already taken Li Jinglong by the shoulders, using their combined strength to send him flying. Hurtling into the entrance hall, Li Jinglong smashed through a window headfirst and landed with a resounding crash in the main courtyard, where he promptly blacked out.

Hongjun grimaced. He had told the others not to hurt him, but in the end, no one had pulled their punches... Looking down, he saw he had sliced his fingers open on Li Jinglong's blade, and his hands were covered with blood. The others hurried forward to examine his wounds.

"Are you all right?" Mergen asked with a frown. "What sort of grudge does this man have against you?"

Glancing around, the carp yao spotted Feng Changqing, who had yet to gather his wits, gaping at them as he slowly backed away from the door. "There's another one over there! Don't let him get away!"

A-Tai and Qiu Yongsi both whipped their heads around. Qiu Yongsi was the first to react, rushing toward Feng Changqing with sword in hand.

Feng Changqing yelped, "M-m-m—monster!"

This was all he could get out before Qiu Yongsi knocked him down and set a foot on Feng Changqing's chest, pressing the point of his blade against the man's throat. A-Tai seized the opportunity to conjure two lengths of rope, which twined themselves securely around Feng Changqing's hands and feet as the man fainted in shock.

In the time it took for an incense stick to burn, Hongjun's hands had been wrapped in bandages, and the two unconscious cousins, Li Jinglong and Feng Changqing, had been tossed into a corner of the main hall.

"His name is Li Jinglong. He's an ordinary city guard with no spiritual powers. I ran into him while I was chasing a monster through the outskirts of Chang'an..."

Hongjun told the story in its entirety, sitting together with the other three in the main courtyard. When he came to the part about the heart lamp, the carp yao coughed loudly beside him. Hongjun paused briefly before skirting around that particular detail.

By the time he had finished, everyone's expressions had turned to ones of surprise.

"So it's just a misunderstanding," Mergen said. "This man, Li Jinglong, thought you were a monster, which is why he attacked you so fiercely. Thank goodness you weren't badly hurt."

Mergen moved to untie Li Jinglong's ropes when the carp yao tapped Hongjun's knee with a rolled-up scroll.

"What's this?" Hongjun asked, puzzled.

"They dropped it at the door," the carp yao answered.

Qiu Yongsi unrolled the document and discovered that it was an imperial edict, which he read aloud:

"Dear respected sir, in light of the propitious omens that have emerged as a consequence of His Majesty's reign, the Great Tang Department of Demonic Exorcism founded by Duke Di during the reign of Empress Shengshen[8] will henceforth be reestablished. In accordance with this imperial edict, you, Li Jinglong, will immediately depart your station in the Longwu Guard and assume the office of the ch-ch-ch-chief of the…D-D-D-Department of Demonic Exorcism…"

Everyone looked up from where they were gathered around Qiu Yongsi to stare at the insensible Li Jinglong. The paper shook in Qiu Yongsi's trembling hands as his mouth twitched in dismay.

---

8   Wu Zhao, reigning as Wu Zetian, was China's sole empress regnant. She took the title Shengshen when she established the Wu Zhou interregnum (690–705) between phases of the Tang dynasty.

9
NEWCOMER

"W E'RE DEAD!" the carp yao cried. "That guy over there is your boss! The chief of the Department of Exorcism! What are we going to do?"

Everyone looked at each other in horror.

"I made this mess," Hongjun said. "I'll wake him up and apologize."

Bracing himself, Hongjun strode into the main hall. The other three exchanged glances—they couldn't allow Hongjun to take all the blame by himself—and followed.

Hongjun knelt and patted Li Jinglong's cheek. "Hey, wake up," he said softly.

"He'll never wake up if you tap him like that," the carp yao said. "Just smack him."

Hongjun was at the end of his rope. "He's our boss! How am I supposed to smack him?!"

The carp yao darted forward and, before anyone could stop him, delivered a series of sharp slaps to Li Jinglong's face, the sound echoing through the hall.

The young exorcists nearly wet themselves from fright. "Stop it!"

Li Jinglong gasped awake, only for A-Tai to wallop him on the back of the head with his barbat. With a dull thud, Li Jinglong was once again knocked unconscious.

"Zhao Zilong, I'm begging you, please don't make any more trouble." Hongjun was near tears.

In a flash of inspiration, Qiu Yongsi said, "Listen—let's untie his ropes and move him to the couch. Later, when he wakes up on his own, we all pretend nothing happened. No matter what he says, we stick to our story and say they both fainted from heatstroke."

"Great idea!" the others exclaimed.

A-Tai loosened Feng Changqing's and Li Jinglong's bindings and lifted them both onto the couch—which they had fortunately cleaned earlier—so that the cousins were lying side by side.

"Excellent!" Qiu Yongsi said. "Now, we return to the outer courtyard and go back to doing what we were before. When they come out, greet them happily and say, 'Chief, you're awake!' We admit nothing, upon pain of death. They have no way to prove we're lying—got it?"

The other three promptly agreed and made to head out.

They had only taken a single step when Li Jinglong spoke up coldly from behind them. "I heard everything."

In the time it took for another incense stick to burn, Li Jinglong's forehead was wrapped in bandages, and he had come to sit on the couch in the main hall with Feng Changqing, who was awake and unharmed. The other four knelt before them, looking up with awkward smiles.

"Chief," Mergen began, earnest. "About today's misunderstanding. When all's said and done, no matter what, you...you shouldn't have attacked before clarifying the situation. You hurt our little brother here..."

"How was I supposed to know?!" Li Jinglong exploded. "Thanks to this idiot, not only have I lost my official position, I've become the laughingstock of Chang'an. Who's going to right the wrongs I've suffered?"

"Huh? But why?" Hongjun poked his head out from behind Mergen and Qiu Yongsi. Mergen pushed him back, keeping him out of Li Jinglong's sight.

"We're all here to do our part for the peace of Chang'an," A-Tai said. "Our intentions were pure. We shouldn't let a misunderstanding sow discord between us. This beautiful little brother of ours is as innocent as a lamb…"

"That's enough!" Li Jinglong was about to keel over from rage.

"Allow me to play you a little something on my barbat, Chief," A-Tai said, smiling brightly. "May the melody of my song melt away your anger, and may the world—"

"Put that thing away!" Li Jinglong bellowed.

Everyone lapsed into silence once again. After A-Tai's rambling, the atmosphere seemed to have taken a strange turn. The distress and indignation in Li Jinglong's heart evaporated, and for a span, he had no idea what to do next.

Feng Changqing chose this moment to speak up. "So this means that there really are yao monsters in Chang'an… Y-y-you…just what kind of yao are you?" Feng Changqing pointed a shaking finger at Zhao Zilong.

"Are you blind?" the carp yao asked in return. "Don't you know a carp when you see—"

Hongjun shoved his fingers into the carp yao's mouth before he could finish.

"Come out." Li Jinglong pointed at Hongjun. "Stop hiding behind them. I'm going to ask you three questions. After that, I'll consider us even."

Hongjun, shoulders hunched to make himself as small as possible, shuffled out from behind Mergen and came to sit cross-legged before Li Jinglong.

"Was it you who fought me in the alleyway outside Pingkang Ward the other night?" Li Jinglong asked.

"Yes."

Li Jinglong glanced at Feng Changqing, but Feng Changqing said nothing.

"Where did you take me after you knocked me unconscious?"

After some thought, Hongjun concisely recounted the events of the night. "...But actually, it wasn't me who knocked you out. It was because you—"

Li Jinglong lifted a hand, cutting Hongjun off. He turned to look at Feng Changqing once more. Feng Changqing nodded his head in silence.

"Did I touch that woman, Sang-er?" Li Jinglong asked.

"No." Hongjun examined Li Jinglong's expression; he had no idea why Li Jinglong would ask these things.

This time, Li Jinglong turned fully to face Feng Changqing. "The people out there are saying I—"

"All four of you, get out," Feng Changqing said.

The group of exorcists padded out, and Mergen closed the door behind them.

Li Jinglong was fit to be tied. "They're all saying I'm the great loser of the Li family. But I exhausted the family fortune for the sake of Duke Di and his dying wish—for the sake of our nation! How many injustices have I had to bear? Not a single person has believed me all this time! Now a monster stands before you! Do you not see it?!"

Li Jinglong jabbed a finger at the carp yao as he spoke. The carp's mouth opened and closed, his eyes huge as he awkwardly observed

Li Jinglong and Feng Changqing from where he squatted on the ground.

"What are you still doing here?!" Feng Changqing snapped at the fish. "Get out!"

The carp yao scurried out into the entrance hall where the others were waiting. While the others had begun discussing what had transpired, Hongjun was drowning in anxiety.

"They're fighting!" the carp yao exclaimed.

"About what?" Hongjun asked.

"Probably about Li Jinglong visiting a brothel," Mergen responded.

A-Tai tiptoed over to the doorway to eavesdrop, and the rest followed in his wake. They all heard Li Jinglong's raised voice, but from Feng Changqing they could hear nothing.

"...The entire Longwu Guard was mocking me today! Yang Guozhong has been saying I'm undisciplined and unruly because my parents aren't around to keep me in line. Did I complain when no one stepped up to defend me against these accusations? No! I endured it in silence. All my life, I've suffered humiliation after humiliation. Even when they looked down on me, in my heart, I've always sneered at these petty men and their unbearable stupidity. But what about you? Now that you've realized you were wrong about me, do you intend to ignore your mistake?!"

"I was wrong; I admit it." Feng Changqing sighed deeply. "What do you want to do now? Do you want to bring that child before Chancellor Yang to clear this up?"

The main hall descended into silence.

Outside, Mergen, A-Tai, and Qiu Yongsi had all turned to look at Hongjun. After listening to their conversation, it was clear that he had more or less ruined Li Jinglong's life. It seemed that even when Hongjun wasn't in the middle of causing trouble, he was always on the verge of it. Yet he had no idea how to fix what he'd done.

"Forget it," Li Jinglong said inside the hall. His voice was cold. "One day, you'll all see."

Outside, the evening drum began to beat.

"You should go," Li Jinglong said.

"A good man has nothing to fear from rumors," Feng Changqing said seriously. "Jinglong, I was wrong to blame you yesterday. It was a mistake on my part..."

But Li Jinglong merely pushed open the door.

The four eavesdroppers scrambled back from the entrance. By the time Li Jinglong emerged, A-Tai was strumming his barbat by a flower bed beneath the parasol tree; Qiu Yongsi was gazing pensively up at the faded red paint of a pillar with his hands clasped behind his back; Mergen was picking up the shattered remains of the broken window; and Hongjun was crouched near the well, amusing himself by poking at the carp yao's mouth with a tree branch.

The beats of the evening drum continued without pause. Li Jinglong watched his cousin leave through the main courtyard.

Feng Changqing limped out with the help of his cane, glancing at the young men as he passed.

"Make sure you hide the carp if Chancellor Yang comes to call," Feng Changqing warned. "Or it'll be carted off and presented to His Majesty and Noble Consort Yang for their entertainment."

"He won't come," Li Jinglong said. "Besides, monster or not, I won't allow that creature to become anyone's plaything."

Hongjun's mouth fell open in surprise as he shared a glance with the carp yao. Zhao Zilong couldn't resist giving Li Jinglong an appraising look as Feng Changqing hobbled away to the pulse of the evening drum.

"You can come in now," Li Jinglong said with dignity.

Everyone filed back into the main hall. Li Jinglong fetched some water and instructed each of them to wash their hands, one by one, before rummaging through the drawers to dig up some sticks of incense.

"Does anyone have a firestarter?" Li Jinglong asked.

A-Tai flicked his fingers, and a tendril of smoke unfurled from the red gemstone in one of his rings before sparking into a flame. Li Jinglong's eyes widened with surprise. A-Tai smiled slightly, his brows lifting as if he'd discovered some secret.

Yet Li Jinglong said nothing as he lit the incense before dividing the handful of sticks between them. Then, with his own three held out reverently before him, he approached the mural and bowed thrice to Di Renjie's portrait.

"Duke Di, today, the Department of Demonic Exorcism resumes its duties. May your spirit in heaven protect us and watch over our nation of Great Tang."

When he had finished, he motioned for the others to do the same, then placed his incense in the old copper burner. He lifted his head and studied the timeworn portrait on the wall for a long moment before finally turning to leave.

"That's it for today. You're dismissed."

The evening drum was still beating in the distance. The four turned and trudged out, their hearts heavy with anxiety.

Mergen crouched in the main courtyard while the other three chatted, glancing periodically toward the east wing. The others still didn't know exactly what Hongjun had done to offend Li Jinglong, but they had surmised it had something to do with dragging him into a brothel and ruining his reputation. Given that Li Jinglong had rushed to attack first and ask questions later, it seemed he was prone to rash behavior. As for Hongjun, he still had not a clue what a brothel was and remained as confused as ever.

But the principal source of their consternation wasn't who had offended whom, or Li Jinglong's explosive temper. It was the fact that Li Jinglong was so ordinary. It stood to reason that any exorcist who came to report for duty would either be well-versed in spiritual techniques or else possess some supernatural abilities that would help them capture and subdue yao—yet Li Jinglong was just a regular mortal man.

"He has an incredibly powerful sword," Hongjun said. "It broke through my pentacolor sacred light."

"No matter how powerful his sword, it's just a magical artifact. What good will he be if he has no abilities of his own?" A-Tai sighed in despair.

Hongjun didn't want to say Li Jinglong had the heart lamp's power inside his body when he hadn't yet verified that this was so. As they talked things over, the four of them grew increasingly dejected: Mergen had expected the leader of the Department of Exorcism to be a highly capable master of exorcism; A-Tai, on the other hand, simply found Li Jinglong to be extremely dull. Qiu Yongsi thought the chief of the Department of Exorcism ought to at least have the power to protect his subordinates. From what he'd seen of Li Jinglong's abilities, even if the man was a skilled martial artist and possessed a divine weapon, he had nothing else to recommend him; Qiu Yongsi couldn't help but lose enthusiasm for the whole venture.

Halfway through their discussion, Li Jinglong emerged from the east wing. He ignored his subordinates and made his way to the outer courtyard to fetch some bedding. Despite their silence, the young exorcists' disappointment with their new chief was painfully obvious.

"So then...what are we going to do from now on?" Hongjun wondered.

"I suppose we wait and see what orders he has for us," A-Tai said with a smile. "We do whatever he tells us to do. Anyway, I'm heading back to my room."

After A-Tai left, Qiu Yongsi spoke up. "I refuse to hunt yao with him. I'd have to waste energy protecting him, and I'm already afraid of dying as it is."

Qiu Yongsi got up as well. Shrugging his shoulders, Mergen was about to ask which room Hongjun was staying in when Hongjun abruptly announced he was going to check on Li Jinglong and hurried away with soft steps.

10
A FRESH START

As the moon reached its zenith, an autumn chill settled over the earth. Standing outside the east wing, Hongjun watched through the paper screen window as Li Jinglong's towering shadow carried a bundle of bedclothes into his room and began to make his bed beneath the lamplight.

"Chief, do you want some help?" Hongjun called.

"Stop dithering," the carp yao piped up from beside him. "If you want to help him, just go in."

"Will you shut up?!"

Li Jinglong didn't answer, but his shadow paused briefly, so Hongjun pushed open the door and went in.

"Get out," Li Jinglong said. "Who taught you to enter your superior's quarters without permission?"

Scratching his head, Hongjun stepped back to watch from outside the open door. The carp yao stood at Hongjun's feet with his head resting against the doorsill to peek inside.

After making his bed, Li Jinglong straightened up and turned to look at Hongjun.

"I caused a lot of trouble for you, didn't I?" Hongjun said. "Is it really bad?"

Li Jinglong took a deep breath. Assuming he was about to get yelled at again, Hongjun took another step back.

"How old are you?" Li Jinglong asked instead, gazing steadily at Hongjun.

When Hongjun had reported his age, Li Jinglong said heavily, "Keep an eye on your yao. If it sneaks off and scares someone, I'll have to send you home. I won't have a repeat of what happened today."

Abashed, the carp yao scuttled off, leaving Hongjun alone. "Please don't send me away," Hongjun said. "I'll be careful. I can't go home now."

Li Jinglong started in surprise.

Hanging his head, Hongjun turned away and followed the winding corridor back to the west wing. His room was covered in dust, and he had no bedding; the best he could do was find a wooden board to sleep on and make do for the night. Spotting a sheepskin hunting jacket spread out on the wooden board—presumably left for him by Mergen to use as a blanket—Hongjun gathered a stack of his dirty clothes to use as a pillow and lay down to sleep.

When Hongjun emerged the next morning, he found Li Jinglong in the main courtyard surrounded by a dozen porters carrying packages of all sizes.

"You can leave those here," he said, counting out money to pay them for their labor.

Astonished, Hongjun stepped forward to get a closer look. The packages contained all sorts of basic household necessities: bundles of bedding, kitchen utensils, stationery supplies for the study... evidently all purchased by Li Jinglong.

"Wow!" Hongjun exclaimed. "Did you buy these for us?"

"We'll split the expenses," Li Jinglong said neutrally. "The cost will be deducted from your salaries."

With that, he strode over to the west wing and kicked open the doors to A-Tai and Qiu Yongsi's rooms.

"Get out here!" he barked. "What were you two doing visiting a whorehouse in the middle of the night instead of sleeping?!"

A-Tai and Qiu Yongsi had gotten barely four hours of sleep after sneaking in from their clandestine adventure. They made for a sorry sight as they sprang from their beds in a panicked flurry. Li Jinglong ordered all four of them to carry their new things to their rooms, then assemble in the courtyard as quickly as possible to set about cleaning and renovating the Department of Exorcism.

Li Jinglong worked like a dog for three days while the four exorcists and one fish slacked off. They idled about in the courtyard, singing along to A-Tai's barbat and making merry as if they had nothing better to do, even as the painters and plasterers Li Jinglong had hired to fix up the walls and pillars stood around waiting for the chief to finish cleaning so they could begin.

By the time Li Jinglong concluded his work, the entire Department of Exorcism had changed beyond recognition. A gilded statue of Acalanatha, the Immovable Wisdom King, now occupied the entrance hall, beyond which snowy-white walls and vermilion pillars extended as far as the eye could see. The doors and windows had been freshly painted, and patches of moss had been planted in the main courtyard, where the seventy-year-old parasol tree stood amid several stands of bamboo that rustled in the breeze. The whole scene was bathed in autumn sunlight that made the roof tiles glow with a liquid luster. Cobblestone had been laid in the entrance hall and the rear courtyard, and wind chimes swayed gently beneath the eaves of the complex's winding, open-air corridors with a bright tinkling sound. There was even a school of red fish swimming in the pond, where a wooden sign labeled *Zhao Zilong* had been erected. This would be the carp yao's new home.

A table bearing a tea set, its cups turned neatly upside down, had been placed in front of a squat new couch in the main hall. Li Jinglong had chosen sleeping quarters in the east wing, apart from the rest of them, near the department's common spaces such as the armory, the infirmary, and the library, the latter of which was occupied by a dozen shelves piled high with books and case records left by Di Renjie.

Each room now had brand new floor-to-ceiling wooden sliding doors, which allowed for a wealth of natural light. As Hongjun ran barefoot along the courtyard's corridors, wiping the floorboards spotlessly clean, he couldn't help but notice the way each of his new friends' quarters had been redecorated by its occupant. Mergen had spread a tiger pelt before the table in his room, displaying the longbow he had purchased in the West Market upon the wall. A-Tai's exceedingly luxurious room was draped in exotic-looking blankets and cluttered with curious objects fashioned from white jade and colored glass. As for Qiu Yongsi, he had hung up famed painter Zhan Ziqian's *Spring Outing* on one of his walls and set out delicately glazed celadon teacups and flower vases, which had been fired in the famous Yue kilns.

Hongjun's room, containing little more than a bed pushed against the wall, was the only one that was bare. When Li Jinglong noticed, he picked out three pieces of art and tossed them to Hongjun, instructing him to hang them up himself. The first was a piece of calligraphy by poet Zhang Xu in cursive script; the second was painter Zhang Sengyou's *Hundred Birds*; and the third was a gold-green landscape painting by another celebrated artist, Li Sixun. Hongjun didn't recognize the artists' seals and had no idea how valuable these works were, so he put them up at random. Zhang Sengyou's *Hundred Birds*, at least, gave him a keen sense of familiarity, reminding him of his days in Yaojin Palace.

Now that the renovations were complete, it would have been no great exaggeration to say the Department of Demonic Exorcism was the most elegantly appointed government office in the city. The premises, purchased by Di Renjie's disciple Luo Jintong when Great Tang's seat of government moved from the divine capital of Luoyang to the current capital of Chang'an, had once been a villa owned by architect Yuwen Kai. It had been blessed with good natural light and plentiful sources of water from the start, and after Li Jinglong's exertions, it immediately became everyone's new home.

The renovations weren't the only changes to the department. The four exorcists had begun to see Li Jinglong, too, in a different light. Having deemed their new chief woefully lacking on day one, Mergen, A-Tai, and Qiu Yongsi were surprised by the tenacity he'd shown in forging ahead with his plans. No matter how they loafed about, Li Jinglong continued his work. In the end, he had even personally cleaned their new rooms, one by one.

"All right," Li Jinglong said as they gathered in the main hall, wiping sweat from his brow before settling down and breaking open a brick of compressed tea.

"I can do it," Qiu Yongsi said, motioning toward the tea leaves.

Li Jinglong allowed him to take over preparing the tea. The autumn sky arched high and clear overhead as water boiled within the copper pot, and everyone took a seat in the main hall to wait for their tea.

"Since the Department of Exorcism has only just resumed operations," Li Jinglong began, his voice low and his face as impassive as ever, "I thought we could use the renovations as an opportunity to work together and get to know each other..."

Hongjun blinked in confusion. Looking left and right, he saw that Mergen, Qiu Yongsi, and A-Tai's expressions had turned a bit unnatural.

"However, I see now that you are all titans among men and have already become brothers-in-arms," Li Jinglong continued mildly. "It seems that, as an ordinary mortal, I will be the one holding you back in our work. You have my sincerest apologies."

An extreme awkwardness settled over the group. It was true that except for Hongjun, they all looked down on him for his lack of supernatural talent. Li Jinglong was keenly aware that his subordinates had no respect for him, but as he dealt with contempt everywhere he went, he had long since grown used to it.

"Now give me your letters," Li Jinglong said. "I'll get you all registered today and report to Chancellor Yang tomorrow."

"Chief, were you the one who sent us these letters?" Mergen asked.

Li Jinglong shook his head. "It wasn't me. I was just about to ask you who sent them."

This made no sense, but Li Jinglong had no reason to lie to them. After a round of discussion, everyone agreed that someone must have summoned the four of them to Chang'an at the exact same time for the express purpose of reconstituting the Great Tang Department of Demonic Exorcism. But if this was the case, how could they account for Li Jinglong's arrival, which seemed to be a matter of purest chance? Was it simply a fateful coincidence?

Hongjun took the initiative and handed Li Jinglong his letter first.

"Kong Hongjun," Li Jinglong said. "Where are you from, and who are your parents?"

The carp yao peeked in from outside the main hall as Hongjun began to recite the story as he had been taught: His adoptive father was a Daoist cultivator who'd long ago retreated to the Taihang

Mountains to hasten his spiritual development, and Hongjun had come to Chang'an to learn and gain experience. As for Zhao Zilong, Hongjun had adopted the carp yao after meeting him through a chance encounter years ago. There was no need to worry that Zhao Zilong might be an agent sent by the yao to spy on them.

Li Jinglong listened in silence as Hongjun spoke. Even as he said the words, Hongjun felt his story was full of holes, yet Li Jinglong seemed to believe him without reservation.

Next up was Mergen. Born into a Shiwei tribe, Mergen also told Li Jinglong that he had come to Chang'an to train. Hongjun felt that Mergen, too, seemed to be hiding quite a lot, but once again, Li Jinglong asked no questions and merely recorded Mergen's name.

A-Tai was a Tokharian noble who had come to study the culture of Great Tang. Qiu Yongsi hailed from Hang Prefecture to the south, and stated in plain terms that he came from a family of scholars. It was his grandfather who had ordered him to come to the Department of Exorcism to improve his courage.

The explanations grew simpler and simpler, the questions discharged with just a few words. By the time everyone was registered, Qiu Yongsi had finished preparing the tea, which he distributed in cups to everyone, including the carp yao.

"Next time, dry your feet before you come in. Don't get the floors all wet," Li Jinglong told the carp yao as he finished making his notes. "Looks like no one else is coming to report for duty."

Everyone watched Li Jinglong in silence, trying to guess what he was about to say. Li Jinglong took a slow sip of his tea. "I don't know who summoned all of you here," he said quietly, not looking up. "But I do believe that although Duke Di has passed, he continues to watch over our nation of Great Tang. The fact that we're all gathered here today is a testament to the mysterious workings of fate."

Li Jinglong looked past the young men sitting before him and up at the mural of Di Renjie on the eastern wall, his eyes filled with some complicated emotion. The others turned to gaze up at the portrait as well.

"Are you saying Di Renjie wrote these four letters in life with the intention of sending them years after his death?" Mergen asked. "You think *he* was the one who summoned us here to revive the Great Tang Department of Demonic Exorcism?"

"How can that be possible?!" Qiu Yongsi exclaimed. Everyone turned to stare at Li Jinglong, as if to say, *Do you think we're stupid?*

"That's...absurd, isn't it?" Hongjun asked in bewilderment.

"No more absurd than a carp with hairy arms and legs," Li Jinglong said, glancing over at the carp yao with no change in his expression. Zhao Zilong gaped back at him.

"True," Hongjun said, bobbing his head in agreement. "Compared to that, sending letters from beyond the grave does seem slightly more reasonable."

Everyone else clapped their hands to their foreheads, exchanging looks of exasperation. But as Li Jinglong had spoken, they didn't dare probe any further. He was the boss; so long as the boss was happy, all was well.

"I'll place the order for our uniforms and authority tokens tomorrow," Li Jinglong said. "Whether you choose to stay, and what salary to request if you do—all of that is up to you. You have one more day to think things over. Regardless of whether you are a Han person of the Central Plains or not, once I submit your name to the chancellor, you will become an official appointed by the imperial court."

In his head, Hongjun was already tracking down the Chen family and his missing throwing knife. Lost in thought, he nodded absently at Li Jinglong's words and noticed the man was staring at him with raised brows, as if waiting for him to speak.

"I'm staying." Hongjun nodded again for emphasis, his heart heavy with anxiety.

"Me too," Mergen said.

"I'll stay as well," A-Tai chimed in.

"I'll be staying too," Qiu Yongsi said. "But what exactly will we be doing as members of the Department of Exorcism? Chief, you must have some work for us, right?"

"You'll definitely have work to do," Li Jinglong said. "Chancellor Yang has said any cases suspected of supernatural involvement—if they can't be solved by the imperial guard and the Court of Judicial Review—will be transferred to the Department of Exorcism. We have no cases yet, so I thought you might take the time to explore Chang'an…but if you're that eager, you can start working immediately."

Li Jinglong finished his tea and got to his feet.

Hongjun spoke up at once. "Chief, everyone…could you help me with something?"

"No," Li Jinglong answered.

Silence fell over the room.

"I know you want to hunt down the monster from the other night," Li Jinglong continued, "but right now, I don't know what any of you are capable of. We've never worked as a team before. If we were to head out on a mission right now, we'd be worse than unprepared; we'd probably cause some disaster. We can revisit it after some time has passed."

Hongjun was terribly distraught, but he knew Li Jinglong was right. He nodded his head.

Seeing Li Jinglong rise, everyone else got up as well. The day's official business was concluded; Li Jinglong left the main hall and made his way back to the east wing.

The moment he was safely out of sight, he slumped against a pillar and panted as if he had just been relieved of a heavy burden, his heart still racing with lingering fright. Realizing he had somehow managed to successfully wrangle this group of exorcists capable of fantastical magical feats, Li Jinglong pumped his fist in victory, the corners of his mouth curling in a rare smile.

When he lifted his head, he found Hongjun standing across from him, a puzzled expression on his face. "Chief, what are you doing?" he asked tentatively.

Li Jinglong coughed before schooling his expression back to seriousness. "What is it now?"

"I was wondering if you could help me with something." Hongjun gazed at Li Jinglong. "I want to find—"

"I said no!" Li Jinglong snapped, displeased.

"Not the monster," Hongjun assured him. "You're familiar with Chang'an. If you can just tell me where Chen Zi'ang's family lives, I can go by myself."

Hongjun's other colleagues in the Department of Exorcism were all new to the city; there was no point in asking them this question. And there were over six hundred thousand households in Chang'an. He couldn't go searching door to door. Now that Li Jinglong had arrived, the man might very well be Hongjun's savior.

Li Jinglong studied Hongjun for a moment. "Let me ask you a question first," he said. "You're a cultivator—do you know if there's a spiritual technique that can make someone forget certain things?"

"A technique?" Hongjun had no idea why Li Jinglong would ask something like this. He thought carefully. "There's no technique, but there's this flower…"

Hongjun had loved to run wild through the Taihang Mountains as a child. All sorts of rare and exotic plants grew in Yaojin Palace's rear courtyard, and now that he considered it, he vaguely recalled a flower transplanted there from the Western Regions with just such an effect.

11
DIVIDE AND CONQUER

LI JINGLONG LEFT his quarters that afternoon with Hongjun in tow. As they passed through the main courtyard, they found Mergen sunning himself beneath the sky well, a stalk of grass held between his lips and one leg slung over the other. Qiu Yongsi was sitting, reading a book, and A-Tai was fiddling with his barbat.

"Get up, all of you. You have your first assignment," Li Jinglong said. "Go to the West Market and find a medicine called oblivion pollen."

"Huh?" Everyone gathered round.

"The oblivion flower is native to the Western Regions," Li Jinglong explained. "Those who inhale its pollen will sneeze and forget their most recent memories. It'll be useful during our investigations to help calm panicking witnesses."

Qiu Yongsi, Mergen, and A-Tai studied Li Jinglong, their faces filled with doubt.

"What if we can't find it?" A-Tai asked.

"Because chances are we won't," Qiu Yongsi agreed.

"If you can't find it, then look until you do," Li Jinglong said. "This is an order, not a negotiation. Now, go."

"Chief, where did you hear about this pollen?" Mergen frowned slightly, sensing something amiss.

Hongjun weakly raised a hand from where he was standing behind Li Jinglong. At everyone's exasperated expressions, Li Jinglong glanced backward. Hongjun shoved his hand back down to his side.

The autumn air was pleasantly crisp, but as Hongjun followed Li Jinglong through the streets of Chang'an, his thoughts were in turmoil. The other three had looked so reluctant as they had headed out. He couldn't help but worry he'd once again placed a burden on his colleagues. If they failed to find this rare flower after spending all day looking, they would no doubt come back and yell at him for making them waste their time.

"Chief, what if they can't find it?"

"Chief…to be honest, I'm not sure whether oblivion flowers really work either."

"Chief, why aren't you saying anything?"

Li Jinglong walked on in silence.

"Huh?" said Hongjun, distracted from his worrying. "Chief, what's that over there?"

Great Tang had flourished into a bustling empire, and the streets of Chang'an thronged with activity. Hongjun was afraid of getting lost; he grasped at Li Jinglong's sleeve. Unsettled, Li Jinglong tried to shake him off, which only made the atmosphere more awkward.

"Kong Hongjun," Li Jinglong snapped. "We're in public—don't cling to me like that!"

As a child of four or five, Hongjun had always held tight to Chong Ming's sleeves as he followed him around Yaojin Palace like a little shadow. It seemed completely normal to him, but confronted with Li Jinglong's displeasure, he quickly let go.

Li Jinglong led him on and on through the winding streets, weaving between wards before finally arriving at the entrance of a family residence. He knocked on the door. A woman's voice floated out to ask who it was, and Li Jinglong stated his name before stepping over the main gate's threshold to enter.

A woman met them in the outer courtyard with an infant in her arms. She looked her guests over curiously.

"Excuse me, ma'am, is Chen Zi'ang at home?" Hongjun asked.

"Chen Zi'ang passed away decades ago," Li Jinglong hissed. "Don't talk nonsense."

Hongjun was shocked. From the dilapidated state of the courtyard, it was clear the owner was terribly poor. "What about his grandchildren or great-grandchildren? Who are you?"

After thinking for a moment, the woman said, "Why don't you come inside."

They sat down at a small table in the dimly lit hall as the infant in the woman's arms, no more than six months old, began to whimper from hunger. Hongjun found the baby adorable and reached out to soothe him, letting the child play with his fingers as his mother spoke.

The great poet Chen Zi'ang had died in prison fifty-one years ago, she told them, after making an enemy of the powerful official Wu Sansi. He was survived by his only son, but as the years passed, the Chen family had continued to dwindle in number. After several generations, only a single living descendant—a failed imperial examinee—remained. The woman sitting before them, whose maiden name was Duan, was his wife. Her husband had studied in poverty and hardship for over ten years to achieve scholarly honors in the imperial examinations, but after failing many times, he caught a terrible cold before he could make his next attempt. After a long and protracted illness, he passed westward, leaving behind a widow and infant son.

"The grave is on the city's outskirts," Mistress Duan said. "Since you're acquaintances of my late husband, I can take you to see him tomorrow, if you like."

Hongjun felt as if his heart had tumbled to the bottom of an icy ravine. Qing Xiong had told him the scion of the Chen family might help him investigate his father's death after he returned the heart lamp. But even if he did manage to return it, there was no way this infant could grow up overnight!

"Have you gotten your answer?" Li Jinglong asked, sipping from the cup of water Mistress Duan had served him. "If so, then let's go."

Hongjun mulled it over but remained at a loss. At least, he reflected, the Chen family line yet lived. He counted out a handful of pearls and gave them to Mistress Duan. "Take care of yourselves," he said. "If anything happens, you can come find me at the Department of Exorcism in Jincheng Ward."

When Mistress Duan saw the lustrous pearls, she immediately tried to press them back into his hands. But Hongjun insisted, so in the end, she had no choice but to gratefully accept.

Surprised by his generosity, Li Jinglong couldn't help but study Hongjun with renewed curiosity.

"Did you also know my husband?" Mistress Duan asked Hongjun in gratitude.

"I did not," Hongjun answered honestly.

An awkward silence fell between them. Li Jinglong had no earthly idea why Hongjun had asked to come here in the first place; regardless, he felt compelled to lend his subordinate a hand out of his awkward predicament. "This kid is a big fan of poetry. He has always admired Censor Chen's literary grace."

"I see." Mistress Duan nodded, understanding at once. Reading poetry was akin to communing with the spirits of the great minds behind the brush; perhaps this boy considered Chen Zi'ang his old friend.

Hongjun sighed, his brow creasing deeply with distress as he stood up to pace the hall. The other two, still sitting at the table, watched him in confusion. "We should be going," Li Jinglong said, lifting his cup to down the rest of his water as Hongjun passed fretfully behind him.

At that precise moment, Hongjun noticed that the woman, her infant, and Li Jinglong happened to form a straight line. Inspired, he thought, *If I could just expel the heart lamp from Li Jinglong's body...*

"Spirit of the body—manifest!"

Speaking the incantation, Hongjun activated his pentacolor sacred light and pressed it to Li Jinglong's back. The light poured into Li Jinglong's meridians in a thrumming rush, causing Li Jinglong, who was sitting upright in his chair, to light up with a dazzling brightness.

Terrified, Mistress Duan clutched her babe to her chest. "Ch-Ch-Ch-Chief Li, you're glowing! Aiya, someone help! Chief Li is glowing!"

Hongjun's sacred light scoured Li Jinglong's body in an instant. But his meridians were completely empty; Hongjun couldn't sense anything of the heart lamp.

Li Jinglong felt blood and qi surge in his chest with such force that his soul nearly shook free of his body. He coughed mid-gulp, and water sprayed from his mouth, soaking Mistress Duan and her baby, who promptly started wailing.

An hour later, inside the Department of Exorcism, Li Jinglong stood before Hongjun in the main courtyard.

"What the hell were you doing?!" he shouted at his subordinate. "I'm docking half a month of your pay for this stunt!"

Hongjun hastily suggested he could dock a full month's pay if it would quell his anger.

"Have I done something to offend you?" Li Jinglong was so angry he was shaking. "Why do you insist on making a fool of me at every turn?"

"The truth is so outlandish, you wouldn't believe me even if I told you!" Hongjun cried, instinctively reaching for Li Jinglong's sleeve as he turned to leave.

Li Jinglong jerked it away. "Go face the wall! Stand there till dinner!"

"What havoc have you wreaked now?" the carp yao asked gleefully as he clambered out of the pond to witness Hongjun's misfortune. "Finally, someone who can keep you in line!"

Hongjun bared his teeth at the carp yao in an unhappy grimace.

A few moments later, Li Jinglong returned. "How outlandish are we talking?" he asked quietly, standing before Hongjun. "Explain yourself. If this really wasn't a deliberate prank on your part, I won't punish you."

At this point, Hongjun had no choice but to come clean. He told Li Jinglong about the heart lamp and what had happened when they'd fought on the night they met. He had hoped, he explained, to force the heart lamp from Li Jinglong's body just now, so he could pass it on to Chen Zi'ang's descendant and complete his mission.

Li Jinglong was silent for a long time.

"If only Qing Xiong were here," Hongjun finished with a sigh.

"So, in other words, the heart lamp entered my body accidentally?"

"I'm not totally sure yet." Seeing Li Jinglong's knit brows relax slightly, Hongjun continued, "But if it's not in your body, I'm in huge trouble. If the heart lamp is gone, I'll have failed my mission, and I won't be able to go home. Chief, I really don't bear you any ill will, and this is such a serious matter; I would never cause trouble for you…"

"That's not necessarily true," the carp yao piped up. "You cause trouble for plenty of people, whether you bear them ill will or not."

"Shut up!" Hongjun and Li Jinglong shouted in unison.

"Go back to your pond!" Hongjun added.

The carp yao flicked his tail and ran off.

"Well, let's confirm it now," Li Jinglong said, picking up where they'd left off. "You have my full cooperation."

"Then…I guess I'll start?" Hongjun asked tentatively.

Li Jinglong led Hongjun to the corridor in the east wing, and the two of them sat down beneath the eaves. Li Jinglong loosened his lapels, revealing an expanse of wheat-brown skin and the lean muscle of his torso under the sunlight.

"Try to relax," Hongjun said. "It might feel a little uncomfortable." He took a deep breath. *Please, oh please let me find the heart lamp,* he thought as he gathered his power and pressed a hand to Li Jinglong's chest, once again infusing his meridians with sacred light.

Li Jinglong shuddered as his blood and qi began to roil. His face flushed and his features twitched as Hongjun's divine energy flowed through his meridians, infusing his skin with a gentle light. After a moment, the pentacolor sacred light reconverged, forming itself into a single band that streamed into Li Jinglong's heart.

Just as Hongjun began to sink into his task, he heard voices behind him.

"What's going on here?! Chief Li! What are you doing?"

Two men, an official of the Court of Judicial Review and an administrative officer, gawped at the scene before them: a bare-chested Li Jinglong with a young man sitting before him, one outstretched hand squeezing his chief's pectoral muscles.

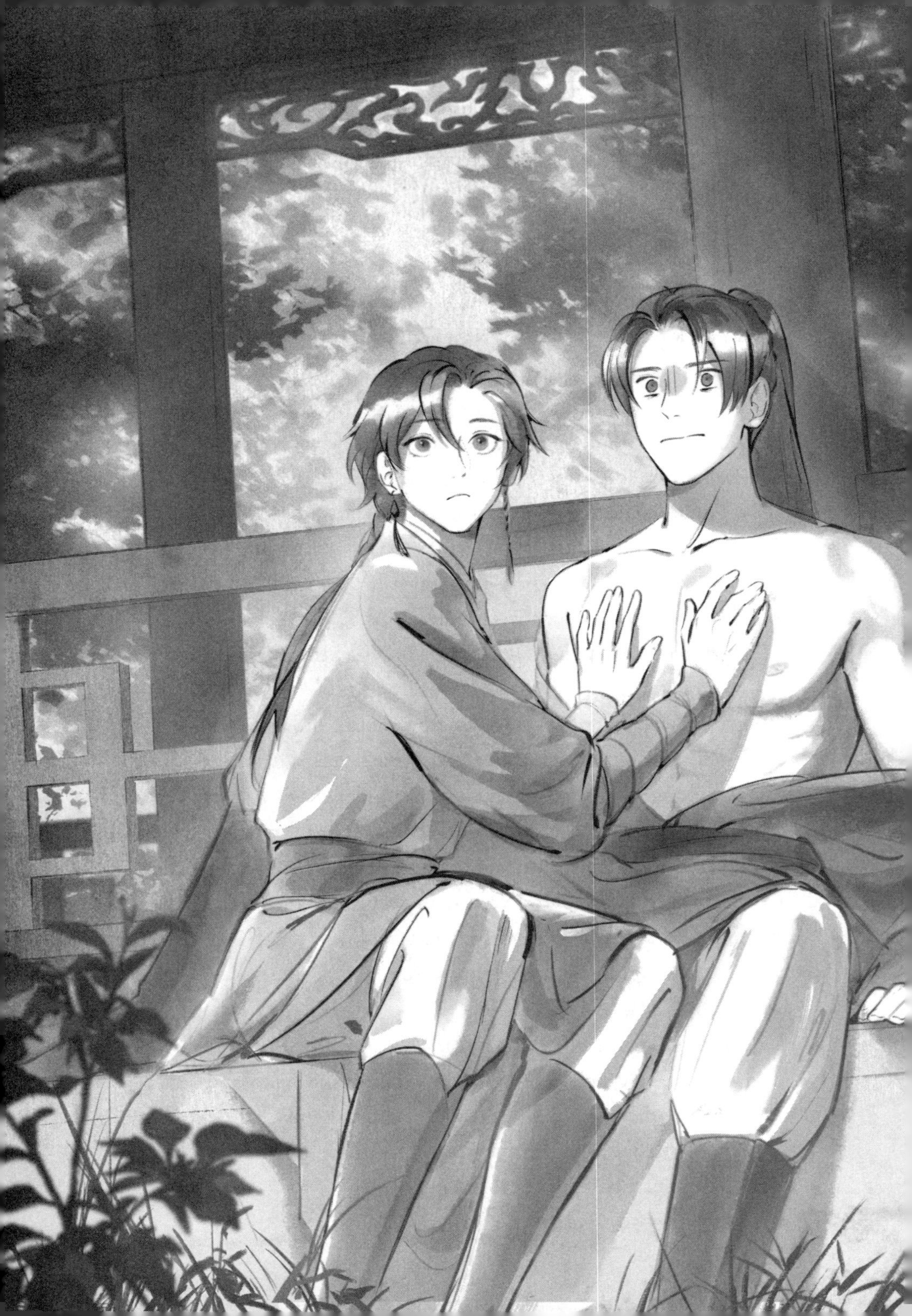

Hongjun snatched his hand back—but in the instant before letting go, he felt it: a weak force, like a dormant seed, buried deep within Li Jinglong's heart.

Cheeks aflame, Li Jinglong shoved Hongjun behind him and hurriedly pulled on his clothes. Anger and awkwardness warred on his face, but he dared not lose his temper. He adopted a dignified tone as he cupped his hands and said, "Justice Huang, please come in and have some tea."

Hongjun was overjoyed. He'd found it! Thank goodness! Now he could finally clean up the mess he'd made. He skipped around the courtyard in joy until Li Jinglong snapped, "Kong Hongjun!"

Hongjun hastily cupped his hands, following Li Jinglong's example, as the chief introduced their guest: Deputy Chief Justice Huang Yong of the Imperial Court of Judicial Review. He and the administrative officer with him watched Hongjun as if observing an idiot.

"There's no need for such formalities," Huang Yong said. "A case has been assigned to you by the Court of Judicial Review. As Chancellor Yang has surely already explained, you'll receive a copy of any cases that don't require our intervention. This is Registrar Lian Hao. Henceforth, he'll handle communication between our departments. Now that the Department of Demonic Exorcism has been officially reestablished, His Majesty and Chancellor Yang both have high hopes for you. You must devote yourself to solving cases for the sake of our great nation."

Li Jinglong nodded, then walked Huang Yong and Lian Hao back out to the main gate. As soon as the door was shut behind them, the sound of laughter erupted beyond the wall.

"What in the world was Li Jinglong doing? Milking himself in his own government office, in broad daylight no less! Ha ha ha ha..."

Li Jinglong stared at the closed door in silence.

ASSUMING OFFICE

"IT'S THERE! It's in your heart!" Hongjun exclaimed as he sat down across from Li Jinglong in the hall. "Thank goodness, I finally found it!"

He felt as if an enormous weight had been lifted from his shoulders. For the last few days, he'd been so caught up agonizing over the heart lamp he'd barely eaten; now he could finally put his biggest worry to rest.

"How do I get it out and return it to you?" Li Jinglong asked.

Hongjun spread his hands helplessly. "I don't know yet. I suppose it'll have to stay in you for now."

Li Jinglong parted his lips as if to speak, but after a brief pause, he simply nodded.

The best thing to do would be to write a letter to Yaojin Palace asking for help. But how would Hongjun send it? Should he dispatch Zhao Zilong to deliver it for him? No—the carp yao was lazy, and he hated walking because it hurt his feet. Besides, it was such a long journey; it would be dangerous for a fish to go alone. And if Qing Xiong wasn't at Yaojin Palace when the letter arrived, it would all be for naught. Should Chong Ming be the one to receive it, his reply would almost certainly be something along the lines of, *So what if you messed up? It has nothing to do with me.*

What a predicament... Hongjun looked up at Li Jinglong as he thought. He could see there was something else the man wanted to say.

"While the heart lamp's inside me," Li Jinglong began hesitantly, "will I experience any changes?"

"Nothing bad will happen." Hongjun hurried to explain, "Of the five organs, the heart is associated with the element of fire, so the heart lamp will protect yours while it makes its home there. The power of the heart lamp is pure and unadulterated. Its light is full of qi, so it won't do you any harm."

Li Jinglong nodded, yet he still seemed to be struggling with something. Puzzled, Hongjun watched him steadily until Li Jinglong finally blurted, "Will it give me any spiritual power?"

"Ah?" Hongjun responded doubtfully. "Probably...not? Your meridians don't show any signs of spiritual power. Even if you're given a spiritual device, you might not be able to activate it."

"I see," Li Jinglong mumbled to himself, eyes downcast. "I really am just an ordinary human."

Hearing the hint of disappointment in his voice, Hongjun was struck by a realization. "You don't want to be ordinary, do you?"

Li Jinglong looked up at Hongjun. "You, Mergen, Hammurabi, Qiu Yongsi—you all have spiritual power flowing through your meridians, don't you?"

Hongjun blinked. Now that he thought about it, the way A-Tai had summoned fire with a flick of his fingers implied that they all knew how to use certain spiritual techniques, even if they hadn't shown off their abilities yet. "Yes," he answered honestly.

"Where does this spiritual power come from?" Li Jinglong asked.

Hongjun was stumped; he had never considered the question.

"They're born with it," the carp yao called from the puddle of sunlight he was basking in outside. Flipping himself over onto his other side, he continued, "There's no point fretting about it. How do you think those powerful exorcist families came to be?"

Li Jinglong hummed in agreement. "Let's keep the heart lamp between us for now."

"Even though you're an ordinary human, you still have your sword," said Hongjun, attempting to console him. "Honestly, it's a pretty amazing weapon. Even my dad can't break through my sacred light with his fire—"

"Oi!" the carp yao shouted, putting a stop to Hongjun's babbling before he could say too much.

But Li Jinglong had perked up at these words. He rose to fetch his sword, which he placed on the table. "This blade once belonged to Duke Di."

Hongjun eagerly examined the sword as Li Jinglong went on, seemingly lost in thought. "I admired Duke Di greatly as a child. I once came across a book that had been passed down by him... It described all manner of grotesque yao beasts; immortals who had retreated to the most distant corners of the realm to live in seclusion; demons born from the convergence of malign energies that would reincarnate once every couple hundred years..."

"So you don't want to be like the ordinary humans—you want to be an exorcist?" Hongjun asked as he ran his fingers over the sword.

"Not necessarily," Li Jinglong said slowly. "Maybe it's just my natural inclination; I've been fascinated with these things for as long as I can remember."

Li Jinglong watched Hongjun's fingers as he spoke. "There was a section at the end of the book... According to Duke Di, the Divine

Land will face a great calamity in the next hundred years. But he was born too early—by the time he made this discovery, he was already an old man. With no successor to continue his work of protecting Great Tang, he feared that when his soul returned to the yellow earth, the nation would fall into utter chaos. Thus Duke Di left a book and sword to be passed down to the next generation. Whoever inherits these items must protect the sacred lands of our nation."

Hongjun found himself rather moved by Li Jinglong's speech. Perhaps there wouldn't be *utter* chaos...but given the mission entrusted to him by Chong Ming and Qing Xiong, and the number of yaoguai that had infiltrated the human realm, it seemed inevitable that Chang'an would suffer at least a little bit of chaos.

"What happened to the book?" Hongjun set the sword back on the table. His dad and Qing Xiong had mentioned a demon called "Mara"; he felt a curl of curiosity as he recalled their conversation.

"My father burned it to ashes," Li Jinglong said. His eyes were focused on the sword under Hongjun's hands. "He never believed any of it. Everyone thought it was just the nonsensical ramblings of a senile old man."

Hongjun pondered this in silence. He knew nothing of the sword's origins, but he could tell it was no ordinary weapon—in fact, he had a nagging sense he had seen it somewhere before. "Where did you find this sword?"

"I stumbled across it at an auction at the Treasure Emporium, many decades after Duke Di passed. Somehow the sword had ended up in the possession of a merchant from the Western Regions. To save it from falling into foreign hands, I sold off a number of family heirlooms to buy it... Oh, I have no idea why I'm telling you all this; we barely know each other."

Hongjun blinked, perplexed.

Li Jinglong sighed. "You're probably the only one who'd believe me," he said quietly.

"Mergen and the others will believe you too," Hongjun said encouragingly.

"Forget it; I don't want to discuss this with them."

Hongjun hadn't known the human realm was filled with such sad stories: having your talents go unrecognized, being born at the wrong time... But as Li Jinglong spoke, Hongjun's initial fear of the man slowly turned to understanding. An idea occurred to him. "Ordinary humans aren't born knowing how to use spiritual techniques, but perhaps you could pick it up through training? I remember..."

"Hongjun!" The carp yao called out, flipping onto his other side again as if pan-frying himself. "You've caused him enough misery!"

Hongjun knew the fish was right: There was a good chance Hongjun, with his penchant for troublemaking, would end up ruining Li Jinglong's life even further. He decided to drop the matter for now.

Li Jinglong had taken Hongjun for an idle, careless young master. Now he was forced to revise his assessment: He was surprised to find the young man wasn't nearly as foolhardy as he'd thought. Just as Li Jinglong was about to subtly probe into Hongjun's past, Mergen burst in with A-Tai and Qiu Yongsi close behind him.

"We found it!" Qiu Yongsi said, mopping sweat from his brow as he placed a box on the table. He was still panting from exertion.

Li Jinglong was already reaching toward the box when Hongjun's hand darted out to keep the lid firmly shut. "You'll want to wait till there's no wind, and hold your nose when you inspect it. If the pollen gets out and you sneeze, you'll forget everything."

"It took us forever to find it. You sent us running all over Chang'an while you two have been sitting here drinking tea?" Mergen asked, exasperated.

Li Jinglong coughed; as the department chief, he needed to maintain some modicum of dignity.

A-Tai, still breathless from their efforts, picked up where Mergen left off. "You're footing the bill, right, Chief? The total came out to three thousand, two hundred taels of silver."

Li Jinglong took out his wallet as A-Tai resumed trying to catch his breath. His hand froze. "Three thousand, two hundred taels of silver?!" Li Jinglong howled. "How is that possible?!"

"Well..." A-Tai began as Mergen and Qiu Yongsi stared at Li Jinglong in confusion. "We bought four taels of pollen. One tael of pollen costs eight hundred taels of silver. Four times eight is thirty-two—did I mess up my calculations somewhere?"

Li Jinglong sat dumbstruck. The other four glanced at each other in puzzlement, apparently unfazed by such exorbitant prices.

"Are exorcists' materials always so expensive?" Li Jinglong frowned.

"Why don't I pay for it this time?" Mergen suggested, giving Li Jinglong an out. After all, Li Jinglong had just spent quite a lot of money fixing up the Department of Exorcism.

"I can offer eight hundred taels." Qiu Yongsi beamed.

"No, no, don't worry about it, I've already paid." A-Tai waved them off.

"Why don't we split it?" Mergen suggested. "A-Tai paid for it upfront, so give him your contribution."

Li Jinglong stood up. "That's not—"

"Chief, please sit down," Qiu Yongsi reassured him. "How can we allow our chief to foot the bill? Ay! After all, you didn't hold a grudge against us for attacking you the other day... Right, Hongjun?"

Grasping his meaning at once, Hongjun began to dig around for his pearls. "That's right, that's right! If you promise not to punish us for what happened, I'll pitch in and pay for this too..."

"Hongjun!" the others shouted in irritation and dismay. While they were out, Qiu Yongsi, A-Tai, and Mergen seemed to have all come up with a plan to coax Li Jinglong into writing off their past offenses. Now that Hongjun had hit the nail so tactlessly on the head, their faces contorted through a variety of conflicting emotions.

Hongjun was baffled. "What did I say?"

Li Jinglong couldn't stand to listen anymore. He raised a hand for silence before placing the box on the top shelf in the main hall. "This is a department expense, so the imperial court will reimburse us for the cost. We'll set the oblivion pollen aside for now, and I'll divvy it up another day."

"What's this?" Mergen asked, noticing the document lying on the table.

"A cold case from the Court of Judicial Review," Li Jinglong replied. "I'd like to get started this afternoon."

"No way!" the three who had just returned groaned. "We have to go out again?"

"Was the oblivion pollen really so hard to find?" Hongjun asked. "Why are you all so tired?"

"There wasn't any to be had in the West Market," Qiu Yongsi said. "A-Tai ended up taking us to the Treasure Emporium's underground black market. The Tajik merchant insisted we put on women's clothes and dance the Sogdian Whirl with him before he would sell it to us. We danced for nearly two hours!"

"Oh? Then why is there grass stuck to your back?" the carp yao sang out from behind them. "You guys rode out to go play in the city outskirts, didn't you?"

After all they had done to cover their tracks, they stood no chance against Hongjun and the carp yao, who seemed to be working together to expose them. Laughing loudly, they quickly changed the subject.

"Aiya! Our first case already!" cried A-Tai. "Time to distinguish ourselves by cracking it quickly!"

"That's right," Qiu Yongsi agreed. "It's our duty to pour all our energies into serving our nation."

Mergen rubbed his hands together. "Tell us, what kind of major case are we talking about? Whatever it is, we'll solve it for you right away, Chief!"

Li Jinglong glanced suspiciously at the three of them. He took a deep breath and pointedly let the subject drop. "As long as no one's life is at stake, you may put it off until tomorrow. Now, let's see what this is about…"

He bowed his head to untie the scroll and spread the case file out on the table. "On the fifth day of the ninth month, a white, long-haired cat of Greater Yuezhi origin went missing from the Duchess of Qin's estate in Daning Ward. The cat in question measures nearly a foot and a half long and has one blue and one golden eye…"

TWELFTH YEAR OF TIANBAO,

TWENTY-THIRD DAY OF THE NINTH MONTH.

The Department of Demonic Exorcism's first case: Locate a missing cat.

Degree of Difficulty: Human.

Location: The city of Chang'an.
Person(s) Involved: All members of the Duchess of Qin's estate
Case Details: According to a maidservant's testimony, on the fifth evening of the ninth month, the Duchess of Qin's beloved cat, Qing-er, escaped from the estate after suffering a terrible fright. The Yulin, Shenwu, and Longwu Guards conducted extensive searches throughout Chang'an, but the cat remains unaccounted for. After ten days and no results, the case is hereby transferred to the Great Tang Department of Demonic Exorcism.
Remuneration: Successful retrieval of the feline will be met with substantial compensation from Noble Consort Yang and her sister, the Duchess of Qin.

The look on Li Jinglong's face could hardly get any uglier.

"Fetch the chief a cup of water," Qiu Yongsi called. "He looks ill!"

"What if we dosed him with the oblivion pollen that we just bought?" Hongjun suggested, looking toward the box.

"Don't be ridiculous!" The others stopped Hongjun in his tracks.

Mergen poured the water, A-Tai delivered the cup, and Hongjun patted Li Jinglong sympathetically on the back. Several seconds elapsed before Li Jinglong managed to swallow his anger. The Department of Exorcism had just been reestablished, and the first case they had been given was to track down Yang Yuhuan's eighth elder sister's pet cat? It was a monumental insult.

"Well, it's certainly a difficult task," Hongjun said. "Chang'an is so big—how will we ever find one lost cat?"

"We'll be doing no such thing!" Li Jinglong slammed the case file back down on the table. "Send it back! They've crossed the line this time!"

Everyone sighed in resignation, as if they had long expected this.

Bright and early the next morning, four young exorcists staggered after Li Jinglong, yawning widely as he led them down one of Chang'an's major thoroughfares. The shops along their path had yet to open.

"Chief, we spent all night thinking about it," A-Tai said, "but there really isn't any spiritual technique that can track down a cat."

"Then look for it with your eyes," Li Jinglong said with a flip of his sleeves. "It's not like we have anything better to do."

The exorcists split up, heading for all four corners of Chang'an to ask around for the missing cat. The imperial guard had surely questioned a number of Chang'an's citizens during their investigation, but who was to say there'd been no new developments since?

Hongjun had been assigned to the south side of Chang'an; it would take him two hours just to walk there. In all honesty, he strongly suspected the cat had already escaped the confines of the city.

"Kong Hongjun!"

Hongjun had just left the main street when he saw Mergen beckoning him over from the mouth of an alleyway. A-Tai and Qiu Yongsi were both with him.

"As your big brothers, we're taking you out to play. Let's go," Mergen said.

"What about work?" Hongjun asked.

"You're not really planning on helping him track down that cat, are you?" A-Tai looked at him in surprise.

"Of course I am!" Hongjun said. "I think the chief's a good person."

After yesterday's events, Hongjun's impression of Li Jinglong had shifted significantly. Carefully speaking in general terms and skipping over the matter of the heart lamp, he told the other three what he'd learned: that Li Jinglong had come to the Department of Exorcism because he genuinely hoped to do something extraordinary for the sake of Great Tang. As an ordinary mortal—one disdained by the imperial court—there was little he could do to serve the nation as he wished to.

Hongjun watched the others' expressions turn strange. He suddenly realized—as exorcists, these three considered themselves brothers, while branding Li Jinglong an outsider.

"The most painful thing in the world is to covet that which can never be yours," A-Tai said with a shrug.

"So that's how it is?" Mergen mused. "But why didn't he tell us?"

Maybe because he has his own convictions and sense of dignity, Hongjun thought. "Anyway, I'm going to help him search for the cat. If I can't find it, we can try something else."

The other three exchanged a look, then nodded in agreement.

Mergen spread open his hands. "In that case, let's…"

For Hongjun's sake, they would help him this once. The four of them agreed to meet up in the East Market at lunchtime before going their separate ways.

13
RETURN TO PINGKANG WARD

Hongjun arrived in Jinchang Ward with a stack of paper in his hands and a fish slung over his back. It was still early in the morning, and Zhao Zilong was half asleep, his fish mouth widening slightly as he yawned.

"Do you think it would help to put up these missing cat posters?"

"With how bad your doodles are, who in the world is going to be able to tell that we're looking for a cat and not a scribble?" the carp yao asked.

Hongjun glanced around. Taking advantage of the emptiness of the streets so early in the morning, he tossed out his grappling hook and swung up onto a nearby roof. He climbed Goose Pagoda, leaping up floor by floor until he reached the top of the tower, where he settled down and hugged his knees.

White clouds scudded across the deep blue sky as a morning breeze washed over tens of thousands of roof tiles. To think the humans of the Divine Land had built such a magnificent city—Hongjun couldn't help but relax and sigh happily at the sight.

He looked down at the stack of cats he had drawn before heading out to search, wishing he were back at Yaojin Palace. Qing Xiong and Chong Ming could both speak to birds. It would be a much faster search if he could dispatch a few hawks to look for the cat instead of searching on foot.

"How long are we going to stay up here?" the carp yao groused. "The autumn winds are always so dry; it's making my scales itch."

"I just feel so bad for him," Hongjun said. "I know everyone has their own struggles. But I still want to help him with the search."

"You feel bad for everyone," the carp yao said. "That bleeding heart's going to get you in trouble one day."

"Do you think those officials will treat him a little better if we find the cat?" Hongjun asked.

He had spent the previous evening learning all about the strict grades and ranks of human society from the carp yao. Although some of it had undoubtedly flown over his head, he'd at least taken away that Li Jinglong had been so unsuccessful in achieving his goals because the emperor and high officials of the imperial court scorned him.

"Don't be silly," the carp yao said. "It's not so easy to eliminate human prejudice. In fact, when they throw caution to the wind, humans are capable of far greater evil than yao. None of Li Jinglong's detractors will ever admit he's a capable man—they may as well slap themselves in the face. The way I see it, they'll continue to send him off searching for lost cats and dogs forever."

"Why did this cat run off anyway?" Hongjun mumbled to himself. "Did something scare it away?"

Li Jinglong's voice floated up from the highest floor of Goose Pagoda. "Looks like we're on the same page. Chances are, it saw something it wasn't supposed to see."

Startled, Hongjun nearly slipped from his perch. It seemed they'd had the same idea: climbing up to the highest point in Chang'an to gaze out over the whole city at once. Hongjun let down his grappling hook, allowing Li Jinglong to climb up and sit down at his side atop the tower.

Hongjun couldn't keep himself from glancing guiltily at Li Jinglong. "When did you get here?"

"Right about the time you said, 'I just feel so bad for him.'"

Hongjun's cheeks burned with embarrassment, but Li Jinglong merely frowned slightly. "I paid a call at the Duchess of Qin's estate just now. The cat saw something that scared it out of its wits that night. Cats are unusually sensitive to the supernatural. They are also picky eaters and don't typically wander away from home for no good reason. There are few places in Chang'an with better food and accommodations for a pampered white cat than the duchess's estate. Whatever the cat saw, it must have been so terrifying it won't go back."

"Maybe it just got lost?" Hongjun asked.

Li Jinglong shook his head. "Unlikely."

"Or maybe someone's hidden it?"

"Who would have the gall to hide the Duchess of Qin's cat?" Li Jinglong countered. "The imperial guard spent ten whole days searching, and they offered ample rewards for its return. If someone saw it, it would have been reported. Unless something truly unexpected happened, as long as it's alive, it's likely hiding somewhere within the city—probably not far from the duchess's estate. So, let's go."

It struck Hongjun then that Li Jinglong was quite intelligent.

Before Li Jinglong could begin to climb down from the tower's roof, Hongjun tossed out his grappling hook and rappelled down Goose Pagoda, leaping to a nearby rooftop and pulling Li Jinglong along with him. The two flitted over the roof's ridge, bounding over to the next one as they reached the end of the first.

A thought occurred to Hongjun. "Do you think there are a lot of monsters in Chang'an?" he asked Li Jinglong, who was walking in front.

"The infernal mist that enshrouds Chang'an has long gone unchecked," Li Jinglong said. "Every night, the yao gather in revelry and Chang'an is transformed, until it no longer resembles the city you see before you now."

"How can you tell?" Hongjun had sensed this as well, but not to the extent Li Jinglong described. Every night, after the three hundred strikes of the evening drum, Chang'an seemed to undergo a strange but subtle alteration, as if unearthly events were unfolding just out of sight.

Li Jinglong wordlessly patted the sword strapped to his waist.

"Did the sword tell you that? How many monsters do you think there are in Chang'an?" Hongjun asked.

"Tens of thousands," Li Jinglong said, glancing back at Hongjun.

Hongjun recalled Chong Ming, too, saying that yao had taken over Chang'an just before they had parted ways, but after so many days in the city, he'd yet to stumble across any more yaoguai. Were they too well hidden, or was he simply too oblivious?

"Monkey," the carp yao called from behind Hongjun.

"What?"

Confused, Li Jinglong and Hongjun stopped on a rooftop outside the East Market just as a flurry of limbs and fur struck Li Jinglong in the face as it flew by. They both jumped at the series of high-pitched chitters and whirled to look—a little monkey was crouched on the roof of Jadeflower Hall, watching them intently.

"What the—"

Li Jinglong was about to shoo the animal away when Hongjun recalled the monkey he had freed that day at the market. "Ah! It's you!"

Smiling broadly, Hongjun held his hand out, and the little creature ran over, its chain clanking along behind it. Since escaping its tamer, the monkey seemed to have been fed by kindhearted passersby, and looked much healthier. At present, it was holding a moldy steamed bun, which it now offered to Hongjun.

Hongjun accepted the moldy token of appreciation. Breaking the bun into pieces, he fed one to the carp yao.

"This steamed bun—" The carp yao grimaced.

"Just eat it." Hongjun shoved the rest into the carp's mouth before producing one of his throwing knives to pry off the collar still locked around the little monkey's neck.

"These monkeys are trained to understand commands," Li Jinglong said. "Seeing as it's been running around this area these past few days, why don't you ask whether it's seen that cat?"

That's right! Hongjun pulled out his missing cat flyers and held them up before the monkey. Li Jinglong nearly slipped and fell from the roof. "These drawings... Are you sure that's a cat?!"

Hongjun's drawing consisted of three circles of varying sizes, with a squiggly, wormlike tail and pointed ears. The picture rather resembled a monster itself.

The monkey cocked its head to the side. Then, with a chitter, it gestured for Hongjun to follow before taking off like a wisp of smoke.

"No way!" the carp yao exclaimed. "It actually understood!"

Hongjun scooped up the carp yao and, together with Li Jinglong, followed the monkey all the way to the boundary of Pingkang Ward. The East Market had just opened, and the streets were bustling with noise down below. Still somewhat traumatized from his last visit to this ward, Li Jinglong stayed low and took the long way around to avoid being seen.

The monkey had barely come to a stop when Hongjun exclaimed in surprise. Curled up on the eaves between the Spring Oriole and the Poetess's Pavilion was a ball of white fluff, lying perfectly still and basking in the sun. "That's the cat, isn't it?!"

"Quiet! Don't move!" Li Jinglong was shocked; he'd never imagined that they would actually find the creature. Catching the cat was nowhere near the kind of victory that would allow them to strut around with their heads held high, but it would at least be a hard slap in the face to the imperial guard. It seemed Hongjun couldn't possibly get any luckier. To think the whole city had been searched from top to bottom, only for the case to be solved practically the moment it fell into his hands—Li Jinglong could scarcely believe it.

"Should we call for Mergen and the others?" Hongjun asked. "What if it's the wrong cat?"

That morning, Li Jinglong had given them all explicit instructions not to catch the cat, if they were lucky enough to find it, without notifying him first. After all, what if they snatched the wrong cat? During his visit to the Duchess of Qin's estate, however, Li Jinglong had learned this was an eye-wateringly expensive breed of cat; even if they searched every corner of Chang'an, it was highly unlikely that they'd find another like it.

"Not necessary," Li Jinglong said, his voice low with caution. "They're probably slacking off anyway. Even if it's the wrong cat, let's catch it first and deal with the rest later. You stay here, and I'll go around behind it. Do you have the net?"

"I do, I do." Responding to Li Jinglong's tone, Hongjun began to grow apprehensive as well.

"We mustn't startle the people on the street, or we'll scare it away again," Li Jinglong warned.

Hongjun nodded blankly and watched as Li Jinglong crouched down, gesturing for Hongjun to do the same before making his way around to the cat's other side.

"There's no need for him to circle around so far, right?" the carp yao asked. "It's just a cat."

"In a bit, can you…" Hongjun began.

"Absolutely not!" The carp yao cut him off. "No way am I going to help you guys with that cat! Have you forgotten what I am?!"

Hongjun conceded the point. The carp yao was a fish, and therefore naturally afraid of cats and bears. He watched Li Jinglong creep over fifty paces away, until Hongjun could barely see him anymore, before inching closer to the cat. Net in hand, Hongjun moved carefully over the rooftop, treading silently forward as the star of this drama lounged lazily in the sun.

The cat remained motionless, seemingly fast asleep. As Hongjun and Li Jinglong drew closer and closer from either side, its fluffy white fur rose and fell gently with each of its breaths. When Li Jinglong was less than ten feet away, he stopped and gestured toward Hongjun. Crouching down, Hongjun edged closer, a step at a time, with the net clutched in both hands.

Suddenly, the cat opened its eyes and spotted Li Jinglong. Man and feline stared at each other for a stunned moment before Li Jinglong shouted, "Now!"

Hongjun opened the net and dashed forward as Li Jinglong dove for the cat.

Li Jinglong had expected the cat to run straight into Hongjun's net as it tried to escape his grasp. Instead, the creature swerved and slipped like a pale shadow through the gap between Li Jinglong's legs as Li Jinglong froze in astonishment.

A breath later, Hongjun dropped and slid between Li Jinglong's legs as well. "Get back here!" he shouted. Hongjun stretched out his arms to make a grab for the cat when he stepped on a loose roof tile, and his foot slipped out into empty air. A single thought flashed through his mind—

This cat is way too cunning! Are we sure it hasn't cultivated into a yao?!

Hongjun pitched from the roof of the Spring Oriole, careening toward the lower levels of the Poetess's Pavilion and the food stalls that had just opened for business in the alley below, only to be saved at the last second by Li Jinglong's sturdy grip on his ankle.

Hongjun glanced down at the giant pot of soup bubbling in the noodle stall below as Li Jinglong dragged him back to safety. *That was way too close!* he thought. Even if Hongjun had managed to escape unscathed, that pot would have been the end of the line for Zhao Zilong.

"Shhh." Li Jinglong shushed him as he ducked back out of sight, pulling Hongjun along with him. The two of them watched as the cat hopped down onto the third-floor balcony of the Poetess's Pavilion and disappeared through an open window.

Hongjun's chest heaved as he caught his breath. "I did my best..."

"Don't worry about it," Li Jinglong said. "It'll be easier now that we know where it is. Let's go!"

They leapt over to the next roof and cautiously climbed down the side of the Poetess's Pavilion.

"I'll go in," Hongjun whispered. "Aren't you afraid of damaging your reputation again...?"

"I can't be *that* unlucky," Li Jinglong whispered back.

Favored by Chang'an's literati, the Poetess's Pavilion was an elegant building, clean and lavishly furnished. After slipping through the brothel's window, Hongjun and Li Jinglong found themselves in a narrow corridor. The interior wall was lined with doors, each labeled with the names of various famous poems, including

"An Invitation to Wine," "Spring Morning," and "Jade Terrace in Spring."[9]

"Let's split up and search," Li Jinglong said. "Zhao Zilong, you too. And the monkey—Hongjun, tell it what to do."

Before the carp yao could protest again, Hongjun had already set him down. He had little choice but to cautiously stick his head through the first half-open door, his fins quivering with fear. Meanwhile, having received its orders from Hongjun, the monkey promptly scampered off in a different direction.

"If you find the cat, stay quiet and come find me," Hongjun told Zhao Zilong. "You don't have to catch it by yourself." He shoved the carp yao toward another room.

"You go left, and I'll go right," Li Jinglong said, his voice low.

By now, the sun had risen high in the sky. It was anyone's guess where the girls of the Poetess's Pavilion were at this hour. Hongjun entered one of the rooms, the scent of rouge and powder assaulting his nose as he looked this way and that. The rooms here were all extravagantly decorated, the furnishings expensive yet tasteful—the girls to whom they belonged were likely the most popular courtesans of the establishment. Li Jinglong had guessed correctly; the cat had indeed found a place near the Duchess of Qin's estate to hide.

The carp yao entered another room. He still felt parched from the moldy steamed bun he'd eaten earlier, so he ran over to a basin and took a sip of the water. After one gulp, he noticed something was off.

"Ugh, footbath water." He grimaced and stopped drinking at once.

Glancing around, he spied Zhang Xuan's *Brocade Carp Swimming through a Creek in Springtime* hanging on the wall. The willow branches in the painting seemed to sway gracefully in an imaginary

---

9   A famous poem by Tang dynasty poet Li Bai; a famous poem by Tang dynasty poet Meng Haoran; and the name of a cipai (词牌 / "tune") used as the basis for ci lyric poetry.

breeze over a stream populated by vividly lifelike fish. Zhao Zilong gaped at the painted carp, going perfectly still.

"A beauty! A beauty!" The carp yao drew closer, practically drooling.

The scrape of claws across wooden floorboards behind him shook him from his stupor. The carp yao froze, all the hair and scales on his body standing on end. A tiny squeak slipped out as he looked around in terror.

Crouched atop a cabinet high above was that long-haired cat, staring at him with evil intent in its blue-and-gold eyes.

The carp yao's soul nearly fled his body as he began to shriek. "Help—!"

Next door, Li Jinglong and Hongjun heard the shout and rushed toward the sound like twin blasts of wind.

The cat leapt down from the cabinet, lunging for the carp yao. Scared out of his wits, the fish scuttled under the bed.

Hongjun and Li Jinglong shoved open the door just in time to see the cat slip beneath the bed with a "mrow." The carp yao screamed hysterically as he scurried back out, his tail flapping as he sprinted desperately across the room and dove into a chest of drawers.

"Gotcha!" Li Jinglong cried, shutting the door behind him. The cat wouldn't get away this time.

Hongjun crouched down and groped under the bed for the cat, but this bed was different from his own. Carved from a rare rosewood, it was set against the wall, and the base of the three outward-facing sides was sealed off with a frame made of multiple wooden slats. Hongjun could see the cat hiding in the darkness, studying him with its two-toned eyes.

Li Jinglong reached under the bed as well, but the cat shrank even further away.

"What are we going to do?" Hongjun asked beside him.

Li Jinglong's arm was too thickly muscled; it got stuck between the slats as he tried to reach for the cat again. The two looked at each other awkwardly.

Hongjun tried his luck again, stretching his arm as far as he could under the bed. The cat licked its paws, unruffled, as if these humans were completely beneath its notice.

"Let me try lifting the bed," Li Jinglong offered.

"It'll escape the moment you do," Hongjun said. "Maybe try lifting it just high enough for me to scoot underneath and grab it."

The ornate bed weighed well over four hundred pounds. With a shout, Li Jinglong gathered his strength and lifted the massive frame, creating a gap that could just barely accommodate a single small person. Hongjun didn't hesitate—he dropped to the ground and rolled in.

It was a tight fit; the underside of the bed was obviously used for storage, piled with wooden poles and painted scrolls. The cat hissed and puffed up its fur, trying to escape, but Hongjun reached out and grabbed a paw. "Got it!"

"Hold on tight!" Li Jinglong called out. "Don't let it get away again!"

It was then that a voice drifted in through the closed door: "I can't come at night, so I can only see you during the day..."

Li Jinglong whipped his head around, his pupils contracting. Something about the man's voice was incredibly familiar. He immediately let go of the bed frame.

Clutching the cat, Hongjun braced his knees against the bed, straining to keep the furniture aloft. "Chief, could you please lift the bed again so I can get out of...?"

But before he could finish, Li Jinglong had rolled in to join him. Pressing his hands up into the frame, he took the weight from

Hongjun's knees and carefully lowered the heavy piece of furniture down onto the ground.

Before Hongjun could question him, Li Jinglong grabbed him from behind, pulling Hongjun tight against his chest. He pressed a hand over Hongjun's mouth, ensuring he couldn't make a sound. An instant after the wooden bed settled back onto the ground, the door opened. The heavy thumps of a man's steady footsteps approached, accompanied by a woman's tinkling laughter.

The couple settled on the bed, and the man's voice rumbled above them. "After that idiot Li Jinglong got caught visiting the Spring Oriole, the Censorate submitted a memorial accusing the Longwu Guard of all sorts of transgressions. It's been days since I've been able to come. I've missed you so much."

Hongjun's eyes were huge as he tilted his head back to glance at Li Jinglong. Slowly releasing his mouth, Li Jinglong motioned for him to keep silent before reaching over to muzzle the cat, still tucked between Hongjun's arms.

Squished in the narrow space beneath the bed, Hongjun was distinctly aware of Li Jinglong's arms around him as they held the cat secure. His skin was hot against Hongjun's own, and he could feel the man's heart pounding in his broad, firm chest.

Behind him, where Hongjun couldn't see, Li Jinglong's features were contorted in fury—the man who had come to visit the Poetess's Pavilion was none other than his former superior, Captain Hu Sheng of the Longwu Guard. It was his refusal to believe Li Jinglong that led to the vicious mockery he'd endured from the entire imperial guard and the ridicule he'd suffered from Yang Guozhong.

For a time, the only sounds in the room were Hu Sheng's moans of "Jinyun" as he fondled and kissed the courtesan. Jinyun began to gasp, and their talk grew increasingly licentious as they tumbled on the bed.

Hongjun's heart galloped in his chest. In all his sixteen years, he had never encountered anything of this nature. He'd certainly never imagined that he would end up here, listening to an amorous couple panting above him while Li Jinglong held him from behind in such a suggestive position. The sounds alone were shocking—not to mention the indecent way Hu Sheng spoke. Just listening to it made Hongjun blush.

As if that wasn't mortifying enough, he could hear Li Jinglong's breathing growing heavier and feel something stiff pressing against him.

Hongjun swallowed hard as Li Jinglong subconsciously tightened his arms around him, which in turn made Hongjun tighten his grip on the cat. Uncomfortably squashed, the cat began to struggle and claw at its captor. As Hongjun grabbed at the cat's paws, worried the noise would alert the paramours on the bed, the animal's claws caught on the linen of a nearby cloth bundle.

With a yank of the cat's claws, the cloth pulled loose, revealing the gaunt head of a corpse.

"Ah!" Hongjun shrank back with a cry.

Aghast, Li Jinglong clapped one hand over Hongjun's mouth and covered his eyes with the other, pulling him tightly into the protective circle of his arms.

As luck would have it, Hongjun had cried out just as Jinyun began to scream on the bed above; Hu Sheng, intoxicated by their lovemaking, remained oblivious. Hongjun felt his hair standing on end. He had never been so close to a corpse before. His breath came too fast as he tried to regather his wits; he felt like he was about to lose his mind from fright. Li Jinglong's face, too, was a mask of shock. He could scarcely believe what he was seeing. Nevertheless, he tightened his arms once more around Hongjun, signaling to him not to be afraid.

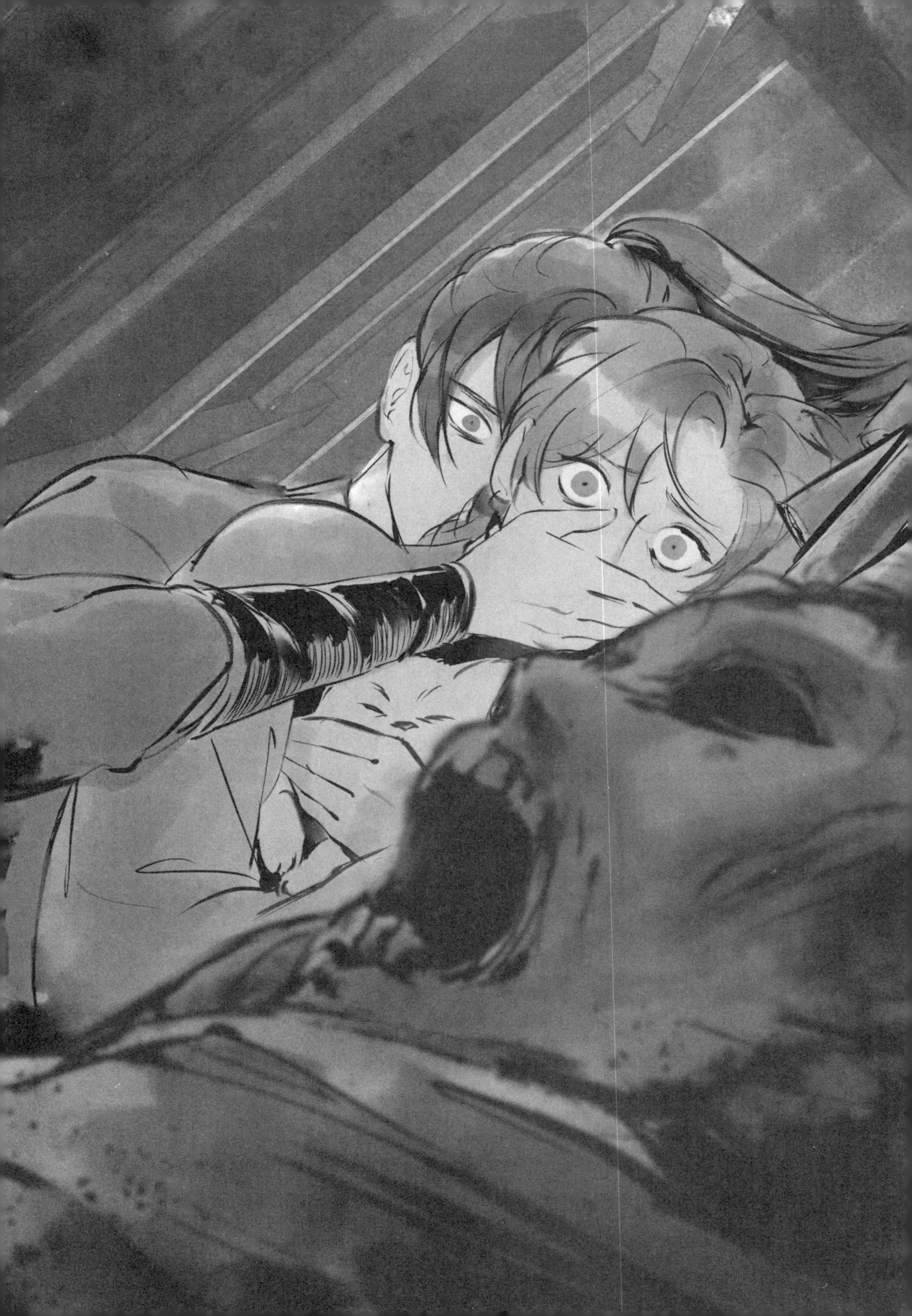

Hongjun examined the corpse's face through the gaps in Li Jinglong's fingers and realized it had likely been here for quite some time. Its mouth gaped open, and the skin of its face had long since become dark and desiccated. All that remained of its eyes were two dark sockets. Li Jinglong carefully reached out and pulled away that piece of cloth to reveal the dried-out corpse's body, dressed in white robes and curled tightly in a corner under the bed, as if huddling in terror.

Hongjun touched Li Jinglong's arm and found that he had broken into gooseflesh.

On the bed, Hu Sheng was also breathing hard. Apparently finished with his business, he murmured a few more words to Jinyun. "I have to go," he said, a smile audible in his voice.

"You're leaving already?" Jinyun asked, reluctant to part from him.

"I'll come see you again another day."

Hu Sheng embraced Jinyun once more and kissed her on the cheek with a wet smacking sound before pulling on his clothes and moving toward the door. Jinyun followed to walk him out.

As soon as their footsteps faded, Li Jinglong and Hongjun climbed out from under the bed. Gasping for breath, Li Jinglong met Hongjun's eyes, and the pair stared at each other in bewilderment.

"What now?" Hongjun asked.

After some thought, Li Jinglong said, "We can't stay here. This is too big—we can't afford to alert the culprit."

14
THE BODY UNDER THE BED

AT NOON, Hongjun arrived at the agreed-upon restaurant—a sizable establishment called Dragon's Gate—to meet with Mergen and the others. Yet to recover from his fright, he burst out with, "Something huge happened earlier!"

Qiu Yongsi, Mergen, and A-Tai had just taken their seats. Puzzled, they greeted Hongjun and said, "Well, go on then—wait, where's the chief?"

"He went back to headquarters with the cat. He said to get started on lunch first, and he'll explain everything when he gets here."

"He actually found the cat?" Mergen asked in surprise.

The three of them exchanged a glance and began pressing Hongjun for details. Hongjun told a truncated version of the story: After securing the cat, Li Jinglong went to the Court of Judicial Review to inquire about recent missing persons' cases. This was a case within a case—after they'd found that *thing* under the bed—with potentially huge implications, so it was imperative that they gather as much information as possible.

"Let's eat," he concluded. "I'm starving."

The waiter recited the restaurant's menu, but no one was familiar with the dishes he named. A-Tai hailed from a faraway land and had yet to try any of Chang'an's delicacies. Mergen had grown up in the grasslands and had never attended any high-end banquets, and Hongjun had been granted even fewer such opportunities.

"You guys go ahead and order," Qiu Yongsi said modestly. "I'm fine with whatever you pick."

Throwing his hands up in exasperation, the carp yao took charge, ordering from where he was hidden behind Hongjun. "Six bowls of pheasant soup, one plate of rapid stir-fry, one whole scallion-vinegar chicken, okra with iced orange dressing, and rainbow veggie rolls. With it, we'll have six bowls of the Divine Queen Mother's imperial yellow rice, and for dessert, a tray of sweet snow, to be served at the end of our meal. And a catty of Mount Li shaochun wine, please. For any dishes that require fish, use anything but carp."

The waiter's face turned pale. "Wh-who's speaking?!"

"It's ventriloquism!" Hongjun said.

"The four of you are eating six portions?" The waiter glanced at the empty seat beside A-Tai, petrified.

"The last guest hasn't arrived yet," Hongjun said. "We'll order for him now so you don't have to come back after the food's served."

"Who would want to eat carp, anyway?" the waiter muttered under his breath. "They have so many bones."

"What did you say?!" the carp yao shouted from behind Hongjun, his eyes round with fury at the insult.

The waiter looked around in bewildered terror.

"It's nothing, you may go," Hongjun said, hastily dismissing the man.

The waiter, still on edge, quickly returned with the food, and the table was soon spread with an exquisite array of delicacies. Hongjun realized that the meals he'd eaten on the road to Chang'an could hardly be counted as food. The pheasant soup was served in porcelain bowls fashioned to look like bamboo stems, and the rapid stir-fry was a heaping pile of the most succulent fish and lamb he'd ever tasted. The scallion-vinegar chicken had been steamed, the white meat and yellow skin delicately fragrant, and the Divine Queen Mother's imperial yellow rice was topped with a perfect soft-boiled egg. The four exorcists and one fish swept through the lot like a whirlwind through clouds.

"Zhao Zilong used to live in a restaurant in Chang'an," Hongjun said as he ate. "We're lucky he learned a lot during his stay."

"Oh?" Mergen smiled. "As a chef? I'd never have guessed."

"As an ingredient," the carp yao corrected.

There was a brief, awkward silence before Hongjun clarified, "He was on sale at the market and got sold to a restaurant, where he was kept in a fish tank. A kindhearted monk bought him later and released him—that's how he came to be with us today."

After eating his fill, the carp yao buried his head in his cup and swallowed a few more mouthfuls of wine. He took a few swaying steps across the table before falling over with a *whump*, dead drunk.

"Come," A-Tai said. "Lunch is on me. Let us raise a toast to our friendship, and our absent chief—"

The four of them lifted their cups. This was the first time since joining the Department of Exorcism that they had all come together for a meal. The other three had already been slacking off together and had grown quite familiar, but Hongjun never partook in their fun. At once they began to ask Hongjun questions about Li Jinglong. Hongjun gave vague answers to a few of their queries, but considering how little time he had spent with Mergen and company, he was equally eager to learn more about his companions.

"My dad sent me here to Chang'an..." Hongjun paused, considering his next words. Before setting off, he'd been specifically instructed to keep quiet about certain things. With Zhao Zilong snoring away on the table, Hongjun was afraid he might say more than he should. In the end, he settled on, "He told me to expel the monsters from Chang'an."

A-Tai burst into laughter. "What monsters could there possibly be in Chang'an?"

Mergen began to laugh as well. "If there aren't any monsters, then what are we all doing here?"

"But the chief told me Chang'an is filled with yao, it's just that they rarely come out," Hongjun said.

Hongjun had never had alcohol before. It was his first time drinking wine, but he gulped it down like water; assuming Hongjun could hold his drink, the others did nothing to stop him. Hongjun had finished half the catty of Mount Li shaochun wine by the time the effects hit him. As his mind fogged over, Hongjun's world seemed to tip sideways and he slouched over, falling fast asleep.

Li Jinglong arrived shortly after Hongjun passed out. When he saw Hongjun slumped to the side, he immediately flew into a rage. "What are you doing, drinking during work hours?" Li Jinglong demanded. "And you even got Hongjun drunk too! This is—"

"Chief, please come and sit down!" A-Tai hastily interjected. "Today's lunch is on me!"

Li Jinglong took his seat with a frown. All the dishes on the large table had been reduced to remains, but Li Jinglong didn't seem to mind as he tucked into food that had long since gone cold. The other three hurried to ask Li Jinglong what had happened. When he reached the part about the Poetess's Pavilion, whatever they'd been doing—drinking tea, sipping wine, eating dessert—the three exorcists fell still, turning in unison to stare at Li Jinglong.

"You found a corpse under the bed?" Mergen asked.

Li Jinglong grunted in affirmation. "So, you're finally interested?

I stopped by the Court of Judicial Review just now, but no one has been reported missing recently."

"That makes no sense." A-Tai's brow creased. "Why hide the corpse under a bed?"

"Whether or not this case falls within our remit remains to be seen," Li Jinglong said blandly, "which is why I wanted to discuss it with all of you."

"This is definitely the work of a monster!" Mergen cut in.

"And that monster hasn't escaped yet," Qiu Yongsi said with a knowing smile.

"What do you mean? Explain." Li Jinglong continued to pick at his food, but the furrow in his brow grew deeper.

After studying Li Jinglong for a few beats, A-Tai said, "Perhaps my good brothers should do the explaining here."

"No, no, no, you can speak first…"

"No, go ahead, you can start…"

The three of them bickered until Li Jinglong snapped, "Enough!"

There was a brief pause. Finally, Mergen explained. "Hidden under the bed like that, the body should have begun decomposing within a matter of days—the smell would have attracted notice. It doesn't make sense to take the time and effort to dry out a corpse just to store it under a bed. It would be much easier to simply bury the body."

"So…Jinyun hid this body because she plans to use it to practice the yao arts?" Li Jinglong frowned.

Everyone stared at Li Jinglong with odd expressions on their faces, trying their best not to laugh.

"Am I wrong?" Li Jinglong asked, perplexed.

"Uh…" Qiu Yongsi began. "About that, Chief—I think the victim was desiccated on the spot, resulting in the corpse you saw today."

"So that's what happened," Li Jinglong murmured, grasping his meaning immediately.

"A monster likely sucked that man dry of all his blood and essence," Mergen continued. "With no other way to dispose of the body, it probably just shoved it under the bed. At least that's my guess."

Li Jinglong mulled this over as A-Tai glanced at the other two.

"Shall we go for a walk tonight?" he asked. "I thought there was something queer about Pingkang Ward...and as expected, the enemy has slipped up."

Qiu Yongsi shot A-Tai a look, warning him to silence.

It dawned on Li Jinglong then why A-Tai and Qiu Yongsi had gone brothel-hopping the night before: to hunt monsters.

"There are yao in Pingkang Ward?" Li Jinglong asked.

"It practically reeks of yao energy," Qiu Yongsi chuckled. "In Chang'an, the energy is strongest in Pingkang Ward, Daming Palace, and Xingqing Palace."

Several seconds elapsed, but Li Jinglong didn't say a word. He had thought long and hard about whether he should notify the Shenwu and Longwu Guards about the dead body in the Poetess's Pavilion immediately, or whether he should secretly capture the yao responsible first. With his rotten luck, it was unlikely anyone would believe him; even if he did capture that woman, Jinyun, he would probably only make more trouble for himself. But he hadn't expected his subordinates to be so aware of the delicate situation at hand.

"In that case, tonight will be the perfect opportunity to see what all of you are made of," Li Jinglong finally said.

"Hongjun can take the lead on this one," Mergen said with a smile. "He should be capable of capturing a puny little yao or two. The rest of us will back him up if he needs it."

Thunder rumbled overhead, and a light rain began to fall over Chang'an as the group exited Dragon's Gate. Li Jinglong strode briskly ahead while Mergen carried the lolling Hongjun on his back. A-Tai and Qiu Yongsi brought up the rear as they hurried back to the Department of Exorcism.

A group of young women taking shelter beneath the eaves spotted them and began whispering among themselves, nudging their companions as they did. Li Jinglong was tall and handsome; Mergen was dashing and leanly built; A-Tai was as pretty as a pearl; Qiu Yongsi was elegance personified; and as for Hongjun, presently being toted on Mergen's back, his face was flawless as white jade, even with a salted kipper—nay, carp—on his back.

The young women trailed behind them, hoping for another look. Mergen glanced back at them as A-Tai said, "Ay, what a bother. Why are there always so many people chasing after us? Let's hurry up and get out of here."

Back at headquarters, everyone settled in the main hall to listen to the patter of the rain. Li Jinglong had leashed the lost cat to a pillar next to the corridor with a length of rope, upon which it pulled fiercely, yowling as it tried to escape its restraints. Given everything that had happened, Li Jinglong decided to put off returning the cat until tomorrow.

The carp yao lay inert in the courtyard, soaking in the rain.

Hongjun was still asleep as well, slumped over the table in the hall. Li Jinglong dug out all of Di Renjie's old case files, and as if through some wordless agreement, the other three divided up the pile and began searching for any information pertaining to the presence of yaoguai in Pingkang Ward.

Based on Di Renjie's accounts, even if there had been yao back in the day, most of them had appeared in the divine capital of

Luoyang. There were very few records of yao-related incidents after the Son of Heaven permanently transferred the seat of government to Chang'an.

"What kind of yao cultivates by absorbing human blood and essence?" Li Jinglong asked.

"There are many," Mergen replied absently as he sorted through his stack of scrolls. "Animal yao, like foxes and snakes... Flowers, too. Even objects like paintings, if they're significant enough..."

"We shouldn't jump to conclusions," A-Tai said. "What if the body is merely Jinyun's lover?"

Everyone was shocked.

"You must be joking!" Qiu Yongsi exclaimed. "A-Tai, don't tell me you're into that stuff!"

"Of course, I would prefer for her to be a yao." A-Tai laughed.

"Didn't you all arrive at the Department of Exorcism at the same time?" Li Jinglong suddenly asked.

"Yes, just about," A-Tai said brightly.

"Then why does it seem like you've known each other much longer?"

Everyone went quiet. His comment seemed innocuous, but Li Jinglong was carefully observing their reactions. After a pause, he broke the silence. "I'll be looking to all of you for future guidance. As for our plans tonight, I leave them in your hands."

The three of them nodded as Li Jinglong turned to look at Hongjun, still sleeping off his excesses.

Mergen reached out to shake him. "Hongjun?"

Worried he would remain in a stupor till evening, Mergen was about to rouse him in earnest when the carp yao stirred in the courtyard. He tipsily rose to his feet and swayed in place. "We're back? Mm..."

The carp staggered to and fro as he drifted beneath the shelter of the open-air corridor. The cat's interest was immediately piqued, and with a hard yank, it finally pulled its head free of the rope and lunged at the fish.

Zhao Zilong stared for a few dumbstruck breaths as the cat shot toward him before shrieking in naked terror. "Help! The cat's loose!"

His screams were so loud they woke even Hongjun. Li Jinglong had taken care not to tie the cat's restraints too tightly, afraid the creature would strangle itself; he never imagined it would be able to escape. Realizing their hard-won prize was about to slip away, everyone scrambled up to give chase.

"Come into the main hall!" Li Jinglong yelled to the fish.

The carp yao charged straight in, and the cat followed. "Quick, close the door!" Hongjun shouted after him.

Mergen, A-Tai, and Qiu Yongsi threw themselves at the doors as the carp yao dodged this way and that to avoid the cat, ready to wet himself from fright. Hongjun yelled at him to stand still, but the carp yao was faced with his natural predator—the sheer terror easily countermanded Hongjun's order.

The carp yao flopped up onto the table before flinging himself onto the altar in a blind panic. Then, as if the promise of imminent death had unleashed some heretofore unknown potential in the fish, he took a flying leap and sprang to the very top of the cabinet like an arrow loosed from its string.

A-Tai and Mergen dove for the cat from the left and right, only for the agile creature to scamper up the cabinet after the carp in a pale flurry of movement.

Li Jinglong sensed at once that something terrible was about to happen. Kicking off the wall, he rushed in to salvage the situation—

—too late.

"Shit!" the carp yao yelped as he bounded back down to land in Li Jinglong's arms just as the cat turned to swipe at its prey, sending the box of oblivion pollen flying.

Everyone watched helplessly as the box sailed from its place atop the cabinet in a clean arc and smacked Hongjun neatly in the head. There was a soft *click* as the box sprang open and pollen filled the air.

The windows and doors had been sealed shut against the rain. As the pollen dispersed through the room, the five men issued a single, earth-shattering sneeze before launching into their own individual attacks.

"Achoo—!"

"Achoo!"

"Achoo! Achoo! Achoo! Achoo! A—choo!"

"Achoo!"

The sounds of sneezing erupted through the main hall as the five cycled between shock and confusion.

"What happened?" Hongjun asked, dazed. "Achoo!"

"Who am I?" A-Tai wondered. "Achoo!"

"You guys...where...?" Mergen began haltingly. "Where am I? Achoo!"

"Achoo!" Qiu Yongsi sneezed. "Excuse me good sir, if I could please...? Achoo!"

Even the cat was sneezing. One moment, it would look at the carp yao with hunger in its eyes, its expression turning puzzled a moment later as it sneezed.

The cacophony continued without end. Everyone went from curious to confounded and back again, unable to make sense of anything.

"Maybe we should get out of here...?" Li Jinglong said before his words were eaten up by another violent sneeze.

The carp yao hopped down from his arms and ran over to the entrance, mostly unaffected by the oblivion powder—his nose only worked underwater, and his tiny nostrils were usually stuffed up. Leaving the cat wandering about disoriented, he hurried to push open the door.

"Out you go, quick!" the carp yao hollered.

As Hongjun oscillated between confusion and clarity, he heard someone calling his name. Staggering out the door, he soon joined the carp yao in shouting at the others inside the hall until they all stumbled out, one after another.

Dazed, Hongjun looked down at the carp yao, then up at Li Jinglong and the others. He strained to remember what had just happened, but his brain was a chaotic mess.

The cat bounded out of the room, seemingly as stumped as they were as to where to go next. The carp yao promptly shouted, "Hongjun! Grab that cat!"

Hongjun reflexively scooped the creature up. The carp yao fetched a brush and dustpan and left to clean up the oblivion pollen in the main hall.

"What happened just now?" Li Jinglong asked.

The other four looked at each other brainlessly. A-Tai was first to speak as the wheels began to turn in his head again. "You're Chief Li!"

"Ah!" Li Jinglong said. "That's right, I'm Li Jinglong, and this is the Department of Exorcism."

"That's right, that's right!" As if waking from a dream, everyone nodded along.

"But why am I holding a cat?" Hongjun asked.

"Mrow?" The cat looked this way and that.

"What...were we doing?" Li Jinglong wondered.

Their memories were a great and vast blank. Mergen wandered aimlessly around the main courtyard. "I vaguely remember…we all came to the Department of Exorcism to report for duty."

"We've already done that, right?" Qiu Yongsi said. "Why do I feel like we all know each other? This doesn't seem like our first meeting."

"Calm down," Li Jinglong ordered. "Something must have happened just now…"

Inside the hall, the carp yao finished sweeping the oblivion pollen scattered all over the ground into a pile, which he tipped into a palm-sized, silk brocade pouch. "You guys inhaled oblivion pollen," he called out.

"That's right, that's right!" Everyone nodded as they began to string the sequence of events together.

Two hours later, the group had recovered most of their memories. No matter how they tried, however, none of them could recall the most critical piece of information: namely, what exactly they had been doing right before they inhaled the oblivion pollen.

Li Jinglong and his subordinates settled down in the main hall with their chins in their hands and began to rack their brains. Although the carp yao had summarized in bits and pieces how they had captured the cat, he didn't know the specifics of what had transpired after that. Their inability to remember what they had forgotten thus became their most pressing problem.

The cat, in the interim, had been stuffed into a cage. It stared longingly at the carp yao from within its prison.

"But what in the world were we doing?" Li Jinglong wondered with a deep frown.

"Maybe we were just drinking tea?" Qiu Yongsi suggested.

"No, that doesn't make sense," Li Jinglong muttered to himself.

"Why would there be so many scrolls on the table if we were just drinking tea? There's something strange about this—we must have been working on an important case. We know that when we were chasing after the cat, Hongjun and I ended up hiding under a bed..."

"This happened after I drank the footbath water," the carp yao interjected.

While Li Jinglong pieced together his fragmented memories, Hongjun was still trying to figure out who he was and where he came from. Muttering to himself, he gradually recalled that he hailed from Yaojin Palace, and the details of his childhood returned to him one by one. After a few more moments, Hongjun remembered Chong Ming—more specifically, the first time he ever met him.

Hongjun sighed in relief. Yet just as he leaned forward to join the conversation, he froze, caught in a memory.

Li Jinglong's voice slowly faded to nothing. The sunlight streamed down, and the flickering shadows cast by the parasol trees lent the courtyard an intense air of surreality, as if everything beneath the dazzling sun was but a dream. In this dream, his own awareness seemed to wane as time began to swirl like a twisting maelstrom, taking him back to that first evening in Yaojin Palace.

Countless images flew by in reverse before the scene suddenly sharpened on a certain day.

Somewhere far away, the carp yao was saying, "Hongjun said you guys found a dead body under the bed..."

"A dead body?"

The others turned to stare at the carp yao, who recounted everything he knew about what had happened in the brothel.

Hongjun's pupils remained tightly contracted as he found himself reliving the night he arrived at Yaojin Palace—how the first thing he'd seen, the moment he'd opened his eyes, was Chong Ming's tear-streaked face.

His memory lurched backward once more, returning to darkness. He was suddenly standing amid the wreckage of a building, looking around in confusion. An unfamiliar male voice sounded in his ears.

"He's the only child I have…"

15
THE HAZY PAST

"So it's settled. We need to go back to that room to see... Hongjun?"

Li Jinglong frowned. Everyone turned to look at Hongjun as he rose from his seat, coming to stand beneath the eaves of the open-air corridor.

This place was familiar to him, but in his recollection, it looked completely different. Hongjun glanced around, overwhelmed by the feeling that he was recalling a memory he'd never had—

What was happening? Was it because of the oblivion pollen...? But didn't oblivion pollen cause memory loss? Why was it showing him scenes from the past?

"Daddy—! Daddy!"

In the memory, Hongjun was crying hysterically. A dark shadow swooped down and landed in the courtyard.

Qing Xiong!

Hongjun turned to see Qing Xiong from the past. As he stepped forward, the fabric of his robes and qun billowed around him.

"That's enough killing, isn't it?" he asked grimly.

Hongjun looked up. Inside the hall, beneath the golden rays of the sun, lay a man and a woman. Their faces were indistinct, but it was clear they had died in each other's arms. Hongjun tried to throw himself at their bodies, sobbing and screaming wildly, but Qing Xiong grabbed him by the collar and hauled him back.

"Daddy!" Little Hongjun continued to wail in misery as Qing Xiong's voice echoed in his ears.

"Shhh. Look at me, look at me." Qing Xiong dropped to one knee and grasped Hongjun's shoulders, turning the child to face him. He met the boy's eyes, and his lips moved as he said something Hongjun couldn't make out.

Hongjun looked around the courtyard in a daze. Pressing a hand to the back of his head, Qing Xiong forced him still. He spoke again, but again the words turned into an indecipherable burr of sound.

What did Qing Xiong say? Hongjun's brow furrowed. Whatever it was, Hongjun had the feeling that he said it often, yet he couldn't seem to remember. But what had happened to the Department of Exorcism and the dead couple?!

"Hongjun!" everyone shouted.

Li Jinglong strode into the main courtyard and waved a hand before Hongjun's face. "Are you all right?"

Hongjun couldn't help but feel that Qing Xiong had said something of vital importance, but instead of remembering his words, he could only grasp at fleeting images from other strange scenes. He closed his eyes and shook his head hard, trying to dispel these muddled memories.

"What's wrong?" Li Jinglong asked in concern.

Hongjun took a deep breath and held up a hand to indicate that he was okay. Returning to the main hall, he took his seat and asked about the outcome of their discussion with raised brows.

"We act tonight," Li Jinglong said. "We have a rough idea of what happened. You and I found something suspicious in the Poetess's

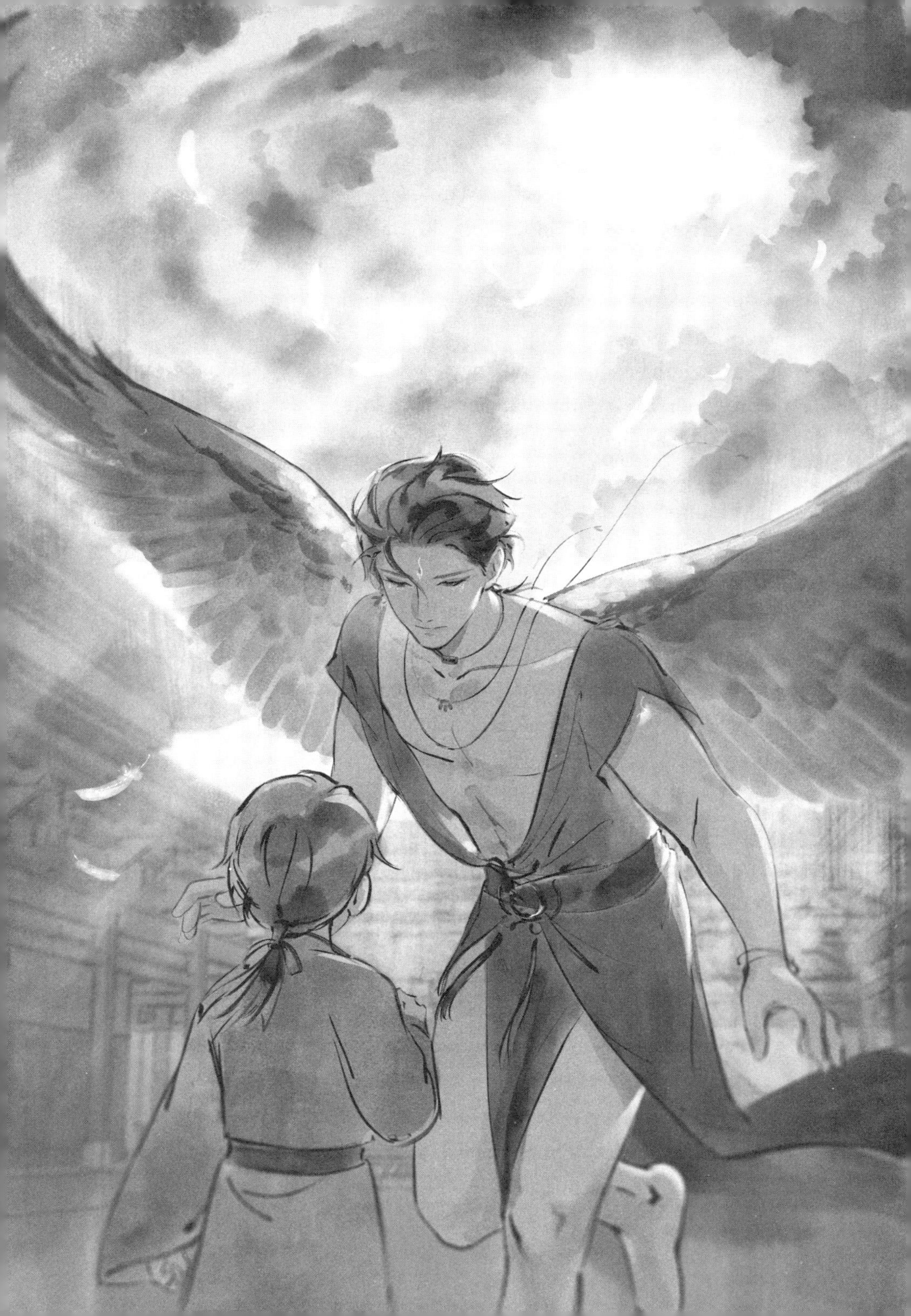

Pavilion, so we'll just have to verify what it is. Everyone get some rest; we'll move out later this evening."

Mergen, A-Tai, and Qiu Yongsi nodded, but instead of leaving for their rooms, they all glanced at Hongjun. Only once Hongjun assured everyone again he was fine did they finally disperse.

Hongjun had just settled down to sleep when Li Jinglong arrived at his door. He let himself in and took a seat beside Hongjun's bed.

"Kong Hongjun, what was going on with you earlier?" Li Jinglong asked, placing his hand atop Hongjun's.

Hongjun's heart began to race. He was overcome by the wild urge to grasp Li Jinglong's hand and tell him everything he'd just seen. But even he had no idea what had truly happened, and after a moment, all that came out was, "It's nothing, I'm fine."

"You can talk to me at any time, if you ever have something on your mind," Li Jinglong said. He withdrew his hand. "If the oblivion pollen made you sick, then it'd be best to get you help as quickly as possible."

Hongjun assured him that it had nothing to do with the oblivion pollen. Li Jinglong nodded and, apparently satisfied, turned to leave. Hongjun could keep his eyes open no longer; with a yawn, he rolled onto his side and promptly fell asleep.

As the sun sank into the west, the shadows of the mountains stretched over Daming Palace. A woman dressed in sumptuous robes swept through the gloom beneath the palace walls, moving as soundlessly as a wraith.

"It's in Chang'an—I can feel it."

A man dressed all in black with a deep scar on his forehead kept pace in grim silence.

"Fei'ao, go take a look," the woman instructed.

"Feed me," the man called Fei'ao said, bloodlust emanating from him in the dark.

"You'll get plenty later," the woman responded, hushed. "We must find this person. Mara remains unstable…"

"Feed me!" Fei'ao snapped, baring a mouthful of wicked teeth.

"They are not for you!" The woman stepped forward threateningly. "Bring them back. Your hunger will be sated when the time comes."

Her eyes flashed red, and Fei'ao took half a step backward. After a moment of stillness, he turned and vaulted over the palace wall, disappearing into the gloaming.

"My lady, there you are!" A maidservant hurried over. Surprised to find her mistress alone, she asked hesitantly, "Were you speaking to someone? My lady…"

The woman turned to her, and the maidservant let out a blood-curdling scream. "Help—!"

The word had barely escaped her lips before she was swallowed by black mist. A fur-faced monster dressed in opulent robes now stood before her. The girl's throat rattled as she stared wide-eyed at the creature, her flesh beginning to shrivel on her bones. In the blink of an eye, the maidservant had been transformed into a skeletal corpse, which toppled to the ground with a soft *thud*.

The well-dressed woman strolled into the sunset. Gazing out at the mountain range, she gave a loud whistle, and a number of wild foxes leapt over the wall. In no time at all, they had dragged the maidservant's body out of Daming Palace and tossed it down a deep ravine.

"Hongjun, wake up." It was Mergen, patting him on the shoulder. Hongjun woke with a splitting headache, but swung his feet over the bed to stand up.

Mergen pressed his hand to Hongjun's forehead, checking his temperature—no fever. "Do you feel sick? Do you want to sleep a little longer?"

Hongjun waved away Mergen's concerns. He'd had a long and strange dream, but it had vanished from his memory the moment he woke up.

Stepping out of his room, he saw everyone was busy preparing for their mission that evening. Li Jinglong, with a bow slung over his back in addition to his sword, had already mounted his horse and was in the middle of assigning everyone their tasks.

Recalling the way Li Jinglong had placed his hand over Hongjun's own earlier in the afternoon, Hongjun suddenly felt he could trust this man with anything. He took a step closer, wavering over whether to say something about what he'd seen. But with everyone else present, Li Jinglong merely nodded at him and said nothing.

The carp yao was sitting astride Li Jinglong's horse, his hairy arms and legs dangling limply as he dozed with his head propped on Li Jinglong's back.

"Mm...let's go," Hongjun said. He set aside the lingering unease from that dream—it'd be best to forget about it.

The riders mounted their horses as the evening drum began to sound.

Upon arriving in Pingkang Ward, A-Tai and Qiu Yongsi split off to take the main street, while Li Jinglong, Hongjun, and Mergen filed into a back alley. With a quick nod at the other two, Mergen scaled a wall to enter the rear courtyard of the Poetess's Pavilion.

"Hammurabi and Qiu Yongsi will provide a distraction to keep everyone occupied," Li Jinglong said as he lifted the carp yao off the horse. Seeing Hongjun glancing all around, he explained, "Mergen will act as lookout. He'll keep us apprised of any unexpected developments while we search the room again."

"Wow, it's so lively here," Hongjun remarked.

It was Hongjun's first time truly exploring the city after the evening drums had sounded. After sundown, Chang'an seemed to undergo a dramatic transformation. The red lanterns above the street had been lit, dyeing the intricately carved balustrades of the brothels' balconies a deep crimson. Lamps in brilliant colors shone everywhere, and music drifted through the air in competing strains.

The sound of a pipa spilled like a cascade of pearls down a drum from the Spring Oriole on his left; dozens of konghou harps tinkled like an endless stream of spring water melting snow inside the Poetess's Pavilion on the right. The two establishments stretched high into the sky, their windows draped in billowing red gauze, beyond which Hongjun could hear the cheers of scholars and merchants and the ceaseless laughter of serving girls. Tall, brightly lit buildings stretched from the Poetess's Pavilion as far as the eye could see, their beautiful silk curtains hiding every sort of gilded and bejeweled splendor within. Revelers came and went like shadows flitting across a revolving carousel lantern. Pingkang Ward was said to be three miles of earth where song and dance never slept, and it lived up to its reputation.

"What do people actually do in these places?" Hongjun asked. He had been pondering this question for days now.

It seemed impossible to Li Jinglong that Hongjun didn't know what a brothel was. He studied Hongjun, trying to decide whether he was truly that naive or merely faking it. But the lad appeared entirely guileless. "Are you serious?"

Hongjun blinked in confusion.

"It's a..." Li Jinglong began awkwardly. "Listen, all you need to know is it's not a good place."

"But why did everyone mock you when I took you to the Spring Oriole?"

Li Jinglong pressed a hand to his brow and flapped the other at Hongjun to signal him to stop talking. What civil or military officials of Chang'an *didn't* visit the brothels of Pingkang Ward? They were simply using his public embarrassment for their own ends.

But Hongjun was like a dog with a bone. "Did you ever come here before that night?" he pressed.

"No," Li Jinglong said.

At that moment, a scholar turned into the little alleyway with a beautiful young woman in his arms, clearly drunk and looking for the back door. Li Jinglong swiftly pulled Hongjun back to hide in the shadows. Hongjun watched the couple, his curiosity having grown to nearly unmanageable proportions. He didn't seem to be faking his ignorance. Li Jinglong finally admitted with a serious expression, "I don't like it."

"You don't like what?"

Hongjun turned back to look at him. The two of them were pressed tightly together, so Li Jinglong rather awkwardly took a step back. "I don't like those sorts of short-lived entanglements."

Hongjun had only the vaguest idea of what Li Jinglong was talking about and looked back at him in puzzlement. Li Jinglong was flabbergasted. "Why are you so clueless about everything? Never mind your parents, hasn't that carp yao taught you anything?"

"Well, why don't *you* tell me then?" Hongjun pricked up his ears at once. The more Li Jinglong tried to skirt around the topic, the more intrigued he became.

Li Jinglong had no idea how to respond.

In the main entrance of the Poetess's Pavilion, A-Tai smiled broadly as he spread his arms in greeting. "Hai mie hou bi!"

"Oh—he's back!"

"That foreigner! The foreigner with the lute's come back!"

"My darling..." A-Tai lifted the procuress's chin and mimed a kiss.

The woman flushed a charming scarlet as she laughed. "Young Master, how good to have you back! It's been days since your last visit—the girls have been pining."

A-Tai beamed. "It couldn't be helped. Ay, as a newcomer to Chang'an, it's important that I remain in my boss's good graces. I came as soon as I had the time, didn't I?"

"Ahh—"

The moment A-Tai entered, young women swarmed down the staircases, squealing as they hurried to welcome him. They made such a ruckus that the other clientele seated behind the screens in the parlor couldn't resist peering around the sides to see what the fuss was about.

"Young Master Qiu's here too!" another girl exclaimed. "Won't you compose a poem for us today?"

"Tell us more about your cousin!"

Qiu Yongsi smiled. "Let's hear A-Tai play his barbat first."

As A-Tai strode toward the middle of the parlor, all the dancing girls left their spots and crowded over. A-Tai wrapped an arm around one of the young women and brushed a kiss over the soft skin of her cheek before taking his place on a couch at the center of the room.

"Shall we have some wine?" Qiu Yongsi suggested with a smile.

The attendants jumped up to serve them. Among the brothel's clientele tonight was a group of scholars who had traveled from all over the country for the autumn imperial examination. Growing increasingly displeased as they watched their female companions crane their necks, they grumbled, "What's so special about some foreigner?"

"Shhh." One of the girls gestured for quiet before peeking out from behind their screen once more.

The second and third floors were filled with young women and their clients, who had all crowded out onto the mezzanine to see what was going on. Beneath the glittering lamps suspended high above, they watched as A-Tai, with his dark brown curls, sea-blue eyes, and milky pale complexion, flashed his audience a radiant smile.

A-Tai settled down cross-legged with his barbat in his arms as a hush fell over the room. But his hands didn't go to the strings; instead, he cleared his throat and began to sing in a clear voice:

"*How many deserts were once gardens filled with flowers...*
How many palaces are now walls reduced to rubble..."

As the notes trailed off, A-Tai began to pick at his barbat's strings, allowing them to vibrate without cease. A strange power seemed to flow from his fingers, like moonlight spilling over a glowing white stag as it ambled through an overgrown courtyard to the sound of silver bells, snowy flowers blossoming in the wake of every light step.

"*Intoxicated by your eyes, I have long since forgotten about lost times...*"

A-Tai's profile was breathtakingly handsome as he turned his head aside and closed his eyes. The doors to the rooms on the second and third floors of the Poetess's Pavilion flew open, one after another, as everyone heard the music and tiptoed down the stairs to watch. The whole building seemed to fall under his spell, the bodies of its occupants no longer their own under the influence of the music.

Qiu Yongsi smiled faintly, his ears stuffed with wads of cotton as he nodded along to the beat.

In the back alley, Hongjun's face had turned a remarkable shade of crimson as he listened to Li Jinglong's explanation.

"Really?" he asked, torn between curiosity and excitement.

Li Jinglong never wanted to repeat what he'd just said to Hongjun so long as he lived. Technically speaking, Hongjun was already sixteen, and the customs of Great Tang were comparatively liberal: Youths as young as thirteen or fourteen could be considered adults. What was more, it was commonplace for a man to visit the brothels of Pingkang Ward; Li Jinglong had never forbidden his subordinates from discussing such things as a commanding officer of the Longwu Guard. But standing before Hongjun, he felt an inexplicable prickle of guilt. "Don't tell anyone what I just told you—that's an order!"

"But this place is so nice—why don't you ever come?" Hongjun asked.

"Of course I don't come here!" Li Jinglong nearly blew a fuse. "Didn't I just say I'm not the type?"

Mergen peered out from the rear courtyard and whistled, waving them in. Li Jinglong gave Hongjun a severe look, as if to indicate that he had better keep his mouth shut—though it seemed hardly necessary.

"Time to get to work!" Li Jinglong nudged the carp yao awake. "Go keep watch in front of the building."

With that, he and Hongjun turned and sprinted into the rear courtyard.

They found the second and third floors completely deserted—whatever A-Tai and Qiu Yongsi had done, it seemed to be effective. Hongjun flung out his grappling hook, and he and Li Jinglong swung to the second floor where Mergen was waiting, pressed to the wall. He handed Li Jinglong and Hongjun some cotton. Li Jinglong promptly stuffed his ears, but Hongjun merely accepted his handful in confusion, unsure what it was for.

Li Jinglong took the lead. As they approached the balustrade, Hongjun leaned over the top rail and glanced down. The strains of A-Tai's barbat floated up like the music of the gods. Everyone within the Poetess's Pavilion sat enraptured as they listened, entirely motionless, like puppets on a string.

Hongjun went still. A-Tai's voice painted pictures of flowing moonlight and a beautiful courtyard... Mergen grabbed Hongjun's hands and stuffed the wads of cotton into his ears, cutting off A-Tai's song and yanking Hongjun back to reality.

Li Jinglong tugged Hongjun along behind him. "Don't listen to it," he said, his voice low as he pulled him into a room. Mergen took his place at the door to guard against unexpected interruptions. "Hurry up and get to work."

Hongjun couldn't help but glance back once more toward the music. "That's A-Tai playing his barbat?!" he said as he dropped to his knees to check beneath the bed. This must be A-Tai's magical technique, but he had never used it on them while playing to amuse himself at the Department of Exorcism.

After clearing the room, Li Jinglong sheathed his sword and came over to lift the bed. "You haven't heard him play before?" he asked, gritting his teeth as he heaved.

"Not like this... Found it!"

There was indeed a long, cloth-wrapped bundle under the bed. Hongjun dragged it closer and, as he flipped back the fabric, was once again met with the sight of the dead man's shriveled head.

Hongjun yelped in terror. "It's this thing again!"

A quick tap came on the door from the outside, and Li Jinglong assured Mergen that all was well in the room.

"Huh? Why did I say *again*?" Hongjun muttered to himself.

"Pull it out," Li Jinglong instructed.

Hongjun hauled the desiccated corpse out from beneath the bed, and Li Jinglong set the frame back down. This time, he had come prepared: Donning a pair of black silk gloves, he showed no sign of fear as he unwound the makeshift shroud and began to inspect the body. Hongjun looked on, half hidden behind him in horror.

"Male, thirty to forty years of age... Look at his clothes—he doesn't seem like a merchant or a government official. Perhaps he's a scholar who came to the capital for the imperial examination... Hongjun?"

"I'm too scared to look!"

The corpse had blackened in death, and its mouth yawned open, gums pulled back over white teeth. Li Jinglong had stripped it of its clothes, and under the unforgiving glare of the lamps, the shriveled corpse was so unspeakably disgusting Hongjun's hair stood on end.

"Don't be scared," Li Jinglong said. "It's not like it'll jump up and eat you. Now look—what kind of yao sucked him dry of both blood and essence? This can't possibly be the result of natural decomposition."

"Could the monster who did it be the owner of this room?" Struck by inspiration, Hongjun began to dig through the cabinets and drawers beside the bed.

"Don't move anything around; they'll notice," Li Jinglong warned.

Engrossed in his search, Hongjun called over his shoulder, "If it's a monster, it'll have some spiritual devices or malign artifacts nearby—but there's nothing here."

Li Jinglong considered this as A-Tai's song continued downstairs.

"Are you still not done?" Mergen called from outside.

After rummaging through most of the room, Hongjun rendered his verdict: "There are no yaoguai living in this room."

"Let me ask you something," Li Jinglong said. "Can you sense any yao energy right now?"

Hongjun shook his head. Li Jinglong thought for a moment. "The yao must be in the building. As things stand, our only option is to take a risk. Hongjun, lend me your grappling hook. You and Mergen go stand on opposite sides of this floor and keep a close eye on the crowd in the parlor downstairs. Be ready to throw your knives at any moment."

"I only have three left."

"Leave it to me; I'll make sure you get them all back."

In the parlor of the Poetess's Pavilion, A-Tai's melody unspooled with all the urgency of drifting clouds and flowing water as his song reached its intoxicating climax. The music swelled like a nimbus cloud pushed by the wind to swallow the moon, like countless leaves swirling through the air to cover heaven and earth.

"In this roaring tempest, I continue my search..."

A withered corpse with a grappling hook around its neck fell from above with a loud crash.

Caught entirely off guard, Qiu Yongsi and A-Tai jumped in surprise. The music came to an abrupt halt as A-Tai instinctively glanced upward in confusion.

The crowd in the parlor stared vacantly at the dead body for a handful of breaths before bursting into horrified screaming. The procuress screeched wildly as the customers began to flee in panic. Chaos overtook the building—shrieks filled the air as several young women fainted away on the spot.

Li Jinglong, Hongjun, and Mergen had never taken their eyes off the crowd as they watched from three different angles on the second floor. Now, they marked a young woman in a corner of the room—while everyone ran about in panic, she stepped back, and her face took on a sharp edge. Two more girls in opposite corners started in surprise, turning away from their clients to glance at the first woman. As one, all three looked up toward Jinyun's room.

Three throwing knives sliced through the air faster than anyone could blink. Though they had yet to realize their cover had been blown, the women sensed the danger. With a wave of their hands and a flick of their exquisite silk sleeves, streams of purple light shot out in defense—but the throwing knives were immune. Blazing with fire, the blades plunged into each of the women's shoulders.

"Follow the knives!" Li Jinglong shouted. "Don't let them get away!"

Li Jinglong vaulted over the balustrade, dropping through the air to land on the parlor floor. The entire building had long since descended into pandemonium. A-Tai gathered up his barbat before charging out of the brothel with Qiu Yongsi in tow. On the second floor above them, Mergen pushed off the railing and took off in pursuit.

Pinned with the knife, the woman standing nearest the main entrance cried out in pain. All three grabbed at the blades embedded in their shoulders, screaming wildly in agony as the hilts burned their hands. Realizing they had run afoul of a fearsome foe, the women dared not stay and fight; they turned tail and ran.

Just before bounding out the window, the first woman, whose level of cultivation appeared highest among them, turned and shot a stream of fire from her fingertips.

"Hongjun, look out!" Li Jinglong called.

Hongjun had just jumped from the second floor and was still airborne. He jerked his head to the side as the fire hurtled past him—the woman wasn't targeting him, but the corpse hanging from the railing. The body burst into flames, turning to ash in an instant.

Another woman had made it to the front doors. Mergen, who had used his shoulder to smash through the second-story window, nimbly drew his bow and unleashed three arrows in rapid succession before his feet hit the ground. As his target dashed through the door, she couldn't resist slowing to look back at her pursuers. It was her fatal mistake—the moment she glanced backward, Mergen's first arrow pierced her through the neck. With a humming sound and a flash of white light, the woman disappeared. In her place was a brown-furred, blue-eyed fox with three tails, its mouth gaping open as blood ran from its neck. Two more arrows followed right behind—one striking the creature's abdomen, one its leg—killing it instantly.

"Don't use excessive force!" Li Jinglong bellowed. "This is your only warning! Where did the other two go?!"

Mergen landed, and with a wave of his hand, his arrows tore themselves from the three-tailed fox's body, splattering blood everywhere as they whistled back to their master.

"I didn't mean to shoot it in the neck!" Mergen called back, pleading his innocence.

Hongjun emerged from the building a second after the fox. Behind him, in the Poetess's Pavilion, shock had turned into mayhem as people shoved at each other trying to escape, trampling any who fell underfoot.

"They're foxes?" Hongjun asked in shock. He beckoned, and his throwing knife returned to his hand.

"Fox yao," Li Jinglong corrected. "Where are your other two knives? Quick!"

"They're..." Hongjun looked around. "They're in the alleyway!"

"Where's Zhao Zilong?!" Li Jinglong demanded. "Move it! How are you all so bad at teamwork?"

"I'm coming! I'm coming!" the carp yao huffed as he ran over, his tail swishing behind him and a silk brocade pouch in his hands.

Li Jinglong punted the carp yao straight through the doors into the building before turning to pursue the fox yao with Hongjun and Mergen close behind.

16
LATE-NIGHT FOX HUNT

A-TAI AND QIU YONGSI had raced out the door in hot pursuit of the remaining two women. Their quarry split up at the boundary of Pingkang Ward, transforming into their fox forms in the East Market. One disappeared into the shadows of the market stalls, while the other sprang to the rooftops and fled southward, disappearing into the darkness like an arrow on a moonless night.

The two young men skidded to a halt just outside an alleyway as Li Jinglong, Hongjun, and Mergen caught up. Before either of them could speak, Li Jinglong gave orders: "You two—chase the one on the roofs; we'll take the one on the ground. Go!"

Without another word, A-Tai and Qiu Yongsi leapt up to the rooftops as Li Jinglong, Hongjun, and Mergen plunged into the depths of the closed-down market.

The guests were still trembling in fright as the carp yao scurried into the Poetess's Pavilion. One patron cried, "Someone alert the Longwu Guard!"

The carp yao threaded its way through the crowd, yelling, "Ephemeral as passing clouds!" He scooped a handful of oblivion pollen from his brocade pouch and tossed it into the air, setting off a deafening chorus of sneezes.

"A—choo!"

"All phenomena are mere fabrications!"

The carp yao hopped onto a table on the dais in the middle of the parlor and tossed out even more pollen.

"A—choo!"

He skittered up to the third floor, tugged open his brocade pouch, and scattered the remaining pollen down over the crowd. "A lifetime away!"

"A—choo! Achoo!"

"Eat, drink, and make merry; I'll be on my way—"

With this, the carp dove out the window to reconvene with Hongjun and the others.

The East Market was silent, so dark one's own outstretched hand disappeared into the shadows.

"Do you sense any yao energy now?" Li Jinglong whispered.

"It's faint; I can barely sense it," Hongjun replied softly. He pointed. "But I saw a flash of light over there just now."

Mergen stared into the darkness.

"Can you see it?" Li Jinglong asked.

Mergen frowned. "I can't, it's too dark."

The Shiwei tribesman had excellent eyesight and carried a set of seven nailhead arrows forged from the finest steel, each one covered with charmed inscriptions. In the open desert or wide, grassy plains, he could shoot down any bird in flight. Unfortunately, no matter how keen his eyes, they were useless in the unrelieved darkness of the market.

"Or maybe...it was over there." Hongjun turned in a different direction, an uncertain look on his face.

"Chief." Mergen patted Li Jinglong's arm. "Your sword... It's glowing?"

Li Jinglong drew his sword and pointed it toward where Hongjun had indicated. To Hongjun and Mergen's surprise, the script carved into the blade lit up with a faint glow. He turned the sword in a different direction. The blade glowed brighter, then dimmed.

"What does it mean?" Hongjun asked in wonder.

"Either the sword can sense yao energy," Li Jinglong said, "or it can sense your throwing knife."

He began to sweep the blade left and right, the sword glowing and dimming with his movements. Next, he moved it in a slow arc; the blade settled into a steady glow.

"The fox is running circles around us," Li Jinglong said. "It's trying to throw us off the scent by taking a circuitous route out of the East Market. Cut it off!"

Foxes were crafty creatures at any time, to say nothing of one that had cultivated into a yao. Afraid any hesitation would allow it to escape, taking another one of Hongjun's throwing knives with it, Li Jinglong ordered Mergen and Hongjun to show no mercy—they were to capture the creature dead or alive.

The exorcists scattered, closing in on the fox from three different directions.

A-Tai panted as he and Qiu Yongsi sprinted across the rooftops. "Qiu-xiong,[10] you go on ahead. Let me catch my breath."

"But I'm only shadowing you," Qiu Yongsi said, perplexed. "I said I wouldn't be capturing any yao."

Speechless, A-Tai pushed himself to keep running. "Why does our chief keep changing the plan? We never discussed any of this ahead of time..."

---

10 A word meaning "elder brother." It can be attached as a suffix to address an unrelated male peer.

Qiu Yongsi laughed. Lending A-Tai a hand as they leapt across a gap between the eaves, he said, "Actually, this Li guy is quite clever. Meticulous attention to detail isn't enough. There's no such thing as a foolproof plan. When all else fails, you might as well shake things up. It's not like our investigations until now have yielded any results. Tossing that dried corpse into the parlor to catch the fox yao off guard finally made them show their tails!"

"But now whoever they answer to will be on alert." A-Tai was breathing hard. "It'll make things harder in the long run."

"That's not your problem," Qiu Yongsi replied, laughing again. "Maybe he had a backup plan in mind all along?"

"I doubt it," A-Tai remarked.

"Ah—it's over there!"

"Quick, after it!"

The throwing knife flashed up ahead, and the two of them set off in pursuit.

Down below, the other fox with a knife through its shoulder stumbled, its steps coming slower and slower. The creature had taken a wide arc through the East Market.

Mergen and Hongjun, having quietly circled round to cut off its escape, prepared to attack on Li Jinglong's signal.

As if sensing the impending danger, the fox sniffed the air and came to a stop.

Without warning, Li Jinglong charged out of the darkness and silently swung his sword. Darting back, the fox gave a hoarse shriek as a cloud of smoke billowed from its mouth. An arrow cut through the air and disappeared into the smoke. Cornered, the fox yao transformed with a bright flash, and the vulpine scream of fury was replaced with a woman's cry.

"Shameless mortals! This goes too far! What have I ever done to you?!"

"Murderers must pay with their lives." Li Jinglong's voice was cold. "Chang'an is not your hunting ground."

When the fox charged out from the smoke, it had grown to ten feet in height. Unsheathing its sharp claws, it lunged toward Li Jinglong.

Li Jinglong brought up his sword, yet one swipe of the fox's paw knocked it to the ground with a resounding *clang*. He'd had no idea fox yao could grow to such a size—the insolent creature wasn't fleeing, but luring them out here to finish them off!

Another of Mergen's arrows buried itself in the fox's shoulder. But the fox yao—the same who'd set fire to the corpse in the Poetess's Pavilion—had reached an advanced stage of cultivation. It had no fear of his seven nailhead arrows.

Eyes glowing bloodred, the fox yao breathed a column of flame. Just as Li Jinglong was about to be burned to a crisp, Hongjun somersaulted in front of him, throwing out his sacred light to shield them both. The fox yao screamed in pain as its face was burned by its own deflected fire.

The flames went out, and the fox yao careened into a market stall, toppling it with a crash that echoed in the silence. Li Jinglong threw his arms around Hongjun, rolling them away from the falling stand.

Ducking low, Mergen rushed over. "Chief!"

"I'll distract it. Aim for its heart." With that, Li Jinglong strode calmly toward the yao.

Hongjun and Mergen peeked out from behind a pile of rubble. The fox yao staggered to its feet, Mergen's arrow and Hongjun's throwing knife both protruding from its shoulder. It appeared to be reaching the end of its strength.

Fearing it would breathe fire again, Hongjun readied his final throwing knife in his right hand, his left beginning to glow with sacred light. Mergen gave Hongjun a quick pat on the shoulder and tiptoed away.

The fox yao panted, staring Li Jinglong down. Hongjun's nerves were stretched to the breaking point, but Li Jinglong appeared utterly unafraid. He advanced with sword in hand.

"Evil creature," he said coldly. "Great Tang's Department of Demonic Exorcism may have lain dormant for half a century, but so long as this sword is here, Chang'an will never be yours!"

Li Jinglong raised his blade to point at the fox yao, and the knife embedded in the fox's shoulder flared with light in answer. Perched atop a pile of wood at the other end of the East Market, Mergen nocked an arrow and drew his bow. Hongjun's palm was slick with sweat as he tightened his grip around his final throwing knife.

"You think you're so strong?" the fox yao sneered. "Well, there's no harm in telling you: Chang'an no longer belongs to humankind. Just you wait…"

Li Jinglong started in surprise, but before he could reply, the fox yao bared its fangs and threw itself at him, claws that could gut a man in a single swipe glinting in the scant illumination of the moonless night. Li Jinglong swung his sword in a feint before springing backward.

A patrol from the Longwu Guard chose this moment to arrive, their presence announced by the ringing of hooves on stone. Their commanding officer yelled, "Who's causing a ruckus in the middle of the night?!"

Mergen let down his bow as Hongjun's head snapped around. In the instant Li Jinglong dodged, the fox yao seized its chance and rushed toward the Longwu Guard soldiers.

"*Run!*" Li Jinglong bellowed.

The Longwu guards thought they must be dreaming as the giant fox lunged toward them. The fox yao was on them before they could recover from the shock, bowling over soldiers and horses alike. Close on its tail, Li Jinglong sprang onto the fox's back and thrust the point of his sword into the base of its neck.

The horses whinnied and shied back as the soldiers tripped and fell in the dark. Li Jinglong yelled again, "Run, now!"

At last, the soldiers scrambled to their feet and began to flee. The fox yao let out a furious roar and tossed its head, hurling Li Jinglong to the ground. Hongjun's throwing knife was ready in his hand, but he couldn't get a clean shot, afraid to injure Li Jinglong.

As the fox raised its claws to strike again, Hongjun tugged the jade peacock feather from his belt, infused it with spiritual energy, and sent it skidding across the ground.

"Don't worry about me!" Li Jinglong shouted. Leaving his sword buried in the fox yao's neck, he grabbed one of the guards' spears, but he'd hardly raised it when a single strike from the fox yao's claws split the mortal weapon in two. Just as those claws were about to spill Li Jinglong's guts, the peacock feather landed at Li Jinglong's feet with a burst of sacred light and blocked the fox yao's blow with a bright *clang*.

"Ignite!" Hongjun yelled as he released the throwing knife.

Li Jinglong bent backward and out of the way, but the fox yao was prepared for Hongjun's attack. It turned on the spot, allowing the knife to plunge into its stomach, and charged toward Hongjun.

Li Jinglong ran to help Hongjun as the youth ducked and dodged. He had no spiritual devices left; if he was struck now, he was sure to be badly wounded. Crashing into Hongjun, Li Jinglong shoved him to the ground, narrowly avoiding the fox yao's attack.

A howl split the air as an enormous gray wolf appeared on a rooftop at the other end of the market. The beast was as tall as a man, though still much smaller than the fox yao. Leaping down, it clamped its jaws around the fox yao's throat, lupine teeth digging into flesh.

"Where did the wolf come from?" Hongjun was shocked.

"Now!" Li Jinglong shouted.

Snapping back to his senses, Hongjun pointed two fingers of each hand to form sword seals and swiped them through the air. His two throwing knives tore free, trailing twin arcs of the fox yao's blood as they returned to his fingertips. Gripping a throwing knife in each hand, Hongjun flung them simultaneously as the fox yao sailed overhead.

"Strike!"

Both blades flashed with light, one covered in frost and the other crackling with flame. They whipped past Li Jinglong, sending his hair fluttering, before piercing the fox yao through the heart. Ice hissed and fire raged; the explosion that followed hollowed out the fox yao's chest, leaving nothing but a scorched, gaping hole rimmed with crystals of frost in its wake.

The creature's body hung in midair as it spasmed in death. The bloody light in its eyes dimmed, and it quickly shrank, until it was only a small fox dangling limply from the giant wolf's jaws. The two throwing knives, an assortment of arrows, and the sword embedded in its flesh clattered to the ground, one by one.

The giant wolf spat out the fox and looked steadily back at Hongjun and Li Jinglong.

"Mergen?" Hongjun asked as Li Jinglong pulled him to his feet. The giant wolf huffed and bared its teeth, its lips pulled back as if in a smile.

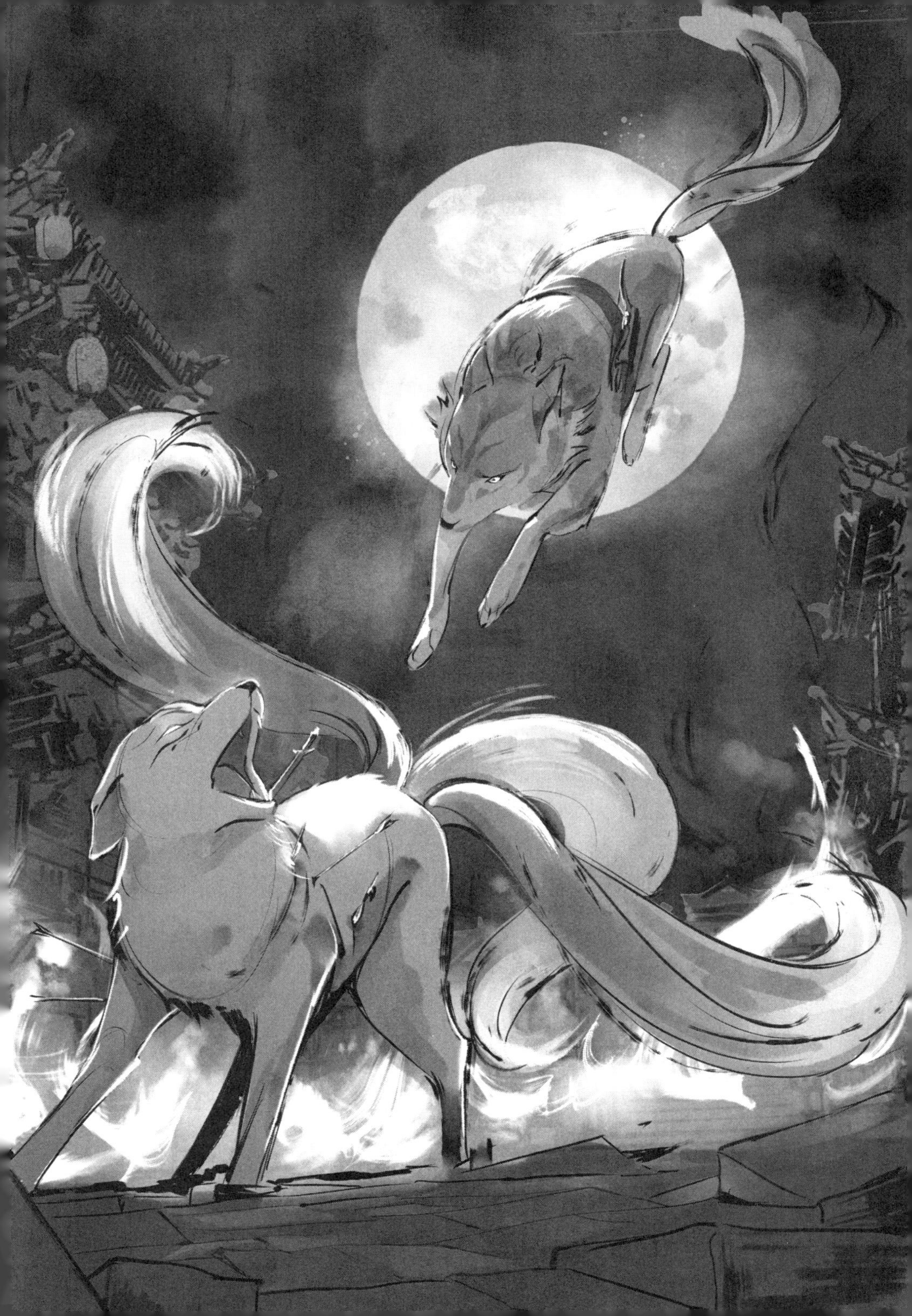

Li Jinglong signaled Hongjun to leave it for later. He hurried over to check on the dazed Longwu guards, who were beginning to rise cautiously to their feet.

"Commandant Li!"

Many of the soldiers in this patrol were in fact his former subordinates. Awe showed through the shock and fear on their faces as they greeted him—worlds apart from the way they had looked at him when he was still a member of the Longwu Guard.

Li Jinglong asked after each man in turn, ensuring there were no casualties, before turning back to Hongjun. "Where's the fish? Give them some oblivion pollen."

Moments later, the carp yao finally showed up, dragging his brocade pouch behind him. "We're out."

The guards yelped in fright. "Ahh! A monster!"

Li Jinglong was briefly lost for words. "Three thousand, two hundred silver's worth?! Used up all at once?!" he sputtered, his hard-earned composure slipping in an instant.

The carp yao was quick to defend himself. "You all inhaled nearly three and a half taels last time; there was less than a tenth of an ounce left in the bag..."

At the reminder of the earlier disaster, Li Jinglong dropped the subject. The soldiers watched in stupefaction as Li Jinglong scolded a monster.

"Don't speak of what happened tonight to anyone but Captain Hu," Li Jinglong told them, resorting to a verbal warning in lieu of the depleted oblivion pollen. "I'll submit a report to the Longwu Guard in person tomorrow. Tell your brothers-in-arms that if there's another disturbance tonight, no one is to investigate."

The soldiers nodded. Unsure whether his poor substitute for oblivion pollen would have any effect at all, Li Jinglong resolved to accept this stroke of misfortune and smooth things over as best he could later on.

Once the patrol departed, Li Jinglong turned back to Hongjun and the great wolf. "Let's see you; are you injured anywhere?"

Hongjun had scraped his elbow when he fell, but he and Mergen were otherwise unharmed. It had been the most intense battle Hongjun fought since leaving the mountain, and it took several moments for him to process everything and return to his senses.

A ball of flame rose into the air like a firework some distance away.

"They got it," Li Jinglong said. "Let's go."

"Ride on my back," Mergen said to Hongjun in his gray wolf form, seeing how tired he was. "I'll carry you there."

Hongjun clambered onto the gray wolf's back. He took off northward as Li Jinglong jogged along behind them.

"Mergen?" Hongjun quietly asked.

"Hm?" The gray wolf slowed and turned his head.

Hongjun signaled him to continue running. "Are you a yao?"

"Of a sort," the gray wolf replied. "This ability hasn't appeared in my tribe for nearly a century. I don't know exactly what I am, either. Don't tell A-Tai and the others."

The wolf seemed not to want Li Jinglong to overhear too much of their conversation. When they came to a courtyard, he bounded up the wall and leapt onto the rooftops.

The dark clouds over Chang'an slowly parted to reveal a bright moon. The gray wolf ran silently along the rooftops with the young man on his back.

"You won't arrest me, will you?" the wolf asked.

Hongjun laughed and leaned down to the wolf's ear. "I'm half yao, too."

"Hm?" The gray wolf flicked his ear, surprised. "You don't seem like one."

"My dad was a—"

"Shh," the wolf said, "you don't need to tell me. My dad once said there isn't much difference between humans and yao; the only real difference is between good and evil."

The wolf paused and looked around from his perch atop the roof ridge. Spotting dark traces of blood on the ground, he took off again to follow. "Hongjun," the wolf asked, "have you ever seen a glowing white deer?"

Hongjun hummed in thought. He had only ever lived in the Taihang Mountains. There were plenty of deer, but he had never seen a white deer like the one the wolf was describing. When Hongjun said so, the wolf fell silent again.

"My main goal in coming to Chang'an was to search for the white deer," the wolf said. "If you could let me know if you come across any clues to its whereabouts…"

Even after transforming into a gray wolf, Mergen's leather belt, bow, and quiver were still strapped to his back. It was difficult to balance on the back of a running wolf, and Hongjun had to grab the belt to avoid slipping off.

As they approached the palace, another series of flashes lit up the sky in the distance. The gray wolf stopped to let Hongjun slide off his back, then slowly rose onto his hind legs and transformed back into the Mergen he knew. Hongjun peered behind them, looking for Li Jinglong, who'd commandeered a horse from who knew where and taken a shortcut to catch up.

"They're here, they're here!" Qiu Yongsi and A-Tai said as they huddled at the base of the palace wall.

"Where's my throwing knife?" Hongjun asked.

A-Tai pointed at the other side of the wall, the picture of innocence.

"We injured it with a fireball, but it fled into the imperial palace," Qiu Yongsi said.

"I'm the one who injured it," A-Tai said. "Qiu-xiong, you didn't do anything!"

"We didn't dare barge in after it," Qiu Yongsi explained. "We don't want to make more trouble for the chief, so we decided to wait for you to catch up."

Li Jinglong, arriving at the scene at last, jumped down from his horse. He listened in shock as they told him the fox yao had fled into the imperial palace.

"You…" Li Jinglong was about to expire from fury. "All this, and you still let it get away?"

"It hasn't gotten away yet!" protested A-Tai. "Shall I go in and capture it for you now?"

Li Jinglong frowned deeply. The fox could be anywhere in the vast grounds of Xingqing Palace—how were they to find it? But when he cast a questioning glance at A-Tai and Qiu Yongsi, the two merely smiled knowingly.

Quickly catching on, Li Jinglong gave them a sharp nod in response. The two fox yao had split up, one fleeing to the East Market to lure their enemy away. The other had likely gone to seek reinforcements. Rather than dealing the creature a fatal blow, A-Tai and Qiu Yongsi had tailed it to see where it would go. In that case, were their reinforcements other monsters lurking inside the imperial palace?

But Hongjun's throwing knife was still embedded in the fox yao's flesh. Li Jinglong was determined to fulfill his promise to retrieve it.

As countless possibilities swirled through Li Jinglong's head, a faint clinking sound in the distance caught his attention.

It was a quiet night—no insects chirped this late in autumn, and no wind blew in Chang'an. The clink was crystal clear even from a hundred paces away: the sound of a throwing knife striking glazed tile as the fox sped across the rooftops above the rear hall of Xingqing Palace.

Li Jinglong shushed Hongjun, who had opened his mouth to speak, and listened with bated breath. He was rewarded with another sequence of scrabbling sounds.

"It hasn't gone far. It's on the roof of the rear hall, trying to pull out your knife," Li Jinglong whispered. "I can hear it."

"That doesn't change anything." Qiu Yongsi shook his head. "It'll run the moment we come near. Fox yao are clever. We can't make a ruckus in the imperial palace."

Li Jinglong unslung his bow from his back. Everyone looked at him in shock.

"My arrowheads are forged from common steel. They can't kill yao." Li Jinglong turned to Mergen. "Lend me one of yours."

Mergen couldn't believe his ears, though he nevertheless handed him an arrow. "You think you can hit it?!"

Li Jinglong carefully fit the arrow to his longbow in the dark. "I can try."

Hongjun had been playing with throwing knives since he was a child. He knew how difficult such a shot would be. Neither he nor any of the others could hear the sounds Li Jinglong was describing. Even if he could, Hongjun would never be able to hit a target from a hundred paces away by sound alone—not on the first try.

Li Jinglong cocked his head, listening carefully to the far-off sounds. His mounted archery skills had been one in a hundred in his youth. In those days, he had liked to boast that he was the Flying General Li

Guang's true successor. But he had suffered years of scorn and never had a chance to take to the battlefield, and since he refused to participate in frivolous displays of marksmanship to entertain lords and nobles like a circus monkey, he rarely had the chance to show off his abilities. Over time, people spoke less and less of his talents, and with no way to prove a connection to the famous Li clan of eight hundred years ago, his youthful boasting had become a joke to the citizens of Chang'an.

Despite his calm exterior, he couldn't keep his hand from trembling ever so slightly as he took aim.

On the rooftop of Xingqing Palace, the fox yao seemed to scent danger in the air. Gazing into the boundless darkness beyond the high palace walls, it lifted its paw and began to slink away deeper into the palace complex.

"Let's head back," Hongjun whispered. "We'll find it eventually, Chief, and I still have two more knives. It's no big deal."

Li Jinglong sucked in a deep breath and drew the bow. As he locked eyes with Hongjun, the crisp clink of metal on tile again reached his ears.

He let the arrow fly.

It pierced the air without a sound, sending withered leaves flying as it swept aside the curtain of willow boughs blocking its path over the palace walls. Streaking in a meteoric arc from the ground, it ended its hundred-pace flight by silently striking the fox yao in the belly as blood sprayed into the night.

Li Jinglong, listening carefully at the base of the wall, heard no cries of pain from the creature. He heaved a weary sigh and looked at Hongjun again, an apology in his eyes. "It's been too long since I trained; I'm out of practice." Li Jinglong frowned in vexation. He had a sudden urge to snap his bow in half.

Just as everyone was about to comfort their chief and tell him he had really done very well, the fox's body rolled over the edge of the roof, landing in the pond with a small splash.

"He hit it?" Mergen was astounded.

"He hit it," Hongjun said. "I'll go take a look."

He flung out his grappling hook and, in the next breath, had scaled the courtyard wall. Everyone else stared at Li Jinglong in shock.

"Come back as soon as you find it!" Li Jinglong called.

Hongjun jumped back over the wall a moment later and tossed the third fox to the ground. The arrow had buried itself between the creature's ribs on its right side, and it was on the brink of death.

Li Jinglong sighed in relief and smiled. "I promised I'd get your throwing knives back."

The chief had never smiled in their presence before. Rather than lighten the mood, the atmosphere turned awkward as everyone looked at each other in turn. A-Tai and Qiu Yongsi were dumbfounded, still struggling to process everything that had transpired since nightfall.

"You look pretty nice when you smile, Chief." Hongjun grinned. "You don't have to go around with that stern look on your face all the time, you know."

Li Jinglong coughed stiffly, his voice going cold once again. "Let's go. We can continue this discussion back at headquarters." With that, he turned to lead the way.

17
LEAVING THE BAIT

"Come with me, but don't say anything," Li Jinglong instructed Hongjun as he woke him early the next morning.

Autumn was on the cusp of turning to winter, and the maple tree in the main courtyard had turned crimson, though the parasol tree was still verdant. Red and green leaves formed a vivid contrast which, along with the blue sky and white clouds reflected in the pond, combined to paint a colorful scene.

Three foxes, two dead and one heavily injured, were laid out in a row in the courtyard. The surviving fox appeared to also be the youngest. It had a gash in its shoulder from Hongjun's throwing knife, and A-Tai's fire had charred the fur and skin of its leg, which was now cracking to show bloody flesh underneath. Li Jinglong's final shot had nearly dealt the fatal blow, impaling the fox through the chest. Mergen's arrows were barbed; they had had to tug the arrow all the way through—fletching and all—to extract it, leaving the creature howling in pain. It was only thanks to the medicine Hongjun had brought from Yaojin Palace that the little fox had survived this long.

"This one's cultivation was most advanced." Qiu Yongsi, pacing through the courtyard, pointed at the larger of the two dead foxes. "Mergen killed this one right outside the front door, so it's difficult to determine its strength. The one that survived is the greenest."

The little fox had its eyes tightly shut, unmoving where it lay.

"Shall I deliver you to Captain Hu and let him see what you look like now, Jinyun?" Li Jinglong examined the little fox. "It hurts, doesn't it?"

The fox opened its eyes but turned its head away.

"Jinyun, Tuying, Ziying." Li Jinglong tossed down a stack of paper: the contracts of the three girls who had disappeared from the Poetess's Pavilion the night before. "Place of residence: Xinyang; age: sixteen; one of three girls from the same hometown who came to Chang'an together to seek a new life for themselves.

"If you were just an enlightened creature of the natural world that had cultivated to human form, holding only good in your heart, there would be no issue. At most, I would have driven you out of Chang'an." Li Jinglong paused, then sat down on the stairs to the open-air corridor and looked the little fox in the eyes. "Why did you have to commit murder?"

The little fox didn't answer.

"Who was the dead man under the bed?" Li Jinglong's voice was cold. "Speak."

Silence.

"I'll find out, whether you talk or not," Li Jinglong said. "But I'll give you one last chance: Tell me who killed that man."

Met again with silence, Qiu Yongsi said, "Maybe we should just kill it."

After an extended pause, Li Jinglong said, "Let's close this case. Yongsi, write up a memorial; I'll submit it to Chancellor Yang first thing tomorrow morning. We'll hand the creature over to Hu Sheng today—he must have received a report about what happened last night, and we owe him an explanation. We can let him take it from there. We'll head out shortly; lock up the fox for now."

Mergen secured the little fox in a cage and placed it in a side courtyard. Qiu Yongsi plastered the cage with talismans to keep it from escaping, though the measure was likely unnecessary. Even if the fox wished to flee, it clearly hadn't the strength.

When everyone had reconvened in the main courtyard, A-Tai frowned. "Do you think it'll fall for it?"

Hongjun was mystified.

"You can talk now," Li Jinglong said to Hongjun.

He was about to ask what A-Tai meant when Li Jinglong explained: "Searching the entire imperial palace for a single yao is like looking for a needle in a haystack. It's much easier to keep an eye on one fox in the care of the Longwu Guard."

Hongjun finally understood—Li Jinglong was trying to trick the little fox by telling it the case was closed; his real objective was to draw out the yao behind the scenes. "You're trying to lure the snakes from their nest!" exclaimed Hongjun.

Everyone looked at Hongjun in awkward silence. Li Jinglong nodded. "Smart—you've got it."

Mergen cut in, "But what if no one comes to save it?"

Li Jinglong replied, "Someone will come to save it for sure. Or at the very least, they'll kill it to make sure it doesn't talk. Look, it's clever; it knows the only way to keep its life is to say nothing at all. Its compatriots must know it's clever too. But they won't let it live too long, or it might start to reveal their secrets. If Hu Sheng sets it free, that makes our job even easier; we would only have to follow it as it escapes."

Hongjun didn't have enough brains for all this scheming. Listening, he felt perhaps his companions were the real monsters.

"If we can pull it off, this will be a major case for sure," Qiu Yongsi said.

"Let's get moving," Li Jinglong said. "Hopefully we can follow this vine all the way to the melon at the end."

The way A-Tai, Mergen, and Qiu Yongsi looked at Li Jinglong this morning was entirely different from how they'd looked at him a few days ago, particularly after Li Jinglong's display of marksmanship last night. Li Jinglong rose to his feet. Before the others could scramble up as well, he said, "I'll return the cat with Hongjun. You all should rest."

"I'll get some more oblivion pollen," Qiu Yongsi said with a smile.

Li Jinglong glanced at Qiu Yongsi, then nodded. He instructed Hongjun to fetch the white cat.

A change came over the other three's faces as soon as the gate door closed behind them.

"You two weren't there last night," Mergen said. "When the second three-tailed fox yao appeared, the chief was ready to lay down his life to protect Hongjun and the Longwu guards who stumbled into the fight. It's no easy thing for an ordinary mortal to display such courage."

A-Tai pondered Mergen's words, pacing back and forth across the courtyard. "Perhaps he really does have what it takes to defeat the yao king?"

Qiu Yongsi crouched in the corridor and sighed in exasperation. "Isn't it a bit early to be saying such things? We've barely tackled a single case."

"I was ready to pack up and leave a couple days ago!" Frustrated, A-Tai looked back at Qiu Yongsi with his hands on his waist. "Do you know how I despaired? Huh? Can't you be a little more optimistic?"

"Hey, Tokharian pretty boy!" The carp yao, having just woken up from his nap, was digging through the fish food kept next to the pond for a snack. "So you three are conspiring together?"

All three of them froze on the spot. They had forgotten the walls had ears, and now they had a big, fish-shaped problem on their hands.

"Zilong-xiong," said A-Tai, struck by inspiration. "What kind of lady fish do you like? Shall I buy one for you?"

Munching on his fish food, the carp yao said, "That's not necessary. I must abstain from desire for the sake of my cultivation. Hongjun is depending on all of you to take care of him. Regarding everything you've said today, my mouth is sealed."

The trio let out a collective sigh of relief.

"However…" the carp yao continued. They tensed up again, only for the carp to say, "You guys are a mess right now; you can't even work together to catch a fox. How do you intend to defeat the yao king of Chang'an?"

"Ay, my dear fish brother," A-Tai said, "that's where you've got it wrong. We're sincerely worried that Chief Li might get hurt, or even die…"

"All living beings are equal in the eyes of the world," the carp yao said. "The monk who released me from slaughter said humans and yao are alike; they all have things they want to protect. Is that not true?"

The other three fell silent.

"The way I see it," Qiu Yongsi said, "we don't need to keep it from him any longer. We should find a chance to have a proper talk with the chief and bring everything out into the open."

After finishing his meal, the carp yao seemed to have already put the matter from his mind. "Time to wash Hongjun's clothes," he muttered. As they watched, he dragged a washboard over to the well, pulled out Hongjun's undergarments, and began to scrub.

The other three flushed with embarrassment—to think they had been exorcists for so long, only to find themselves less enlightened than a carp.

Li Jinglong walked into the slanting rays of dawn as Hongjun followed after him with the cat, heading for the Duchess of Qin's estate to return her pet.

"Pay close attention to the people in the Duchess of Qin's estate," Li Jinglong said to Hongjun. "A great deal of information can be derived from a person's expression."

Hongjun both admired and pitied Li Jinglong. How had he ended up in such a sad situation, getting bullied left and right? To him, it made no sense. But Chong Ming was wont to say that everyone had their own convictions, and there were many things that shouldn't be forced.

"Zhao Zilong always says I have no knack for observation," said Hongjun.

"Sometimes, ignorance is bliss," Li Jinglong said weakly. "It's not a bad thing. Forget it, there's no need to strain yourself. Just say as little as possible once we arrive."

The moment Li Jinglong and Hongjun entered the duchess's estate carrying the cat, the gatekeeper cried, "Qing-er is back! Quick, everyone! Qing-er is home!"

The housekeeper hurried out to welcome them in person.

"Is this...?" Li Jinglong began.

Overjoyed, the housekeeper snatched the cat away before he could finish his question. "It is, it is! Where on earth did you find her?!"

Even Li Jinglong felt a bit awkward about the fanfare that accompanied their arrival. The entire estate sprang into action as if preparing to receive the emperor himself, doing everything short of bringing out musicians and dancing girls. Every maid and servant turned out to joyfully escort the cat to the main hall, where the housekeeper reverently set it down in the seat of honor atop a perfumed cushion of fine silk. He produced a jadeite food box filled with delicacies like sea cucumber and longsnout catfish, then set a gilded bowl of luminous stone beside it, which he personally filled with crisp spring water from a bottle of creamy mutton-fat jade.

The cat was on the verge of a hunger strike after so many boring meals of rice and sauce in the Department of Exorcism. Returned to its rightful place, it dug into its meal with relish, looking like it was on top of the world.

"Kowtow to Commandant Li!" the housekeeper shouted.

All the serving girls organized themselves into rows outside the main hall and kowtowed thrice toward the entranceway.

Li Jinglong was speechless.

"It's Chief Li," Hongjun corrected on his behalf.

Face clouding over, Li Jinglong got up to take his leave. The housekeeper bustled forward to stall him. "My lady is visiting the palace. Please wait until she returns so she can offer her gratitude in person."

Li Jinglong waved him off and turned to summon Hongjun—but the chief's instructions were the last thing on Hongjun's mind. He had spotted some pastries on a nearby table and, having missed his breakfast, immediately began to wolf them down.

"Delicious...mmph..." Hongjun took a sip of tea to wash down his feast.

Li Jinglong muttered to the housekeeper, "This is my subordinate."

"A lion among men!" It was only out of consideration for his own status that the housekeeper didn't kneel and kowtow to them himself. He grabbed Li Jinglong's hand again. "I must offer my sincerest personal gratitude to Chief Li. I never thought you would be the one to save our lives... Ay..."

The housekeeper had a silver tongue. Just a few days ago, when Li Jinglong came to question them about the cat, the servants had scarcely given him the time of day. They'd never expected he would actually find the creature. The way the man tripped over himself in excitement now grated on Li Jinglong's nerves.

Li Jinglong glanced around the estate but found no suspicious servants nor odd-looking characters. He ordered Hongjun to finish eating quickly so they could beat it as soon as he was done.

Hongjun, still drinking his tea, held up a hand for Li Jinglong to wait another moment. He had never eaten such delicious pastries, and he couldn't resist grabbing a few extra.

"If you like them, this servant will prepare some more and deliver them to the Department of Exorcism!" the housekeeper said at once.

Fuming, Li Jinglong turned the topic back to business. "Were there any guests staying at the estate when the cat ran away?"

"The noble consort, the Duchess of Guo, and Chancellor Yang paid a visit that night," the housekeeper said. "The estate was all in a tizzy, ay..."

Li Jinglong frowned. Hongjun, listening in, stopped chewing and glanced at Li Jinglong.

"We're leaving as soon as you're done," Li Jinglong reminded him.

The housekeeper attempted to delay them again, but Li Jinglong waved him off and led Hongjun outside. When the housekeeper tried to present them with a reward of gold and silver at the gate, he finally lost his patience. Li Jinglong spun around to face the man. "It was nothing. We barely lifted a finger. There's no need to thank us."

He turned to Hongjun. "The soldiers who bloody themselves in battle to defend Great Tang's borders are paid a mere two taels of silver a month. They live lives far inferior to that of a cat in the Duchess of Qin's estate. If these aristocrats are merely frittering away their own ancestors' fortune, outsiders have no call to comment. But if not, who's to say how their lavish lifestyles are funded?"

The housekeeper recoiled a little at this sudden barb. The pair was already strolling through the gate before he could lay into Li Jinglong, so he was forced to content himself with a final remark. "Your talents aren't fit for anything more than finding lost cats, anyway," he muttered, his voice dripping acid.

Li Jinglong pretended not to hear. As he and Hongjun headed for the Court of Judicial Review to look for relevant case files, Hongjun pulled a pastry from his pocket and offered it to Li Jinglong. "Here."

"I don't eat the people's lifeblood," said Li Jinglong.

"These are called 'the people's lifeblood'? They're delicious," said Hongjun. "Have a taste. I know you want some. Why do you always say the opposite of what you mean? That's no good…"

"I'm not saying the opposite of what I mean; I'm really not going to eat it!"

They pushed and shoved in the middle of the street. Li Jinglong was utterly helpless against Hongjun; he couldn't bear to beat him for his impudence. Judging by the crowds along the streets of Chang'an who were beginning to look their way, more rumors were sure to start flying about him any moment. He had no choice but to take the pastry to placate Hongjun.

The pastries were actually called gold dumplings, a steamed dessert consisting of a crystalline layer of sticky rice wrapped around a center of egg yolk, a soft, sweet cheese, osmanthus blossoms, and honey made from early summer blossoms. Li Jinglong claimed he wouldn't eat, but he was hungry too. In the end, he gave in and began to feast on the people's lifeblood.

"Delicious, isn't it?" Hongjun prompted.

"Mm."

Li Jinglong glanced around as he and Hongjun walked down the long avenue, afraid they'd be spotted by someone he knew. The Li family had had some wealth in the past, but their kitchen had never been as refined as the ones in the Yang sisters' estates. Li Jinglong pondered the housekeeper's words, thinking idly as he did that the pastries were truly of exceptional quality.

"Say, could the creature we're hunting be at the emperor's side?" Hongjun asked.

Li Jinglong frowned. "If it is, then His Majesty is in great danger. What if—"

"I wouldn't be too worried about that." Hongjun spun around and paused at the entrance to an alley. "The mortal Son of Heaven is protected by the Ziwei Star. No matter its level of cultivation, no yaoguai should be able to directly use its techniques against him. But this yao we're looking for—could it be Chancellor Yang? Or the Duchess of Guo? What about the noble consort?"

"That's not possible." Li Jinglong's response was immediate.

"Why not?" Hongjun asked, bemused. "Wouldn't that make a lot of sense?"

Li Jinglong was unable to speak for a long time; he stood dazed, as if Hongjun's words had woken him from a dream. This theory shattered Li Jinglong's entire worldview. One of the people right at the emperor's side—the chancellor, the noble consort, or her sister—a monster?

He glanced at Hongjun. "Let's go. Why are you standing here?"

Hongjun looked at the noodle stall in front of them, then at Li Jinglong.

Li Jinglong stared back.

"Those noodles look really good. Chief, don't you want a taste?"

The cook was pulling dough behind the stall to form golden noodles. As they watched, the golden strands took a tumble through a pot of boiling water before being crowned with braised pork trotters, soybeans, dried tofu, and sundry other toppings, then finished off with a handful of seasonings. The tempting scent curled toward them through the air.

"Didn't you just finish all those pastries?" Li Jinglong asked. "How are you still hungry?" But recalling the way Hongjun refused to move at the sight of food, Li Jinglong was afraid onlookers would laugh at him again if he tried to argue. "Fine, fine, we can eat."

Li Jinglong ordered two bowls of noodles and sat down, taking the break as a chance to digest Hongjun's outlandish theory. A cloud of gloom seemed to hang over his head; thinking back on it now, he realized the cat seemed to have been trying to show them something. Unfortunately, the animal couldn't talk, and Li Jinglong had forgotten many of the details after inhaling the oblivion pollen. For the most part, he would have to rely on guesswork.

If a member of the Yang family was a yao, that was no small thing. Or perhaps Yang Guozhong and his cousins were *all* yao? Li Jinglong scarcely dared entertain the thought. But as he pondered, he found his attention drawn to Hongjun, who was already digging into his third bowl of noodles.

"Do you always eat this much?" Li Jinglong asked.

"I'm growing." Confused, Hongjun asked, "What's wrong with eating a lot? It's not like I'm eating from your pantry."

Li Jinglong said nothing for a moment. "If someone were to provide for you in the future, you'd eat them out of house and home." Li Jinglong awkwardly averted his gaze.

"I'm providing for myself," Hongjun said, ever earnest. "My dad gave me a lot of money. My goal is to taste every delicacy in the land. Mortal food is too delicious!"

"Mortal food?"

Hongjun pressed his lips shut, realizing he'd slipped up. Li Jinglong tactfully let it lie. "You're all rich," he said as he counted out coins to pay, pausing briefly to warn Hongjun to stop eating before he gave himself a stomachache. Hongjun dug into his own wallet, but Li Jinglong wouldn't hear of it. "Or perhaps we're all rich here—a tael of pollen costs eight hundred taels of silver. No one from a poor family would be an exorcist."

Li Jinglong had spent the entirety of his savings on renovating the Department of Exorcism, and they were still down three thousand, two hundred silver for the oblivion pollen. Now Hongjun had eaten through at least two days' worth of his food budget in a single meal, and Li Jinglong wouldn't receive his salary until next month. He considered the twelve copper coins left in his wallet. If they didn't go to any more restaurants and only ate inside the department for the next few days… It was the twenty-sixth today. He should be able to hold out until the fifth of the next month. The outlook was bleak, but unable to confess the truth of his financial woes to Hongjun, he could only grit his teeth and bear it as they continued on.

It was Hongjun's first time visiting the Imperial Court of Judicial Review. Hongjun had been wondering what sorts of games were played on an imperial court, but it turned out to be just another government office. Officials streamed in and out of the gloomy, oppressive main hall, while pained screams sounded in the distance—presumably a far-off interrogation. The place had a discomfiting air of malice from the moment one stepped through the gate.

The case should have been closed after recovering the corpse and capturing the yao responsible. Li Jinglong had found the fox yao's choice to burn the corpse highly suspicious, however—this was obviously a move to keep him from investigating further. Several peculiar points had arisen during the case of the lost cat and the case of the fox yao alike, and it was becoming increasingly apparent that they wouldn't be able to mark these cases concluded so easily. Li Jinglong had a vague premonition that an even larger riddle lay behind both incidents.

Li Jinglong led Hongjun to the back room, where the case records were kept. They had been digging through old records for some time when Hongjun said, "Hey, Chief, take a look at this."

Hongjun could just about keep up with some of Li Jinglong's conjectures now: There were many things that appeared perfectly normal yet hid strange truths beneath their surface. In the case he was holding, three scholars from Gong District, described as men between thirty and forty years of age, had come to Chang'an for the imperial examinations, opened a tab for several days' worth of expenditures in a certain restaurant, then absconded before paying their bill. Unable to collect, the restaurant owner had submitted a report to the Court of Judicial Review.

"We'll take it." Li Jinglong pulled out the case file and stepped outside to complete the procedures to transfer the case from the Court of Judicial Review to the Department of Exorcism.

The records clerk took one look at the case and broke out in uproarious laughter. "So this is what the Department of Exorcism does? Find lost cats and collect debts?"

Refusing to dignify this with any comment, Li Jinglong stamped his seal on the proper forms in stony silence. The two exited the Court of Judicial Review and set out for the Longwu Guard Garrison, which was surrounded by a wide training field.

The great general Yuchi Jingde had founded the Xuanjia Army for Li Shimin, co-founder and second emperor of the Tang dynasty. After over a hundred years of history, the army had split into two branches dubbed Shenwu and Longwu. In the interim, the capital had moved to Luoyang, then back to Chang'an, but the Longwu Guard's training fields were as awe-inspiring as ever, filled with soldiers moving through their morning drills.

Mergen, A-Tai, and Qiu Yongsi had arrived before them, carrying the caged fox. Li Jinglong instructed Hongjun to wait with them outside while he took the fox into the administrative office to meet with Hu Sheng.

Li Jinglong caught a snicker from a group of soldiers off to the side. "Everyone, look, Li Jinglong's caught a yao! It's a little fox!"

It was clear the Longwu soldiers figured Li Jinglong must have caught an ordinary fox somewhere and simply papered the cage with talismans so he could demand recognition for his grand accomplishments.

"Look at our poor chief. His old colleagues have no respect for him at all." A-Tai chuckled.

Mergen frowned, apparently more anxious than A-Tai over Li Jinglong's situation. "A man that smart ought to have a little tact. He needs to make some compromises. Why is he so stubborn about these things?"

"Even common people have their burdens," Qiu Yongsi said. "The only one who can solve his problems is him."

As always, his companions' sly exchanges left Hongjun in a fog of confusion. He cut in, "Can't you guys say things a bit more clearly?"

The other three each gave Hongjun an odd smile.

"The less you understand, the fewer worries you'll have." A-Tai studied Hongjun, using his gilded blue fan to lift Hongjun's chin with a teasing smile. "Isn't it nice having your big brothers worry about things on your behalf?"

"Ignore him," Mergen said earnestly. He slung an arm around Hongjun's shoulders and tugged him to his side.

"That's not very nice of you, Mergen," said Qiu Yongsi. "Are you trying to steal the chief's man?"

Mergen laughed. "He reminds me of my little brother. What's wrong with that?"

"You have a little brother?" Hongjun asked, astonished.

"Four little brothers and two little sisters."

So Mergen was the eldest sibling in his family. No wonder he felt like such a dependable older brother.

"What did you guys do this morning?" A-Tai asked warmly.

Hongjun took a moment to organize his thoughts, then summarized their adventures at the Duchess of Qin's estate and the Court of Judicial Review. Just as he finished, a Longwu Guard soldier showed up to shoo them away from the training grounds.

"Hey! Blades don't care who they hit; stop squatting on the training grounds. Move it!"

They were a strange group no matter how you looked at them. Mergen was dressed in hunter's garb, and Qiu Yongsi sported scholar's robes. Hongjun was wearing a set of clothes he'd purchased at random after arriving in Chang'an, and though A-Tai was sumptuously attired, he was a foreigner. The soldier scoffed as he walked away. "Li Jinglong's department of freaks."

A chorus of laughter followed. Hongjun flushed with anger, but before he'd taken more than a few steps forward, Mergen caught him by the shoulder.

"What are you doing?" Qiu Yongsi asked. "Let's just mind our own business."

Mergen didn't say anything, but he pulled out a copper coin and tossed it to A-Tai. As A-Tai looked at him in confusion, Mergen selected a longbow from the weapons rack. He picked three arrows, hefting them in his hand, then walked to the center of the training field.

Inside the administrative office, Hu Sheng's face was slack with shock as Li Jinglong finished recounting last night's events.

"You... Is this true?!"

"What, you think I've conspired with an entire patrol's worth of witnesses to trick you?" Li Jinglong countered.

"But this... It's unbelievable! You mean to say that this fox is one of the women from the Poetess's Pavilion?"

"It's a fox yao," Li Jinglong said, his voice cool. "And her name is Jinyun, the young lady you patronized so often."

"This is preposterous! Li Jinglong, you—"

"Believe me or don't; it's up to you," Li Jinglong said. "The creature is yours to do with as you wish. But once it's discovered that three women have disappeared from the Poetess's Pavilion, it will be only a matter of time before the Court of Judicial Review comes knocking at your door."

Hu Sheng suddenly realized he had a larger problem—though he hadn't spoken widely of his relationship with Jinyun, the procuress of the Poetess's Pavilion, the servants, and the other girls had seen him more than a few times. Jinyun must have spoken of him to others as well, and he knew she kept the brocade pouches and other gifts he'd given her in her room. Even a cursory investigation would uncover the link between them.

Li Jinglong had backed him into an impossible corner.

"Okay, little Flying General." Hu Sheng began to laugh in frustration. "I certainly have underestimated you."

His eyes drifted again and again to the fox, countless thoughts flashing through his mind. Although he didn't know what scheme Li Jinglong was hatching, Jinyun's disappearance was an irrefutable fact. If the Court of Judicial Review were to investigate, they would hound him about it until he was forced to admit his indiscretions.

But if he testified that yao were involved, he would merely have to kill this fox before the Court of Judicial Review, and that would be the end of it. Perhaps he could even claim he was helping Li Jinglong catch yao infiltrators all this time… With Li Jinglong as a shield, no one could accuse him of misconduct as an official of the state for spending his nights at a brothel.

"All right," Hu Sheng said. "If the Court of Judicial Review comes to me, I'll explain—but they may still wish to interview you personally."

"I'll take responsibility for closing the case, of course. All we have to do now is wait for their investigation to begin."

Both men turned at a sudden din from outside. Frowning, Li Jinglong went to the window to look.

"You brought your people here?" Hu Sheng asked.

Li Jinglong strode outside. The training field was packed with onlookers as Mergen and a commandant of the Longwu Guard competed in an archery contest. Each time the officer's shot struck true, a cheer ran through the crowd of soldiers; but whenever the dust settled to reveal Mergen's arrow cleanly piercing the bull's-eye, the Longwu Guard went silent as the dead.

After the first three shots, Mergen selected another three arrows. He signaled to A-Tai, then called out to the crowd, "Shooting stationary targets doesn't make for an exciting competition. Shall I have our youngest member assist for a few rounds?"

A-Tai spread open his fan, copper coin balanced atop its flat surface. He flicked his wrist and called, "Go!"

The copper coin flew up, spinning so fast it buzzed in the air. Catching on, Hongjun let his throwing knife fly.

"Strike!" he cried.

The knife shot out and struck the copper coin with a sharp *ting*. The coin changed course, spinning furiously through the air, a blinding ball of light beneath the glaring sun as it flew toward the far corner of the training field.

The commandant had nocked an arrow, guessing Mergen planned to have them shoot the coin, but he couldn't track the trajectory of its flight. His hand shook as he tried to steady his bow.

Hongjun hurled another throwing knife, which first struck a roof tile on the eaves of a building opposite the field before rebounding to hit the coin again with a deafening ring.

The crowd held their breath. Hongjun released his third throwing knife, cutting off the copper coin's path once more. There was another resonant chime as the coin was launched straight up into the sky.

Hongjun sheathed his knives, which had returned to his hands as fast as they shot out, with a smile. "Your turn."

Mergen's bow was already drawn. The commandant drew his too, sweat streaming down his forehead. Both of them fixed their eyes on the spinning coin, now a tiny black dot in the sky. Once it began to fall, they would shoot.

The coin flew higher and higher. A smile tugged at the corner of Mergen's lips. Just as he was about to let his shot fly, another arrow came hurtling from a different direction, stringing itself through the square hole in the center of the coin with a *clang*. Weighed down by the coin, the arrow plummeted toward the earth and nailed itself into the ground at the far corner of the training field.

A thousand heads turned to see Li Jinglong, longbow in hand, standing atop the steps of the Longwu Guard's administrative office at Hu Sheng's side.

"We're going!" Li Jinglong called. "Did you enjoy yourselves, showboating for a crowd?"

His subordinates stowed their weapons and strutted away after him. Li Jinglong wore a scowl on his face, and he was silent the rest of the way back. Hongjun watched him with growing unease.

"You are exorcists," Li Jinglong said once they returned to the Department of Exorcism. "Your skills are naturally superior to those of ordinary men. Is it really so impressive to win against them?"

The others looked down, chastened. But hadn't they merely been trying to stand up for their chief? No one bothered to argue the point; Li Jinglong didn't seem to appreciate the sentiment.

As each went their separate ways, Li Jinglong called, "Starting tonight, we'll be staking out the Longwu Guard Garrison. With any luck, we'll catch ourselves a big fish."

"All right..."

"Yes, sir."

Qiu Yongsi gave Hongjun a look—*See, your attempts at flattery got you nowhere.* Hongjun scratched his head with a smile.

A thick cover of clouds rolled in with the night, and the exorcists gathered once again. After briefing everyone on the results of the day's investigation, Li Jinglong led them back to the Longwu Guard Garrison.

18
THE PALACE IN THE NORTHERN OUTSKIRTS

THE DEPARTMENT OF EXORCISM had fallen into the habit of napping from noon to dusk and working by night. As it was said: Reverse day and night, and your hair will never go white. None of them, including Hongjun himself, could stop yawning by day, but by a few hours after sundown, they were up and raring to go.

Qiu Yongsi and Hongjun sat on a rooftop, from which they had a clear view of the entire Longwu Guard Garrison. Mergen was crouched on the wall between Hu Sheng's room and the rear courtyard, while A-Tai kept watch outside the captain's door.

Hu Sheng's lamps remained lit well into the night. While the captain had a residence of his own within the city, he often stayed overnight at the garrison, eating and sleeping alongside the men of the Longwu Guard. Tonight he seemed restless, pacing back and forth and casting frequent glances at the talisman-covered cage in the corner.

Although he couldn't bring himself to believe the little fox was really Jinyun, he found the injured creature quite pitiful. "Where did you come from?"

The little fox replied, "Captain Hu, set me free."

Hu Sheng yelped in alarm.

Mergen and A-Tai heard his cry from outside. Both had started forward to investigate when Li Jinglong appeared in the courtyard, signaling them to wait.

"Patience," Li Jinglong whispered. "Don't act without orders unless it makes a run for it."

Li Jinglong sprang up onto the wall and disappeared among the rooftops.

Within, Hu Sheng felt as if he was in a dream. "Y-y-you...you can speak?"

"Captain Hu?" a Longwu guard called, rapping on the door.

Hu Sheng assured him that nothing was amiss and hastily dismissed the guard before returning his attention to the little fox. Its eyes brimmed with tears.

"Captain Hu," it said quietly, "I know you were always sincere with me. I once thought...if I wasn't a yao..."

"Y-y-you..." Hu Sheng stumbled backward, terror written across his face.

"My sisters and I cultivated in Xinyang." The little fox pressed up against the side of the cage as it spoke. "But I wanted to see the mortal world, so Dajie and Erjie[11] brought me to Chang'an. We never harmed anyone, but we had no one to rely on. We had no choice but to sell ourselves into service in Pingkang Ward. Even so, Li Jinglong refused to show us mercy..."

"That bastard wasn't lying to me." Hu Sheng's heart was still palpitating. "You really are a yao!"

"Captain Hu!" the fox yao cried. "The Buddhists say humans cherish all living beings, and so they are virtuous. If you let me go, I will repay my debt to you, even if I must carry jade hoops and braid

---

11 Dajie, a word meaning "eldest sister." Erjie, a word meaning "second eldest sister."

THE PALACE IN THE NORTHERN OUTSKIRTS

ropes of grass,[12] like your stories say... Do you remember the tale I told you when we first met?"

Hu Sheng drew in a steadying breath. He recalled his first meeting with Jinyun, while setting lanterns afloat beneath Qushui Bridge on the night of the Hungry Ghost Festival three years ago. Jinyun had told him a story about a fox yao and a scholar. It was a romance between a talented young man and a beautiful woman, but because humans and yao walked divergent paths, it inevitably ended in tragedy.

Hu Sheng's heart welled with pity. He had heard many such tragic tales over the course of his life, but having one unfold before his eyes now still left him uncertain and suspicious.

Some distance away, Li Jinglong leapt onto the rooftop where Hongjun and Qiu Yongsi had been chatting quietly. The pair immediately fell silent.

Li Jinglong shot them a quizzical look, but both remained mute. In fact, Hongjun had been questioning Qiu Yongsi about Pingkang Ward—he was sixteen after all, at the age when his blood was running hottest, and he was curious about everything. The more Li Jinglong warned Hongjun not to ask, the more he burned with curiosity. Thus Qiu Yongsi had ended up giving him a full, whispered briefing.

"Have you seen anything odd?" Li Jinglong asked.

"Not at all," Qiu Yongsi answered promptly.

Face crimson, Hongjun echoed, "Not at all."

Both looked like they were waiting for Li Jinglong to leave; Li Jinglong sat down beside them instead. Feeling as if he'd been caught red-handed, Hongjun fidgeted in place.

---

12 An idiom referencing two folktales about repaying debts which first appear in the Zuo Zhuan. The first tells the tale of a finch that gifted a man who saved it with blessed jade hoops to ensure the future of his descendants, while the second tells the tale of a father who braids a rope of grass to trip the enemy of the man who spared his daughter's life.

"I've put you all to a lot of trouble," Li Jinglong said. "Once we close this case, I'll make sure everyone gets a nice, long vacation. I'll take you out—somewhere fun."

Li Jinglong looked at Hongjun and Qiu Yongsi. Excited at the prospect, Hongjun blurted, "We were just—"

Qiu Yongsi swooped in before he could finish. "It's our duty to serve our nation. How can you call it trouble?"

Unseen in the shadows, the ground bulged like the spine of some great beast moving below the Longwu Guard's training field. As the bulge reached the main hall, it crashed into the building's foundations with a *thud*, retreated, and turned laboriously to take a different path along the courtyard wall.

Li Jinglong was on his feet at once. "What was that sound?"

Hongjun and Qiu Yongsi looked at him, perplexed. A moment later, Qiu Yongsi said, "Just now... I think I felt a tremor beneath us."

Expecting more fox yao, everyone had trained their focus on the walls and rooftops. No one had anticipated an approach from below.

"What type of monster can travel underground?" Li Jinglong asked.

But Hongjun knew instantly—it was the ao fish he had chased for over five miles the other day.

Li Jinglong jumped down from the roof. "Meet me in the rear courtyard!"

The ground swelled. A dark mist rose into the air and coalesced into the form of a tall, slender man with a bloody scar on his forehead, dressed entirely in black. The door to Hu Sheng's room creaked as the man let himself in.

Inside the room, the cage door yawned open as a pale-faced Jinyun lay the unconscious captain on the bed. She drew the blankets up over him, tears in her eyes. "Captain Hu, I'm truly sorry... I never wanted to..."

"You actually fell for him," the black-clothed man murmured grimly.

Startled, Jinyun whipped her head toward the door. She frowned. "Fei'ao?"

"The boss ordered me to escort you out of Chang'an."

Jinyun sighed in relief, tears rolling down her cheeks. "Dajie and Erjie are both dead at their hands. Have you recovered from your injuries?"

Fei'ao stepped forward and lifted Jinyun's chin. "This generation's Department of Exorcism is surprisingly tough. But just you wait; I'll avenge your sisters for you. Let's go."

Jinyun stumbled over her own feet as she walked toward the door. Noticing her wounds, Fei'ao swept her up in his arms. He gathered his yao energy in his left hand and set it atop her head, pouring energy into her to heal her injuries. Jinyun's face slowly regained some of its color.

Outside, the five exorcists had moved into position around the courtyard. Mergen stood atop the wall, slowly drawing his bow and taking aim at the two figures inside the room. Qiu Yongsi and Li Jinglong crouched outside the door, eavesdropping. A-Tai and Hongjun hid in the shadows, the former gripping his fan while the latter held three throwing knives ready between his fingers.

"We're about to face a powerful enemy. You shouldn't waste your cultivation on me," Jinyun said softly.

"After tonight, run far away from this place. Don't come back to Chang'an," Fei'ao replied. "Not until you and I have both grown stronger."

Jinyun was shocked. "They told you to kill me?"

"As long as I'm here, no one will touch a hair on your head."

"What about my other sisters? Li Jinglong won't stop his investigation."

"If your erjie hadn't been so careless, all the bodies would have been disposed of long ago. What's there for him to investigate? Is he going to capture all of your sisters and interrogate them one by one? By the time next year's palace examinations are over, Li Jinglong will be dead without a body to bury! It would be letting him off easy to kill him now."

Qiu Yongsi and Li Jinglong's expressions were bleak. Li Jinglong's hand—raised in anticipation to signal their attack—froze in midair.

Holding Jinyun in his arms, Fei'ao stepped through the door.

Mergen loosed his arrow before Li Jinglong could call out his orders. In the space of a heartbeat, Jinyun sensed the danger and shoved Fei'ao aside; she fell to the ground with a cry as the arrow struck her instead.

"Stop him!" Li Jinglong shouted.

Fei'ao knew it was a trap as soon as he saw the arrow sprouting from Jinyun's body. Quick to react, he charged out the door, one hand dragging Jinyun alongside him.

Li Jinglong drew his sword as Fei'ao took a sharp turn and lunged at him with a furious roar. "Die!"

The others started in alarm, fearing Li Jinglong would be no match for their enemy. Arrows and throwing knives hurtled toward Fei'ao, who bellowed in rage as a blast of vapor exploded from his body.

Li Jinglong, closest to the epicenter of the attack, went flying backward as Hongjun threw up his light barrier to shield himself and A-Tai. Just as he was about to jump in to help, Li Jinglong planted a foot against a pillar, shifting his sword into a two-handed grip.

"Evil creature!" he shouted. "You'll be the one to die today!"

The sword seemed to be an extension of Li Jinglong's body as he launched himself at Fei'ao and swung the blade down. Fei'ao raised an arm to block the blow, sending Li Jinglong flying again as he deflected the strike.

"Fei'ao, run... Forget about me..." Jinyun choked out.

"I'm going to kill them!" Fei'ao snarled, his chest heaving.

"You and what army?" A-Tai scoffed.

Hongjun dropped his shield as A-Tai snapped his blue fan open. The instant the shield was down, he flicked his wrist, raising a funnel of wind from the stagnant air. The wind whipped Fei'ao's mist into a typhoon, which slammed into Fei'ao with a thunderous crash that demolished the doors and windows of Hu Sheng's room. Mergen released three arrows in a flash, each one burying itself in Fei'ao's flesh before he hit the ground.

Unfazed, Fei'ao transformed into a giant fish in midair.

"Hongjun!" Li Jinglong shouted. "Your throwing knives!"

Hongjun hurled another blade, which whipped through the air to plunge into Fei'ao's body beside Mergen's arrows.

The monstrous fish exploded through the back wall and dove for the ground, taking another one of Hongjun's throwing knives with it as it fled the Longwu Guard Garrison.

By now, every last soldier of the Longwu Guard had heard the commotion and come with torches to investigate.

"After it!" Li Jinglong shouted at the exorcists, "This time, we can't let it get away!"

They burst through the crumbling rear wall to find the garrison boiling with chaos.

"Follow my throwing knife!" Hongjun yelled.

Just as it had the other night, the ground surged upward as the ao fish sped toward the north of the city, Hongjun's throwing knife lodged in its side.

"Please go anywhere but the imperial palace... After it!" Li Jinglong shouted.

The exorcists redoubled their pace, chasing after the ao fish. This was Hongjun's best chance to get his first throwing knife back; he couldn't let the creature escape again. He flung out his grappling hook and flew to the rooftops, Mergen at his heels.

A-Tai waved his fan and conjured another burst of wind to lift himself onto the roof as well. A few paces behind them, Li Jinglong vaulted up with a few nimble steps.

"You guys... Wait for me!" Qiu Yongsi yelled.

Li Jinglong looked back in astonishment. Qiu Yongsi was still trying to scale the wall. After he tried and failed twice, Li Jinglong turned back to lend him a hand. By the time they were both steady, the other three had disappeared into the distance.

"Hurry up!" Exasperated, Li Jinglong sprinted off after them.

The ao fish circled around the imperial palace and passed it, charging northward. Hongjun yelled, "It's leaving the city! It'll have to surface!"

"Hongjun! Give me a lift!" A-Tai yelled.

The ao fish was fast—it had already reached the northeast gate. Hongjun had no time to think; he tossed out his grappling hook and swung upward through the air—

A-Tai leapt from the rooftop, twisting in midair, and caught Hongjun's hand. Holding him by the wrist, Hongjun used every ounce of strength in his body to launch A-Tai skyward.

Mergen followed close behind, grasping Hongjun's wrist as the arc of his swing took him back in the other direction. "Thanks for the boost!"

Hongjun swung through the air again and flung Mergen onto the city wall above the gate. It was late at night, and quiet; the sentries posted on the gate were busy trading that day's rumors.

"I heard Li Jinglong caught a fox and delivered it to the Longwu Guard, claiming it was a yao!" The man laughed along with the rest.

"How desperate is he for attention?! The man's gone mad. Maybe tomorrow I'll bring in a dog…"

"What was that sound?"

The ground rumbled beneath their feet as the clear calls of A-Tai and Hongjun reached their ears. The sentries rushed to the ramparts of the gate tower and peered down at the commotion.

Li Jinglong and Qiu Yongsi overtook the others just as the ao fish broke through the stone at the base of the tower and leapt into the air.

A-Tai was still suspended above the ground. The ao fish roared as it flew toward him, its bloody maw gaping wide, poised to crush him between its jaws. A-Tai whipped his barbat from his back and raised it overhead. "Get—down!"

He smashed the instrument against the ao fish's nose.

A deafening *boom* erupted at the moment of collision, sending the thirty-foot fish hurtling toward the city wall. Bricks went flying, and the creature tumbled down the ramparts.

"You're kidding!" Hongjun yelled. "It really *is* a blunt-force weapon?!"

A-Tai shrugged. "Yeah?"

Mergen burst out laughing. Feet skipping across the chunks of brick flying through the air, he took three shots in quick succession, striking the three compound eyes on the ao fish's forehead. The creature howled as the arrows were recalled, yanking each eyeball from its socket.

The ao fish slammed into the ground outside the city wall, Li Jinglong and Qiu Yongsi sprinting after it.

"Open the gates!" Li Jinglong yelled as they approached. The guards stood frozen, on the verge of a nervous breakdown. "This is urgent business of the Department of Exorcism! Take another second to open the gate, and you'll be held accountable!"

The guards hurried to follow his orders. Without another word, Li Jinglong ran out, dragging a wheezing Qiu Yongsi behind him.

"Where are the horses?!" Li Jinglong looked around.

"Where's the monster?" Mergen was also scanning the darkness.

Li Jinglong pointed north, in the direction the ao fish had fled.

"A-Tai, you're so powerful!" Hongjun was still recovering from his shock.

"This is nothing," A-Tai said modestly. "I'm nowhere as strong as you, Xiao-di."[13]

"No, no, your spiritual techniques are awesome!" Hongjun looked at A-Tai with a new admiration—especially after that swing of his lute.

Qiu Yongsi added his voice to the stream of flattery. "A-Tai is the great magus of the Western Regions..."

"That's enough out of you!" A-Tai said. "Qiu Yongsi, have you done a single thing these past few days besides watch us dance about like circus monkeys? Isn't it high time you demonstrated your abilities?!"

"I really can't..."

"Cut the chatter!" Li Jinglong interrupted them. "Get over here! I found the horses!"

Hongjun had already resigned himself to losing another of his throwing knives as the yao got away again—but somehow, there

---

13   Xiao-di consists of the prefix xiao-, meaning younger and -di, meaning younger brother. In this case, it's used as an affectionate address for Hongjun as the youngest of the group.

were horses at the city gate. Mergen and Li Jinglong led a couple over, and the group quickly mounted and set off down the road at a gallop.

Li Jinglong drew his sword atop his horse; the blade lit up as he pointed it northward.

"Where did the horses come from?" Hongjun asked, confused.

"I made arrangements this afternoon," Li Jinglong replied. "Each of the four gates have horses tied up outside."

Their steeds charged through the night. Li Jinglong's sword glowed brighter and brighter as they sped down the road. The ao fish was clearly slowed by its injuries as it tunneled through the bare, postharvest fields, heading for the mountain range to the north.

"This sword can definitely sense your throwing knife." Li Jinglong held the reins in one hand and his sword in the other, the bright gleam of the blade illuminating the road before them.

"Perhaps they were forged of the same material," said Qiu Yongsi. "Spiritual devices of the same origin often resonate with each other."

They reined their horses to a halt in front of the outer walls of Daming Palace. Li Jinglong's brow was twisted in a knot of worry. The sword's glow had stabilized—the creature was inside.

"Do we break in?" Mergen asked.

"We break in," Li Jinglong said.

With a few swings, Hongjun threw his grappling hook and scaled the ten-foot wall encircling Daming Palace's rear courtyard. The others followed, climbing up the rope one by one.

Daming Palace was one of Li Longji's imperial residences, but as he much preferred Xingqing Palace within the city, he rarely visited. Daming Palace was outside of Chang'an proper, connected to the city on only one side. Only a few hundred servants attended to it, and at this hour, they were long asleep.

A wisp of moonlight on the horizon cast the palace in its hallowed, mournful light. Li Jinglong signaled his subordinates to follow after him as he crept past the palace halls, his sword shining brighter and brighter. An autumn breeze played with the gauze curtains in the rear courtyard as a furious roar echoed against the palace walls.

Fei'ao, once again in human form, knelt beneath the open sky, sobbing in anguish over the dead fox in his arms. "Why... You've left me, just like that..." Fei'ao rasped.

Hongjun's eyes stung at the sound of his raw grief. As if guessing his thoughts, Mergen put a hand on his shoulder.

Li Jinglong spoke at a hush. "This is it. Whatever cards you've got up your sleeve, now's the time to use them. Hold nothing back. Especially you, Qiu Yongsi."

Qiu Yongsi smiled uncomfortably.

"Don't forget," Li Jinglong continued, "we want to take him alive. We need to bring him in for interrogation. Subdue him as quickly as possible; don't damage the palace."

The others murmured their assent. Thinking it over again, Li Jinglong decided that the preservation of human lives was more important than material objects. "On second thought, never mind what I just said. Do your worst."

At his signal, everyone silently scattered to the far corners of the rear courtyard. Once they were in place, Li Jinglong walked out into the open, sword in hand. The throwing knife, still embedded in Fei'ao's back, pulsed with light.

Hongjun, Mergen, and the others watched him closely, nerves strung tight. Hongjun frowned. Li Jinglong always put himself forward as bait to distract the enemy—it was too dangerous.

Li Jinglong stopped ten paces from Fei'ao, facing him from across the wide courtyard. "Let's do this," he said. "Seeing as we've come this far, there's no need for chat."

"Li Jinglong," Fei'ao rasped. "Tell me, do you have a lover? What is her name?"

Li Jinglong kept his silence, carefully watching Fei'ao for any sign of movement.

"If you don't kill me today," Fei'ao continued, "I'll flay the skin from your lover's body, inch by inch; I'll gnaw the flesh from her bones, bite by bite, and pull the tendons from her joints, strand by strand. And one day, I'll use her cured tendons to garrote your neck."

Watching from afar, Hongjun shuddered at the malice in Fei'ao's gaze. Never had he seen such intense hatred in a yao's eyes, as if a mass of black energy was on the verge of erupting from his pupils. Fei'ao opened his mouth, and his face warped as wickedly sharp teeth sprouted from his jaw.

Li Jinglong's hand tightened on his sword. "Unfortunately, you won't live to see that day."

"Even if you manage to kill me now," Fei'ao rasped, "others will take vengeance on my behalf!"

"Now!" Qiu Yongsi shouted, surprising everyone as he broke the silence before Li Jinglong could give the order.

Hongjun, too, feared Li Jinglong wouldn't survive Fei'ao's final, desperate attack. A throwing knife flew from his fingers as countless flashing teeth shot out from Fei'ao's throat. Li Jinglong leapt backward, and the throwing knife swept toward the yaoguai's gaping jaws to intercept the ominous rain of bone. The blade ricocheted back and forth, colliding with teeth in all directions.

"Li Jinglong!" Hongjun shouted.

This time, Li Jinglong was prepared. He made a quick retreat to evade Fei'ao's grasp as everyone readied their attacks. But Fei'ao's first strike was only a feint; he quickly turned and ran inside Daming Palace's rear hall.

Mergen loosed all seven of his nailhead arrows, each of which made a sharp turn midair to follow Fei'ao into the hall. Hongjun and A-Tai were just behind this volley, sprinting after the creature as it disappeared from sight.

"Wait!" Li Jinglong called out.

"Hongjun's spiritual device can take a beating!" Qiu Yongsi shouted. "Don't worry about him! Chief, let's go!"

Li Jinglong, Qiu Yongsi, and Mergen sped into the hall. The ao fish had destroyed the wooden door, and they could hear crashes coming from farther ahead as another structure fell victim to its charge.

Gripping his fan, A-Tai slammed his hand against the ground: The red, blue, yellow, and green rings on his fingers flared to life. The floor began to rumble and shake as the entire rear hall briefly lifted into the air, floating above the ground.

Unable to retreat into the earth, the ao fish turned with a roar and launched itself at A-Tai. In the blink of an eye, Hongjun was between them, deploying his sacred light to form a giant, impenetrable shield that took the collision head-on. "Get—*lost*—!"

An explosive burst from Hongjun's shield sent the ao fish flying backward. The enormous creature tumbled through the hall, demolishing porcelain and furniture. The guards outside Daming Palace rushed toward the hall in a panic, their shouts filling the air.

"You..." Seeing the absolute devastation as he ran into the hall, Li Jinglong could scarcely imagine how much they would have to pay in damages after the dust had settled. "Lead it outside and fight there!" he ordered immediately.

"Doing my best!" Hongjun shouted back. He took off after the creature, with Mergen right behind. Mergen made a beckoning motion mid-sprint, and the seven nailhead arrows came flying back, converging into a single arrow that cast a brilliant light ahead of his bow as he nocked it to the string.

Hongjun held his jade peacock feather in one hand to summon the pentacolor sacred light and formed a sword seal with the other as he rained throwing knives down on the ao fish, striking one after another like a rain of shooting stars. A-Tai waved his fan thrice, and cyclones infused with lightning, frost, and blowing sand spiraled up from the ground.

The ao fish had left the rear hall in shambles. As it charged toward the wall to escape into the side hall, Mergen finally released the arrow and yelled, "Retreat!"

Hongjun was at the front fending off the ao fish's charges. He took a few stuttering steps back before Li Jinglong grabbed him by the collar and hauled him backward. The luminous bundle of the seven nailhead arrows screeched through the air, punching through a pillar before piercing the ao fish's abdomen.

Three cyclones swept in behind them. The ao fish was sent flying once again, crashing through yet another wall as it hurtled toward the open plaza beyond Daming Palace's rear hall, the ground trembling with aftershocks in its wake.

19

FEI'AO SLAIN

THE AO FISH SHRANK BACK into human form. Stumbling and unsteady, he struggled to his feet, still holding the little fox in his arms. There was nothing but a bloody hole where his stomach had been, yet when the exorcists followed him outside, a wry smile touched the corner of his mouth.

"Well...so much for that..." Fei'ao muttered. "It seems there's no escaping...my fate today..."

Woken by the commotion, the servants of Daming Palace had gathered in the plaza outside the rear hall to gawk. As Fei'ao spoke, a black mist swept in to cover the ground from every direction, swelling with a life of its own.

"All of you, hide!" Li Jinglong shouted. "It's a monster!"

Many turned and fled, though a few braver eunuchs and guards remained, retreating into the corners of the plaza to watch from a distance.

The black mist flowed inexorably toward Fei'ao. Low-voiced, Li Jinglong asked, "Is there some charm or talisman that can seal him?"

"No," Hongjun panted. "All we can do is beat him until he stays down... He hasn't shown the true extent of his abilities yet. Maybe... we can try...stabbing him with your sword?"

This fish could really take a beating. It was a good thing Hongjun hadn't kept chasing him that day, or he would have found himself badly outmatched.

Li Jinglong hefted his sword in his hand. "Cover me."

The plaza was silent, the air heavy with a strange atmosphere. Fei'ao muttered an incantation from the heart of the black mist, which had by now spread in a growing cloud all around him. He looked up at the exorcists and said, quiet, "Even if I die, I'll—"

Hongjun threw out a sacred light barrier to shield the others as Fei'ao exploded with a *boom*.

In an instant, the black mist transformed into thousands of dark flames that shot outward from the center of the plaza. The remaining guards and servants collapsed as the flames rushed over them, wailing in agony as they thrashed and writhed on the ground. By the time their cries stopped, they had all transformed into rotting, black ao fish eager to launch themselves at the exorcists.

The plaza was packed with decaying ao fish, their gaping mouths revealing countless wicked teeth as they charged toward the five exorcists. Hongjun raised his shield, but he was reluctant to kill any of the transformed creatures lest the humans inside die with them.

"Get him!" Li Jinglong shouted.

He ran for the raging black inferno at the center of the plaza, sword held out at his side. Hongjun raised his sacred light, throwing himself to one side to open a path through the putrid throng of black ao fish for Li Jinglong. A-Tai summoned whirlwind after whirlwind, and Mergen loosed his seven nailhead arrows again and again, but there was no end to the creatures.

Qiu Yongsi looked around and yelped. "Don't come near me! Don't! Hongjun, where are you going?!"

A-Tai and Mergen let out simultaneous roars of fury as wave after wave of ao fish launched themselves at them. "Qiu Yongsi!" yelled A-Tai.

Mergen, too, had reached the end of his patience. *"Do something!"*

Smiling, Qiu Yongsi said, "You can do it. I'm cheering you all—"

Before he could say *on*, Mergen let an ao fish slip past him to crash into Qiu Yongsi. Qiu Yongsi shrieked, terrified out of his wits. He scrabbled inside his lapels without a trace of his usual elegant demeanor, but the ao fish pinned him to the ground before he could grab whatever he was looking for.

"Get it off me!" Qiu Yongsi wailed.

The ao fish opened its gaping maw. Its tongue, damp and sticky with saliva, darted out to wrap around Qiu Yongsi's neck.

Finally snapping, Qiu Yongsi roared, "Get the fuck off me!"

His hand emerged from his pocket clutching an ink brush. A-Tai and Mergen, fending off the waves of ao fish swarming them like a school of migrating carp, suddenly felt their feet float off the ground.

"Aaaaaaaaahhhh—" Qiu Yongsi screamed, hysterical. "Get the hell away! Get away from me!"

The others stared, speechless.

The brush stabbed a series of points in the air. With a soft rustling sound, the ao fish leading the charge melted into a puddle of ink, which was whisked away as if by some overwhelming force.

A-Tai and Mergen looked back at Qiu Yongsi. Chest heaving as he recovered from his shock, Qiu Yongsi clutched a white marble brush, quaking in his boots. The brush flashed with light, and countless trails of ink emanated from its brightness like the tails of a thousand comets.

"Monster!" Qiu Yongsi wailed, raising his brush again.

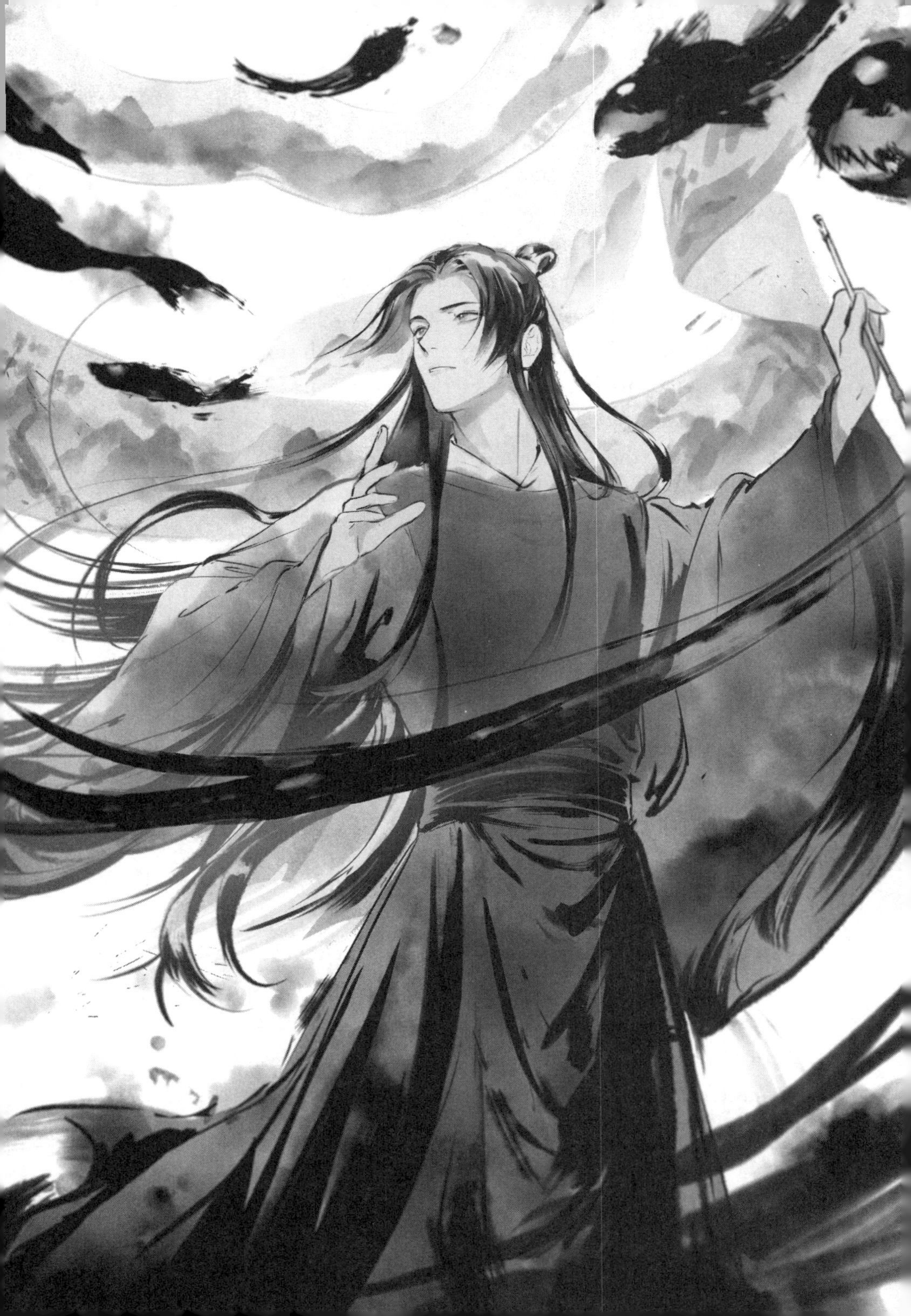

Mergen and A-Tai both paused their attacks. Qiu Yongsi swished his brush—in a blink, the entire plaza transformed, becoming an ink painting. Every ao fish dissolved into swimming traces of ink that were whipped away as the space between heaven and earth turned white as a sheet of paper. Dark ripples spread outward from Qiu Yongsi's feet as the columns, the palace walls, and even the surrounding hills were pulled into the painting.

Swept up by that strange power, the ao fish swam laps around the plaza. Qiu Yongsi's brush had somehow transformed the dangerous scene into a beautiful work of art depicting a hundred fishes dancing in the warmth of spring.

"Took you long enough!" Mergen roared.

A-Tai could have died from fury. "Why didn't you use your spiritual device sooner?!"

Qiu Yongsi gasped for breath, his expression blank with bewilderment.

"Wow, he did it! He did it! Look! What happened?" Hongjun could tell the world had changed around them, but he couldn't say exactly what the strangeness was. As he watched, the scenery began to warp and twist.

"Stop gawking!" Li Jinglong shouted. "This is our chance, quick!"

"Wait, hold on…" Hongjun felt himself floating, his feet lifting off the ground.

Li Jinglong drew his arm back to stab at the cloud of black energy that was Fei'ao when he, too, began to levitate. The edges of the ink painting spread at a speed visible to the naked eye as the black energy continued to vibrate and howl, attempting to flee but finding it impossible to control its own movements.

"Stop using your technique!" Li Jinglong looked down and shouted at Qiu Yongsi.

"Stop playing around!" A-Tai and Mergen yelled in unison.

"First you tell me to attack, and now you tell me to stop! What do you want from me?!" Qiu Yongsi cried, his temper flaring.

The entire plaza had turned into an enormous ink painting laid flat against the ground. All the surrounding scenery had been sucked in and flattened, becoming part of the picture. A ball of black fire charged back and forth across the surface, trying to escape, while Qiu Yongsi clutched his brush and cried in a trembling voice, "I can't hold it much longer! I'm releasing it! Watch out, everyone!"

"Do it!" Li Jinglong yelled.

Shrouded in dark fire, Fei'ao let out a furious roar, using the last of his strength to hurl a wave of scales from his own body.

The burst of yao energy tore Qiu Yongsi's painting to shreds. Qiu Yongsi stumbled back a step, spitting blood from the force of the backlash. At the same time, Hongjun and Li Jinglong began their descent. Hongjun swiped a hand through the air to block the roiling black energy with his sacred light.

"Your sword!" Hongjun yelled.

As they neared the ground, Li Jinglong pulled Hongjun close. Wielding his sword one-handed, he stabbed through the shield of sacred light, piercing the barrier to plunge the tip of the sword into Fei'ao's chest as the yaoguai gave one last enraged howl.

Fei'ao's cries ground to a halt. A shock wave rippled out from where he stood as he slowly turned to ash, sending brick and tile flying. With the painting ripped, the clouds of black energy dissolved around each of the swimming ao fish, who recovered their human forms as they tumbled toward the corners of the plaza.

At the moment of its death, the yaoguai exploded into plumes of black energy. Face to face with Hongjun as they fell, Li Jinglong pressed a palm to the flat of his blade and spun it through the air, flipping their positions to cushion Hongjun's fall.

Li Jinglong grunted in pain as he landed flat on his back. A split second later, Hongjun crashed down on top of him, kneeing him in the stomach as he slammed into the ground. Li Jinglong flailed like Zhao Zilong flopping around on land. Qi and blood roiled through his body, and he went limp on the marble tile.

The morning sun had begun to rise in the east, cresting the mountains as it spilled its golden light over Daming Palace and the Divine Land. With effort, Hongjun climbed off of Li Jinglong and shook him by the shoulders. "Chief! Chief! Are you all right?!"

Li Jinglong felt as if he'd been trampled by a herd of elephants. "My ribs…" he groaned. "Are they broken? I think I have internal injuries…"

"I have medicine!" Hongjun said. "I promise, you'll be better in no time."

Li Jinglong didn't know what to say.

A-Tai, Mergen, and Qiu Yongsi ran over as Hongjun slung Li Jinglong's arm over his own shoulders and helped him upright.

The rear plaza was littered with unconscious servants and guards, and Daming Palace's rear hall, side hall, and courtyard were utterly destroyed. Broken shards of pottery and gilt vessels lay strewn across the ground; the structural casualties included seven pillars and three walls, as well as countless windows, doors, and colored-glass folding screens.

The sun slanted over the walls, turning the shattered baubles into a sea of gold.

"Chief, is there something you wanted to say?" Hongjun looked up at Li Jinglong, whose expression had turned queer.

"I was going to say..." Li Jinglong sucked in a deep breath and cried in dismay, "The damages—just how much are we going to have to pay, huh?!"

Have to pay, huh? ...to pay, huh? ...pay, huh?

His cry echoed through the mountains beneath the rising autumn sun.

The carp yao was washing Hongjun's clothes in the courtyard under the same bright sunlight. His efforts always left Hongjun's clothes smelling of mud and raw fish, but Hongjun never cared. He was lucky enough to have someone washing his clothes for him when he was away from home.

The carp yao did care, however. He cared whether Hongjun was getting laughed at when he wasn't there to see, and he worried that Hongjun smelled too strongly of fish. He always insisted the boy spend time with his new friends, but him? Well, he would simply stay home and mind the house.

At least that's what he told himself. How could the carp yao not feel a bit dejected when he was left behind, as if he wasn't needed anymore? He could only comfort himself with the thought that all kids grew up someday.

"I should light some incense to scent these clothes," the carp yao muttered, "so Hongjun won't be excluded."

He bounded off to find the incense, sighing as he went.

Outside the courtyard, the exorcists had arrived at the gate. The group was supporting Li Jinglong, who looked as if he was on death's door.

"Let's lay him down here," Hongjun said to the others.

"You're back?" the carp yao asked. "How did it go?"

Everyone sprawled out haphazardly in the entrance hall. Li Jinglong slumped over, his eyes dead and spiritless.

"You failed?" The carp yao was secretly pleased. "I just knew I should have gone with you."

"We slew the yaoguai, but we didn't find my throwing knife," Hongjun said.

The carp yao consoled him at once, assuring him that they could keep searching.

"You've all worked hard today," Li Jinglong said, "Go get some rest; as for everything else…I'll think of something."

Everyone came forward to give Li Jinglong sympathetic pats on the shoulder, then retired to their rooms.

Li Jinglong, however, stumbled to the main office. He pressed a hand to his forehead, spacing out behind his desk. The carp yao, having followed him in, asked, "What's the matter?"

"Give me some time to myself; I want some peace and quiet…"

"If it all becomes too much, you could try taking a sniff of oblivion pollen. We've already restocked," the carp yao said on his way out.

With a pained smile, Li Jinglong asked, "How much did it cost?"

"Three thousand, two hundred taels, same as last time," the carp yao said. "A-Tai told the shopkeeper to put it on a tab so we can pay on the first of the month."

Li Jinglong stared ahead in silence. He obviously couldn't pull a hit-and-run after leaving Daming Palace in that state. Nor could he make everyone sniff oblivion pollen, or the palace servants' heads would roll.

The yao were already gone, but he still needed to explain the mess he'd made of the palace, the city gate, and Hu Sheng's residence in the Longwu Guard Garrison. He fetched a brush to write out and sign an official statement. If the Shenwu Guard and the Court of Judicial Review came to investigate or the emperor were to inquire, or if the Ministry of Works needed to make repairs, they could use the signed statement to hold him responsible.

Ah, forget it. Sleep comes first. Li Jinglong peeled off his dirty outer robe and tossed it aside, lying down right then and there. He could worry about it after he woke up.

Everyone's doors were closed, the exhausted exorcists having passed out without even taking breakfast. After finishing the laundry, the carp yao returned to the pond to watch the clouds drift across the sky in a daze.

The sun began to dip toward the west, but no one stirred even after it had long passed its zenith.

Late in the afternoon, the sound of hoofbeats and rolling wheels marked the arrival of one carriage after another, until no fewer than five different vehicles were parked outside the department's gates.

The carp yao, ever vigilant, stuck his head out of the water. His mouth opened and closed as he pondered whether to wake Li Jinglong.

"His Majesty, the enlightened and valiant Son of Heaven has arrived—" a eunuch's voice declared from outside the gate.

"The noble consort has arrived—"

Recalling Feng Changqing's voice warning that he'd be taken to the emperor and his consort "for their entertainment" if discovered, the carp yao leapt from the pond and hid himself in the bamboo growing thickly along the wall.

"The Junior Grand Chancellor has arrived—"

"The Duchess of Qin has arrived—"

"The Duchess of Guo has arrived—"

All the doors inside the Department of Exorcism were still tightly shut, its residents sound asleep.

"Where is the chief of the Department of Demonic Exorcism, Li Jinglong? Come out at once. His Majesty has arrived—"

"There's no need for such formality. We shall go inside and take a look..."

"Oh my, the decor in here is rather unique..."

"Huh? Jiejie, which Buddha is this?"

"He is called Acalanatha, a vanquisher of evil."

"Oh! Well, it's quite appropriate for the setting, then, isn't it?"

"Mrow—"

"We heard Duke Di purchased this little courtyard residence when he was still in Chang'an. As time went on, it fell into disrepair. We were considering sending some workmen to fix it up."

"Your Majesty, it seems your concerns were unfounded. The Li family was once a prominent clan, and though it has fallen on hard times, I see its members still appreciate the finer things... Where is Li Jinglong? Li Jinglong?!"

Yang Guozhong, Li Longji, Yang Yuhuan, the Duchess of Guo, and the Duchess of Qin all stood in the main courtyard as the eunuch shouted, "Chief Li! His Majesty is here to see you!"

Li Longji sucked in a deep breath and unleashed a shout worthy of the Son of Heaven, his voice ringing like a bell. "Li Jinglong!"

Everyone broke into laughter as Li Jinglong, well and truly frightened, ran out from the main office, barefoot and dressed only in his undergarments. He gawked at the visitors in the courtyard, his hair mussed from sleep.

"Where is everyone?!" Yang Guozhong blustered. "Does the Department of Exorcism have no one in its employ?"

"Who is it?" A-Tai ran outside, clad in silk pajamas. Hongjun, Qiu Yongsi, and Mergen followed, all barefoot as they stood in the courtyard, staring left and right.

Li Longji had arrived in casual clothing, and Li Jinglong hadn't recognized him at first glance—but he would know Yang Guozhong anywhere. His heart lurched in his chest.

"Why is everyone asleep in the middle of the day?" Li Longji chuckled.

No one could muster a response.

Li Jinglong inwardly sighed. "We were on a yao hunt last night and didn't sleep until after dawn. My apologies, this subject has been lax in enforcing discipline."

He dropped to one knee, but Li Longji stepped forward to pull him to his feet, evidently unoffended by their state of undress. He walked over to the others lined up behind Li Jinglong, smiling brightly. "Then you must be Jinglong's subordinates? What are your names?"

One by one, the exorcists cupped their fists and answered, but none bowed nor offered any more formal show of obeisance. The customs of Great Tang were relaxed with regard to etiquette, and it wasn't mandatory to kneel when greeting the emperor—but none of these young men held official positions. It was the first time the emperor had encountered ordinary citizens who unabashedly refused to offer their sovereign a formal greeting.

Yang Guozhong had drawn himself up to scold them when the noble consort Yang Yuhuan waved him off with a small smile, signaling that it was no great matter.

"You all helped my sister find Qing'er," Yang Yuhuan said warmly. "We came today to offer our gratitude. Qing'er is my sister's entire life, and she cried over her many times in the days she was lost."

"Sister!" the Duchess of Qin interrupted Yang Yuhuan as Li Longji dissolved into laughter. The noble consort's interjection had lightened the atmosphere considerably.

This was Hongjun's first time meeting the Son of Heaven, bearer of the Ziwei Star's protection. Curious, he threw glance after glance at Li Longji's face. He had an energetic sort of visage, with the imposing aura appropriate for a ruler, but the way he spoke was casual. The faintest of shadows hung over his brow.

Yang Yuhuan, meanwhile, had an astonishingly lovely face, which seemed almost to shine like the bright moon; her very presence bathed the Department of Exorcism in a luminous glow. She was picturesque from every angle. Standing behind the noble consort was the Duchess of Qin. Her comeliness faded in comparison, though she herself was a gentle beauty comparable to one of the legendary four, Xi Shi. At the back of the group was the Duchess of Guo, who was a few years older than her sisters. She had a dignified and imposing air and wore no hint of a smile on her face.

Their cousin, Chancellor Yang Guozhong, had a stately mien and was exceptionally tall in stature. When he stood before Li Jinglong—especially as Li Jinglong lowered his head—it was clear that he was in fact a bit taller than the towering chief exorcist.

"In any case, we came to express our gratitude..." Yang Yuhuan began again. She smiled easily, as if she had many sources of joy in her life.

"My thanks to the noble consort for your favor," Li Jinglong replied hastily.

Like Hongjun, the other three exorcists brazenly looked their visitors up and down, not missing a single detail.

"Here." Yang Yuhuan personally lifted the lid from a box packed with Hongjun's favorite pastries. "The housekeeper said there was a lad here who enjoyed these. Which young man was that?"

"So much of the people's lifeblood?!" Hongjun cried out upon seeing the pile of golden sticky rice cakes. "Amazing!"

There was a long stretch of awkward silence before Yang Yuhuan said, "What?"

She still hadn't quite processed the words when Li Jinglong jumped in: "Thank the noble consort for her favor!"

"Thanks!" Overjoyed, Hongjun accepted the box stacked with three layers of the little pastries, each one piled higher than the last.

Yang Yuhuan looked pointedly from Li Jinglong to Hongjun before turning back to Li Jinglong again. "Jinglong," she said with a smile, "His Majesty said we should offer you a reward. But I told him seeing your special someone happy is better than any reward for yourself. Isn't that right?"

Li Jinglong was dumbstruck. Li Longji patted him on the shoulder. "It's about time you settled down."

He hadn't quite puzzled out what the emperor meant by this odd remark when A-Tai burst out laughing. Hongjun, still basking in the joy of his new box of pastries, wore a look of confusion.

Unbeknownst to them, the Duchess of Qin's housekeeper had given her a full account of Li Jinglong's visit to return the cat, including the fact that he'd been accompanied by a young man who'd taken a great liking to the estate's pastries. Amused, the duchess had in turn recounted the story to Yang Yuhuan. The three sisters were sharp women. Noting that Li Jinglong had yet to marry and now seemed to enjoy the company of a young man, they hit upon the idea of catering to his interests by lavishing this young man with the delicacy he'd so favored—thereby resolving the tricky issue of how to reward Li Jinglong. They'd been giggling about the clever ploy they'd devised the whole carriage ride over.

These days, the customs of Great Tang were quite open. Li Longji had no particular fondness for cut-sleeves, but since Yang Yuhuan had expressed her support of the two, he let her do as she wished.

Li Jinglong had a talent for reading people. Noting their reactions, he quickly guessed at some of these twists and turns of their convoluted reasoning, and his handsome face went red to his ears.

"Just a little joke," Yang Yuhuan said cheerfully. "Jinglong still deserves a reward, of course."

She raised a hand, and the attending eunuchs brought over trays containing twenty small silver ingots, each two taels in weight, and ten bolts of navy-blue silk brocade. Li Jinglong hurried to express his gratitude. Yang Guozhong shook a scolding finger at Li Jinglong, but didn't elaborate. After a quick tour of the premises, Li Longji and the rest prepared to depart.

"Come, Qing'er, say goodbye to Chief Li." The Duchess of Qin waved the cat's paw at Li Jinglong.

Li Jinglong hesitated, unsure whether he was supposed to take the animal's paw. Hongjun laughed and came over to stroke the cat's head. The cat stretched its front paws toward Hongjun, as if it wanted to crawl into his arms. Li Jinglong could have screamed in frustration. *Hurry up and see these guests out; why are you courting their attention?*

Fortunately, the Duchess of Qin merely smiled and carried the cat away, climbing gracefully into her carriage. The exorcists stepped out the front gate to see them off.

"The Son of Heaven departs for Mount Li!" the eunuch outside announced.

The procession that followed, replete with ceremonial arms and accompanied by both the Longwu and Shenwu Guards, left Hongjun slack-jawed as it wound its way out of the alley and headed for the hot springs of Huaqing Pool at the base of Mount Li.

The exorcists, still dressed in their plain white undergarments, were left standing in the courtyard barefooted. Seeing the coast was clear, the carp yao finally slipped out of the bamboo and dove into the pond with a *plop*.

20
PERSIAN PRINCE

As the exorcists took their places at the table for their dinner that night, Li Jinglong pointed an accusatory chopstick at his subordinates. "Look at you all. You should at least kneel before the emperor, even if it's just for show."

"Who can remember all of that?" said Mergen.

A-Tai was the picture of innocence. "My family has a special dispensation. We didn't even kneel before the Taizong Emperor."

Li Jinglong blinked.

"To tell the truth, Chief," Mergen said, "my family's status is special too. We're not required to kneel before the emperor of the central lands; a simple greeting suffices."

At a glance from Li Jinglong, Qiu Yongsi offered, "My family... counts sages among our ancestors. We don't have to kneel...um, we don't have to kneel to ordinary mortals."

Li Jinglong raised a hand to stop him. *Okay, fine, well I knelt, so it's not your problem.*

Hongjun was still munching on his mountain of pastries, on which he had been snacking since noon. Li Jinglong gave him a look. "So, what are your glorious origins?"

"My dad said our family doesn't even kneel to the Jade Emperor or the Buddha."

Everyone stared in stunned silence.

"Hongjun!" Portioning rice into bowls beside the table, the carp yao admonished him before he could spill too many details about his background.

"But if you remind me ahead of time," Hongjun continued, "I don't mind kneeling. My dad won't know either way. I'm just worried that if I were to kneel to someone of a lower status, it would take years off their lifespan... Isn't that what people say?"

Qiu Yongsi burst out laughing. "The next time you see a monster, just drop to your knees and knock your head on the ground a few times, and you can rob it of its lifespan all at once. Think of the effort we'll save!"

"That's right!" Hongjun thought the idea made quite a bit of sense. Maybe next time he would give it a try.

"All of you..." Li Jinglong was at the end of his patience. "Hurry up and eat. Hongjun, stop stuffing yourself with those pastries; you won't have room for dinner."

Hongjun scoffed, taking it as a challenge. "You're underestimating me!"

Li Jinglong was still beset by worry. After a day's sleep, he'd still made no progress toward resolving any of his concerns. With so many loose ends, the Department of Exorcism couldn't mark the case closed. Hongjun's throwing knife had yet to be found, and Daming Palace would soon come knocking to seek compensation for the wreck they'd left it in. The conversation they had overheard between Fei'ao and Jinyun hinted at some greater plot... *Ah, forget it. Dinner first, the rest after. Worries are always worse on an empty stomach.*

Everyone ate in silence, absorbed in their own thoughts. At last, Li Jinglong set down his bowl and heaved a sigh. Qiu Yongsi rose to make tea, while A-Tai comforted Li Jinglong with a sunny smile. "Chief, no obstacle is insurmountable. Let's have a chat."

"What is it now?!" Li Jinglong's scalp prickled. "No more!" He looked at his subordinates dubiously, afraid they were up to some new trouble.

"There are certain things we can't keep from you forever..." A-Tai began.

Li Jinglong's heart sank like a stone. But whether he listened or not, he was doomed, so he said, "Fine! It's my unlucky day—just say it. Even if I lose my head, it'll only be a scar the size of my neck."

"It's not quite that serious," A-Tai said. "Chief, to be honest... I lied before. My surname isn't Hammurabi. It's Yazdegerd—my full name is Tigra Yazdegerd. I'm not Tokharian. My ancestral home is in Persia."

Li Jinglong was mystified. "So what? Yazdegerd..." He trailed off, stunned, upon realizing the significance of the name. Voice shaking, he squeaked, "You...you're the Sasanian...crown prince?!"

"Crown prince of the *former* Sasanian dynasty, to be precise," A-Tai said with a touch of melancholy. "After all, my father, grandfather, mother—my whole family—have all passed. I'm the only one left."

Hongjun hadn't the faintest clue what this "Sasanian dynasty" might be, but hearing A-Tai speak of his family reminded him of his own experiences. He couldn't help but pat A-Tai's shoulder in sympathy.

Li Jinglong was still thunderstruck. Frowning, he asked, "Why haven't you...gone to see His Majesty?"

"My clan failed to fulfill a promise we once made." A-Tai ran a hand through his curly brown hair and quietly continued, "In the Battle of Talas, my great-grandfather lost the Protectorate to Pacify the West, which was granted to him by Great Tang. My grandfather borrowed troops from Great Tang to restore our nation, but..."

"But the troops left after escorting him to Tokharistan," Li Jinglong supplied.

A-Tai looked at him in surprise. "You know his story?"

Li Jinglong responded with a question. "What happened next?"

A-Tai sighed and explained: The House of Sasan lost Persia many years ago, when their capital was seized by the Tajik army; the royal family had lived in exile ever since.

Three generations ago, A-Tai's great-grandfather, Yazdegerd the Third, had borrowed troops from Great Tang to successfully establish the Protectorate to Pacify the West, as well as the Area Command of Persia in Jiling City later on. But the good times didn't last. Within a few years, Persia's last surviving territory also fell to the Tajiks, even with Tang aid.

A-Tai's grandfather, Peroz, took his father, Narsieh, and returned to Chang'an to borrow troops once again. Emperor Gaozong, Li Zhi, acquiesced to their request and deployed the army to escort the Persians to their ancestral lands. However, the military commander in charge, Pei Xingjian, departed after escorting the unfortunate prince of Persia to Tokharistan. With no Tang troops to support him, Peroz's mission was suspended for decades. Morale plummeted, and his army splintered.

By the time Narsieh made his way back to the Central Plains, he found a completely different Great Tang awaiting him. The Emperor Zhongzong, Li Xian, granted him the title of General of the Left Flank, but made no mention of lending troops. A short two years later, seeing no hope of restoring his nation, Narsieh returned to Tokharistan. Ten years later, he had a son named Tigra—this was A-Tai, who stood before them now.

Since the fall of Persia, four generations of its princes had traveled far and wide, from the Western Regions to the Central Plains and back again, in pursuit of the distant dream of restoring their kingdom. Spoken from A-Tai's lips on this autumn night, it was a desolate and despairing tale.

"Pei Xingjian was my grandfather," Li Jinglong said at last.

A-Tai was silent.

"I'm sorry about what happened back then." Li Jinglong sighed.

"Oh, what does it have to do with you?" A-Tai suddenly let out a laugh. "Had it been me, after realizing there was no hope, I wouldn't have sacrificed the lives of twenty thousand soldiers in the Western Regions, either."

Li Jinglong sighed again as Mergen spoke up. "Tajik has a fierce army of brave soldiers. It's unwise to fight them head-on for long. You must find a way to defeat them from within."

A-Tai nodded. "I know. Before my father passed, he told me to give up. He said, 'A-Tai, I hope you can live your own life. Don't do what your grandfather and I did, and devote your entire life to…'" He trailed off and fell quiet.

After a long silence, Hongjun said, "But you still want to do it, don't you?"

A-Tai smiled, though it was a mournful expression. Hongjun understood. Just before he left the mountain, Chong Ming and Qing Xiong had expressed similar wishes for him. They had both said not to worry about the tasks he'd been set, yet Hongjun was still determined to complete them.

But what made him feel the greatest sympathy for A-Tai was the fact that the person who had placed those burdens on his shoulders was already dead.

"How many of your men remain?" Li Jinglong asked. "Did you bring them with you?"

A-Tai's eyes sparked with hope at Li Jinglong's direct questions.

"They're all in Tokharistan," he said. "Just over a hundred men. A friend of mine is leading them, for the time being."

Li Jinglong heaved one more long, deep sigh and rose to leave the courtyard. After thinking for a moment, he asked, "A-Tai, where did you learn all of your skills?"

Zoroastrianism, the national religion of Persia, had been suppressed after the fall of the Sasanian Empire, A-Tai explained. The last dastur of Persia had taken A-Tai as his sole disciple, teaching him how to summon whirlwinds with his holy fan and wield his four rings of fire, earth, lightning, and water. A-Tai was regarded as the sacred prince who would restore their sect and nation to their former glory—but in the end, the dastur died even before his father, Narsieh, who was already fifty years old when A-Tai was born. There were quite a few followers of Zoroastrianism left in the Central Plains, but the religion was practically extinct in the Tajik empire.

"What can I do to help you?" Li Jinglong asked.

"I'm willing to devote my strength to the service of Chang'an," A-Tai said. "Great Tang has always been Persia's most faithful ally. I will do anything you command, but I hope that one day, the emperor of Great Tang may be willing to lend me an army to restore my nation."

Everyone knew this was no easy ask. Forget the problems posed by offending the Tajik empire—even if the emperor was to send his men, what were their chances of victory?

"I'll do my best," Li Jinglong said, earnestly. "But we'll have to take it one step at a time."

A-Tai nodded. "I've known this since before I came to Chang'an. Every era of prosperity is as fragile as a basket of eggs. If we cannot defeat the yao king in Chang'an, Great Tang will be in danger itself, and there will be no army for me to borrow."

Li Jinglong frowned. "The yao king?"

"Anywhere a large number of yao gather," Qiu Yongsi said placidly, "a yao king will appear. The Chang'an of today has two kings: The Son of Heaven and descendant of the Imperial Dragon we met today rules in the light, while the yao king who controls the thousands of yao in this city rules in the shadows."

Mergen hesitated before speaking. "I don't know about Hongjun, but to tell the truth…the rest of us are all here for the yao king."

"And where is this yao king?"

Li Jinglong had only just finished his question when a guest appeared at their door.

"Chief Li of the Department of Demonic Exorcism." It was the registrar, Lian Hao, who had visited them some days ago. He politely declared from the door, "Deputy Chief Justice Huang Yong of the Court of Judicial Review extends his invitation."

Li Jinglong's heart thudded in his chest—the destruction in Daming Palace had been discovered. The others looked at each other and prepared to stand up, but Li Jinglong held a hand up to forestall them, insisting he'd smooth things over himself.

"They're not gonna tie him up and beat him, are they?" The prisoners' screams Hongjun had heard the last time he went to the Court of Judicial Review had left a strong impression.

"Of course not," Qiu Yongsi comforted him. "If he's not back by tomorrow morning, we'll come up with a plan to save him."

"We've spent all our money, and now we've gotten ourselves into a heap of trouble," A-Tai said. "We don't know anyone in Chang'an. How are we supposed to save him?"

Mergen put a hand to his forehead. They had gone to so much effort to catch those yao, and now they had to rescue their own boss. Where had it all gone wrong?

"Come on now!" Seeing that the atmosphere had gotten heavy, A-Tai suggested, "Forget all these troubles. Let me play you a song!"

"Do you think the chief took what we said about the yao king seriously?" Qiu Yongsi couldn't help asking.

Plucking the strings of his barbat, A-Tai said, "I think he did. As for the rest of you... It's best if you don't say too much."

Hongjun furrowed his brow in confusion.

"That includes you," Mergen said to Hongjun. "Hongjun, you trust people way too easily."

Hongjun had never expected A-Tai to be the exiled prince of Persia. He figured the other two must have secrets of their own as well. "Are you guys princes too?" he asked.

He thought Mergen and Qiu Yongsi would laugh, but to his astonishment, Mergen nodded. "In a sense."

"Um..." Qiu Yongsi said. "It's hard to say. I'm not sure, but I can probably be considered one, if you stretch the definition—if you're willing to accept me."

The carp yao crawled out of the pond and rested his head on the ledge. "My Hongjun is a prince too. Who isn't, these days?"

Everyone laughed at that. A-Tai leaned forward to give Hongjun a high five. "I knew it!"

"That's great!"

Everyone felt much closer after learning of their shared status. A-Tai was about to start playing when Hongjun said, "A-Tai, wait. I do want to listen to your song, but let me ask one last thing. Where is the yao king?"

A-Tai looked up, and everyone went quiet for a beat.

"You're looking for him too?" Mergen asked.

Hongjun made a few mental calculations, then looked to the carp yao. When Zhao Zilong didn't jump to interrupt, he nodded in response.

"Why?" Qiu Yongsi asked.

"Ah, forget it." Mergen signaled Qiu Yongsi not to press him and said, "It doesn't matter right now. Hongjun, you're on our side."

"Of course." Hongjun could see what Mergen was trying to tell him. He said firmly, "Whether we subdue or slay him, I am his enemy."

Everyone's expressions showed their relief. Qiu Yongsi paced back and forth across the courtyard and said, "The yao king has yet to reveal himself. No one knows his identity nor his true form. But one thing is certain: He is very close to the emperor, perhaps even right by his side."

"It's a black jiao," Hongjun said.

The other three started in surprise. Mergen unconsciously licked his lips as Qiu Yongsi declared, "I knew it! Let's just keep our eyes peeled; there'll be some sort of clue eventually. I'm not so worried about where it's hiding—I'm more concerned whether we'll be a match for it with our current ability."

Hongjun sighed. "My four throwing knives can only be used to their full potential if I can recover the lost lightning blade. Right now, they're only useful against low-level yao. They won't be anywhere near enough."

Out of all of them, there was no doubt Hongjun was the most mysterious. He hadn't mentioned where he came from, but given his naivete about the mortal world, he was likely the disciple of some ascended immortal. Since he never spoke of his background, the others hadn't pried.

"So then, Kong Hongjun, you came to Chang'an to defeat the yao king too," A-Tai said.

All three looked intently at Hongjun as he nodded. "Yes."

The other exorcists looked like a burden had been lifted from their shoulders. Clearly, they had discussed Hongjun's true identity in depth. The most common hypothesis was that he was a yao—he was escorted by a carp yao, after all—and might not really be on their side. But as long as their immediate goals were the same, there was plenty of room for compromise.

"To celebrate our common goal of subduing the yao king of Chang'an," A-Tai said, "let us have a fervent and impassioned battle song!"

Everyone whooped in joy. No matter what struggles lay ahead, there was still room for an occasional bit of mindless fun. A-Tai began to strum his lute, while Hongjun beat out a rhythm on the bottom of a bowl. Everyone raised their voices in song.

Across the city, Li Jinglong stood in the brightly lit interrogation room of the Court of Judicial Review, exhausted in body and soul. The carp yao had put too much salt in their dinner that night, so he was thirsty to boot.

Facing him were the Minister of Works, Qin Xiaokang; the Minister of Justice, Wen You; Deputy Chief Justice Huang Yong of the Court of Judicial Review; Li Jinglong's former superior and captain of the Longwu Guard, Hu Sheng; Captain Tu Ziwen of the Shenwu Guard; the Minister of Rites; the steward of Daming Palace; and, front and center, Gao Lishi, the Chief Eunuch—a full assembly of the highest officials of the imperial court. It was an inquiry in name only; in truth, it was only a set of manacles short of an interrogation.

If only he had Qiu Yongsi's spiritual techniques, Li Jinglong reflected, he could pack all these people into a painting with a wave of his hand, restoring quiet to his ears and peace to all of Great Tang.

"I have told the entire tale, from beginning to end, three times," Li Jinglong said. "I swear, I haven't missed a single detail."

Gao Lishi's power was like that of the midday sun—direct and inescapable. The Department of Exorcism technically fell under Yang Guozhong's supervision and, by virtue of the chancellor's reputation and position, could get away with causing minor disturbances. But this time, Li Jinglong and his subordinates had destroyed at least a tenth of Daming Palace, only to claim afterward that they were capturing a yao monster. How were they meant to resolve this mess?

"I believe you, myself," Gao Lishi said with a smile. "But what am I to report to His Majesty?"

"The truth." Li Jinglong didn't let a trace of fear show on his face. "Yao have threatened Chang'an for a long time now. This is only the beginning. We will find the yao king behind all of this sooner or later—the great General Gao will have all the more to report to His Majesty then."

Everyone was startled by this pronouncement.

Wen You, the Minister of Justice, had already lost patience with the questioning. "This is absurd. Li Jinglong, have you gone mad?"

Li Jinglong burst into laughter. "Have I? Then how do you explain the testimonies of the Daming Palace servants who witnessed the incident with their own eyes, or the sentries who saw the monster overleap the city gates? Captain Hu, you've apparently gone mad, as well!"

A strange expression came over Hu Sheng's face as he finally realized he had fallen into Li Jinglong's trap. This time, it seemed, Li Jinglong was determined to have a witness on his side no matter what;

Hu Sheng could find no excuse to demur. "It's as Li Jinglong says—I did see a fox yao with my own eyes. I know nothing about the rest."

Gao Lishi's eyebrows shot toward his hairline. Qin Xiaokang, the Minister of Works, interjected, "Even if this is true, how do you intend to explain the destruction of Daming Palace?"

"The monster destroyed it," Li Jinglong said. "It was no fault of mine, nor of my subordinates."

"Do you mean to say we should go find the monster to demand recompense?" the Minister of Rites asked, laying a deliberate emphasis on each word.

Frustration crept into Li Jinglong's voice. "My lords, do you know how many people might have died if we hadn't stopped those monsters from rampaging through Chang'an?"

"Li Jinglong." Gao Lishi frowned, impatient. "That's enough. Don't make any more excuses for yourself. You're dismissed."

Li Jinglong was struck by a wave of fury. Before he could entirely lose control and shout at the ministers, a pair of guards from the Court of Judicial Review grabbed him from both sides and began to escort him from the room.

"The noble consort personally assigned this madman to his position," Qin Xiaokang was saying. "We meant to appease him with a meaningless title. We never expected him to cause so much trouble right after taking up his post..."

These were the last words Li Jinglong heard before the doors of the interrogation room closed behind him. The guards brought him to the pitch-dark training field outside the courtroom and told him to await the results of the deliberation there.

"Well, do any of you believe him?" Gao Lishi asked.

The officials all looked at each other in turn, no one brave enough to speak first. They did believe him, for the most part—there was no other explanation for the many strange things that had occurred. But they couldn't simply tell the Son of Heaven that yao monsters were running wild in Chang'an.

"The way I see it," Huang Yong offered, "we'd be better off saying a stray whirlwind swept through Daming Palace in the middle of the night and destroyed some buildings that were weak in their construction. We close this case, and the Ministry of Works can simply send some skilled workmen to complete repairs with all haste..."

The Minister of Works harrumphed, as if to say, *Why should my Ministry of Works take the blame for trouble caused by your Court of Judicial Review?*

Gao Lishi spread his hands, a smile on his face. "The Department of Demonic Exorcism falls under Chancellor Yang's purview. What else can we do?"

"It seems the Right Chancellor does not yet know of these events," said Wen You, the Minister of Justice.

"This time, we'll smooth things over out of respect for the Right Chancellor—but what about the next?" Qin Xiaokang scoffed. "Are we to do the same for every new disaster?"

"What more can I do?" Gao Lishi asked with a genial expression. "I'm frustrated too. I should be at home enjoying a drink right now, yet instead I was summoned here in the middle of the night to listen to this tall tale."

"If you believe it's true," Huang Yong said, "then it's not a tall tale. Di-lao[14] established the Department of Demonic Exorcism precisely for..."

"Whether it's true or not," the Minister of Justice cut in, "if this gets out, the people of Chang'an will panic. Who knows what will happen then? No, we can't let him continue on like this. We must

---

14 *A suffix attached to the surname of venerated elders.*

shut down this ridiculous department. No matter how fierce yao may be, they are still creatures of flesh and blood. Is the Court of Judicial Review really so incapable of capturing them?"

Wen You was Huang Yong's immediate superior. Now that he'd spoken, Huang Yong could only shut up and nod.

"The noble consort personally appointed..." Gao Lishi began.

"General Gao." Wen You sat forward. "Not even Chancellor Yang will be spared if you allow this bastard to continue to go around causing mayhem!"

Gao Lishi's eyes swept back and forth, but he didn't speak further.

"If Daming Palace collapses, it can be rebuilt," the Minister of Rites said. "But what if the next thing they destroy is an imperial ancestral shrine?"

Gao Lishi shuddered and finally conceded the point. "In any case, we must at least notify the chancellor," Gao Lishi said thoughtfully. "We have to show the noble consort sufficient respect."

"Of course," the others agreed. As they reached a consensus, the court clerk immediately set to writing up the transfer order for Li Jinglong.

"Don't go through the Chancellery," Wen You chimed in. "I'll pay a visit to the Ministry of Personnel myself tomorrow. Li Jinglong's reassignment order for the Department of Exorcism can't have been fully processed yet; I'll simply intercept it."

Gao Lishi nodded. "I'll take care of His Majesty's imperial edict and Chancellor Yang. Captain Hu, as his former commanding officer, I'll leave the next arrangements for Li Jinglong to you. Don't let him get up to any more mischief. I'll also trouble you to notify Feng Changqing."

What could Hu Sheng say? He nodded, bending his mouth in a smile.

With a final bang of the gavel, the deed was done. The Department of Demonic Exorcism was to be abolished, lest those troublemakers cause all of them to lose their official titles and heads alike. Wise as the Son of Heaven was, he could do nothing when dragged down by deadweight ministers such as these. One had only to consider the Lai Junchen incident of the previous reign—in which even members of the imperial family had been maliciously implicated in false crimes—as well as scores of others like it. Officials might lose their heads as easily as wheat fell to the scythe. Naturally, this decision was fully necessary.

21
THE NAME OF AN ANCIENT SWORD

LI JINGLONG PACED OUTSIDE the doors of the courtroom for nearly a quarter hour before the officials began to exit, walking past him as they left. The final two were Huang Yong, the Deputy Chief Justice of the Court of Judicial Review, and Hu Sheng, Li Jinglong's former commanding officer.

As he watched them approach, Li Jinglong drew himself up, awaiting the results of their deliberation.

Hu Sheng looked Li Jinglong up and down but said nothing, still weighing his options. He had never understood this former subordinate of his. Li Jinglong's reputation had been poor even when he was simply a member of the Longwu Guard. On several occasions, Hu Sheng had privately asked his officers what they had against the man, but his subordinates had all been cryptic with their answers. The bottom line was that they just didn't like him. Some thought him too arrogant, while a few claimed he was a deviant of some kind. Hu Sheng hadn't pressed the matter. But now that they were shutting down the Department of Demonic Exorcism, the question of where to send Li Jinglong was a brand-new headache. Should he send him back to the Longwu Guard?

Li Jinglong stood quietly, waiting for his superiors to speak. Huang Yong was thinking much the same as Hu Sheng. Both felt a pang of sympathy for Li Jinglong—he was a grown man, but his ancestral home had been sold off, and he had nowhere to go but the Department of Exorcism, where he had finally seen some small hope for advancement. Now this, too, was a door shut to him.

"You have a subordinate, do you not? A young man?" Hu Sheng asked as he took a few steps forward.

Li Jinglong blanched, instantly terrified Hongjun had caused some sort of fresh trouble. But as he looked again at Huang Yong, he recalled that Hongjun had been with him when Huang Yong came to find him earlier. Huang Yong must have mentioned him.

"Yes," Li Jinglong said. "What about him?"

"Bring him with you. You'll return to the Longwu Guard," Hu Sheng said. "The rest will be dismissed from their posts, and the Ministry of Personnel will make arrangements for them. The Department of Exorcism's plaque will be taken down on the fifth next month. You have ten days to vacate the premises."

An explosion seemed to go off in the back of Li Jinglong's mind. Thinking he had misheard, he asked numbly, "What?"

"I don't want to hear any arguing," Hu Sheng said. "Over the past few years, you've worn me to the bone. Do you think I wanted this? Get a hold of yourself; we can discuss it again in a few days."

With that, Hu Sheng stepped around Li Jinglong and left.

"Chief Li," Huang Yong said, "I believe yao exist in this world, and I have faith in your good character. But certain things simply won't go your way—this is a difficult truth in life. As the inheritor of Duke Di's sword, you ought to know the merit of lying low..."

Li Jinglong couldn't hear Huang Yong's words over the droning in his ears. He turned and chased after Hu Sheng, but after leaving the Court of Judicial Review's grounds, the captain seemed to have disappeared. Li Jinglong stood in the street, the world spinning around him, at a complete and utter loss.

He couldn't have said how he got back to the Department of Exorcism. Li Jinglong found himself at the doorway in the small hours before dawn, standing in the moonlit entrance hall. Acalanatha was shrouded in gentle light, peacefully watching him with his six spiritual devices in his six hands.

A few cups and bowls lay scattered over the stone of the courtyard. All the seats had been moved outside and placed beneath the parasol tree, and some tea leaves had been tossed on the ground as the others had gathered beneath the tree to while away the evening.

The lamps were snuffed out in everyone's rooms. Clearly, they had gone to bed when he didn't return, so as not to be ridiculed for their inverted schedules if guests again came to call.

Li Jinglong stood in the courtyard, silently taking in the scene before him.

Not far away, Hongjun lay in bed, trapped in a strange dream. In the Chang'an of his dream, the streets were strewn with bodies. The ground was dark with pools of blood, and black smoke coiled between the buildings. Just as those ao fish had done when they ran rampant through Daming Palace, the corpses stretched out their hands, trying to drag him down to join them.

In his panic, he reached for his pentacolor sacred light, but found his meridians completely empty. Hongjun cast nervously about, dearly wishing he could return to the Department of Exorcism. He thought to call for help, but for some reason, the first person who came to mind was neither Chong Ming nor Qing Xiong, but Li Jinglong.

"Chief?" he yelled. "Chief, where are you?!"

He stumbled through the streets of Chang'an, weaving between piles of corpses. Black smoke rolled up behind him, sending a chill down his spine. His foot caught on something, and he crashed to the ground. "Li Jinglong?! Li Jinglong!"

Yet when he tried to scramble to his feet, he felt a stab of unbearable agony, as if a great force was swelling inside him, nearly bursting from his chest. "Li Jinglong—!"

"Hongjun!"

In his room in the waking world, Hongjun tumbled off his bed. Having heard Hongjun call for him in his dream, Li Jinglong charged inside and caught him in the moment before he hit the floor.

Hongjun jerked awake in his arms. Before he could scream again, Li Jinglong hushed him, gazing down at him in shock. Hongjun was covered in sweat, his eyes wide and face pale, panting for breath.

"A nightmare?" Li Jinglong quietly asked as he knelt on the ground, holding Hongjun by the shoulders. Hongjun grabbed the hem of Li Jinglong's outer robe and buried his face in Li Jinglong's arm as he let out a long, shaky sigh.

The lamp in Li Jinglong's room glowed in the darkness before sunrise.

After retrieving some herbs from the east wing to prepare himself a calming draught, Hongjun was walking past Li Jinglong's door when Li Jinglong called out to him. "Come inside; make one for me too."

"I can bring it over once I'm done."

He hadn't forgotten the vehemence with which Li Jinglong had ordered him out of his room last time. Afterward, Hongjun had consulted the carp yao, who had told him that some people didn't like it when others entered their rooms. Hongjun had taken this advice to heart.

"Keep me company for a while," Li Jinglong said.

Hongjun stepped barefoot across the threshold and summoned a flame to light the copper stove set next to the table. He placed a bowl of the same material over the stove and began to measure out the ingredients he'd collected.

"Were you often disturbed by dreams when you were little?" Li Jinglong asked.

Hongjun shook his head. "No. I only started having nightmares after I left the mountain."

"Do you miss your home?" Li Jinglong asked with a sigh. He had removed his outer robe and wore only undergarments cut from a snowy white cloth as he knelt across the table from Hongjun.

Hongjun carefully stirred the medicinal herbs in the bowl with a copper spoon. His handsome, youthful face seemed touched with despondence in the glow of the fire. But when Li Jinglong asked him whether he missed home, he looked up with a smile. Though Li Jinglong lived a life practically devoid of desire, that smile raised a ripple deep within his heart, like the pluck of a string sending a note ringing through the air.

"Zhao Zilong says people lose many things over the course of their lives, and you only ever realize how good something was once it's gone," Hongjun said, his lips curved gently upward. "I miss home because I left home, but I like the Department of Exorcism and everyone here too."

Li Jinglong looked at him with a trace of confusion. "What do you like about the Department of Exorcism?"

"The parasol tree." Hongjun turned and looked out the window. "The pieces of art and calligraphy you gave me; the way you take me out and spend time talking to me..."

"I don't know why, but I feel an odd affinity with you," Li Jinglong said quietly.

Perhaps the calming draught was taking effect. Li Jinglong felt his worries lighten significantly as the scent given off by the medley of herbs rose with the steam through the air. His eyes were drawn to the young man in front of him. Why *did* he take such pains to look out for him?

Was it because he wasn't like the other three, who each had their own agendas? No.

Or was it perhaps because Li Jinglong was charmed by his pretty face? After contemplating this, Li Jinglong decided the answer was also no.

"What happened tonight?" Hongjun asked, looking up from his task.

Li Jinglong saw the wisp of uncertainty in Hongjun's eyes. Suddenly enlightened, he let a chuckle slip free.

There were so many things Hongjun didn't understand. Unlike everyone else, there was no ridicule in his eyes when he looked at Li Jinglong. He never treated others differently depending on their station, like Li Jinglong's old comrades in the Longwu Guard who flattered their superiors and belittled anyone they deemed lower than themselves. Hongjun had no guile in his heart, nor any desire to ferret out others' innermost secrets. He didn't have an overinflated idea of his own intelligence, nor did he put himself down. He had no deeply held opinions about the ways of the world nor the workings of people's hearts; he was ignorant as a newborn babe.

Who wouldn't like to be friends with such an innocent person: They would neither pull you into a battle of wits, nor screw you over in the end.

"Did I get you in a lot of trouble again?" Hongjun asked.

Still delighted by his realization, Li Jinglong chuckled helplessly and shook his head.

Hongjun was mystified. In truth, he had begun to follow most of what his companions meant when they spoke in riddles, and he knew that in this realm, there were many who didn't say exactly what they meant. But just now, he didn't understand what Li Jinglong was thinking at all.

"Were you this carefree at home, too?" Li Jinglong asked. "Getting up to mischief, making trouble for people left and right?"

"Chong Ming is so scary when he's angry, I wouldn't dare," Hongjun said. "I'm just unlucky."

"You are, a bit," Li Jinglong said, chagrined. Ever since he'd met Hongjun, he'd encountered one misfortune after another. These last few weeks had been more dramatic than his first twenty years of life put together.

"None of you understand ordinary mortals," Li Jinglong continued. "Our lives are full of suffering."

Hongjun nodded. "Right, mortal lives are full of suffering. Yao, on the other hand, are wild creatures of the natural world, while demons are the product of the pain and resentment of all living beings."

A thought occurred to Li Jinglong. "They call us the department of 'demonic' exorcism. Why not yao exorcism? I've seen yao, but what about demons? Where are they? Are they also in Chang'an?"

Hongjun thought a moment. Ever since he could remember, he had never had much to worry about. His life had been carefree beneath the protective barrier of Chong Ming's gentle strength. But in the brief two months since he'd left the Taihang Mountains, he had discovered the intensity of the mortal realm's joys and sorrows. He had witnessed poverty, aging, disease, and death here in the Divine Land. The carp yao said that these were the eight sufferings of the mortal realm: birth, age, illness, and death; clashes between bitter foes, separations between loved ones, wishes unfulfilled, and excesses of the five cravings of mind and body.[15] These

---

15   The five skandhas in Buddhist tradition: "rupa," or form; "vedana," or sensation; "samjna," or perception; "samskara," or volition; and "vijnana," or consciousness.

sufferings would disperse into the energy meridians of heaven and earth, cycling again and again, continuously purified by these vast and mysterious forces. Once this pain exceeded what the natural world could purify, malign energies would gather to become these so-called demons.

"They call us 'demon exorcists,'" Hongjun replied after a pause, "because our final duty is to dispel the pain and suffering of the Divine Land. To drive the demons from the hearts of all living beings, and to cleanse the human realm of its fog of lingering demonic energy."

Hongjun had not forgotten Qing Xiong's mention of the heavenly demon Mara, and what he had begun to say before Chong Ming interrupted him. He was deeply curious about the existence of demons, but the carp yao had only explained their origins and nothing more.

Li Jinglong frowned. "Perhaps this is exactly what Duke Di meant when he spoke of a great calamity that threatened the Divine Land."

Examining Li Jinglong's distressed expression, Hongjun said with a smile, "You're always unhappy."

"I can't be happy," Li Jinglong replied, exhausted. He felt a bit lighter after looking at Hongjun again and gave him a relieved smile. "But every time I speak with you, I feel a lot better."

"You haven't even taken the medicine yet." Hongjun picked up the boiling kettle and poured water into the copper bowl to steep the heated herbs. "Did they ask you to pay for the damages? I still have some money left..."

Hongjun reached for his pearls, but Li Jinglong held up a hand. "It won't be enough. Forget it, I'll think of something. The trickiest part is that the entire court dislikes me—though I suppose that's understandable."

"What if you go talk to your emperor?" Hongjun said. "The palace is his. If you apologize and he says it's okay, that should take care of it, right? Actually, I burned down Yaojin Palace before I left the mountains..."

Li Jinglong was briefly speechless. But Hongjun's comment had once again woken him up as if from a dream. He frowned, deep in thought. No matter what, it was Li Longji who held the ultimate authority. A word from him would be more effective than anything else in the world. As long as the Son of Heaven understood what they were doing and trusted Li Jinglong, what could his ministers do? But how was he to convince the emperor and make him believe his account of what had transpired? It was a plan, at the very least—if he could manage it before the fifth of next month...

"I'll think about it," Li Jinglong replied. "But the case is not yet closed, and there are still yao within the imperial palace. Hmm..."

He was beginning to get a firmer handle on the situation. Hongjun pushed the bowl of medicine toward him, but Li Jinglong gestured for him to drink first while he thought.

Hongjun downed half the bowl; Li Jinglong took it and drained the rest.

"I think I put...a little too much...medicine," Hongjun murmured, instantly dizzy.

Li Jinglong had just finished his dose when he saw Hongjun start to tilt sideways, his eyes losing focus. He lunged forward to catch him but was also overtaken by a dizzy spell, nearly tripping over himself.

"You... Hongjun..." Feeling the world spin around him, Li Jinglong quickly sat back down on the ground. Without any support, Hongjun slumped against Li Jinglong, fast asleep.

"Wait... What medicine is this...?"

All the strength left Li Jinglong's body. Leaning against the bed, he groped blindly for something to push himself upright with. In the next moment, his hand went limp as he lost consciousness.

The sun shone into Li Jinglong's room the next morning. As A-Tai passed the door, he spotted Li Jinglong asleep on the floor next to the bed, legs slightly parted, with Hongjun draped on top of him. Both wore only their undergarments, fast asleep.

A-Tai was stunned.

"Qiu Yongsi!" A-Tai looked out into the courtyard and beckoned to his companion.

Qiu Yongsi jogged over, his keen sense for gossip tingling. Both of their mouths fell open as they gawked at the scene inside the room, two spitting images of the carp yao's normal expression.

"Should we show Mergen?" whispered A-Tai.

"Show him what? What's there to see? Close the chief's door; let's go."

"Didn't you hear last night? Hongjun kept calling his name! All 'Chief! Chief! Li Jinglong! Jinglong!' Don't tell me I misheard!"

"Right, right! I heard it too! So that's what it was! But weren't they in Hongjun's room? The sound was coming from the right!"

Their voices faded into the distance.

Li Jinglong woke before they could return. Looking down, the first thing he saw was Hongjun sprawled on top of him. His heart began to pound. He patted Hongjun's face, calling softly, "Hongjun? Wake up!"

While they'd been busy talking, Hongjun had over-brewed the calming draught. He'd been heavy-handed with the dosage in the first place, so the resultant medicine had left him dead to the world.

Li Jinglong's first instinct was to take him back to his own room, but the others must have gotten up already. Forget anyone else—if that carp yao saw them, he'd kick up a huge fuss. Out of everyone, the fish was the one Li Jinglong could least afford to offend. He had no choice but to lift Hongjun onto his own bed and tuck the blankets around him.

In the main hall, Mergen was using a pair of pliers to adjust a leather shield he had gotten from who knew where. A-Tai was fiddling with a piece of crystal, and Qiu Yongsi was brewing tea. When Li Jinglong walked in after washing up, they all bid him good morning and asked what had happened last night with great concern.

Li Jinglong acknowledged their inquiries but said only that everything had gone fine. He finished his breakfast, deep in thought, then accepted a cup of tea from Qiu Yongsi. A-Tai and Qiu Yongsi exchanged a look, while Mergen shot them a questioning glance.

"Then, does this mean the case is closed?" A-Tai asked.

"Not yet," Li Jinglong said. "We'll continue investigating today."

They all watched him, waiting for him to elaborate. Jinglong thought it over, then said, "Can you teach me some spiritual techniques?"

The corners of everyone's lips twitched.

"I don't want to drag you all down." Li Jinglong spoke frankly. "You were right—I'm just a mortal man, and martial ability alone is not enough to capture yao."

Hongjun woke feeling as if the fatigue that had been piling on him for days had disappeared. He stretched his arms overhead and noticed a pleasant scent wafting up from the blankets. Looking around, he realized he wasn't in his own room. How had he fallen asleep in Li Jinglong's bed?

"Chief? Chief Li?!" Hongjun shouted. "Where are you?"

Li Jinglong was still speaking with the others in the courtyard. This was awkward indeed. Before Li Jinglong could begin to explain, Mergen called out, surprised, "Hongjun? What's going on?"

Hongjun ran outside in his white underclothes. "Chief Li? What happened last night?"

The carp yao's cup fell to the ground with a crash.

Li Jinglong frantically waved at him to stop talking, but Hongjun continued, confused, "Why was I asleep in your bed? You even covered me with the blankets!"

Flabbergasted, Mergen looked from Li Jinglong to Hongjun as A-Tai and Qiu Yongsi piped up in unison: "No way! What's going on here?"

"Li Jinglong!" the carp yao shouted. "What did you do to my Hongjun?!"

Fed up, Li Jinglong roared, "Kong Hongjun! You had a calming draught, not a whiff of oblivion pollen. Did your mind get wiped? You had a nightmare and shouted my...shouted out loud, then you borrowed my furnace to brew a calming draught..."

Now Hongjun remembered. He quickly nodded and apologized, then said, "That's strange, why would I shout your—"

"How would I know?!" Flummoxed and furious, Li Jinglong yelled, "Go to your room and put some clothes on!"

"Chief, you don't need to explain in so much detail," A-Tai quickly said.

"That's right," Qiu Yongsi added. "We all understand."

"What the hell do you understand?!" Li Jinglong was about to pass out from fury.

After a change of clothes, Hongjun returned and sat in the corridor to eat a bowl of noodles. Seeing that A-Tai and Qiu Yongsi were attempting to teach Li Jinglong some spiritual techniques in the courtyard, he watched curiously.

"I have no spiritual energy in my meridians," Li Jinglong admitted.

"Actually, Chief," Mergen said, "for an ordinary mortal man, you're pretty impressive."

Li Jinglong sighed. "It's not enough."

When faced with the fox yao and the ao fish, Li Jinglong had relied both times on Hongjun's protection. Had he charged ahead alone, he would have been eaten in no time.

Qiu Yongsi tapped his head. "Wit is the most important thing for anyone. Spiritual power comes second. My grandfather said if you try to use spiritual devices and cultivation to brute force every problem, it's only a matter of time until you get yourself killed."

"Besides, you have Hongjun," A-Tai said.

"Right, you have Hongjun," Mergen and Qiu Yongsi agreed.

Hongjun blinked in confusion.

Li Jinglong set down his sword. Hongjun, having finished his noodles, stepped into the courtyard and said, "I've been wondering for a while... What kind of spiritual device is that sword?"

This was the third time Hongjun had examined the black blade. "Qing Xiong said if one can put a spiritual device to good use, even a powerless mortal can become an exorcist."

"That's true," Qiu Yongsi said. "Many exorcists have no innate power in their meridians. They rely on their skill with a few spiritual devices to defeat their enemies instead... May I take a look at this sword?"

It was the first time Qiu Yongsi, A-Tai, and Mergen had gotten a good look at Li Jinglong's sword.

"It seems to respond to Hongjun's throwing knives," Li Jinglong offered.

Hongjun held his throwing knives between his fingers and experimentally flooded them with spiritual energy. The knives lit up, and the black longsword glowed along with them.

"Whoa!" Everyone started in surprise.

"When my throwing knives are stuck in a yaoguai's body, they're activated by its yao energy," Hongjun said. "Perhaps this sword is made of the same type of metal as my throwing knives?"

"Perhaps," Qiu Yongsi murmured. "Can you make it a little brighter?"

As the sword continued to resonate with the throwing knives, a row of words appeared on the blade, glowing more and more brilliantly.

"This is…" Qiu Yongsi looked up at Li Jinglong, then back down at the sword.

Li Jinglong's brows twisted together. "What is it?"

"How much did you pay for this sword?"

"Five hundred fifty thousand taels."

"If they're five hundred fifty thousand each, I'll take ten." Qiu Yongsi laughed and returned the sword to Li Jinglong. Everyone couldn't help but stand straighter—out of all of them, Qiu Yongsi understood spiritual devices best.

"What kind of spiritual device is it?" Li Jinglong asked.

"It's the Sword of Wisdom," Qiu Yongsi replied.

"What?!" The carp yao was shocked.

"You know it?" Li Jinglong asked.

"Nope."

Li Jinglong stared.

"I just thought someone ought to set the mood."

The others were so appalled they nearly collapsed on the spot.

22
YAO IN THE ACADEMY

Struck by inspiration, Li Jinglong strode into the entrance hall and looked up at the Sword of Wisdom in Acalanatha's hands. The statue was a solemn depiction of the Immovable Wisdom King protecting all living beings. The sword in his hand was identical to Li Jinglong's rusty black blade.

"This is the Sword of Wisdom, subduer of yao and slayer of demons," Qiu Yongsi explained. "It's said it has the power to destroy all the world's demonic energy."

Hongjun frowned in thought. He looked up at Acalanatha, then down at the sword in Li Jinglong's hand. He had only one question—*Why does the Sword of Wisdom break through my pentacolor sacred light?* Chong Ming had said his sacred light was the world's strongest shield–that even if Mount Tai were to crash down upon him, the barrier could still withstand the blow.

"So, Chief, as long as you use this spiritual device well," Qiu Yongsi said warmly, "becoming an exorcist without innate spiritual power is more than a pipe dream. I imagine you'll discover more uses for the sword over time."

Li Jinglong nodded and said he understood, then slid the Sword of Wisdom back into its sheath. Everyone exchanged glances—they all sensed that Li Jinglong had suffered some blow last night, but as he hadn't said anything, no one had wanted to ask. Now it seemed Li Jinglong had recovered some degree of confidence, at least.

"Today, we continue our investigation," Li Jinglong said. "Whatever rumors spread outside, remember to focus on your own duties. Our task has nothing to do with anyone else."

Everyone voiced their agreement. Li Jinglong paired Qiu Yongsi with Hongjun and A-Tai with Mergen. As for Li Jinglong, he would move on his own. Qiu Yongsi and Hongjun were to investigate the temporary lodgings of the scholars taking part in the imperial examination, while A-Tai and Mergen were to go to Pingkang Ward to inquire about any examinees who had recently patronized brothels in the area.

"Is this really necessary?" A-Tai said. "Chief, why don't we think of some way to—"

"Forget about Daming Palace for now," Li Jinglong said. "It can wait until we've completed the investigation; I'm certain more will come to light."

Everyone looked at Li Jinglong, who turned away. "I'm not just hoping for a miracle. Don't you think it's suspicious that we discovered a nameless dried corpse, yet no one has appeared to identify the deceased?"

"All right," Qiu Yongsi finally said. "We'll do as you say and investigate."

"But what about you?" Hongjun asked. "You should come with us."

"I have a different task," Li Jinglong said, distracted. His brows were still knit in a frown.

"Let's go together." Hongjun tugged at Li Jinglong's sleeve.

"Don't cling. This is a government office!" Li Jinglong snapped.

"Have you no sense of propriety?" He strode out the door and was gone in a rush.

By the time Hongjun departed with Qiu Yongsi at noon, he had made neither heads nor tails of Li Jinglong's mysterious behavior. This was Hongjun's first time working one-on-one with a colleague other than the chief. Why had Li Jinglong assigned him to work with Qiu Yongsi?

Qiu Yongsi was tall in stature; he carried a folding fan and walked like the wind. He moved in starts and stops, pausing from time to time so Hongjun could catch up.

"To the Imperial Academy! Let's go," Qiu Yongsi said. "Are you hungry? Do you want a snack, a break?"

Hongjun waved him off. "I'm not a bottomless pit. Who gets hungry that fast?"

Chuckling to himself, Qiu Yongsi said, "Now that the chief has paired us up, I can't slack on the job anymore."

"When will you all show the chief a bit more respect?" Hongjun asked earnestly.

Qiu Yongsi burst out laughing. "The chief is a good man, just not quite what we expected. That was our mistake, I guess. But..." Hitting upon a different topic, Qiu Yongsi snapped his fan closed and looked at Hongjun. "As for you, Hongjun, what made you believe in him from the start?"

Hongjun pondered. "Maybe it's because the heart lamp entered his body."

"The heart lamp?" Qiu Yongsi started in surprise.

Everyone was here to defeat the yao king, so Hongjun figured there was no more reason to hide it. He told Qiu Yongsi the story of how the heart lamp had accidentally taken up residence in Li Jinglong's body.

Qiu Yongsi considered this. "So that's why... You always stuck with Li Jinglong ever since joining the Department of Exorcism; I was wondering if there was something wrong with the rest of us."

Hurriedly, Hongjun assured him there was not. Qiu Yongsi continued, deep in thought, "If he possesses the heart lamp, maybe that guy really will see his wish fulfilled."

Hongjun didn't know much about the heart lamp, but given Qiu Yongsi's breadth of knowledge when it came to spiritual devices, perhaps he knew a way to retrieve it. Before he could inquire any further, however, they arrived at the Imperial Academy. Qiu Yongsi signaled to Hongjun that he would do the talking as they approached the entrance.

People streamed in and out of the Imperial Academy's gates. The metropolitan examination[16] was scheduled for the fifth of next month, and a total of two thousand, five hundred provincial scholars from every corner of the nation had gathered to attend. As the examination approached, guards were set at the gate to search every person who entered or exited the academy in the interests of preventing exam questions from leaking or proxies sitting the exam in another's place. Books from outside were banned, and each visitor was required to display a token of passage to enter.

Standing on the street with Hongjun, Qiu Yongsi held his breath, waiting as people flooded past them. When the crowd swelled to its highest point, he strode toward the gate, pulling Hongjun behind him.

"Hey! Wang-xiong! Wang-xiong, wait for me!" Qiu Yongsi followed a passing scholar. "Quick, I forgot my token..."

With so many people at the gate, the guard only gave Qiu Yongsi a cursory search. "Where's your token?"

---

16 An intermediate phase of the imperial examination, held in the capital. Examinees who pass this phase may advance to the palace examination for a chance to earn the highest scholarly qualifications.

"I forgot it! I'm going back to grab it right now!"

The rest of the line muttered for them to hurry up. Finding nothing of note on his person, the impatient guard waved him through.

Hongjun's guard found nothing on him either. "Your token?" he asked just as Hongjun was about to cross.

"Wait, neither of them have their tokens? You there, halt! Which courtyard are you staying in?"

Hongjun's heart pounded; he had no idea what to do. Qiu Yongsi turned back to the guards. "He's a foreigner; he can't understand what you're saying! He left his token in my room—hey, remember? Your token!"

Hongjun quickly recovered and pasted a smile on his face. "Hai mie hou bi! My dear friends of the Great Tang Empire!"

Hongjun went up to give the guard a hug. Already frustrated by the presence of guards at the gate, the scholars lined up behind them were ready to explode. The guards had little choice but let them through.

Qiu Yongsi led Hongjun through a side corridor, glancing back once or twice to make sure he was following. "Thank goodness we got inside. Now let's go find the registrar."

"Why didn't we just climb the wall?" Hongjun asked.

With his grappling hook, Hongjun could fly into the imperial palace, Daming Palace, or the Imperial Academy as if walking across flat ground—the only difference was the color of the wall. Qiu Yongsi was dumbfounded. Indeed, why hadn't they just climbed the wall?

"You can't solve every problem with brute force," Qiu Yongsi eventually answered.

When they reached the registrar's office, Qiu Yongsi said they were looking for three other scholars from their hometown. He motioned to Hongjun, who wrote down the three names. After hearing from the registrar that the scholars had been staying in the fourth building in the Plum Courtyard, the two of them walked back through the long corridor to enter the courtyard indicated through a side hall.

The side hall was a spacious area where the scholars could drink tea and chat among themselves. As Hongjun and Qiu Yongsi walked down the path bordering the space, Hongjun stopped in his tracks and peered into the hall.

"What is it?" Qiu Yongsi asked.

"Nothing."

"Trust your instincts," Qiu Yongsi said. "We're on a case."

"I just had a strange, sort of familiar feeling."

"Can you describe it?" Qiu Yongsi cocked his head to the side and looked at Hongjun.

What kind of feeling was it, exactly? Somehow, it was just like being at home. Hongjun swept his eyes over the side hall. Nearly forty men were gathered there, all scholars, old and young alike, quietly conversing in groups.

A young man walked by with his head lowered and bumped into Hongjun. Hongjun stumbled; the young man quickly bowed and apologized before looking up at the person he'd knocked into. The stranger was small and slender, likely even younger than Hongjun. Seeing the uneasy look on his face, Hongjun offered him a smile and waved off the offense. The young man smiled back as he turned to move into the side hall, clearly reassured.

The way he moved again reminded Hongjun of Yaojin Palace. All the young men in Yaojin Palace were birds who had cultivated human form, and the whole mountaintop was suffused with yao energy. It was a product of Chong Ming's noble and unsullied character that the yao energy there was purified into something closer to immortal energy, removed from the churning dust of the mortal realm.

"He's a yao," Hongjun said.

Qiu Yongsi was silent as he turned to lead the way inside.

"You felt it too?" Hongjun quietly asked.

"The yao crashed right into us. How could I not?"

Although he didn't have an unveiling glass or any other spiritual device that would force a yao to reveal itself, Qiu Yongsi could sense yao energy at close range.

The two of them chose a spot and sat down. Qiu Yongsi gave Hongjun a refined and gentle smile. "Young gentleman, they have roasted rice. Shall we have a cup of tea?"

"Okay!" Hongjun loved Qiu Yongsi's tea the most. A brew of fresh tea leaves suffused with silky cream, mixed with pounded sesame and topped with roasted rice: It was flavorful and refreshing with a fragrance that lingered on the tongue, a delicacy of the highest caliber.

"Do your usual clueless thing," Qiu Yongsi said with a smile. "Look all around the room—whoever tries to size us up is the yao. Tell me once you spot it."

Hongjun decided to let Qiu Yongsi's comment slide. He craned his neck and looked about, letting his eyes fill with the curiosity of a stranger visiting Chang'an for the first time. The side hall was lined with tables in neat rows, with a teapot and furnace stowed beneath each. Outside, the autumn sky was broad and open, a washed-clean azure blue broken here and there by fluffy white clouds. With the sun shining in, the hall was an excellent spot for leisure and put its inhabitants in a comfortable and lazy mood.

The other scholars were all engrossed in their own conversations. A few people at other tables occasionally looked in their direction, but only with brief glances.

"There are a lot of people looking at us," Hongjun said to Qiu Yongsi. "But if it's as you say, does that mean they're all yao?"

"You got it. We've walked right into a nest of them," Qiu Yongsi said, his smile plastered to his face. "We can't make a move now or we'll destroy the Imperial Academy. The chief would cry."

Hongjun noticed one table where three scholars were having a cheerful discussion while another young man boiled water for them. His three companions all ignored the young man, who looked bored, staring into the courtyard outside with a vacant gaze. In the next moment, he looked in their direction and, meeting Hongjun's eyes, gave him a smile.

That smile was suffused with a lovely, almost feminine charm. Hongjun's heart began to pound in his chest, and his face went red up to his ears as he offered the scholar an awkward smile in return.

"What is it?" Qiu Yongsi asked, noticing his expression.

There was an obvious charm spell woven into that smile. Hongjun turned back to Qiu Yongsi. "That one might be a fox."

A moment later, the young man rose, walked up to them, and sat down at their table. "What fragrant tea," he said with a gentle curve to his lips.

Hongjun started in surprise.

Qiu Yongsi was not at all awkward around the stranger. "It'll be ready in a minute if you'd like to join us. Xiao-xiongdi,[17] how should we address you?"

"Du Hanqing," the young man said, his willow-leaf brows curving in a smile. His eyes seemed shrouded in a layer of mist, while his figure was delicate and slim. He leaned against the table, eyes never

---

17 The prefix xiao- meaning younger and xiongdi meaning brother. Used as a casual address for a younger man.

leaving Hongjun's face and body. He scooted a bit closer and asked, "What about you?"

"Uhh…" *That's close enough,* Hongjun thought as Qiu Yongsi introduced them.

"Qiu Yongsi from Hangzhou. This is my cousin, Xiao-Hongjun. Hongjun, you two look about the same age. You should make a friend."

"Did you just arrive in the capital?" Du Hanqing continued staring into Hongjun's eyes. "The exam is the fifth of next month."

Even knowing he was a fox yao, Hongjun felt unbearably awkward under the weight of his gaze. But before he could think any more on it, Qiu Yongsi kicked him under the table.

Hongjun didn't know what he should do, so he looked back into Du Hanqing's eyes. He soon began to giggle at the strange atmosphere.

Du Hanqing couldn't help but laugh as well. "How old are you?"

After each told their age, Hongjun found that he was two months older than Du Hanqing, whereupon Du Hanqing switched to addressing him as *gege*.[18] When he asked about their lodgings, Qiu Yongsi supplied that they were staying with relatives in the city and had come to the Imperial Academy today to tour the place and meet their prospective instructors.

"You're already taking the metropolitan examination at your age?" Hongjun asked. "How impressive."

Du Hanqing smiled. "My family has always been poor. Everyone's counting on me to earn an official position."

As he spoke, he reached out to play with the jade peacock feather hanging from Hongjun's waist sash. Afraid the pentacolor sacred

---

18   A word meaning "elder brother." It can also be used to address an unrelated male peer, and optionally used as a suffix.

light would lash out and send him flying, Hongjun quickly covered it with his hand.

Qiu Yongsi said, "It's been consecrated; it oughtn't be touched."[19]

Du Hanqing nodded in understanding. Someone called his name from the other table—the water was ready, so Du Hanqing got up to make the others tea.

Hongjun watched Du Hanqing go, wondering if he had killed any people, and if so, how many. Back in Yaojin Palace, Qing Xiong had once told him that fox yao were unmatched in the arts of playing with emotions and bewitching human hearts. Of all the different kinds of yao, fox yao's feelings were the most humanlike. At the same time, they suffered the most, because they could experience what it was to be human but could never escape the fact that they were yao.

"He'll come back in a bit." Qiu Yongsi handed Hongjun a Buddha figurine carved from mutton-fat jade. "Give this to him when he does."

"He won't come back," Hongjun said.

"He will. He's taken a fancy to you; it's quite obvious. It's a good thing Chief Li isn't here."

Hongjun blinked, perplexed by his words.

Just as Qiu Yongsi predicted, Du Hanqing returned after brewing the tea. It seemed his so-called friends kept him around so they could order him about, and didn't intend to spare him more attention than that.

Hongjun stared at Du Hanqing, and this time, it was Du Hanqing's turn to go red. He began to laugh. "Why are you always looking at me?"

"You're good-looking," Hongjun said. He sincerely felt that Du Hanqing's delicate appearance, like a dainty willow vine floating in the wind, had a particular sort of charm.

---

19   In Buddhist and Daoist traditions, certain objects may be consecrated to fill them with divine power. Other people are not supposed to touch these objects, as they may lose their blessing if they are "dirtied."

"Do you like poetry?" Du Hanqing asked Hongjun.

"I do!" Hongjun replied.

"Who do you like?"

"Li Bai," Hongjun said. "He's my favorite."

"I like Wang Changling."

The pair soon struck up a spirited conversation about poetry. Hongjun had to admit, although Du Hanqing was a yao, he was well educated in this domain. Hongjun grew more and more invested in their conversation until he entirely forgot he was speaking to a fox yao. His only goal lay in forcing him to accept the superiority of Li Bai's poetry, while Du Hanqing began to puff up in frustration on the opposite side of the debate.

As the sun slanted toward the west, a smiling Qiu Yongsi said, "Should we get going?"

"You shan't convince me," Du Hanqing said.

Hongjun laughed. "Do you like this?" He set the jade Buddha figurine on the table and pushed it toward Du Hanqing.

When Du Hanqing squealed in excitement, Hongjun said, "You like jade, right? I saw you liked my pendant, but it's from my dad, so I can't give it to you. Here, you can have this one."

Hongjun was always a bit slow with people he wasn't familiar with, but once he became invested in a conversation, he was energetic and expressive, to the point that he couldn't resist slapping Du Hanqing on the back in his excitement. Du Hanqing picked up the jade Buddha and looked at Hongjun, deeply moved.

"I'll come find you tomorrow," he said.

"Eh?" Hongjun was caught off guard. *Bad idea*, he thought. *The Department of Exorcism is way too dangerous for you.*

"We have too many relatives at home," Qiu Yongsi said. "Why don't you meet somewhere else?"

Hongjun nodded and promised to meet Du Hanqing beneath Lishui Bridge at noon the next day.

Evening was falling as Li Jinglong made his way out of the Feng Estate.

Feng Changqing stood at the gate, cane in hand. "You've finally made some progress," he said. "You would never have asked me these questions before."

When Li Jinglong said nothing, Feng Changqing went on. "I understand your ambitions. But holding an important position in the court isn't the grand thing you think. Serving as an official is no more than deceiving your superiors above and lying to your subordinates below. Only when they can truly cover things up no longer will you have your chance."

"I fear that by then, it will be too late."

"To them," Feng Changqing said, "it's never too late. Go on, but plan your next moves well."

The knot between Li Jinglong's brows never eased; if anything, Feng Changqing's words only made him more anxious.

It was twilight by the time Hongjun and Qiu Yongsi finally left the Imperial Academy. Only then did Hongjun remember they hadn't investigated any of the three missing scholars.

"They were right there, in the side hall," Qiu Yongsi said. "All replaced with fox yao."

Hongjun's jaw dropped to the floor. "'Replaced' with fox yao?" he asked.

While Hongjun and Du Hanqing were talking, Qiu Yongsi had been paying close attention to the scattered conversations all around them, taking extra pains to monitor any that mentioned the names of the three missing scholars.

"Well, what else could it be? What fox yao do you think would spend a decade studying beneath a chilly window to make it to the imperial examinations in the capital?" Qiu Yongsi asked. "The foxes must have taken the scholars' places after they arrived in Chang'an. Each and every one of them has a delicately pointed chin and peach-blossom eyes—they're not hard to spot at all. It only took me so long to realize because we never considered the possibility."

"So then—what happened to the original scholars?"

Qiu Yongsi gave Hongjun a bleak look. Both of them recalled the corpse beneath Jinyun's bed, and a chill ran down their spines.

GRASS ROPE AND JADE HOOP

"THE CHIEF WAS RIGHT. This is a major case," Qiu Yongsi said as they stepped through the gateway into the Department of Exorcism. Everyone else was already gathered, deep in conversation, only pausing when they saw their last two members had returned.

Li Jinglong closed the gates, and everyone sat down in the main courtyard. Qiu Yongsi smiled. "Hongjun charmed a little yao."

Everyone looked at him incredulously.

"N-not quite," Hongjun said, then related his and Qiu Yongsi's findings.

"How many yao are there in the Imperial Academy?" Li Jinglong asked.

"It's hard to say without investigating further," Qiu Yongsi said. "At a rough estimate, no fewer than a hundred."

Li Jinglong exhaled slowly. "A major case, all right, of shocking scale."

"We checked all the brothels in Pingkang Ward," A-Tai said. "We found no more yao there. The three fox yao we met arrived there a year ago."

Thank heavens, Hongjun thought to himself.

Li Jinglong said, "Then, our next steps are clear. We need to…"

"Wait a minute." Hongjun chose this moment to jump in—these people always laid out the results of their deductions as if every one of them was plain as day. "Explain in more detail. It might be clear to you, but it's not to me."

Li Jinglong elaborated for his benefit. "For the past year, fox yao have been moving into Chang'an in droves. The first three entered the Poetess's Pavilion. Why there? Because it's the favored haunt of the city's literati."

"The first scholar who went to Pingkang Ward got sucked dry after visiting the brothel," A-Tai continued, "so a fox yao could take his place."

Now Hongjun understood.

Li Jinglong picked up where A-Tai left off. "The Poetess's Pavilion enjoys a constant stream of visitors, and the three fox yao specially selected examinees as their victims. For each one they killed, one of their lackeys took his place. More and more fox yao disguised as scholars began to gather in the Imperial Academy. Meanwhile, the dried-out corpses of the actual scholars were disposed of elsewhere."

"That's why there was a corpse beneath the bed that day!"

"Exactly." Li Jinglong paced back and forth, thinking for a moment. "Perhaps he was a recent victim, or perhaps Jinyun forgot about him. Either way, they didn't have a chance to dispose of the body, and we discovered it by mistake. That's why they had to burn it—even at the risk of personal injury."

"After these fox yao take the scholars' places in the imperial examination," Qiu Yongsi explained, "they can join the ranks of officialdom en masse. At that point, the entirety of Chang'an will…"

Everyone shuddered in fright.

"It'll become yao territory," Li Jinglong finished. "But there's one more thing: They want to enter the court as officials. But how can the fox yao guarantee that they can pass the metropolitan examination, and the palace examination after it?"

Hongjun found the premise absurd. A hundred or more fox yao studying to become jinshi-level scholars?

Li Jinglong looked over his subordinates. "They must have someone in the imperial court—either the yao king or one of his direct subordinates. Whoever it is must be leaking the examination questions, so the fox yao can prepare their essays in advance."

"A civil official?" Qiu Yongsi asked.

"Not necessarily," A-Tai mused.

"I've studied some of the writings about fox yao Duke Di left behind," Li Jinglong said. "We can expect that the fake scholars won't be very advanced in their cultivation. With the numbers they need, I imagine any yao that can take human form and use glamour techniques will be allowed to participate. Their leader will be the one sponsoring these fox yao—Fei'ao must have been the guard dog protecting them."

"The biggest question is the identity of their agent in the imperial court," Mergen muttered. "It must be someone who can access the examination questions, someone who has connections throughout the court…"

"This is not the most urgent question." Li Jinglong spoke slowly. "Whoever it is, they will reveal themselves eventually, especially once we dispatch their subordinates. If we can close this case, this agent will want to destroy us even more than we want to defeat them."

He paused. "Hongjun, if I'm not wrong, you'll find your missing throwing knife in their leader's hands. Let's get a move on—we have much to do in the next few days. Mergen, A-Tai, Yongsi, you three get some rest for now. Tonight, you'll go out and mark all the fox yao in the Imperial Academy. Hongjun, I need you to prepare a drug for me."

Li Jinglong took a few steps, then turned back and held out his left hand, palm facing down. The others piled their hands on top in solidarity, then went off to prepare for their own tasks.

The wind whistled between the buildings as Qiu Yongsi, A-Tai, and Mergen snuck silently into the Imperial Academy in the dark of night.

"I keep thinking we need an unveiling glass," Qiu Yongsi said. "Identifying yao like this is exhausting."

A-Tai felt the same. "Shall we make one?" He peeked into a bedroom and whispered, "Does this one look like a yao to you?"

Mergen shuffled closer to examine the scholar lying on the bed. "It's better to accidentally let one go than to kill an innocent person. Ten years of bitter study could be over all at once if we're wrong."

"He is," Qiu Yongsi said. "I saw him in the hall. Do it."

A-Tai fluttered his fan, sending a stream of medicinal powder through the air to leave a tiny spot on the hem of the fox yao's robes. Mergen beckoned them to another window. There were six people sleeping inside the room—Mergen opened his hand to show them the seven nailhead arrows vibrating in his grip, reacting to the presence of yao energy.

"They're all yao," Qiu Yongsi said after a single glance. "Look at that fox there; it's let its tail slip out in its sleep. They wouldn't let any mortals stay in this room; it would be too easy to be exposed."

A-Tai marked each of the sleeping foxes, one by one. It was late autumn, and Chang'an was already beginning to cool. Braziers of coal were commonplace to brew tea and warm rooms; it was easy to accidentally dirty your hem. The fox yao likely wouldn't notice the marks.

Back at the Department of Exorcism, Hongjun mixed medicine in the main courtyard while Li Jinglong sat by his side, reading through a stack of case files.

"I've given everyone a lot of work," Li Jinglong said. "If the department comes out the other side all right, I'll take everyone out for some fun."

"Comes out all right?" Hongjun cocked his head.

Li Jinglong realized he'd slipped. "After the case is closed," he corrected himself.

"What will we do with the fox yao once they're captured?"

"Burn them to death," Li Jinglong said.

Hongjun fell silent.

Li Jinglong flicked a look up at Hongjun, taking in his expression. "Are you going to beg for mercy on their behalf?"

Hongjun thought of the scholars the fox yao had killed. If the Department of Exorcism didn't give them the justice they deserved, who would? But in truth, he found the little foxes quite pitiful. "Couldn't we spare some of them?"

"Did any one of them spare the victims whose lives they took?" Li Jinglong asked. "You're an exorcist."

Li Jinglong had sensed the danger here ever since Qiu Yongsi had recounted the day's events—if Hongjun befriended that little fox, he'd find himself in deep trouble sooner or later.

"Do you think all yao are bad? But then what about Zhao Zilong?" Hongjun questioned him in response.

"All of these foxes are, at least," Li Jinglong said.

Hongjun's forehead furrowed in a frown, but he didn't argue with Li Jinglong. If that little fox from today hadn't hurt anyone, couldn't they make an exception? But then again, he had been an accessory to the scholars' murders, even if indirectly.

Feeling the atmosphere grow awkward, Li Jinglong changed the subject. "Add a little more. I want a drug strong enough for a single drop to knock them out and force them to show their true forms."

Earlier in the afternoon, Li Jinglong had scoured every apothecary in Chang'an to gather the ingredients for this concoction. Hongjun increased the dosage, grinding everything into powder and carefully packaging the resulting medicine.

"You mustn't inhale this, at any cost." Hongjun thought for a moment, then added, "But, Chief, I trust you won't be so unlucky."

"Don't jinx me, okay?!" Li Jinglong was genuinely scared of Hongjun. He carefully divided up the medicine and stashed it in a number of little bags.

Midnight marked the end of the tenth month; an eventful autumn was drawing to a close. Five days remained until the imperial examination.

After completing their mission, Qiu Yongsi returned to report on their findings. "There are two hundred sixty-six foxes in total."

"Fewer than I imagined."

Even so, Li Jinglong still felt uneasy. He set up a rotating watch to keep an eye on the foxes until the examination, lest the exorcists somehow be caught unawares. Yet strangely, an order came down from the court the next day: This year's fall examination would take place at the Imperial Academy three days ahead of schedule, on the second day of the eleventh month. When Qiu Yongsi brought a copy of the pronouncement back with him after his watch, everyone lapsed into contemplative silence.

"The yao king must know Fei'ao has been slain," Li Jinglong said. "He's afraid we'll disrupt his arrangements, so he moved up the date of the examination."

"Has he learned of our plan?" Mergen frowned.

Li Jinglong waved a hand. "This also means he has fewer powerful subordinates than we feared. Don't panic. We'll stick to the original plan, and just move the date up to tomorrow."

"Should I still go meet Du Hanqing today?" Hongjun asked. Truth be told, he didn't entirely want to. He didn't want to face a little fox who was about to die at their hands.

"Go," Li Jinglong said. "At this point, any bit of intelligence you can glean is of the utmost importance."

The carp yao had just popped up out of the pond to ask what was going on. Afraid he would ruin their plans, everyone quickly shoved him back down.

Hongjun considered for a moment, then nodded and agreed to show up at the promised time. Li Jinglong had already devised a plan to capture all the foxes in one fell swoop just after the imperial examination began, but Qiu Yongsi's stroke of inspiration upon meeting the little fox yao had given them a last chance to gather information. If the yao sensed a threat, they would definitely send someone to probe Hongjun. The little fox yao's demeanor would indicate whether his compatriots had discovered the danger or not.

Whoever had orchestrated this plot had gone too far to turn back now. There was no mundane explanation for over two hundred scholars vanishing overnight. They had practically delivered the keys to their own downfall right into the Department of Exorcism's hands.

At a quarter to noon, Hongjun arrived at the base of Lishui Bridge. Maple leaves danced in the breeze over the water as scraps of red foliage drifted downstream with the current. Du Hanqing leaned against the railing, gazing out at the scenery with an absent look on his face.

"Du Hanqing!" Hongjun called with a smile.

"Hongjun?" Du Hanqing began to smile too. Hongjun found it a bit strange—the young man seemed unusually eager to see him. He walked up the bridge to meet him, and the two descended side by side, heading for the East Market.

Carrying the carp yao in his arms, Li Jinglong peeked out from an alleyway with Mergen at his side. The fish had only just been informed of the whole course of events. "Have they met up yet?" he asked.

Li Jinglong shushed him.

"Couldn't you have just sent Lao-Qiu[20] and Mergen to keep watch?" he continued, undeterred. "Chief Li, why did you have to come in person?"

Li Jinglong slapped a hand over the carp yao's mouth. Hoisting him under his left arm, he checked his surroundings, then left the alley to tail Hongjun and Du Hanqing. The two youths made a charming picture as they strolled through Chang'an's market splashed in the bright autumn sun: Hongjun, handsome as a jade tree in the wind, and Du Hanqing, delicate and lovely.

"I'll take you to the bookstore," Hongjun offered.

"Hongjun, why is that man carrying a fish?"

Hongjun turned just in time to see Li Jinglong whip around to face a fish stall in the market. Carrying the carp yao in his arms, he pretended to haggle with the merchant while Mergen stood beside him, glancing around and feigning nonchalance.

He had never thought he looked funny when he went around toting the carp yao on his back, but seeing Li Jinglong with a fish in his arms, he sputtered with laughter. "Who is that? Going around hugging a fish, how silly!"

---

20 A prefix meaning "old." Can be used affectionately between friends of similar ages.

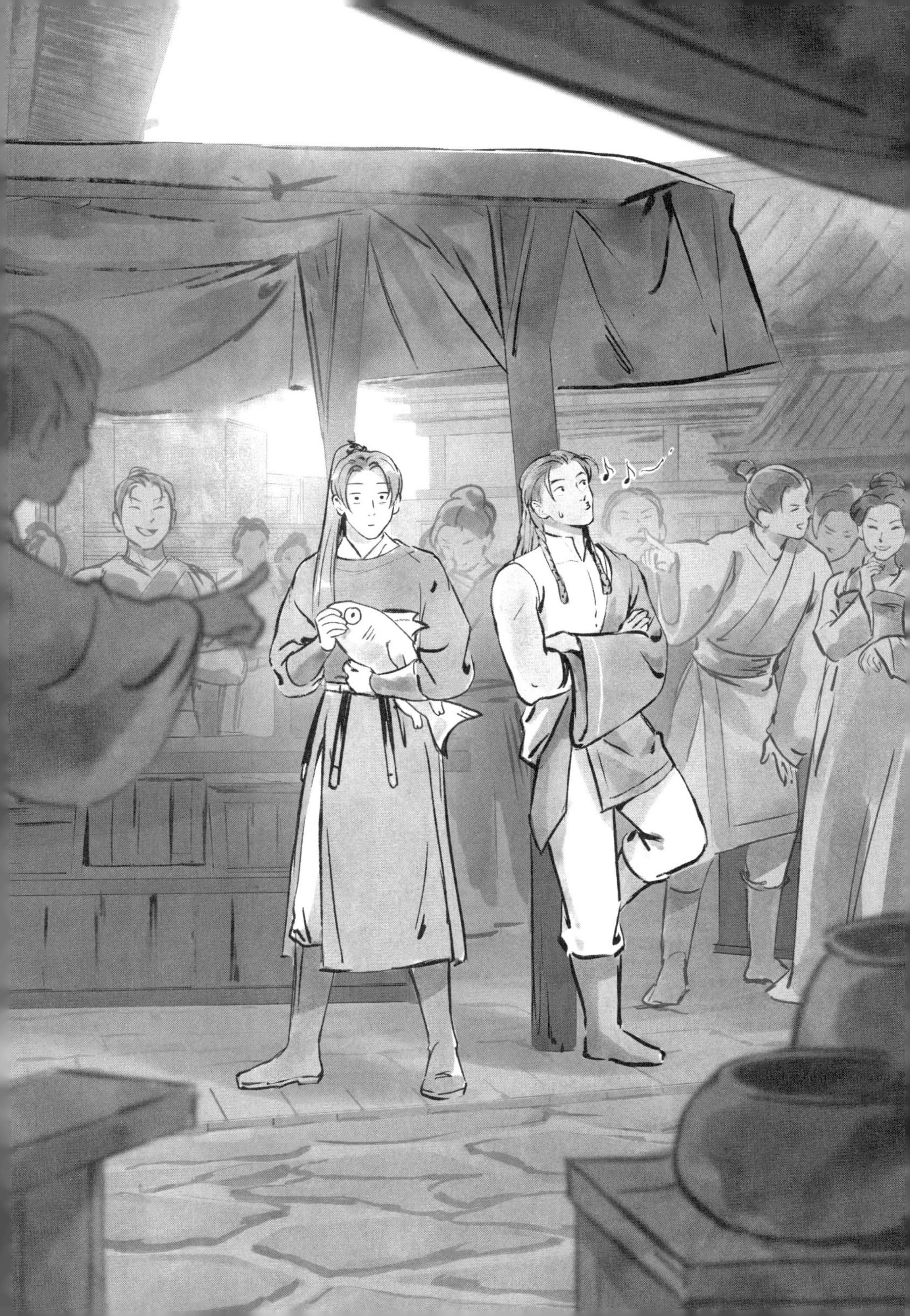

Heads turned from everywhere in the market. "Ha ha, isn't that Li Jinglong?"

Li Jinglong had no words.

Only then did Hongjun realize it was his own fish. How awkward! He grabbed Du Hanqing by the wrist and tugged him into the bookstore.

"Look, there are a lot of books in here," Hongjun said.

"Wow, I've nev—" Du Hanqing quickly caught himself. "I rarely come here."

Outside, Li Jinglong stuffed the carp yao into Mergen's arms with strict orders not to let the carp speak, then darted into the bookstore to eavesdrop from behind a bookshelf. Yet as he listened, he soon grew annoyed—the only thing they were discussing was poetry. *What are you doing discussing Li Bai with a yaoguai?!*

At last Du Hanqing accepted Hongjun's recommendation, and they walked out of the store side by side. Hongjun suggested they go eat and brought Du Hanqing to Dragon's Gate.

Li Jinglong looked at the restaurant in silence.

"Chief, I didn't bring any money." Holding the carp yao, Mergen said, "I can go home and fetch some; wait for me. It's all right, you order first..."

"There's no need. I have money," Li Jinglong lied. "You head back first. Hurry and get that fish out of here."

When the waiter came to take their order, Hongjun racked his brain for what the carp yao had ordered the other day. "One rapid stir-fry, silkie chicken soup..." Hongjun wasn't sure this was right, but managed to finish ordering nevertheless, leaving Du Hanqing gaping in shock.

"This place is way too expensive."

Hongjun assured him it was no problem, turning to him with another brilliant smile.

Du Hanqing's eyes reddened at the rims. "This is the first time anyone has taken me here."

Behind the folding screen at the next table over, the waiter had approached Li Jinglong. "Sir, what would you like to order?"

Li Jinglong was a man of character; he could adapt as circumstances demanded. "Just a cup of water."

"All righty!" the waiter called. "For Commandant Li, one cup of water—!"

The entire second floor of Dragon's Gate erupted in laughter.

Li Jinglong sucked in a deep breath and scooted his chair closer to the screen to eavesdrop on the conversation at the next table.

"What are they laughing about?" Du Hanqing was asking.

Hongjun shrugged; who knew what they were making fun of Li Jinglong for this time. But upon realizing the chief was right next to them, he finally recalled his mission. "The others from your hometown didn't take you on a tour of Chang'an?" he asked.

Du Hanqing heaved a gloomy sigh. "To them, I'm little better than a servant. I'm just there to fetch them tea and pour them water."

Behind the folding screen, Li Jinglong listened to their conversation in silence.

"Perhaps it'll get better once you pass the examination," Hongjun reassured him.

"No way," Du Hanqing said. "I'll probably spend the rest of my life waiting on them."

"How could that be? Once you pass, you'll be an official..."

Du Hanqing gave him a small smile. "How many people are there in your family? You must be very rich."

After a moment of thought, Hongjun replied, "It's just me and my dad, and uhh...a not-blood-related uncle—I don't know what to call him either..." Indeed, what was Qing Xiong to him, exactly?

"Ah? They're both men?" Du Hanqing was surprised. "Are you adopted?"

"Pretty much," Hongjun said. "They raised me. I never had a mom."

Li Jinglong's mouth wouldn't stop twitching. But upon reflection, he was a bit surprised too. Hongjun rarely mentioned his family to them.

Du Hanqing laughed. "No wonder you seemed a bit different."

Hongjun had no idea what to make of this comment. Du Hanqing sighed to himself. "To be honest, I don't know what you see in me."

What I see in him? Hongjun thought. *What is that supposed to mean? I don't see anything in him in particular.*

Li Jinglong scowled.

"I'm very happy to have you as a friend," Du Hanqing continued. "I don't really have any friends in Chang'an. If you have time, come see me at the Imperial Academy again."

Hongjun nodded. By now, Li Jinglong was almost certain the fox yao hadn't noticed anything amiss. He relaxed and sipped his water as he continued to listen.

The waiter served the dishes they had ordered. Du Hanqing had taken a great interest in Hongjun's family, so Hongjun picked some inconsequential anecdotes to answer his questions, hands fiddling with a paper packet as he spoke—the medicinal powder he had just concocted. He hesitated time and again, but never found a good opportunity to open it.

Not only did Hongjun fail to extract any information from Du Hanqing, he ended up spilling more and more details about himself.

At the next table, Li Jinglong twitched in apprehension, afraid Hongjun would sell out the whole Department of Exorcism with the next slip of his tongue.

By the end, Du Hanqing was beside himself with laughter. "Hongjun, I like you so much."

Hongjun grew a bit awkward. Guilt gnawing at him, he quickly changed the subject. Du Hanqing seemed to expect his reaction and let out a soft sigh.

As evening fell, Hongjun walked Du Hanqing to the Imperial Academy's gate to the sound of the evening drums. "I'm heading back. You…take care."

Du Hanqing turned and smiled at Hongjun, then handed him a hoop bracelet of white stone, tied with a knot of straw. "I like the jade Buddha you gave me a lot. This is for you. I don't have any jade, so I substituted stone. I hope you don't find it too crude."

Hongjun accepted the bracelet and nodded, fighting back a surge of unease.

"Let's go on a trip outside the city after the examination ends," Du Hanqing said.

Hongjun agreed and urged him to head inside before curfew. Du Hanqing turned and entered the Imperial Academy just as the evening drum finished its beat.

Dejected, Hongjun carried the bracelet as he wended his way through the streets alone. It was late autumn, and night fell early; before he arrived back home, the city was dark as pitch.

Li Jinglong's voice suddenly came from the side of the road. "Good work."

Hongjun jumped. He was in low spirits, so he simply said, "It was nothing."

Li Jinglong stood tall in his deep blue combat robes, cut from the bolts of brocade Noble Consort Yang had gifted them the other day. The smart clothing only heightened his handsomeness.

Noting the direction of Hongjun's gaze, Li Jinglong glanced down at himself. "Does it look good?"

Hongjun nodded. Li Jinglong continued, "You have a set too. Tomorrow will be our first official mission, and we'll be going in prepared. Everyone will be in uniform."

Humming his assent, Hongjun followed Li Jinglong back to the Department of Exorcism.

"You're upset," Li Jinglong said.

Hongjun hummed again.

Li Jinglong turned around. "Because I won't let you save that fox?"

"Chief Li," Hongjun began, gathering his courage, "are all yao so evil and unforgivable to you?"

Li Jinglong frowned. "Hongjun, you can't take yao for people! Yao understand human emotions, and they can act very much like them, but that fox is only using you. All fox yao want someone to latch on to. Didn't you hear Jinyun that day? Out of everything these fox yao say, how much do you think is the truth, and how much is a lie?"

"But..."

"No buts!" Li Jinglong said. "He's using you! Don't fall for it so easily!"

Li Jinglong's impassioned speech was interrupted by a loud gurgle from his stomach.

There was a brief but pointed silence.

He must be hungry, Hongjun thought. *Hungry people always have a bad temper.*

"You trust others too easily," Li Jinglong went on. "He's trying to charm you. Everything he said today was to try to make you happy and make himself look pitiful. Maybe he made it all up. Not to mention, if we let him go after we kill his whole family tomorrow, do you really think he won't come back for revenge?"

Li Jinglong's stomach let out another audible rumble. Hongjun couldn't take it any longer and dissolved in laughter.

"Don't laugh!" Li Jinglong yelled at him.

Hongjun waved a hand, dismissing the conversation. Stymied, Li Jinglong could only accompany him back to the Department of Exorcism in silence.

Everyone else had been waiting for the two of them to return for dinner. As soon as he stepped inside, Hongjun tossed the white stone hoop on the table to signify that his mission was complete.

"I've already eaten," he said, and headed for his room to go to bed.

"Grass rope and jade hoop," A-Tai said after glancing at the bracelet. "Looks like that little fox intends to pledge himself to Hongjun."

Li Jinglong chased Hongjun across the courtyard, only to find that Hongjun had already closed his door. He had no choice but to return to the table and eat his dinner under a cloud of gloom. Safe in the knowledge that their plan would likely go off without a hitch tomorrow, his companions tactfully probed him no further.

24
IMPERIAL AUDIENCE ON MOUNT LI

That night, Hongjun had another nightmare.

In his dream, Du Hanqing was enveloped in raging flames, blood seeping from splitting skin, beneath which a gory fox pelt had begun to emerge. Racked with agony, the fox struggled free of its human shell, dragging a trail of blood as his fat crackled and burned, howling in pain.

Hongjun bolted upright in bed with a sharp cry.

"Hongjun?" Mergen called from the door. He let himself in and pressed a hand to Hongjun's forehead. Hongjun slumped weakly in his grip, gasping shallowly for air.

This was his second such nightmare. He struggled to sit up straight as he caught his breath. After taking a moment to gather himself, he looked up at Mergen.

"The night the white deer left," Mergen quietly said, "nightmares roared across the plains."

He poured Hongjun a cup of water, then silently recited an incantation over it. Hongjun accepted the water, feeling his racing heart finally begin to slow after drinking it. "What do you mean?"

"The gray wolf is the guardian of the day, while the white deer is the protector of the night," Mergen said. "My homeland has a legend that when the white deer disappears in the dark, children far from home will be beset by nightmares... Are you homesick?"

Hongjun nodded. "A little."

Mergen patted Hongjun on the shoulder with a small smile. "Everyone has to leave home eventually, when they grow up."

"That's true." Hongjun lowered his head and gave Mergen a grateful nod. He felt much better after finishing the water. He lay back down, and this time, slept undisturbed by dreams.

No one else was up when Hongjun woke early the next morning. The carp yao, having heard everything that had happened last night, approached him as he brushed his teeth beside the well.

"Why do you care so much about that fox yao? He's neither family nor any friend of ours, and we hardly have any time to spare after making sure the people of Chang'an will be all right."

Hongjun wiped his mouth as he considered the question. "But am I not a yao too? The chief will find out one day."

"You're not like the foxes," the carp yao said. "The chief doesn't mind me either. If you want to blame someone, blame those foxes for not declaring allegiance to your dad back then. They brought this mess on themselves. Anyway, don't you go around eating anything and everything? I've never heard you talking about how all living things are equal when it comes to eating meat."

"That's not the same," Hongjun protested. "Not eating meat is a choice made out of compassion, but eating meat is also a way of delivering the animals from suffering. Qing Xiong said so."

"Morning, Chief."

Hearing Qiu Yongsi greeting Li Jinglong behind them, Hongjun and the carp yao fell silent. A moment later, Mergen strolled into the courtyard from the street outside.

"You're done?" Li Jinglong asked.

Mergen nodded.

"What did you go out to do, so early in the morning?" Hongjun asked.

Mergen smiled mysteriously and brought a finger to his lips—*You'll find out soon enough.*

Li Jinglong turned to Hongjun. "Don't worry—all I heard this time was the bit about compassion. Let's have breakfast; you can change after you eat."

Troubles the size of the heavens often seemed insubstantial after a good night's sleep. Hongjun's frustrations had melted away, but his awkwardness around Li Jinglong remained. After breakfast, however, Li Jinglong only gave him a cursory look before instructing everyone to change into their official uniforms.

The Department of Exorcism's uniforms had been sewn from the silk brocade gifted to them by the emperor and Noble Consort Yang. The outer garments were constructed from deep navy fabric of the highest quality, bold against snowy white underlayers and cut in a combat style with sleeves gathered at the cuffs, which had the effect of broadening the shoulders and narrowing the waist. Unlike the loose changpao robes worn by civil officials, these uniform hems were cropped short of full length to make it easier to move in a fight, revealing several inches of coal-black combat boots—not to mention making their robes flare much more dramatically as they walked.

Everyone took turns arranging their lapels before the mirror. As the saying went, the clothes made the man—everyone looked incredibly dashing. Even Qiu Yongsi, who was usually to be found dressed in scholars' garb, cut quite the handsome figure in his uniform. But out of the five of them, the best-looking was Hongjun. Since arriving in Chang'an, Hongjun had dressed in robes of coarse cloth with gathered sleeves, with a white top and pale blue trousers:

the garb of a farmer's son. No ordinary person could have made it work, but Hongjun was born with extraordinary good looks and managed to make his humble raiment appear refreshing and youthful. Now, in finer material, he could have been mistaken for a young noble's son, with a beauty so blinding it was difficult to look at him head-on.

"The collar's a bit tight..." Hongjun said, revealing his true nature the second he opened his mouth.

Li Jinglong helped him tug it open. "I forgot about the collar."

He had invited the tailor over earlier, asking them to do a rush order. Hongjun hadn't been in at the time, yet his uniform fit like a glove. Hongjun looked back at him, confused. "No one ever took my measurements."

Li Jinglong coughed awkwardly and said to everyone, "See, I said it would fit."

"Chief, your eye is incredible." Mergen gave him a thumbs-up.

Hongjun cast Li Jinglong a doubtful look. "How did you know my measurements?"

"All right, enough with the questions..." Li Jinglong handed Hongjun a garment like a miniature bathrobe, then pointed to the door. "You're slender, so I had them use the excess material to make an extra set."

"Zhao Zilong!" Hongjun shouted at the top of his lungs, holding the tiny robe.

"What is it, what is it?" Zhao Zilong sprinted over. Though he had lived for so many years, this was his first time wearing clothes. Seeing that Li Jinglong hadn't forgotten him, he exclaimed in joy, then held the bathrobe up and inserted one hairy arm. After he pulled the sash tight, the rear panel just about covered his tail. Li Jinglong also handed him a crossbody bag, presumably for carrying the oblivion pollen.

Everyone burst into laughter.

"Let me have a look," the carp yao said, hopping up and down in front of the mirror.

"We'll stick together today," Li Jinglong said. "This is a day that will decide life or death, existence or demise. Don't use the oblivion pollen without good reason."

Everyone voiced their assent, picked up their weapons, and prepared to head out. Hongjun's heart was hammering in his chest. He finally understood why Li Jinglong had said "*if* the department comes out the other side all right" the other night. The next time he glanced at Li Jinglong, the chief looked back at him with a faint smile in his eyes. *Don't worry,* his expression seemed to say, *everything will be just fine.*

Rain poured down over Mount Li that morning, soaking the robes of the travelers ascending its slopes. Beside the road, a Shenwu guard was saying in panic, "General! Please step aboard the carriage!"

Cane in hand, Feng Changqing struggled up the slope, limping step by step toward the emperor's imperial residence further up the mountain. He waved a hand. "It's no matter. Are you looking down on this general?"

The guards had no choice but to watch in silence as a stooped Feng Changqing made his way up the road. Feng Changqing's parents had died when he was young, and his maternal grandfather had been a victim of a plot orchestrated by former chancellor Li Linfu to have him exiled to Anxi. Feng Changqing had spent his life drifting from place to place, carrying heavy military burdens with his crippled body before displaying his shocking talent under Gao Xianzhi's command when the general had defeated Lesser Patola and Greater Patola in quick succession. Within the span of thirteen years, he leapt up to the status of a fearsome general, comparable to celebrated veterans like Geshu Han.

Feng Changqing had fought and won numerous battles in the Western Regions with his near-flawless command of the field. No one thought twice about ridiculing Li Jinglong, but those same people never had the gall to mock the frail Feng Changqing. He was a commander of vast armies, and his every word naturally carried an awe-inspiring weight. Although Feng Changqing currently held no official position, the day he'd returned victorious to court, he had submitted a memorial of nearly ten thousand words to Li Longji requesting agricultural overhauls in the border regions. This memorial also suggested adopting a policy of conciliation with their neighbors so that soldiers on long expeditions could come home. This had earned Feng Changqing an excellent reputation among the military officials and their troops.

A eunuch hurried into Huaqing Palace on Mount Li, his robes heavy with dew. Within, Li Longji was sound asleep with Yang Yuhuan in his arms. The eunuch feared waking them, but he was equally afraid that Feng Changqing would charge in wielding his cane, and that none of the guards outside would dare block his way.

Overcome with anxiety, the eunuch opened his mouth, but no sound emerged.

"If something's the matter, spit it out. Don't hem and haw." Li Longji's voice came from beyond the bed curtain—the emperor was awake.

"What hour is it?" Yang Yuhuan's languid voice followed.

"General Feng Changqing is waiting outside. He says he must report to Your Majesty about a matter of utmost urgency…"

Li Longji sat up in bed. "What's come up now?" he muttered. "There shouldn't be any problems... We haven't even assigned Changqing any tasks. Did the Ministry of War send him?"

The eunuch had no answer.

"Could it be a military report?" Li Longji pondered. "What about Guozhong? Why didn't he bring it to Guozhong first?"

"He said it is...um, intricately connected with the fate of Great Tang."

"What's this all about?" Li Longji waved an impatient hand. "Tell him that we are aware. When did he arrive?"

"He reached the foot of the mountain before midnight last night and walked up step by step," the eunuch replied.

"But General Feng has difficulty walking," Yang Yuhuan said. "Why has he walked all the way up here? Your Majesty..."

With no other choice, Li Longji wrapped himself in his dragon robes and stepped out of the bedroom, his hair still loose around his shoulders.

In the side hall, he found Feng Changqing leaning on his cane, huffing for breath as he met Li Longji's solemn gaze.

"There's no rush," Li Longji assured him, despite his displeasure. "Fetch General Feng a seat and bring him a drink of water—take your time."

Feng Changqing couldn't stop shaking as he looked up at Li Longji.

Li Longji was getting on in age. Although he took good care of himself, after six decades of life, it was impossible that his body would show no signs of decline. Feng Changqing, on the other hand, had yet to turn sixty, yet he looked years older than Li Longji.

"When this subject was climbing Mount Li today..." Feng Changqing began as he accepted a towel from a eunuch. He wiped sweat from his brow and panted, "...for some reason, I recalled Your Majesty...Your Majesty's handsome figure that year."

"Our handsome figure from which year?" Li Longji began to laugh.

Feng Changqing looked at Li Longji. "The first year of the Tanglong era, when you gathered your troops before Lingyan Pavilion."

Realizing he had been woken up to indulge Feng Changqing's nostalgia, Li Longji didn't know whether to laugh or cry. But his intuition, honed from decades of rule, was telling him that whatever topic Feng Changqing wished to broach with this talk of old times would be no simple matter.

"If you hadn't reminded us, we would have almost forgotten," Li Longji said with a smile. He accepted a bowl of ginseng soup from a eunuch, took a sip, then said, "Oh, give Changqing a bowl too."

That year, imperial guard officers Li Xianfu and Ge Fushun had rebelled, taking over the Yulin Guard to assassinate Empress Dowager Wei, who wished to follow Empress Wu Zhao's example and ascend the throne as a female emperor. Li Longji and his aunt, Princess Taiping, had gathered their troops before Lingyan Pavilion, ready to defend the Li family's reign to the death. They fought their way into the palace and killed the conspirators Princess Anle, Wu Yanxiu, Shangguan Wan'er, and many others to snatch the nation back from their grasping hands.

Those events seemed to have occurred a lifetime ago. But when Feng Changqing brought them up again, Li Longji couldn't help but feel a ghost of the hot-blooded passion that had animated him at the time.

"There was also the first year of the Kaiyuan era,"[21] Feng Changqing said.

---

21   *Kaiyuan, Li Longji's second era name during his reign, spanning the years 713–741. His first era name of Xiantian spanned the years 712–713, while his third and final era name of Tianbao spanned the years 742–756.*

If Li Longji recalled correctly, that was the year he had taken decisive action to thwart the ambitions of Princess Taiping, who was subsequently executed. That event had marked the beginning of a golden age for Great Tang.

"Changqing, you must know that today's age of prosperity is a blessing upon the people," Li Longji said. "It's a good thing that our blade no longer needs to be sharpened." He'd begun to see what Feng Changqing was hinting at, and thus replied in the same veiled manner—no matter what Feng Changqing had to report, the emperor didn't want a major disturbance in court.

"Your Majesty is wise, of course," Feng Changqing said. "It was only that, after thinking about Your Majesty in those days, I couldn't help but recall my own actions in days past."

A faint frown creased Li Longji's brow.

"Has your subject Changqing ever concealed any military report from Your Majesty's court since enlisting under Gao Xianzhi's command?"

"No," Li Longji said. "Though you have exposed many lies from the mouths of others."

"Has your subject Changqing ever lied to Your Majesty?" Feng Changqing asked again.

"In all the world, it is you who are the most likely to tell the honest truth, regardless of whether the situation calls for it." Li Longji's voice carried an unquestionable authority. "Though you may not say what others want to hear, you never lie. Tell us, what is going on in Chang'an?"

Li Longji had been formidable in his youth. Although he had indulged more often in the pleasures of the flesh in recent years, he was clearheaded yet when it came to fundamental issues of right and wrong.

Feng Changqing raised one shaking hand and pointed at his own neck. "If your subject Changqing speaks one false word today, may Your Majesty claim the head which sits atop this neck. This subject will breathe not a word of complaint."

Li Longji's brows knit together. He had no idea what had brought Feng Changqing to him in such a mood. At last, he said, "Speak."

As the sun climbed high in the sky, the bell began to toll at the testing site for the imperial examination on the north side of the city. Nearly two thousand, five hundred scholars were searched and assigned numbered tokens before entering the grounds in single file. Rows of single-occupancy rooms stretched as far as the eye could see, connected by yards and yards of corridors, each door numbered based on the traditional sexagenary cycle.[22]

Each scholar waited at the door corresponding to their token for a proctor to pass by and verify their identity and credentials. Only then could they hang their token at the door and enter. Once the door had been shut behind them, the examination officer placed a seal over the door; each room was completely closed off save for a small window in the door for light, through which servants would deliver standard meals and dispose of the scholars' waste. The examinees would stay within these rooms for the entire three days of the exam.

There were dozens of rows of rooms, with a hundred rooms set along each row. After all the doors were secured, the examination had begun—the enormous testing grounds went silent as a tomb.

---

22 A numbering system traditionally used for recording time. Each term consists of two characters, the first being one of the ten heavenly stems and the second being one of the twelve earthly branches. Both "digits" increment at the same time, so only sixty of the potential one hundred twenty combinations are actually used.

Moving as quietly as possible, the exorcists finished dragging a number of sleeping servants into the corner of a storeroom and wrapped the servants' robes over their new uniforms.

Li Jinglong whispered, "Let's begin."

The carp yao crouched behind the water barrel and portioned out the sedative powder. Medicine in hand, the exorcists split up and departed in different directions.

Hongjun strode quickly through the corridor, keeping his head bowed. He peeked inside every room he passed to look for A-Tai's marks on the sleeves or hems of the scholars' robes. Each time he found one, he left a shallow mark on the door frame with one of his throwing knives.

A-Tai did the same, feigning innocuous glances into each room as he passed.

"Hey!"

A proctor spotted A-Tai as he paced down a corridor and beckoned him over. "Come over here."

A-Tai obliged. Before the proctor could ask why a servant was going about peeking into examinees' rooms, a hand tugged the hem of his robes from behind.

Turning in confusion, the proctor was rewarded with a face full of oblivion pollen, courtesy of the carp yao. "May fortune be with you—"

The proctor sneezed. A-Tai immediately whirled and dashed away like a stiff breeze, while the carp yao darted into a corner and snuck off, leaving the proctor blinking in bemusement.

In another corridor, a guard stopped Qiu Yongsi. "Halt! Why haven't I seen you…"

Once again, the carp yao tossed his pollen—"Good luck and goodbye!"

The guard sneezed, and a vacant look came over his face as Qiu Yongsi and the carp yao quickly went their separate ways.

Hongjun stopped at yet another room and peeked inside. This time, he found Du Hanqing sitting, straight-backed, at the desk. Hongjun hesitated briefly, then walked past the room.

Li Jinglong silently stepped out from around the corner, brows knit as he watched Hongjun's retreating figure. To his surprise, Hongjun soon returned. Li Jinglong ducked back behind cover.

Throwing knife in hand, Hongjun seemed to dither for a moment before steeling himself and scratching a mark on the doorframe. Eyes reddening at the rims, he resolutely walked away.

Moments later, Mergen approached the room and looked down to inspect the mark on the door. He snuck a glance inside, sighed in relief, and deepened the mark with a flick of his wrist before striding away.

Li Jinglong stared, not knowing what to make of this. Just as he was about to leave himself, A-Tai, too, showed up to inspect Du Hanqing's door before speeding away. Next was Qiu Yongsi.

As Qiu Yongsi turned the corner, he nearly ran right into Li Jinglong. He tensed immediately and plastered on a smile. "Oh, Chief, it's you."

"Looks like I worried for nothing," Li Jinglong said coolly. "You're all quite protective of Hongjun."

Qiu Yongsi laughed. "We're just afraid one mistake will ruin all our efforts. We're always on your side when it matters most, aren't we, Chief?" He patted Li Jinglong on the shoulder.

When all the rooms had been marked, everyone returned to the storage room to double-check their numbers.

"Two hundred and sixty-six rooms," Li Jinglong said. "That's all of them. Now we wait for the bell."

Hongjun was silent. No one else spoke either, and the atmosphere turned strained.

Li Jinglong casually placed a hand on Hongjun's shoulder. "After we close this case, let's all go out and have some fun. Tell me, where do you all want to go?"

"For real?!" Hongjun exclaimed, perking up.

Li Jinglong's mouth twitched. *So much for your compassion...*

"Pingkang Ward!" Qiu Yongsi's reply was immediate.

"Pingkang Ward," A-Tai agreed with a smile.

"Is Pingkang Ward okay?" Hongjun asked. "I haven't gone for real yet... Of course, if you don't want to, that's okay too..."

"Pingkang Ward, then," Mergen said. "We won't spend the night; we'll just watch some dancing and listen to some music. That should be fine, right? Pingkang Ward isn't all, uhh...*those* sorts of establishments."

"You too?!" For a moment, Li Jinglong didn't know what else to say. He was utterly unable to understand what went on inside the heads of these subordinates of his.

"I...uhh... I'm saving my first time for the white..." Mergen faltered. "Forget it, I'll tell you another time. But drinking and listening to music is all right."

"Is Pingkang Ward okay?" the carp yao asked. "I want to go back and take a closer look at that painting."

"Pingkang Ward it is!" Qiu Yongsi declared.

"All right!" Everyone cried out in joy, the majority vote crushing the lone dissenter. Li Jinglong pressed a hand to his forehead.

The first toll of the bell put an end to any further conversation; everyone rose and got ready to move out.

At the second tolling of the bell, the proctors picked up stacks of examination scrolls and strode briskly down each corridor, passing one scroll through the window of each room, then hurrying to the next as soon as the exam left their hands. In this manner, all of the rooms were quickly covered.

By now the sun was beating down overhead, and sweat had dampened Hongjun's palms. Outside, someone called, "Water delivery!"

The exorcists melted into the crowd of servants, each carrying a basket of empty water jugs. They kept their heads down as the guards searched each basket, then departed to make their deliveries. Li Jinglong held a sack of the sedative powder in his left hand and a water jug in his right; at every marked door, he surreptitiously tipped a little of the medicine into the jug before handing it to the guard. The guard filled the jug with water and passed it through the window, where it was accepted by the waiting examinee.

Five rows, then five more. Each row had nearly a hundred rooms each, and all the exorcists were sweating profusely by the time they were done. When they returned to the storeroom, Li Jinglong saw that it was about time for the next phase of their plan to begin. "Time to go."

The exorcists hopped over the wall and retreated across the street to observe, all fidgeting with nerves. Their preparations had taken them the entire morning, and the fall air was starting to cool in the afternoon. Hongjun couldn't stop worrying over whether the foxes would drink the water, and whether the dose would be high enough—in retrospect, Li Jinglong had been prescient when he told Hongjun to increase the dosage.

Li Jinglong waited patiently a while longer before sucking in a deep breath—even he seemed a bit nervous. Soon, the ring of hoofbeats along the lane marked the arrival of carriages bearing Gao Lishi and several officials from the Ministry of Rites, come to oversee the examination.

This was the moment Li Jinglong had been waiting for. "Let's move out."

"Wait." Hongjun stopped them. "What if it didn't work? They won't leave any time soon; should we wait a little longer?"

"We tested your drug on those servants earlier," Li Jinglong said. "We know the dose is high enough."

"What if they didn't drink it?"

"I had Mergen sneak into the Imperial Academy this morning and increase the salt in everyone's food by nearly half, just in case."

Hongjun, A-Tai, and Qiu Yongsi boggled at him. Qiu Yongsi was first to speak: "Chief, after today, I'll follow you anywhere!"

A-Tai couldn't believe it. "Who *are* you?!"

"You exaggerate," Li Jinglong said humbly. "Mind your manners when we get back in. Let's go!"

Li Jinglong stripped off his servant's robe to reveal the navy-blue uniform underneath. With the Sword of Wisdom strapped to his waist, he cut a sharp figure in his imperially gifted clothes. The others followed suit and revealed their official uniforms as well, following Li Jinglong as he strode toward the examination grounds.

25
ROUNDUP ON THE EXAMINATION GROUNDS

GAO LISHI HAD COME to patrol the examination grounds accompanied by the Minister and Assistant Minister of Rites, as well as the Grand Secretaries of the Belvedere of Literary Profundity and the Belvedere of Spreading Righteousness. The exam proctors hurriedly gathered in the center of the testing grounds to greet them and receive whatever instructions they had to offer.

Their lighthearted conversation was interrupted by a shout from outside. "This is the site of the imperial examination. No outsiders allowed!"

"The Department of Demonic Exorcism is conducting official business here. Everyone, stand back!"

Gao Lishi was speechless.

The sounds of the argument grew louder as the visiting officials turned from a corridor to peer outside the gate. Qiu Yongsi raised his voice and called, "Li Jinglong, the chief of the Department of Demonic Exorcism under the Imperial Court of Judicial Review, has arrived—"

Li Jinglong shot him a look.

"Li Jinglong! What are you doing?!" Gao Lishi cried.

As the guards swarmed over to stop them, Hongjun deployed his sacred light from behind Li Jinglong. The mortal guards were no

LEGEND OF EXORCISM

match for such a weapon; they were all sent flying backward. The entranceway exploded into chaos. The guards drew their weapons, pointing them at Li Jinglong and his four subordinates.

The exam proctors saw no more than a flash of light, and then Li Jinglong's subordinates had the guards knocked flat on the ground. Gao Lishi knew at once that this was trouble. If Li Jinglong hadn't been lying about that night at Daming Palace, these must be his exorcists. Whether the young man's attack was a parlor trick or a display of true ability, if these people fought here, the guards at the gate would be no match for them. He had no choice but to placate Li Jinglong.

"Let him inside!" Gao Lishi called.

The exorcists streamed into the examination grounds. Li Jinglong offered Gao Lishi an obeisance befitting his station, no more and no less.

"Li Jinglong, the Department of Exorcism has been formally dissolved," Gao Lishi said. "The extra time afforded to you was only so you could vacate the building. Why are you here causing a disturbance?"

The Minister of Rites scoffed, scanning Li Jinglong from top to bottom with a sneer on his face.

This was the first the Department of Exorcism had heard of this. They all looked at Li Jinglong in shock.

Li Jinglong didn't even blink. "We are here today on orders from His Majesty to supervise the imperial examinations and eliminate the evil creatures threatening the examination grounds."

The proctors exchanged looks, and a few began to laugh. "Li Jinglong, are you quite well?" asked the Minister of Rites. "Let's find you a doctor…"

"His Majesty is on his way back from Mount Li, but we needn't wait for his return," Li Jinglong said firmly. "Before he arrives, I ask that all the esteemed officials here serve as our witnesses. This way, please."

He didn't wait for a response before stepping into the corridor.

"Li Jinglong! What are you doing?!" Gao Lishi shouted.

Hongjun and the others fell into step behind their leader. Gao Lishi and the rest jogged after them, and the exorcists moved to either side to make way for the government officials.

"Li Jinglong!" snapped the Grand Secretary of the Belvedere of Literary Profundity. "The integrity of the imperial examination grounds is inextricably tied to the future of the nation. There is no place for your disrespect here!"

Hearing raised voices outside, the examinees peeked out their windows in curiosity. They were greeted by the sight of Li Jinglong striding down the corridor as Gao Lishi trailed behind him, roaring, "Li Jinglong! You've lost your mind! Guards! Arrest him—"

"Which of you dares to try?!" At this single shout from Hongjun, none of the guards risked advancing. Everyone stood stunned as Li Jinglong walked up to a room and kicked in the door, shattering the lock in one blow.

"What are you doing?!" one of the officials cried.

The scholar inside yelped in alarm, looking at Li Jinglong with wide eyes. Hongjun's heart thumped, and he felt as if he had been drenched in ice water. The corridor was deathly still as the same thought passed through every exorcist's head—*We're doomed.*

"Wrong door; my apologies." Li Jinglong shut the door.

Everyone was shocked speechless.

Li Jinglong kicked open another door. Beside himself with anger, Gao Lishi bellowed, "Li Jinglong!"

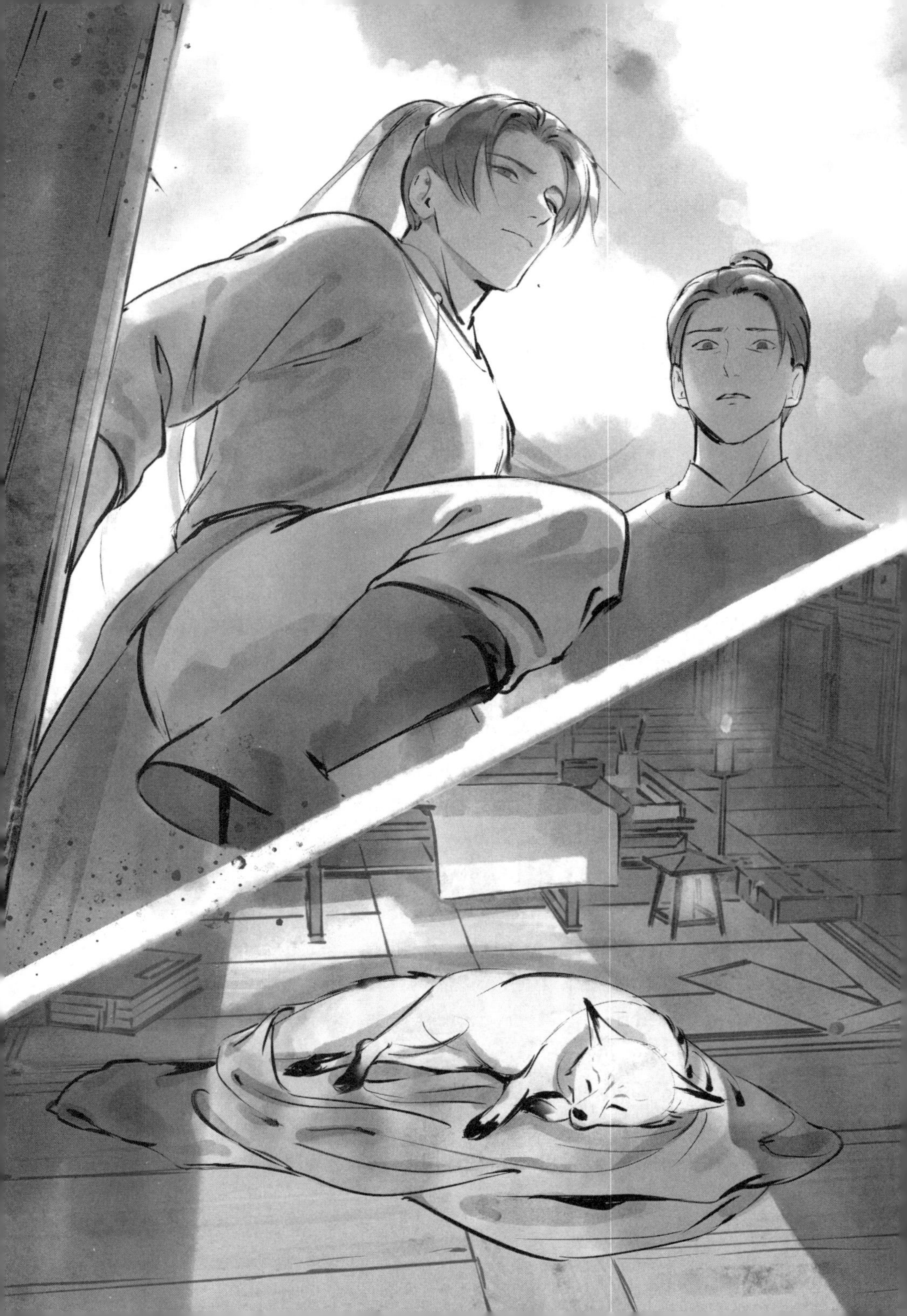

Yet he fell silent the instant Li Jinglong stepped aside. Inside the room, a pile of clothing was heaped before the desk, within which was nestled a sleeping gray fox.

Hongjun nearly crowed in joy, while the others let out quiet sighs of relief.

"What is this?" Gao Lishi glared at each of the proctors in turn, as if he suspected he was the victim of the world's greatest prank.

The Minister of Rites peered around him, then reeled backward and fell on his rear in fright. "This…this…" he stuttered. "What is the meaning of this?!"

"Where's the examinee?!" a proctor cried in shock.

Li Jinglong scanned the faces around him. The other exorcists did the same, searching for any tiny slip in emotion.

Mergen subtly shook his head—the plot's mastermind didn't appear to be present. When the scholar in the next room poked his head out to look, Qiu Yongsi stuffed the man back inside, while Hongjun twisted the lock into place.

"Detain the fox," Li Jinglong said coldly. "Take the token and clothing too. Now, on to the next."

"There're more?!" The proctors were stunned.

Gao Lishi had yet to collect himself when Li Jinglong kicked in the next door. "Wait!"

"Wait for what?" Li Jinglong asked. "General Gao, a skulk of foxes is sitting Great Tang's imperial examination as we speak. Are you not the least bit afraid that our official ranks will be overrun by yao?"

He had struck right at the heart of the issue. All the officials present—the proctors, the Grand Secretaries, the Minister and Assistant Minister of Rites—felt a chill run down their spines as they realized the severity of the problem.

"Watch." Li Jinglong kicked in several doors in a row, then stepped back to allow the officials to take a good look before ordering Mergen to collect the foxes inside and bring them into the middle of the grounds. Qiu Yongsi stuck a few talismans on the parade grounds to form a spiritual array and tossed all the sleeping foxes inside.

As more and more foxes were revealed, Gao Lishi's remaining composure seemed to unravel. "Wait! Li Jinglong, you need to explain what exactly—"

"Let me kick down a door too," Hongjun said.

"Go ahead," Li Jinglong told him. "A-Tai, take the others and capture the rest."

"Stop, stop!" One of the Grand Secretaries was on the verge of hyperventilating, as if Li Jinglong was somehow transforming the scholars inside into foxes each time he burst through a door.

"Li Jinglong! What sorcery is this?!" Gao Lishi was shouting.

Hongjun satisfied his destructive urges with a few solid kicks, and Li Jinglong plucked the foxes from the rooms.

After another three doors, the Minister of Rites yelled, "The circumstances of this case are still unclear! Li Jinglong! Provide a proper explanation before you kick *any more doors*!"

"The Department of Exorcism is not under the purview of the Ministry of Rites. Go summon the Minister of Justice," Li Jinglong said.

"Li Jinglong!" Gao Lishi roared. "I don't know how, but this is all your doing! You...you're intent on getting vengeance!"

Li Jinglong glanced at Gao Lishi, then turned from the doors and walked back toward the officials. Terrified, Gao Lishi and the others shrank back, afraid they, too, would turn into foxes under Li Jinglong's boot.

Their standoff was cut short by a declaration that echoed through the corridors:

"His Majesty has arrived—!"

The examination grounds boiled over. The examinees, who had no idea what was going on, all rushed to their little windows, desperate for a glimpse of Li Longji's face. The emperor was dressed in casual robes, striding ahead while Feng Changqing hobbled behind him on his cane.

Li Longji paused at the edge of the parade grounds to stare at the foxes piled within the array, shock written stark across his face. He looked back at Feng Changqing, who only waved his hand in a gesture of invitation: "Your Majesty."

All the officials bowed in salutation as Li Longji arrived before them.

Li Jinglong cupped his fist. "Reporting to Your Majesty; General Gao and the other gentlemen here are currently assisting this subject with the arrest of these fox yao."

Li Longji cast a glance at Gao Lishi. "Is this true?" he asked, grim.

Gao Lishi was shaking in his boots. Li Jinglong had made quite the fine play—there was no choice but to agree. "Yes...yes... Though this subject is not yet aware of why..."

Li Longji came to a stop before one of the rooms. "Open the door. Let us see."

The proctor's hand was shaking so badly that he was having trouble inserting the key into the lock. Hongjun darted ahead and kicked the wooden door open with a resounding *bang*.

Li Jinglong raised a hand to stop Li Longji before he could march right into the room, but Feng Changqing waved him off. The Son of Heaven was as imposing as ever. Li Longji entered the room himself and lifted the unconscious fox by its ear to examine the creature. "How many more are there?"

"Reporting to Your Majesty, there are two hundred and sixty-six in total," Li Jinglong responded.

Fury darkened Li Longji's face. At the next room, no one had to open the door; the emperor kicked it in himself.

Lo and behold, it was yet another fox.

Two hours later, a veritable mountain of sleeping foxes lay piled on the parade grounds. Hongjun had prepared an extremely potent drug, and none of the fox yao had yet woken.

Li Longji sat in a chair someone had fetched, panting for breath. Li Jinglong saw the unspoken fear in the emperor's eyes when he glanced in Li Jinglong's direction.

"This one is for you." Li Jinglong plucked a little fox out of the pile and handed it to Hongjun. A jade Buddha was tied around one of its front paws.

Greatly relieved, Hongjun opened his mouth to thank him when Li Jinglong said, "But I need you to do me a favor, Hongjun."

At dusk, the little fox awoke inside a cage in the imperial study at Xingqing Palace. It opened its eyes with a shudder, spotting the talismans pasted over the cage. Its eyes darted around the room.

"Don't worry," Hongjun said from the other side of the room. "You're safe here; they won't find you."

Every hair stood up on the little fox's body. It stared at Hongjun in disbelief. Hongjun sat on the windowsill, one foot drawn up on the ledge while the other dangled freely, a beautiful silhouette against the rosy evening sky.

"I'm sorry," Hongjun said. "I came to the Imperial Academy that day to investigate all of you."

"You...you... Who are you?"

"An exorcist," Hongjun quietly replied.

"You lied to me!" the little fox cried.

"But I also saved your life," Hongjun said. "Or else you'd already be dead."

"Where are the others?" the fox asked in a trembling voice.

"Their true forms were revealed. Who sent you here?"

The little fox flinched. Hongjun tilted his head and offered the creature a smile. "Tell me who orchestrated all of this, and I'll let you go."

The little fox was quiet a moment, tears pooling in its eyes as it shook like a leaf. "I don't know," it sobbed. "I'm begging you, let me go."

"You killed so many scholars," Hongjun said. "You're not exactly innocent, are you?"

"I didn't kill anyone! I really didn't!"

"But what about the others?"

The little fox went silent.

"You conspired to kill two hundred and sixty-six scholars, among them many future officials of Great Tang."

"But I really didn't. They never let me absorb essence from mortals. When I arrived, the others had already sucked that child dry."

Hongjun shuddered, the hair rising on the back of his neck.

"They told me to replace a scholar, so I did as I was told. I'm begging you! Hongjun, please!"

Hongjun jumped down from the windowsill and sighed. He crouched to examine the little fox, his eyes shadowed with guilt. "I'm sorry," he said at last.

As he reached out to scatter medicinal powder into the cage, the little fox snapped at his finger. Hongjun yelped in pain, but the fox was soon unconscious once again.

Li Jinglong rushed out from his hiding place behind a bookshelf and grabbed Hongjun's bitten index finger. "Are you hurt? Let me see."

"It's nothing," Hongjun said. "On the mountain I used to get nipped by animals all the time."

A moment later, Li Longji also stepped out from behind the bookshelf—he had heard the entire conversation.

Hongjun straightened up. Li Jinglong said for him, "Your Majesty, this subject wishes to beg mercy for this fox yao on Hongjun's behalf. It has never harmed a human…"

"Fine." Li Longji waved a hand. "We leave this decision to you."

The emperor seemed to age decades in the light of the dying sun, his sure steps becoming a tired shuffle as he exited the imperial study. Hongjun breathed a sigh of relief and followed him out, Li Jinglong at his side.

"Had we not seen it with our own eyes," said Li Longji without breaking his stride, "we would never have believed something so fantastical."

Yang Yuhuan stood on the steps to Xingqing Palace's rear courtyard, lit by the setting sun as she gazed at the sleeping foxes piled in the middle of the palace grounds with naked shock. The Duchess of Guo and Yang Guozhong, arriving after her, turned ashen as they laid eyes upon the scene. Feng Changqing and Gao Lishi stood to either side as eunuchs retrieved chairs from inside the palace, offering seats to the members of the imperial family who had just returned from Huaqing Palace.

Yang Yuhuan could scarcely believe her eyes. "So this was what General Feng meant…"

"Yes," Feng Changqing replied. "These are all fox yao that disguised themselves as scholars with the intention of throwing Great Tang into chaos."

Qiu Yongsi, A-Tai, and Mergen stood guard in front of the foxes, weapons in hand, prepared to strike in an instant should the fox yao suddenly wake.

Li Longji strode past the mountain of fox yao without a sideways glance. With a deep sigh, he sank into the chair set at the top of the staircase. Yang Yuhuan looked down at the foxes, then at Li Longji, who placed his hand in hers. "Jinglong," the emperor said, "tell everyone the story."

Standing at the base of the stairs, Li Jinglong solemnly began his tale. "Your Majesty, Your Grace, lords and ministers, this story starts when Hongjun first arrived in Chang'an…"

He began with Hongjun's encounter with the great fish Fei'ao. At his mention of Pingkang Ward, Yang Yuhuan frowned. "So that's what happened. You were in Pingkang Ward to investigate a case?"

Li Jinglong paused. Steeling himself, he said, "Yes, this subject discovered…yao energy in Pingkang Ward."

Before Hongjun could blurt a protest, Li Jinglong silenced him with a glance.

Deceiving one's sovereign is a capital offense… his other subordinates thought. *Oh well, we'll give you a chance to repair your reputation. It was Hongjun's fault, anyway.*

Li Jinglong proceeded to describe their ventures into Pingkang Ward, their discovery of the fox yao, and how the clues had led them to discover Fei'ao's involvement—the only piece he omitted was the matter of Hongjun's lost throwing knife. Hu Sheng and the guards who had been at the city gate that night were summoned as witnesses to corroborate the story.

Li Longji, Noble Consort Yang, and the rest of the Yang family were astonished by this tale. Voice unsteady, the Duchess of Guo said, "You fought these creatures in Daming Palace?"

Yang Guozhong frowned. "How are you so certain these foxes truly replaced the scholars, that this isn't some illusion..."

Li Longji cut him off with a raised hand. "We witnessed evidence of this with our own eyes. There is no doubt about this detail. Li Jinglong, continue."

Li Jinglong described everything that had occurred in Daming Palace. He added, "The creature was terribly difficult to subdue, and many gold vessels and treasures in Daming Palace were destroyed in the struggle. Your subject Jinglong fears..."

"Your accomplishments today have more than made up for the losses," Li Longji said. "No need to worry. We shall take responsibility for the damages."

All five members of the Department of Exorcism felt a burden lift off their shoulders—they could kiss this debt goodbye.

Li Longji had already heard the full tale from Feng Changqing, but it was even more shocking coming from Li Jinglong's mouth. In the end, Li Jinglong concluded, "These fox yao intended to overthrow the order of the court. Their crimes are unforgivable. This subject urges Your Majesty to eliminate them without delay."

"We will do as you suggest," Li Longji coldly said. "The Ministry of Rites shall notify the families of the deceased and offer compensation for their loss."

The Minister of Rites bowed in acknowledgment. Yang Yuhuan sighed, her eyes filled with pity.

"This subject has a subordinate named Tigra Yazdegerd," Li Jinglong continued. "He is the heir to the throne of the former Persian Empire..."

"Yazdegerd?" A look of recognition came over Li Longji's face. "What is his relationship to Narsieh?"

"Narsieh was my father." A-Tai stepped forward and bowed to Li Longji.

Li Longji examined A-Tai. "You've returned?" he asked, voice grave.

A-Tai let out a long exhale and gave him a small smile. "Yes. I wish to serve the interests of Great Tang."

Li Longji frowned, seemingly lost in some memory. Li Jinglong spoke up again. "Tigra is a disciple of Zoroastrianism and excels in the art of wielding fire. Incinerating the fox yao is a task he can perform with ease."

Looks of reluctance stole over the faces of Yang Yuhuan, Yang Guozhong, and the Duchess of Guo, but Li Longji's voice was filled with only hatred. "Burn them!"

These fox yao had deceived everyone to replace hundreds of scholars in the imperial examinations. If this were to get out, the prestige of Great Tang's court and the reputation of its emperor would suffer irreparable damage, and the imperial examination itself would become a joke. The thought was intolerable. Li Jinglong took a step back and gestured for A-Tai to begin.

"If you don't want to watch, you can be excused," Li Jinglong whispered to Hongjun.

"It's all right," Hongjun replied.

A-Tai murmured an incantation. As the bloody rays of the setting sun slanted over the plaza, thousands of beams of red light burst from the ring on his hand and sparked into raging flames. With a wave of his fan, fire and wind whipped into a cyclone, sweeping toward the mountain of fox yao.

All two hundred some foxes awakened, their horrible screams rising from within the crackling conflagration—but there was no escape. Their cries were snuffed out within the space of a few breaths, and a morbid silence fell over the palace grounds as the flames licked at the sky, giving off an acrid stench. Once all the foxes had perished, a frightening burst of energy surged into the air.

Li Longji trembled, and everyone blanched.

This was the manifestation of the resentment and malign energies released by the fox yao upon their deaths. It boiled up without end, streaking into the sky in the form of a black flame.

This was totally outside Li Jinglong's expectations. "Protect His Majesty!" he shouted.

At that moment, Hongjun felt an overpowering wave of hostility threaten to burst through the walls of his heart, every kind of sorrow and rage pouring out from within him. Li Jinglong dragged him aside and stepped in front of him.

The wrathful energy weakened as soon as Hongjun was behind Li Jinglong. That black flame rose higher and higher, then hurtled into the heavens in a curving arc, like a meteor shooting across the sky, until at last it disappeared entirely.

Yang Yuhuan frowned. "What was that?"

"Reporting to Your Grace," Mergen said, "that was a manifestation of the malicious energy evil creatures accumulate after absorbing the essence and blood of mortals. Now that the monsters have been slain, the souls of their victims will return to the heavenly meridians. There is no need for concern."

Beneath the velvet veil of night, the pile of fox yao corpses crackled, burned to a crisp. Not one of the witnesses dared to break the heavy silence over the palace grounds, each caught up in their own quiet calculations.

26
COMPASSION

"Li Jinglong, you and your subordinates stay in the palace," Li Longji said. "Everyone else is dismissed. It's getting late. Guozhong, patrol the examination grounds with Changqing tomorrow."

After everyone had bowed and taken their leave, Li Longji and Yang Yuhuan retreated to the rear hall of Xingqing Palace. Li Jinglong sensed that today's events had been a great shock for the emperor; he would need time to sort through his thoughts. He drew his sword and began prodding through the fox yao's burnt corpses.

"You should treat your sword with more care," Qiu Yongsi said. "It's not a poker."

Li Jinglong glared at Qiu Yongsi, but Mergen began to laugh. "So we don't need to pay damages for Daming Palace anymore?"

"Excellent news!" A-Tai replied with a smile.

Seeing that Hongjun merely sighed, Li Jinglong asked, "What is it? I already did as you asked and made an exception for that fox. Why are you still so glum?"

Hongjun thought back to what Li Jinglong had said the night before—he had no idea whether the little fox had lied about killing humans. He felt Li Jinglong had been right, and the thought dismayed him.

"Thank you," Hongjun said. "It's just that I feel like I've been tricked. Do you think Du Hanqing…"

"Sometimes, ignorance is bliss." Li Jinglong waved a hand. "Don't take it to heart; turn the page and forget him. We'll give him some oblivion pollen and release him later, and it'll all be over."

"Don't make yourself miserable," Mergen said with a smile.

"All right." Hongjun began to smile too.

Before long, a eunuch arrived to invite Li Jinglong to the side hall, where the emperor had ordered a meal to be set out for them. The servants assigned to clean up the mess of char that had been the foxes had also arrived, so the exorcists followed the eunuch through Xingqing Palace's imperial gardens to take a late supper.

A meal personally bestowed by Li Longji—this show of favor was on a different plane than any they had experienced before. Yang Yuhuan had even ordered the cooks to prepare a batch of "the people's lifeblood," which Hongjun scarfed down without a care. Li Jinglong, however, still seemed to have something on his mind.

"The case is closed now, right?" Qiu Yongsi prompted him.

"Yes." With that reminder, Li Jinglong began to smile again. "Thank you for your hard work, everyone."

Li Longji summoned them again as they were enjoying the tea after their meal. Everyone washed their hands, wiped their faces, and followed the eunuch to an elegant building named Gold Blossom's Fall.

"Tigra is summoned for an audience with the emperor," the eunuch announced.

No one had expected Li Longji to summon A-Tai first. Li Jinglong gave him a nod and an encouraging smile. A-Tai exhaled slowly, removed his boots, and stepped inside the hall. A second message soon arrived from Noble Consort Yang bidding the others to enjoy the flowers and tea outside Gold Blossom's Fall while they waited.

It was a bleak autumn night; Li Jinglong didn't know what flowers they were supposed to be enjoying. With little better to do, he leaned against the wall and took a brief nap. The past few days had exhausted him. As he dozed, his head drooped toward Hongjun's shoulder until he was slumped against him. Hongjun wrapped an arm around his waist to hold him up as he quietly chatted with Mergen and Qiu Yongsi.

Two hours later, A-Tai emerged, and Li Longji summoned Qiu Yongsi and Mergen.

Li Jinglong jerked awake and wiped the drool from his mouth. "Were we summoned?" he asked, disoriented.

"Not yet." Hongjun thought it was strange too. Why was he summoning them individually and in pairs? But Mergen and Qiu Yongsi returned shortly, gone just long enough to have exchanged a few words.

"He said the three of us should head back without you; we won't be needed any more tonight," Mergen said.

"Go ahead," Li Jinglong said. "Zhao Zilong is still waiting back at headquarters."

He and Hongjun saw them off, Li Jinglong rubbing his face in a sleepy daze. Soon enough, the two of them were summoned as well; Li Longji had requested that Li Jinglong enter along with Hongjun.

Gold Blossom's Fall had a clear pool in the center of its courtyard, beside which stood a low couch backed by an eight-sided folding screen painted with celestial cranes. Lanterns flickered, and qin music drifted from the distance in sporadic flurries of notes.

A century-old ginkgo tree grew from the center of the pond, its golden leaves rustling to the sound of the qin like a vast field of gilded flowers. It made for a beautiful scene.

Li Jinglong scrubbed a hand over his face. Li Longji was sitting on the low couch, while Yang Yuhuan assembled medicinal pills to his side. Li Jinglong began to dip in an obeisance when Li Longji stopped him. "There's no need. Take a seat."

The imperial attendants brought out another low couch, and Li Jinglong and Hongjun made themselves comfortable. They sat in silence while they were served tea before Li Longji began to speak.

"Jinglong, this is a great achievement. Tell us, what reward do you desire?"

"This subject was merely performing his duty and dares not accept rewards for acting in the service of the nation. This subject is already overcome with gratitude that Your Majesty is willing to forgive the disturbance we caused at Daming Palace."

Although his words were humble, Li Jinglong spoke them with a quiet dignity. Yang Yuhuan still looked troubled, but a small smile appeared on her face then. "See, this consort guessed correctly."

Li Longji began to laugh, and the serious atmosphere lightened considerably.

"But evil must be pulled up by the roots," Li Jinglong went on. "In a few days, this subject will bring his subordinates to Pingkang Ward again to see if any yao slipped through our fingers."

Li Longji nodded in approval. "If it's for official business, then go where you must."

"I'm afraid the people of Chang'an will once again…" Li Jinglong began.

"Shall we issue an imperial edict?" Li Longji asked.

Everyone laughed again. "This subject wouldn't dare request such a thing," Li Jinglong said.

Hongjun scratched his neck. "Your Majesty, we still owe the shop six thousand, four hundred silver for the oblivion pollen. Could you cover that for us too?"

Li Jinglong was aghast.

"What is oblivion pollen?" Yang Yuhuan asked. "Why is it so expensive?"

As Hongjun began to explain, Yang Yuhuan looked flabbergasted. "Is there really such a thing in this world?"

"A powder that can erase all debts, grudges, affection, and resentment, and relieve people of pain," Li Longji said. "A mystical drug such as this must be one of the rarest in the world."

Yang Yuhuan smiled. "But no matter how much trouble one's joys and sorrows might be, they are still your own. Is this not what gives life meaning? Even if someone offered it to me, I would never take it."

Li Longji laughed. "You're right. If someone offered it to us, we wouldn't take it either. Though we fear there are certain things even oblivion pollen cannot erase."

Yang Yuhuan sniffed. "Well, I don't know about that."

Hongjun and Li Jinglong hadn't the slightest idea what this exchange was about—probably some little quarrel between them. "The next time I buy some, I can get some for you too," Hongjun offered.

"Get a promissory note from Guozhong," Li Longji said without a second thought. "Since our beloved consort has spoken, we won't be in need of any."

Hongjun nodded. He thought about asking for more food, but Li Jinglong elbowed him in the ribs. *Stop while you're ahead; don't ask for more.*

"Today has proved that the fated encounter I had as a child was real," Yang Yuhuan said softly. "You exorcists commonly interact with strange forces and rare deities. Are there any interesting tidbits you can share with me?"

Although Li Jinglong had gotten a true first taste of exorcism these past weeks, in the end, he was still a mortal who hadn't grown up alongside these things like the others. "Why don't you tell Her Grace some stories?" he suggested.

Hongjun quite liked Yang Yuhuan. He felt refreshed every time he interacted with her, as if he was bathing in a spring breeze. She had a talent for putting those around her at ease; it was no wonder the emperor liked her so much. Hongjun picked a few tales about yao to begin. Eager to hear more, Yang Yuhuan prompted him with question after question, and Hongjun lectured about this and that, from the heavenly meridians to the earthly meridians, to Laozi's "mystery beyond mystery, the gate to all essential truths,"[23] and how heaven and earth were first created from chaos.

Li Jinglong had had no idea Hongjun was so knowledgeable. He was the only one in the Department of Exorcism who had no interest in showing off, nor took excessive pride in his identity and status. He was wont to simply nod or agree quietly with what everyone else said, but in fact he could summon an endless stream of words about the mysteries of heaven and earth.

"Are you a Daoist?" Li Longji asked.

"Um…" Hongjun didn't quite know what school he belonged to. If he had to say, Qing Xiong had probably expounded on Buddhist doctrines to him more often than he did Daoist philosophies. "I might count as a Buddhist, I guess?" Hongjun considered a moment, then said, "Qiu Yongsi seems to be a Daoist."

---

23   From the opening lines of the Daodejing, one of the central texts of Daoism.

"And what about your Shiwei colleague?" Yang Yuhuan asked.

Hongjun hesitated. "Maybe a Shamanist?"

"And Tigra is the sacred prince of Zoroastrianism." Li Longji laughed. "If the four of you were to get into a fight, you would each end up calling upon different gods. How novel!"

"There are many spiritual techniques in the world, but they're all different manifestations of the same underlying principles," Hongjun replied. "My dad taught me there's no need to get caught up on the particulars, so long as your intentions are honorable."

Everyone slowly nodded.

Li Jinglong had thought the emperor summoned them because he had lingering questions about the case and wanted to discuss Li Jinglong's upcoming plans. Little did he know they would spend forever chatting about demons and deities in the middle of the night. All this, and the emperor simply wanted to fantasize about achieving immortality?

What a waste of time. He might as well have gone home to sleep.

"Well, young man," Yang Yuhuan finally said, "there is one more thing I wanted to ask."

"Yes?" Hongjun didn't stand on etiquette, brazenly holding his teacup in one hand as he threw one ankle over Li Jinglong's knees as if Xingqing Palace was his own home.

"Is there anything in this world that is eternal?"

Li Jinglong couldn't restrain his own curiosity. He slapped Hongjun's foot back down and glanced sidelong at him.

Realizing he'd been too sloppy, Hongjun sat up straight. He thought for a while, then said, "No, there isn't."

"There isn't?" Yang Yuhuan asked.

"There isn't," Hongjun said firmly. "If I had to name something, there is only the heavens above and the earth below."

Hongjun gestured with his teacup at the autumn sky spangled with stars over Yang Yuhuan and Li Longji's heads. Smiling, he recited, "'The heavens and earth live eternal; they do not live for themselves, and thus they are truly eternal.'[24] If all beings seek immortality, they only do so for themselves. Thus, between heaven and earth, nothing is eternal."

For a moment, Li Jinglong felt as though Hongjun, holding his cup of tea, would face the Son of Heaven, the noble consort, and even the gods of the world themselves with the same lack of fear. His gaze had a pristine quality that moved the hearts of all who looked into his eyes.

Hongjun lowered his eyes from the stars, turning back to Yang Yuhuan and Li Longji, and smiled. "But I think sometimes reincarnation and reaching nirvana are their own forms of immortality. Those who have departed this life may meet again in the next, though there is nothing that is eternal; that is the working of fate."

"Then, is there any medicine that can extend a person's life?" Yang Yuhuan asked softly.

Li Longji took Yang Yuhuan's hand, and she looked up at him.

"The more simply you live, the closer you are to heaven and earth, and the longer you'll live," Hongjun said.

Li Longji began to laugh. "Forget it; don't fret about it any longer. Kong Hongjun, you are a wise child."

Yang Yuhuan sighed. "If it could allow Your Majesty to live a thousand or ten thousand years, this consort would willingly cultivate into a yao to extend your lifespan."

"Living an ordinary human life is much better than living a muddled life as a yaoguai without a higher level of consciousness," Hongjun said. "Cranes may live a thousand years, and tortoises may

---

24 From the seventh chapter of the Daodejing.

live ten thousand, but all beings have their own fates. This is not something that can be changed."

"Come to think of it," Li Jinglong added, "if you offered most mortals a chance to change places with a tortoise and spend their long life crawling through the muck, hardly anyone would take it."

Yang Yuhuan and Li Longji both laughed. Li Longji muttered to himself, "Indeed."

A thought occurred to Hongjun. "Actually, there is one way to extend one's lifespan."

The three others gasped in shock. "What is it?"

"Become a Buddha," Hongjun said.

"All right, all right," Li Jinglong said. "Don't get too excited."

Li Longji and Noble Consort Yang both clapped a hand to their foreheads as Hongjun went on. "All living beings have the potential within them. Delivering living things from suffering includes delivering oneself."

"What a bright child you are," Noble Consort Yang said with a smile. "Just now, when you said, 'become a Buddha,' you suddenly reminded me of someone."

"Who is it?" Hongjun smiled back.

As Noble Consort Yang gazed at Hongjun, her smile faded and her brows knit together, as if she was struggling to recollect something. "I can't remember—I just keep feeling as if I've seen you somewhere before."

"Perhaps we were fated to meet?" Hongjun suggested.

"Mm... The first time I saw you..." Noble Consort Yang pressed her fingers to the space between her brows. "Your smile seemed so familiar. But I can't figure out who it is you resemble."

"In that case," Li Longji said, "perhaps it may be left up to fate. Too much has happened today already. Go get some rest. Chief Li, bring your young friend back to discuss the mysteries of the world again another day."

Li Jinglong knew a dismissal when he heard one, so he tugged Hongjun to his feet to say their goodbyes. Yang Yuhuan, however, beckoned him over. "Hongjun, come here."

"Don't tell me you're looking to adopt another son?" Li Longji asked with a chuckle.

Yang Yuhuan selected a pastry from a plate nearby and handed it to Hongjun. As Hongjun thanked her, Yang Yuhuan said, "This child is just too pretty. My cousin has so many children, but none are as charming as he is."

When Li Jinglong and Hongjun finally exited the imperial palace, the night was deep around them. Li Jinglong held the cage containing the little fox as they proceeded slowly down the streets.

Hongjun plucked a leaf from a roadside tree and turned back to look at him. "Did I say anything wrong today?"

"No." The corner of Li Jinglong's mouth curled up in a smile. "You did well. You're getting smarter."

He could tell Hongjun was a quick learner. Compared to how anxious he'd been when he first joined the Department of Exorcism, he was far more adapted to life in Chang'an now.

"I'm just too stupid," Hongjun said, embarrassed. "I never understand when you all start speaking in riddles."

In truth, Hongjun had simply followed everyone in confusion for the entirety of this case, only beginning to understand the twists and turns involved as they approached the very end. Li Jinglong, Qiu Yongsi, Mergen, and A-Tai seemed to have a tacit understanding between them, while he was always the one foolishly trailing behind.

"Your colleagues are all sly foxes," Li Jinglong said with a smile. "It's actually normal if you can't follow their logic."

As Hongjun studied Li Jinglong, the smile dropped off Li Jinglong's face.

"Keep smiling," Hongjun said. "You look good like that. Come, give us a smile!"

A vein popped on Li Jinglong's forehead. "Who taught you to say that?!"

But Hongjun sincerely felt that Li Jinglong looked good when he smiled. He was always so stiff and severe, like a stoic general, but he seemed much more approachable with a smile on his face.

"Let me give you a test. Tell me, where are we going now?" Li Jinglong said, serious again.

Hongjun looked around—this wasn't the way back to the Department of Exorcism. He scratched his head. "Where are you taking us so late at night?"

The two of them entered a back alley. Li Jinglong handed the fox's cage to Hongjun and scaled the rear wall of a building.

"Is there another case?" Hongjun cried in surprise.

There was no response from the other side of the wall, but a moment later, Li Jinglong walked out, leading a horse.

"You stole their horse…"

"I'm just borrowing it. Let's go!"

The alley had led them to the Longwu Guard Garrison's rear gate. Li Jinglong swung astride the horse, then pulled Hongjun up behind him. Their hoofbeats rang crisply through the silent streets as they rode for the west gate.

They left the city behind and finally came to a stop atop a hill.

"Come on." Li Jinglong handed the cage to Hongjun and peeled off the talismans keeping it sealed.

"Right here?" Hongjun asked.

"Where else?" Li Jinglong said. "Did you want to take it back to the Department of Exorcism?"

Hongjun figured this place would suffice. He took the little fox out of the cage, and Li Jinglong reached out and stroked its chin with a few fingers.

Qiming, the morning star, twinkled above the horizon, and the sky had begun to pale to a fish-belly white on the eastern edge. As the Divine Land shifted from night to day, Hongjun looked up at the intersection of dark and dawn at the blue rim of the world: at the beautiful colors cast by the heavenly meridians as they joined with the earthly meridians, like a giant wheel that would turn until the end of time.

"Hey, wake up." Li Jinglong's voice was much gentler than usual as he scratched the little fox's chin.

A chuckle escaped Hongjun. "I didn't use too much of the drug the second time."

The little fox woke with a yowl, looking at Li Jinglong in alarm. Li Jinglong bent his finger and rapped it on the forehead. "I haven't gotten back at you for biting Hongjun yet."

Hongjun told him to forget it, and the fox whipped around to look nervously at him, then at Li Jinglong. It had barely realized what was going on when Li Jinglong snapped his fingers in front of its nose.

With that crisp *snap*, oblivion pollen scattered from between Li Jinglong's fingers. The little fox sneezed, its eyes filling with confusion. Hongjun let go, and the fox jumped to the ground and shot off into the undergrowth like an arrow.

"Don't come back to Chang'an again," Li Jinglong called. "If we find you've returned, we'll show you no mercy."

The little fox peeked out from a bush. Hongjun bade it farewell with a touch of sorrow, then walked back down the hill with Li Jinglong.

The sun rose, and the land woke to a new morning, all the birds in the mountains breaking out in song.

"Chief?" Hongjun said.

"Hm?" Li Jinglong walked ahead of him, leading the horse.

Hongjun suddenly threw himself at him, jumping onto his back. "I like you so much!"

"Get off—this is improper!"

"There's no one else here."

Li Jinglong plucked Hongjun off his back. "Are you a child?"

"You don't hate yao at all, do you?" Hongjun asked, pleased.

"I don't hate yao that commit no acts of evil," Li Jinglong said, serious.

"You like little foxes a lot, too, right?"

"Who doesn't like cute things?" Li Jinglong asked. "But just because they're cute doesn't mean they can do whatever they please." He poked Hongjun in the forehead, then mounted their horse, urging Hongjun to hurry up as well.

Hongjun felt like he'd been subtly insulted, but he wasn't sure how. Once he was settled behind Li Jinglong, he asked, "Chief, when will you take me to Pingkang Ward?"

Li Jinglong went mute.

Their hoofbeats faded as the tolling of the morning bell echoed from Chang'an, a single horse kicking up clouds of dust as it galloped through the first rays of dawn.

It was a clear, bright autumn morning. The other exorcists had yet to rise, and Hongjun had fallen asleep on the back of the horse.

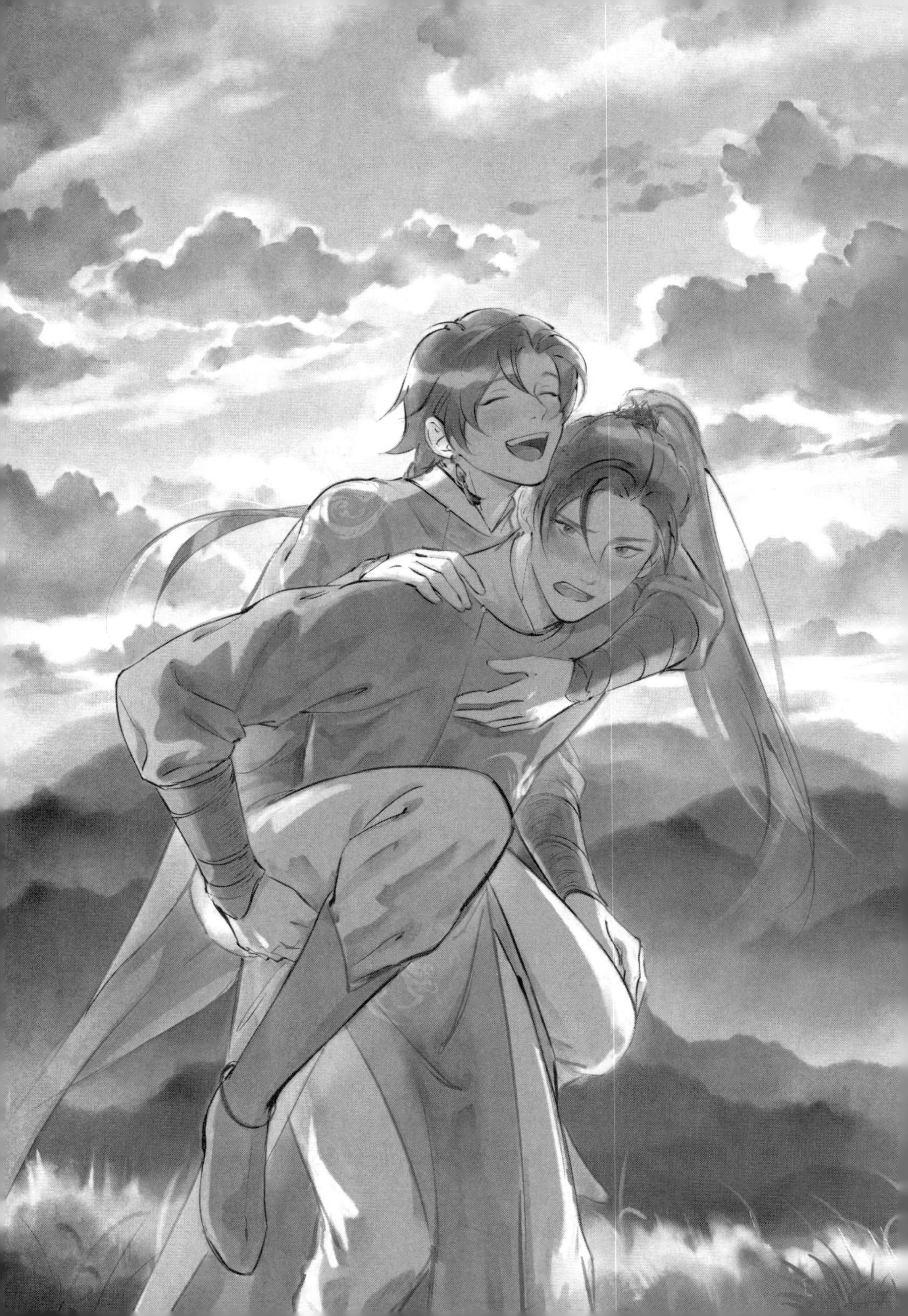

Li Jinglong carried him into his room, placed him on his bed, and sighed. "Get some sleep."

By the time Li Jinglong got back from returning the horse to the garrison, their rewards had arrived. He didn't wake his subordinates, bowing as he received the edict himself. This time, their salary and reward added up to ninety taels of silver, plus a bonus of innumerable pastries. In addition, there was a promissory note from the National Treasury, which could be used in place of silver to pay the merchant for the oblivion pollen.

With everything finally taken care of, Li Jinglong at long last collapsed into bed and slept until dusk.

"A descendant of the Yazdegerd clan, a Shiwei tribesman, the heir of the Qiu family, plus a mortal with absolutely no spiritual power..."

"If you ask me, that young man is the most mysterious in origin, and the most suspicious."

"I don't care how mysterious he is! How could you allow this to happen right before your eyes?!"

"And just what did you expect me to do?" The man in simple black robes spread his hands. "Your vulpine sons and grandsons fell into a trap. Don't gamble if you're not prepared to lose—isn't that what they say?"

The noblewoman gasped in fury, her eyes glowing red as if they were about to drip with blood. "I demand vengeance..."

The man and woman stood in the gathering darkness of Xingqing Palace, the slanting rays of the setting sun lengthening their shadows into savage, snarling beasts.

"Disposing of him would be easy," the man murmured into the woman's ear, "but the human emperor is wary now. If you expose Mara too early..."

The woman looked the man in the face and said quietly, each word deliberate, "It will only be a handful of years before his fate, and the fate of Great Tang, will come to an end."

"Yet you are still helpless against him," the man said coolly. "Get that through your head. Don't introduce any new variables. No matter how strong this generation of exorcists may be, they can't stand against the reincarnation of Mara. If you insist on spoiling our grand plan out of personal weakness, don't say I didn't warn you."

The woman shuddered, her voice filling with malice. "Did you know from the start?"

The man gave her a small smile. "You are too paranoid."

"You knew of their plan, but to avoid getting involved you..." The woman's voice trembled. "You abandoned all of my children!"

The man said no more. As he turned to leave, the woman screamed behind him, "Why else would you avoid the examination grounds?! Mark my words, I'll make you live to regret this day!"

THE STORY CONTINUES IN
Legend of Exorcism
VOLUME 2

CHARACTER GUIDE & GLOSSARY

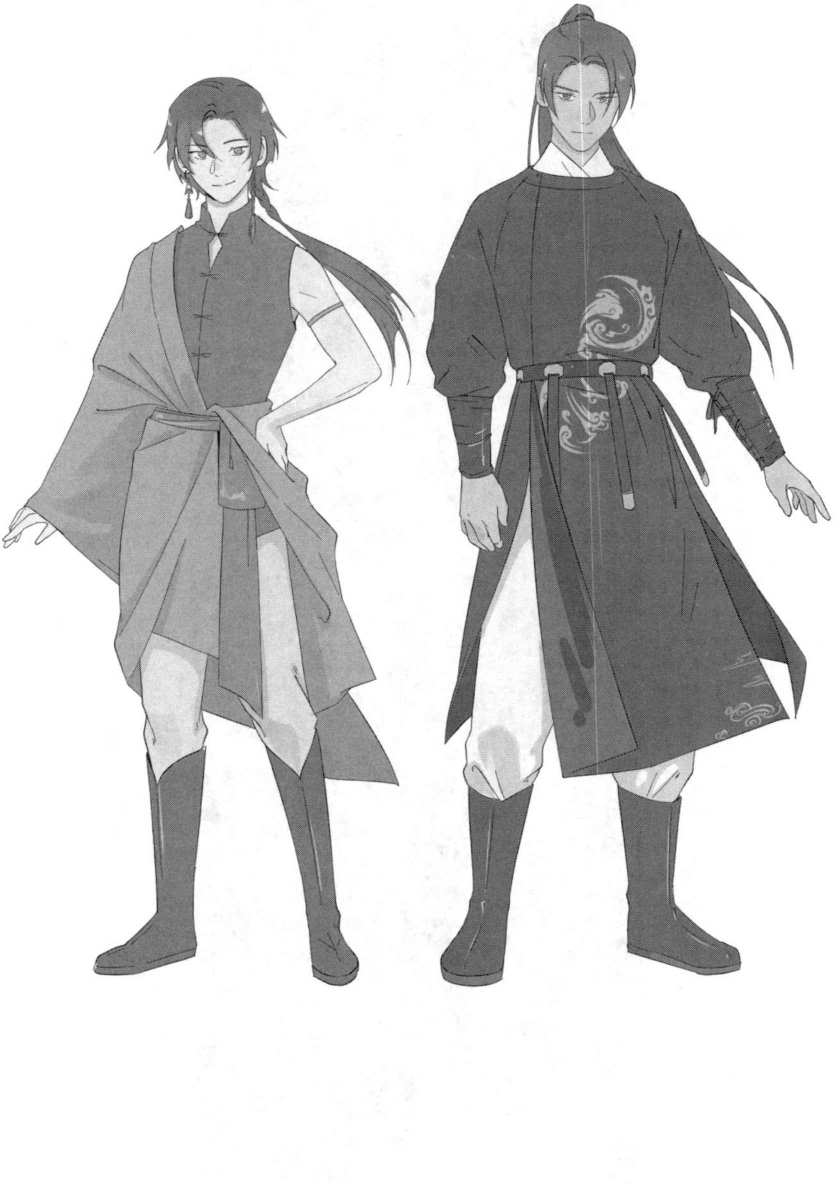

CHARACTER & NAME GUIDE

HISTORICAL PERIOD

Legend of Exorcism is set during the Tianbao era (742–756 AD), the third regnal period of Emperor Xuanzong of Tang. The Tianbao era saw the decline of the Tang dynasty, commonly regarded as the pinnacle of imperial Chinese civilization.

Many of the characters who appear in *Legend of Exorcism* are fictionalized versions of real historical figures contemporary to the setting, including Emperor Xuanzong himself, Li Longji, as well as Noble Consort Yang Yuhuan and Right Chancellor Yang Guozhong. The main members of the Department of Exorcism are fully fictional, though some of their family members are real historical figures.

CHARACTERS

MAIN CHARACTERS

KONG HONGJUN 孔鸿俊: A half-yao boy from Yaojin Palace who is sent on a mission to expel the yao king of Chang'an.

LI JINGLONG 李景珑: Formerly a commandant of the Longwu Guard, an ordinary mortal who becomes the chief of the Great Tang Department of Demonic Exorcism.

SUPPORTING CHARACTERS

THE DEPARTMENT OF DEMONIC EXORCISM

ZHAO ZILONG 赵子龙: A carp yao and Hongjun's closest companion.

MERGEN 莫日根: A Shiwei tribesman with the ability to transform into a gray wolf.

TIGRA YAZDEGERD 泰格拉·伊思艾 (A-TAI 阿泰): A Persian prince and last surviving descendant of the House of Sasan, as well as a disciple of Persian Zoroastrianism.

QIU YONGSI 裘永思: A Jiangnan scholar from West Lake sent to Chang'an to build his courage.

YAOJIN PALACE

CHONG MING 重明: Leader of the three yao kings of Yaojin Palace and Hongjun's adoptive father; a phoenix.

QING XIONG 青雄: One of the three yao kings of Yaojin Palace; a peng.

KONG XUAN 孔宣: One of the three yao kings of Yaojin Palace and Hongjun's birth father; a peacock.

CHANG'AN

DI RENJIE 狄仁杰: Statesman and founder of the Great Tang Department of Demonic Exorcism (deceased).

DU HANQING 杜韩青: A young fox yao that Hongjun encounters while on a mission.

THE DUCHESS OF GUO 虢国夫人: Yang Yuhuan's elder sister.

EMPEROR XUANZONG 唐玄宗 (LI LONGJI 李隆基): The reigning emperor of Great Tang.

FENG CHANGQING 封常清: A general of Great Tang and Li Jinglong's elder cousin.

GAO LISHI 高力士: Chief Eunuch.

HU SHENG 胡升: Captain of the Longwu Guard and Li Jinglong's former superior.

HUANG YONG 黄庸: Deputy Chief Justice of the Imperial Court of Judicial Review.

YANG GUOZHONG 杨国忠: Right Chancellor and Yang Yuhuan's cousin.

YANG YUHUAN 杨玉环: Beloved consort of Emperor Xuanzong, also known as Noble Consort Yang.

NAME GUIDE
NAMES, HONORIFICS, AND TITLES

Diminutives, Nicknames, and Name Tags

A-: Friendly diminutive. Always a prefix. Usually for monosyllabic names, or one syllable out of a disyllabic name.

DA-: A prefix meaning "big" or "elder," which can be added before titles for elders, like "dage" or "dajie," or before a name.

LAO-: A prefix meaning "old." Usually added to a surname and used in informal contexts.

XIAO-: A prefix meaning "little" or "younger," which can be added before names or titles for juniors like "xiaodi." Often used in an affectionate and familiar context.

-ER: Affectionate diminutive. A suffix meaning "son" or "child." Usually for monosyllabic names, or one syllable out of a disyllabic name.

-LAO: A suffix attached to the surname of venerated elders. Denotes a particularly high degree of respect.

-SHI: A suffix attached to the surname of a woman to denote her maiden name.

Family

DI/DIDI: A word meaning "younger brother." It can also be used to address an unrelated (usually younger) male peer, and optionally used as a suffix.

GE/GEGE: A word meaning "elder brother." It can also be used to address an unrelated male peer, and optionally used as a suffix.

JIE/JIEJIE: A word meaning "elder sister." It can also be used to address an unrelated female peer, and optionally used as a suffix.

XIONG: A word meaning "elder brother." It can be attached as a suffix to address an unrelated male peer.

XIONGDI: A word meaning "brother." It can be attached as a suffix to address an unrelated male peer.

PRONUNCIATION GUIDE

Mandarin Chinese is the official state language of mainland China, and pinyin is the official system of romanization in which it is written. As Mandarin is a tonal language, pinyin uses diacritical marks (e.g., ā, á, ǎ, à) to indicate these tonal inflections. Most words use one of four tones, though some are a neutral tone. Furthermore, regional variance can change the way native Chinese speakers pronounce the same word. For those reasons and more, please consider the guide below a simplified introduction to pronunciation of select character names and sounds from the world of *Legend of Exorcism*.

More resources are available at sevenseasdanmei.com

NOTE ON SPELLING

Romanized Mandarin Chinese words with identical spelling in pinyin—and even pronunciation—may well have different meanings. These words are more easily differentiated in written Chinese, which uses logographic characters.

Tiānbǎo Fúyāo Lù
Ti as in **tea**, ān as in **en**d
B as in **b**oy, ǎo as in h**ow**
Fú as in **foo**l
Y as in **y**es, āo as in h**ow**
Lù as in **loo**p

Hóngjùn
Hó as in **ho**ld, ng as in so**ng**

J as in jeep, ún as in bin, but with lips rounded as for boon

Lǐ Jǐnglóng
Lǐ as in leap
J as in jeep, ǐng as in sing
Ló as in low, ng as in song

GENERAL CONSONANTS

Some Mandarin Chinese consonants sound very similar, such as z/c/s and zh/ch/sh. Audio samples will provide the best opportunity to learn the difference between them.

X: somewhere between the **sh** in **sh**eep and **s** in **s**ilk
Q: a very aspirated **ch** as in **ch**arm
C: **ts** as in pan**ts**
Z: **z** as in **z**oom
S: **s** as in **s**ilk
CH: **ch** as in **ch**arm
ZH: **dg** as in do**dg**e
SH: **sh** as in **sh**ave
G: hard **g** as in **g**raphic

GENERAL VOWELS

The pronunciation of a vowel may depend on its preceding consonant. For example, the "i" in "shi" is distinct from the "i" in "di." Vowel pronunciation may also change depending on where the vowel appears in a word, for example the "i" in "shi" versus the "i" in "ting." Finally, compound vowels are often—though not always—pronounced as conjoined but separate vowels. You'll find a few of the trickier compounds below.

- I U: as in **ewe**
- I E: **ye** as in **yes**
- U O: **war** as in **war**m

GLOSSARY

BUDDHISM: The central belief of Buddhism is that life is a cycle of suffering and rebirth, which souls only escape by reaching enlightenment (nirvana). Buddhists believe in karma, that a person's actions will influence their fortune in this life and future lives. The teachings of the Buddha are known as the Middle Way and emphasize a practice that is neither extreme asceticism nor extreme indulgence.

CULTIVATION: A practice in Daoism-inspired Chinese myth through which humans can achieve immortality and non-human creatures can acquire higher forms, more humanoid forms, or both. *(See Yao/Yaoguai for more information)*

DAOISM: Daoism is the philosophy of the dao (道 / "the way"). Following the dao involves coming into harmony with the natural order of the universe, which makes someone a "true human," safe from external harm and able to affect the world without intentional action. Cultivation is a concept based on Daoist beliefs.

DRAGONS: The long (龙 / "dragon"), or zhenlong (真龙 / "true dragon"), is a legendary creature that features prominently in Chinese mythology. Commonly depicted as a horned, snake-like creature with four legs, it is an auspicious symbol of the divine and historically associated with the emperor and imperial power.

According to one myth, the jiao (蛟) or jiaolong (蛟龙 / "flood dragon"), a variety of hornless aquatic dragon, can transform into a "true" dragon by cultivating and passing heavenly tribulations.

According to another, a carp can transform into a dragon if it swims upstream against the current and leaps over the falls of the Yellow River at the Dragon Gate.

IMPERIAL EXAMINATIONS: The official system of examinations in ancient China that qualified someone for official service. It was a supposedly meritocratic system that allowed students from all backgrounds to rise up in society, but the extent to which this was true varied across time.

The imperial examinations were divided into three rounds consisting of prefectural, metropolitan, and palace examinations. Those who passed the highest-level palace examinations were given the title of jinshi.

MANDATE OF HEAVEN: The Mandate of Heaven is the approval of heaven that justifies and legitimizes the rule of the emperor, also known as the Son of Heaven, over the people. If the emperor is not a virtuous ruler and fails to fulfill his obligations, then he would lose the mandate and the right to govern. Signs of a loss of mandate include societal unrest and uprisings, foreign invasions, natural disasters, and so on.

OFFICIALS: Civil and military officials were classified in nine hierarchic ranks, with rank one being the highest. Their salaries ranged according to their rank. The imperial examination was one path to becoming a court official, the other being referral by someone in a position of power, such as a noble, a eunuch, or another official.

TRADITIONAL CHINESE MEDICINE: Traditional medical practices in China are commonly based around the idea that qi, or vital energy, circulates in the body through channels called meridians similarly to how blood flows through the circulatory system. Acupuncture points, or acupoints, are special nodes, most of which lie along the meridians. Stimulating them by massage, acupuncture, or other methods is believed to affect the flow of qi and can be used for healing. The appearance of the acupuncture points can also indicate a person's health; for example, darkness of the Yintang point between the brows portends an ill fate or even death.

TRUE FIRE OF SAMADHI: The true fire of Samadhi is a magical technique used by various fictional characters in Chinese literature including Red Boy and Sun Wukong from *Journey to the West* and Jiang Ziya from *The Investiture of the Gods*. Its primary characteristics are that it is unquenchable by water and can be shot from the eyes, nose, and mouth.

YAO/YAOGUAI: Living creatures and inorganic objects that have gained higher consciousness through absorbing the energy of the natural world and years of spiritual cultivation. Yao who have attained sufficiently high levels of cultivation can assume human form.

ZIWEI STAR: Ziwei, also known as Polaris, the North Star, represents the emperor or leadership. Under its protection, the emperor is believed to be immune to a number of supernatural attacks.

Fei Tian Ye Xiang (Arise Zhang) is a Chinese novelist who has been active since 2008. A romantic who crafts fantasy worlds suffused with eastern mythology, he has published a number of books in places such as Mainland China, Taiwan, Hong Kong, Southeast Asia, and Germany. Many of his works, including *Legend of Exorcism* and *Dinghai Fusheng Records*, have received manhua and popular animated adaptations. He considers writing to be the act of bringing boundless adventure to the mundane life of the real world, allowing his readers to follow his characters in exploring the endless possibilities of time and space. He hopes every world will leave his readers with everlasting memories.